big NATE

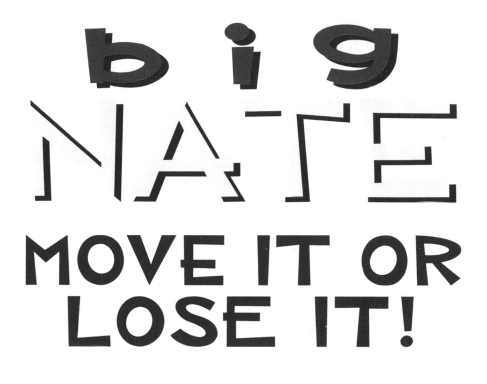

MOVE IT OR LOSE IT!

Complete Your *Big Nate* Collection

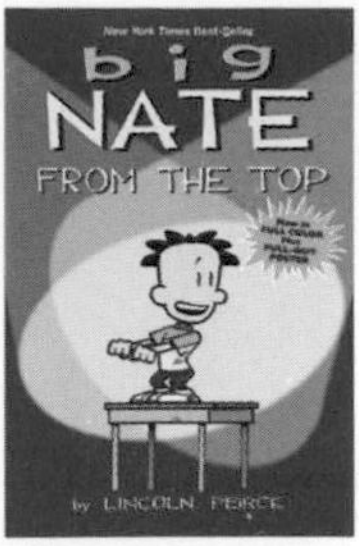
big
NATE
FROM THE TOP
by LINCOLN PEIRCE

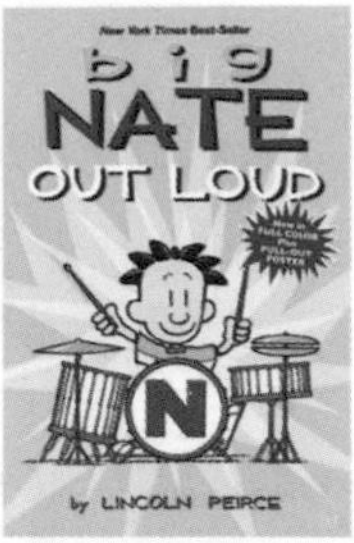
big
NATE
OUT LOUD
by LINCOLN PEIRCE

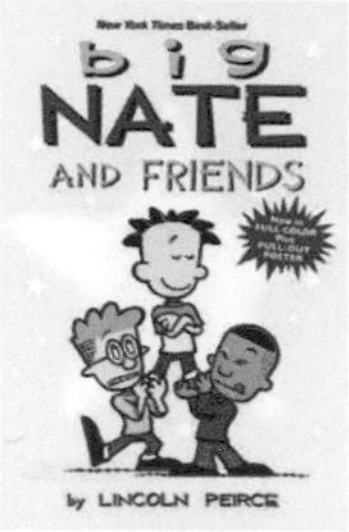
big
NATE
AND FRIENDS
by LINCOLN PEIRCE

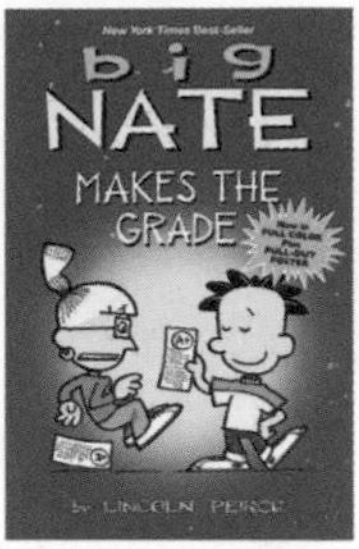
big
NATE
MAKES THE GRADE
by LINCOLN PEIRCE

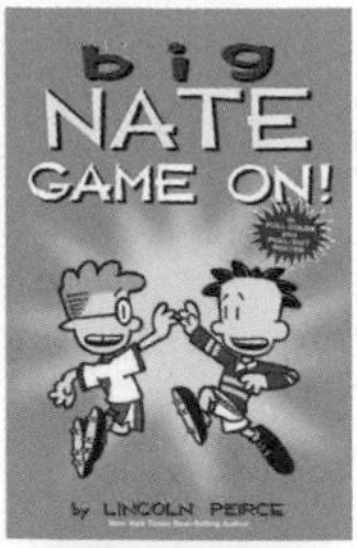
big
NATE
GAME ON!
by LINCOLN PEIRCE

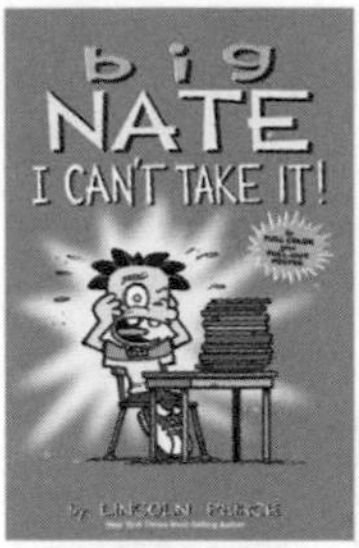
big
NATE
I CAN'T TAKE IT!
by LINCOLN PEIRCE

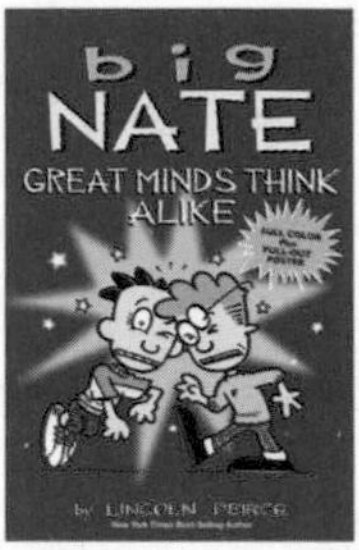
big
NATE
GREAT MINDS THINK ALIKE
by LINCOLN PEIRCE

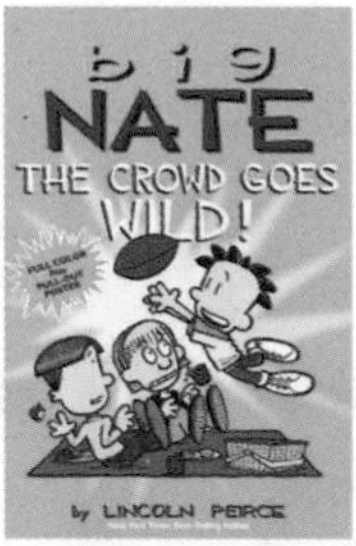
big
NATE
THE CROWD GOES WILD!
by LINCOLN PEIRCE

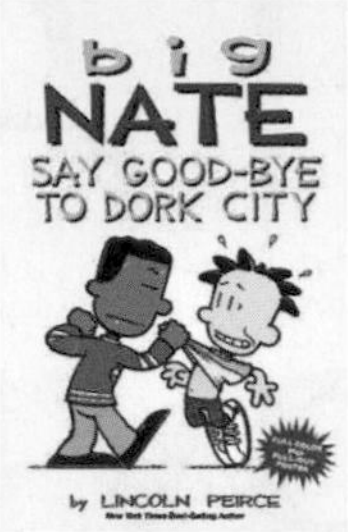
big
NATE
SAY GOOD-BYE TO DORK CITY
by LINCOLN PEIRCE

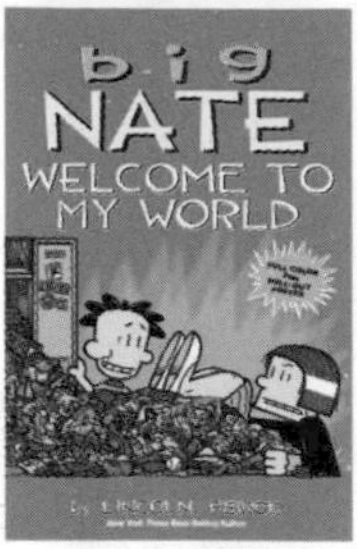
big
NATE
WELCOME TO MY WORLD

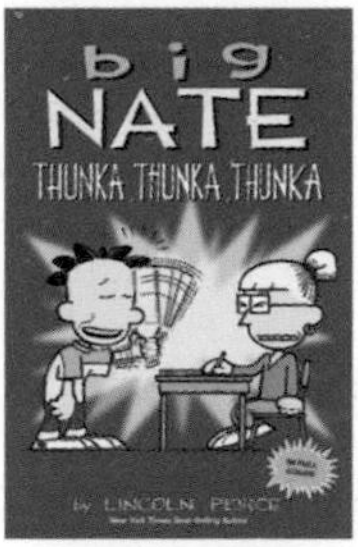
big
NATE
THUNKA THUNKA THUNKA
by LINCOLN PEIRCE

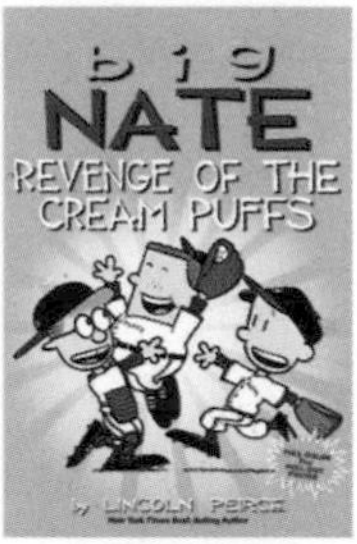
big
NATE
REVENGE OF THE CREAM PUFFS
by LINCOLN PEIRCE

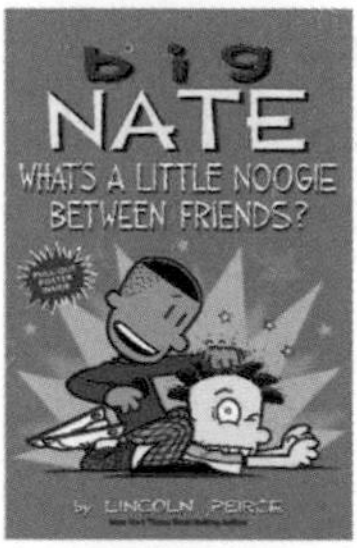
big
NATE
WHAT'S A LITTLE NOOGIE BETWEEN FRIENDS?
by LINCOLN PEIRCE

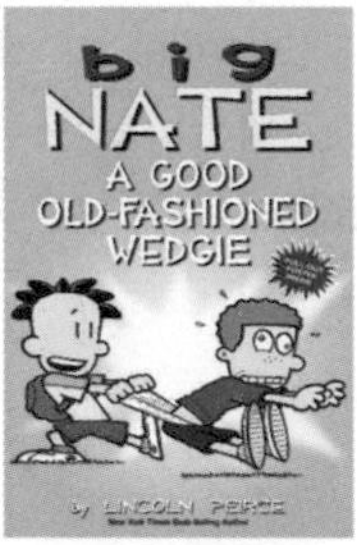
big
NATE
A GOOD OLD-FASHIONED WEDGIE
by LINCOLN PEIRCE

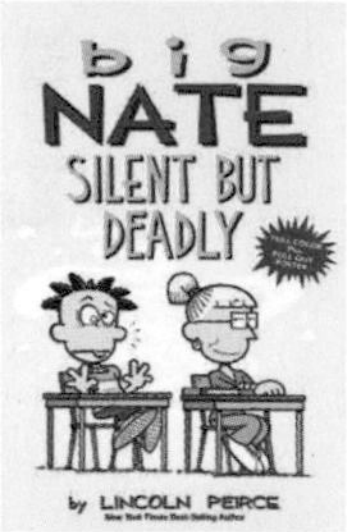
big
NATE
SILENT BUT DEADLY
by LINCOLN PEIRCE

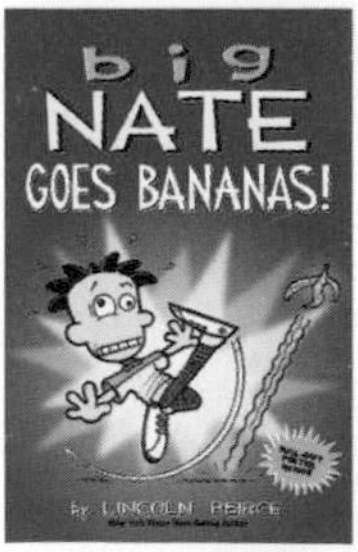
big
NATE
GOES BANANAS!
by LINCOLN PEIRCE

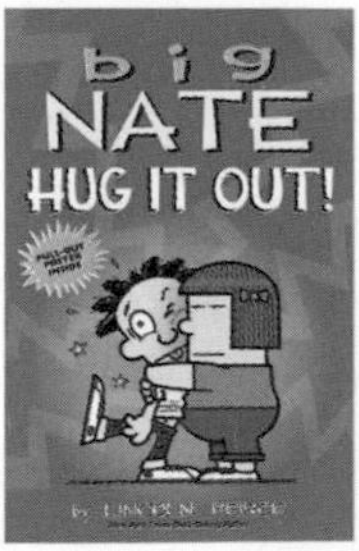
big
NATE
HUG IT OUT!

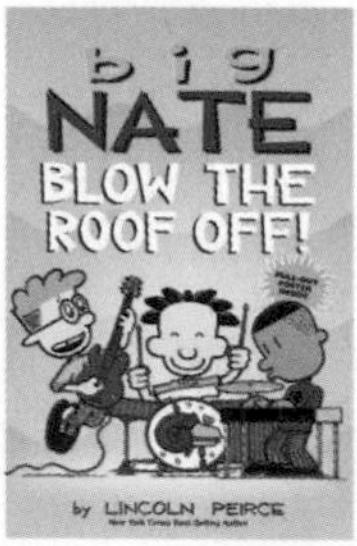
big
NATE
BLOW THE ROOF OFF!
by LINCOLN PEIRCE

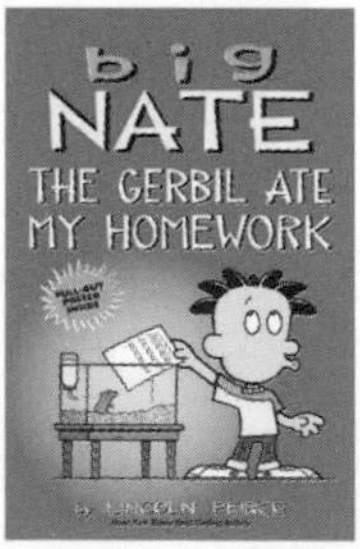
big
NATE
THE GERBIL ATE MY HOMEWORK
by LINCOLN PEIRCE

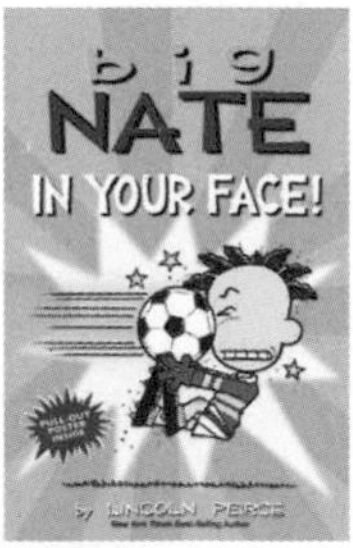
big
NATE
IN YOUR FACE!
by LINCOLN PEIRCE

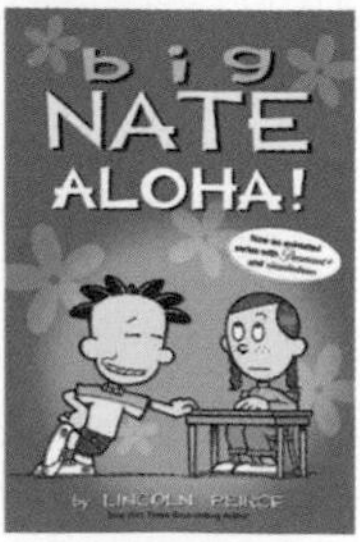
big
NATE
ALOHA!
by LINCOLN PEIRCE

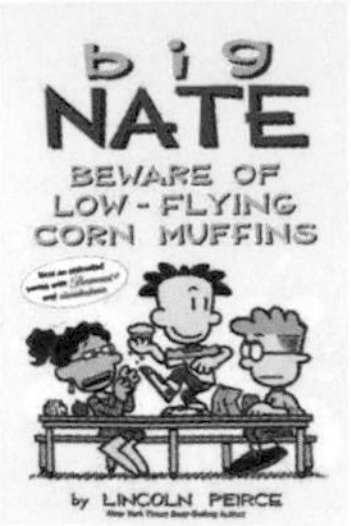
big
NATE
BEWARE OF LOW-FLYING CORN MUFFINS
by LINCOLN PEIRCE

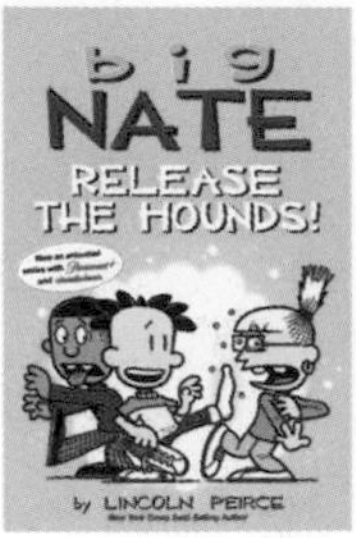
big
NATE
RELEASE THE HOUNDS!
by LINCOLN PEIRCE

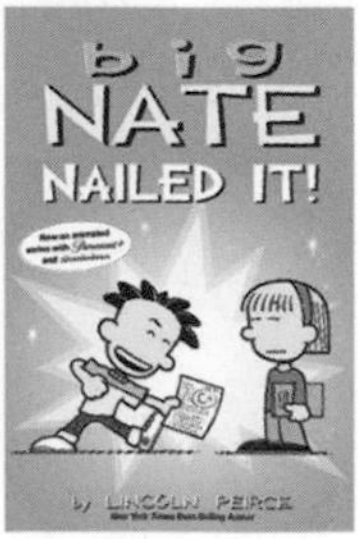
big
NATE
NAILED IT!
by LINCOLN PEIRCE

big NATE

MOVE IT OR LOSE IT!

by LINCOLN PEIRCE

Andrews McMeel
PUBLISHING®

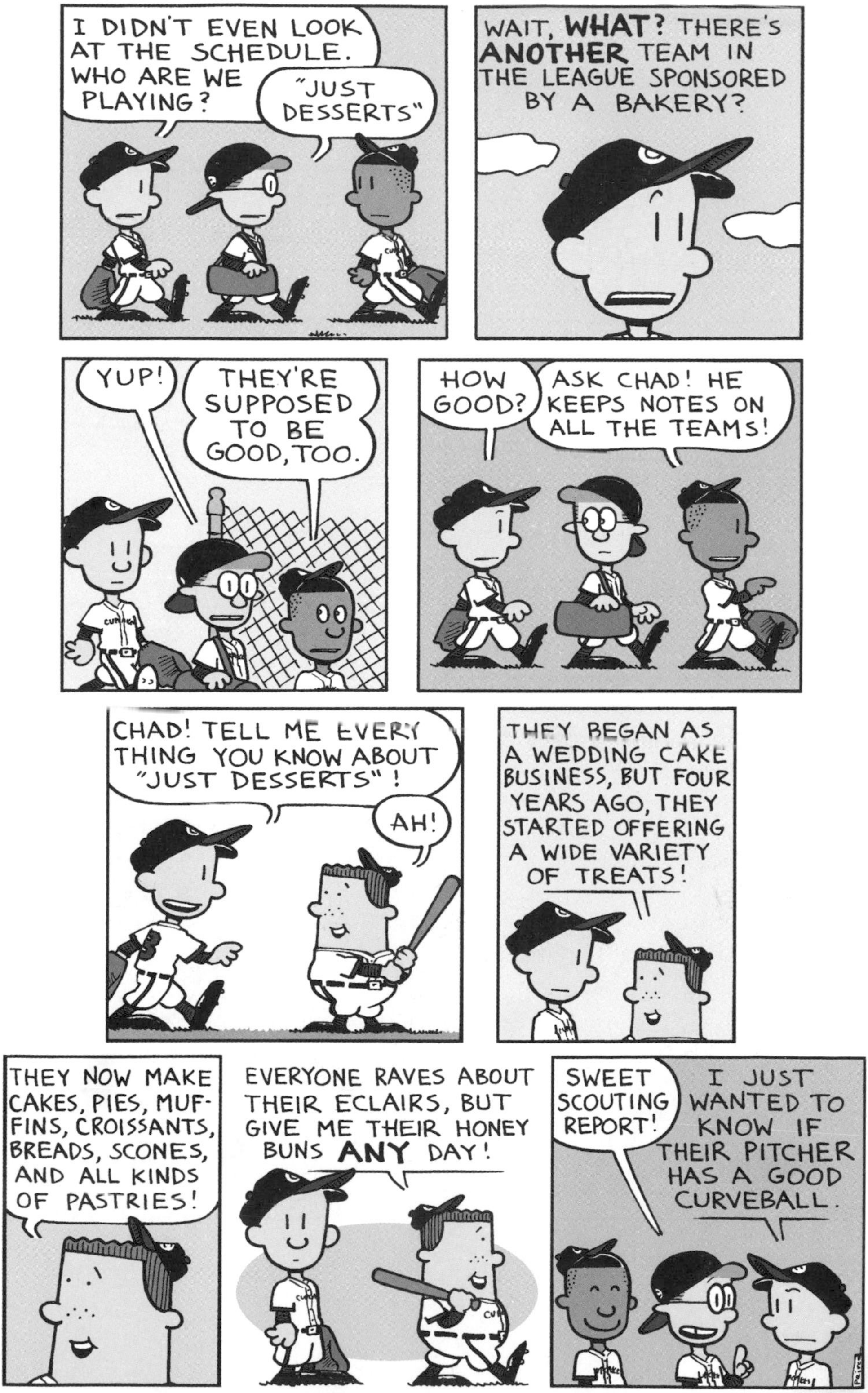

I DIDN'T EVEN LOOK AT THE SCHEDULE. WHO ARE WE PLAYING?
"JUST DESSERTS"
WAIT, **WHAT**? THERE'S **ANOTHER** TEAM IN THE LEAGUE SPONSORED BY A BAKERY?
YUP!
THEY'RE SUPPOSED TO BE GOOD, TOO.
HOW GOOD?
ASK CHAD! HE KEEPS NOTES ON ALL THE TEAMS!
CHAD! TELL ME EVERY THING YOU KNOW ABOUT "JUST DESSERTS"!
AH!
THEY BEGAN AS A WEDDING CAKE BUSINESS, BUT FOUR YEARS AGO, THEY STARTED OFFERING A WIDE VARIETY OF TREATS!
THEY NOW MAKE CAKES, PIES, MUF-FINS, CROISSANTS, BREADS, SCONES, AND ALL KINDS OF PASTRIES!
EVERYONE RAVES ABOUT THEIR ECLAIRS, BUT GIVE ME THEIR HONEY BUNS **ANY** DAY!
SWEET SCOUTING REPORT!
I JUST WANTED TO KNOW IF THEIR PITCHER HAS A GOOD CURVEBALL.

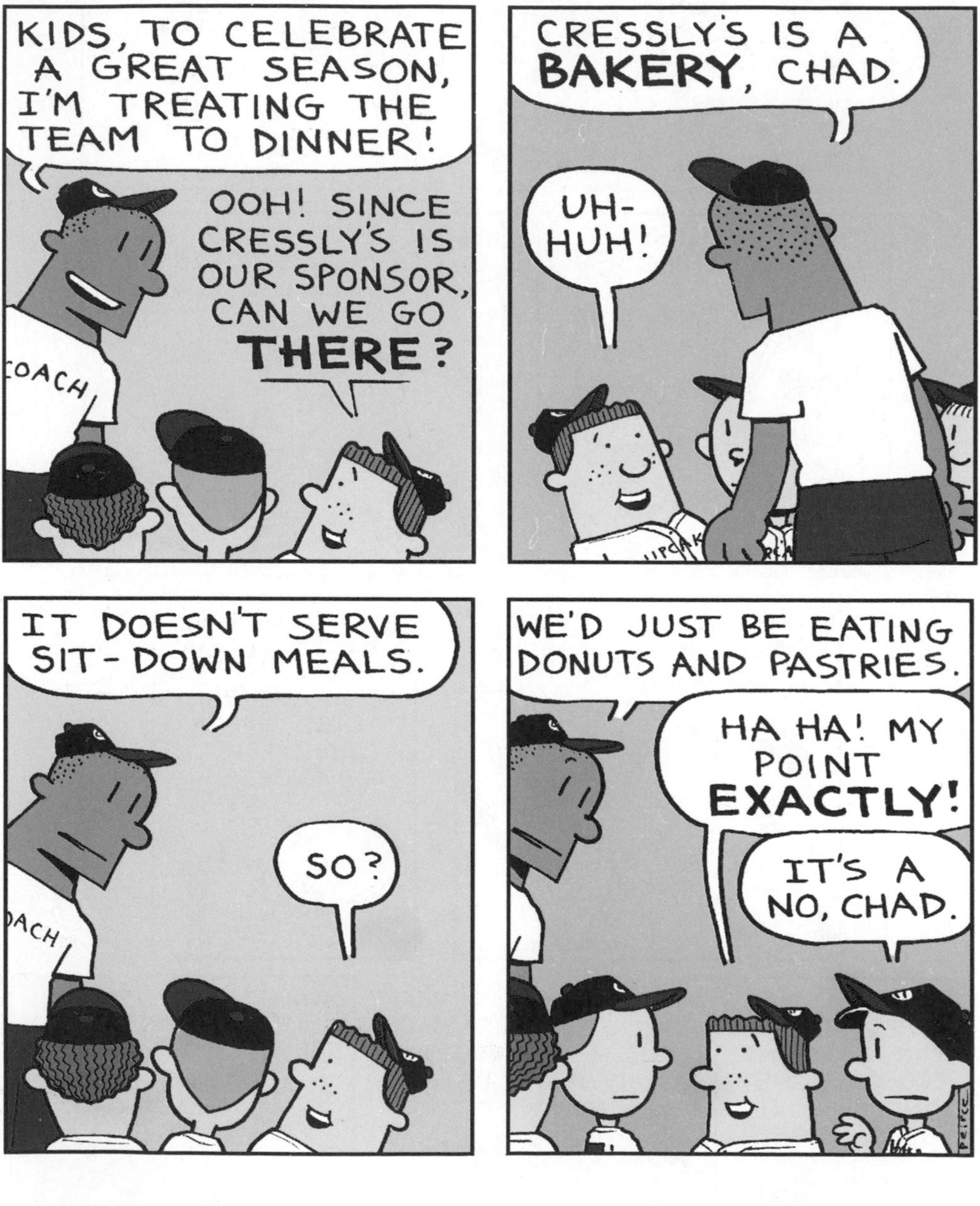
KIDS, TO CELEBRATE A GREAT SEASON, I'M TREATING THE TEAM TO DINNER!
OOH! SINCE CRESSLY'S IS OUR SPONSOR, CAN WE GO THERE?
CRESSLY'S IS A BAKERY, CHAD.
UH-HUH!
COACH
IT DOESN'T SERVE SIT-DOWN MEALS.
SO?
WE'D JUST BE EATING DONUTS AND PASTRIES.
HA HA! MY POINT EXACTLY!
IT'S A NO, CHAD.

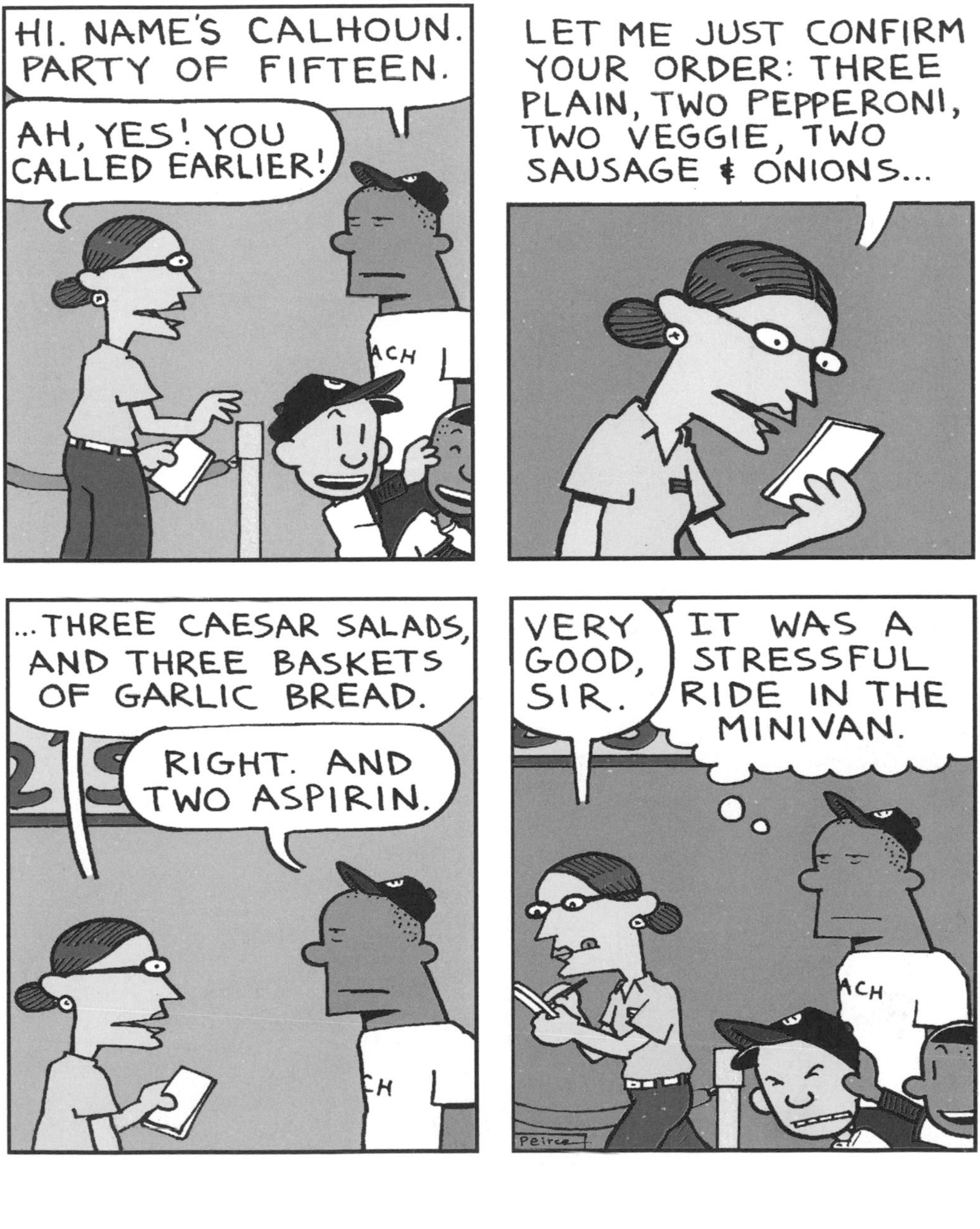
HI. NAME'S CALHOUN. PARTY OF FIFTEEN.
AH, YES! YOU CALLED EARLIER!
ACH
LET ME JUST CONFIRM YOUR ORDER: THREE PLAIN, TWO PEPPERONI, TWO VEGGIE, TWO SAUSAGE & ONIONS...
...THREE CAESAR SALADS, AND THREE BASKETS OF GARLIC BREAD.
RIGHT. AND TWO ASPIRIN.
VERY GOOD, SIR.
IT WAS A STRESSFUL RIDE IN THE MINIVAN.
ACH
Peirce

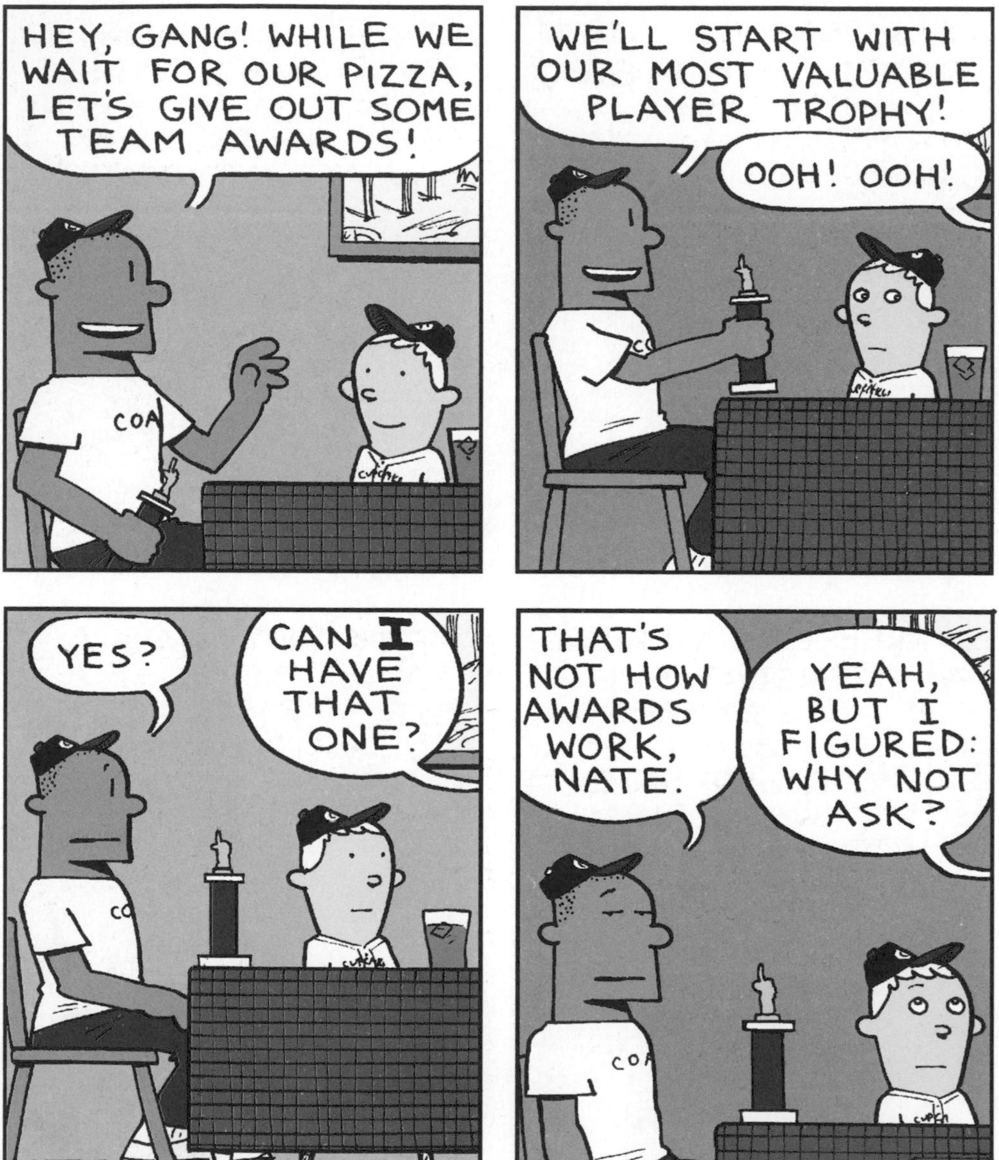
HEY, GANG! WHILE WE WAIT FOR OUR PIZZA, LET'S GIVE OUT SOME TEAM AWARDS!
WE'LL START WITH OUR MOST VALUABLE PLAYER TROPHY!
OOH! OOH!
YES?
CAN I HAVE THAT ONE?
THAT'S NOT HOW AWARDS WORK, NATE.
YEAH, BUT I FIGURED: WHY NOT ASK?

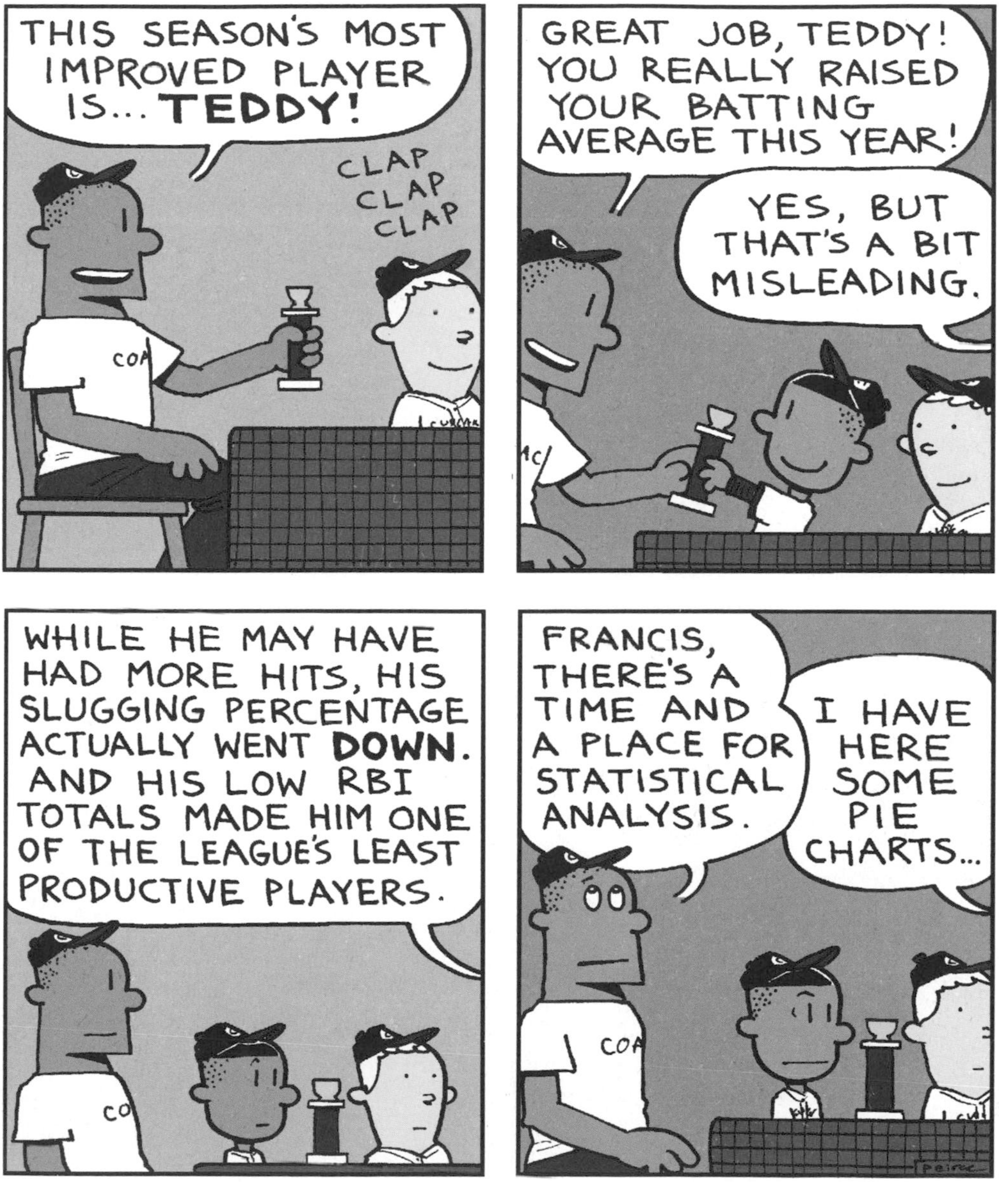
THIS SEASON'S MOST IMPROVED PLAYER IS... **TEDDY!**
CLAP CLAP CLAP
GREAT JOB, TEDDY! YOU REALLY RAISED YOUR BATTING AVERAGE THIS YEAR!
YES, BUT THAT'S A BIT MISLEADING.
WHILE HE MAY HAVE HAD MORE HITS, HIS SLUGGING PERCENTAGE ACTUALLY WENT **DOWN**. AND HIS LOW RBI TOTALS MADE HIM ONE OF THE LEAGUE'S LEAST PRODUCTIVE PLAYERS.
FRANCIS, THERE'S A TIME AND A PLACE FOR STATISTICAL ANALYSIS.
I HAVE HERE SOME PIE CHARTS...

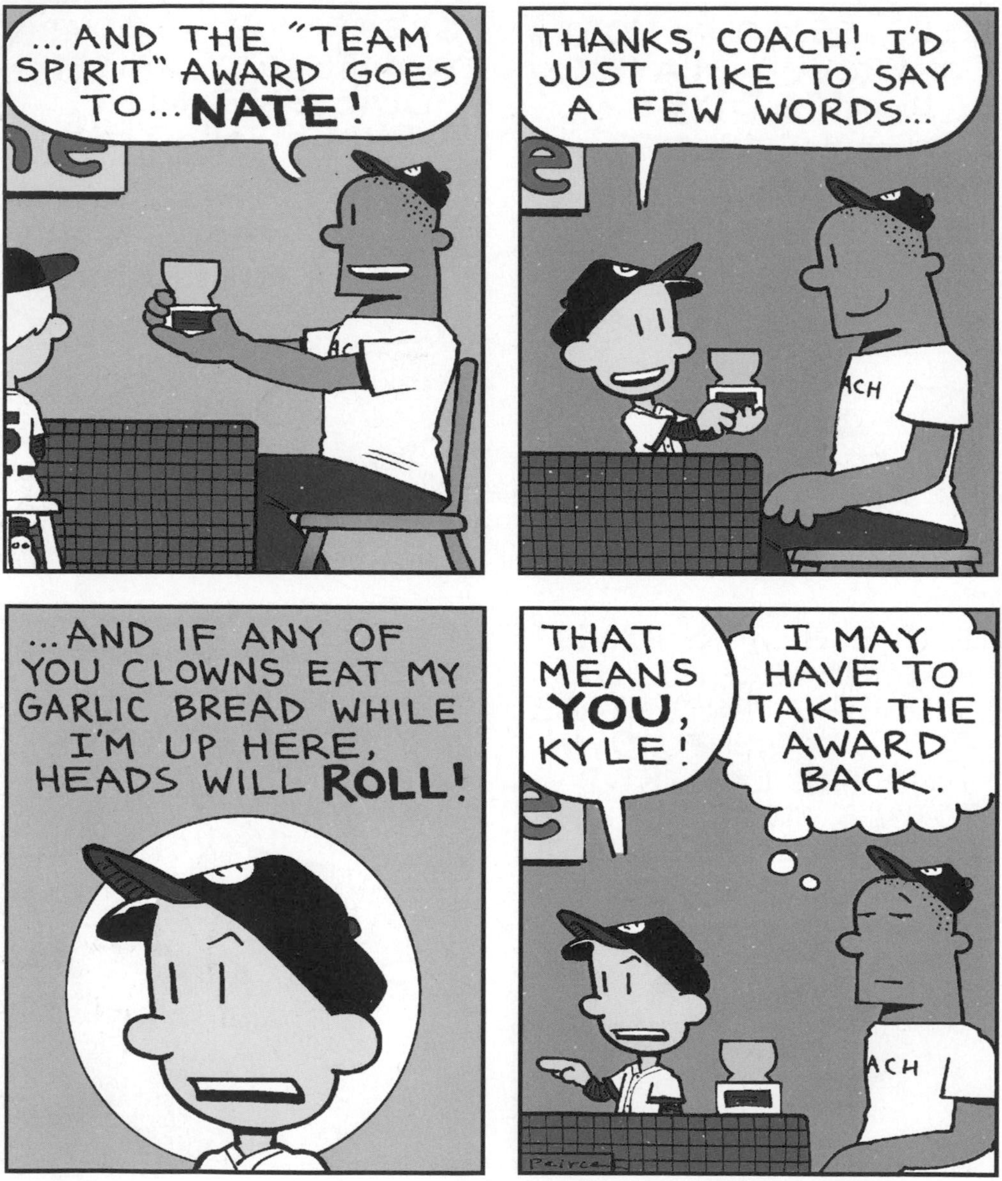
...AND THE "TEAM SPIRIT" AWARD GOES TO... NATE!
THANKS, COACH! I'D JUST LIKE TO SAY A FEW WORDS...
...AND IF ANY OF YOU CLOWNS EAT MY GARLIC BREAD WHILE I'M UP HERE, HEADS WILL ROLL!
THAT MEANS YOU, KYLE!
I MAY HAVE TO TAKE THE AWARD BACK.
PEIRCE

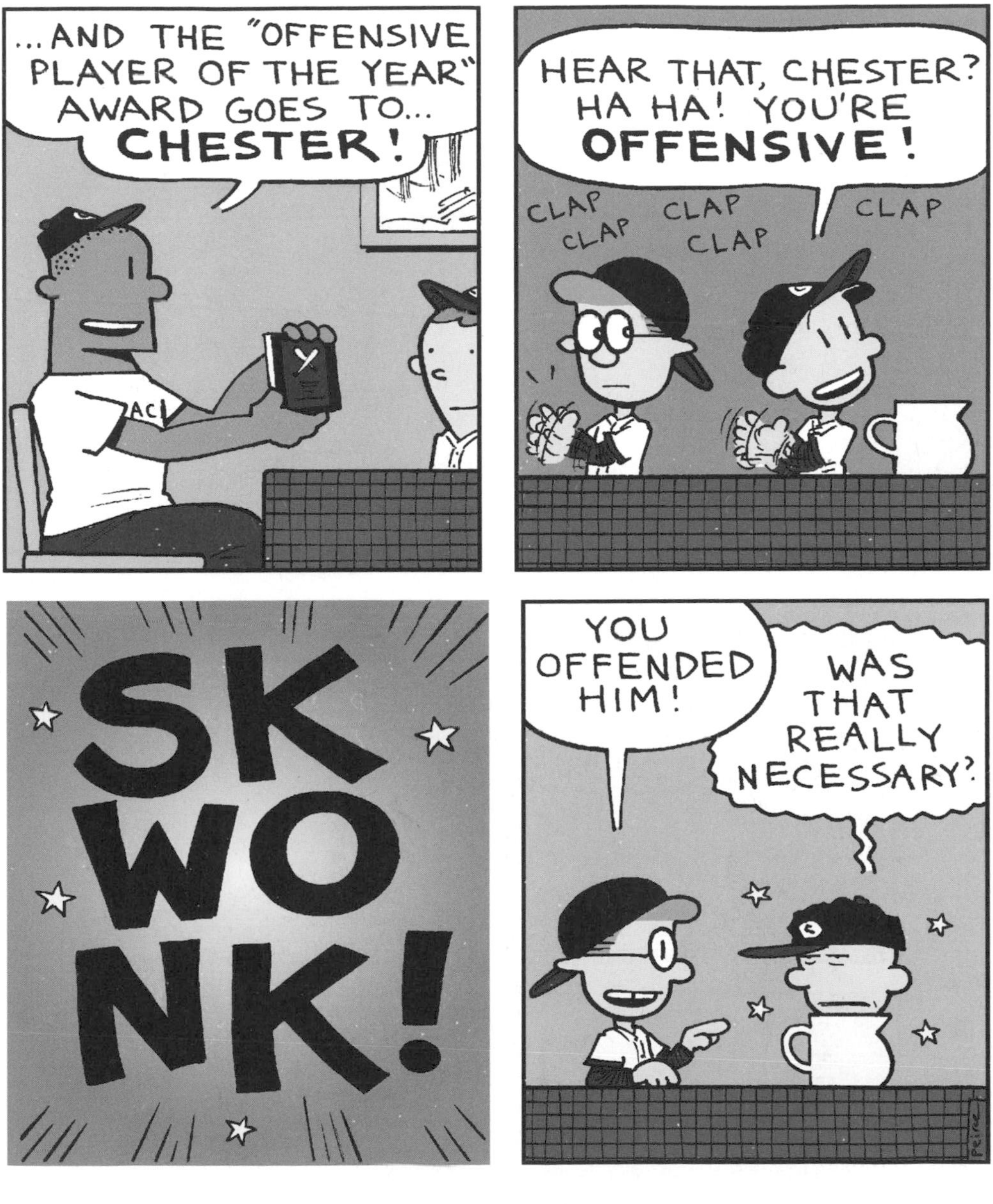
...AND THE "OFFENSIVE PLAYER OF THE YEAR" AWARD GOES TO... CHESTER!
HEAR THAT, CHESTER? HA HA! YOU'RE OFFENSIVE!
CLAP CLAP CLAP CLAP
CLAP
SKWONK!
YOU OFFENDED HIM!
WAS THAT REALLY NECESSARY?

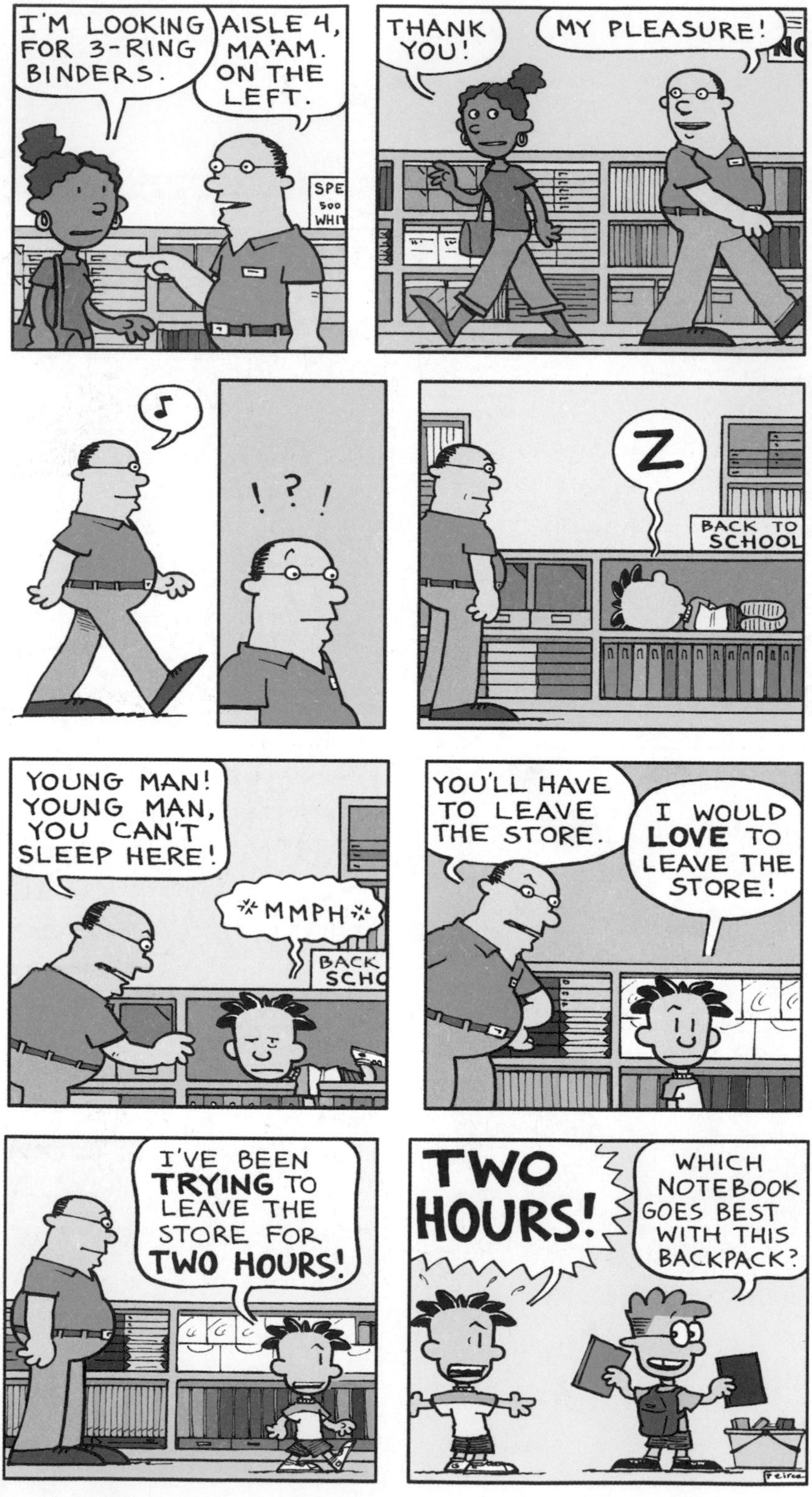
I'M LOOKING FOR 3-RING BINDERS.
AISLE 4, MA'AM. ON THE LEFT.
SPE 500 WHI
THANK YOU!
MY PLEASURE!
♪
! ? !
Z
BACK TO SCHOOL
YOUNG MAN! YOUNG MAN, YOU CAN'T SLEEP HERE!
MMPH
BACK SCHO
YOU'LL HAVE TO LEAVE THE STORE.
I WOULD **LOVE** TO LEAVE THE STORE!
I'VE BEEN **TRYING** TO LEAVE THE STORE FOR **TWO HOURS!**
TWO HOURS!
WHICH NOTEBOOK GOES BEST WITH THIS BACKPACK?
Peirce

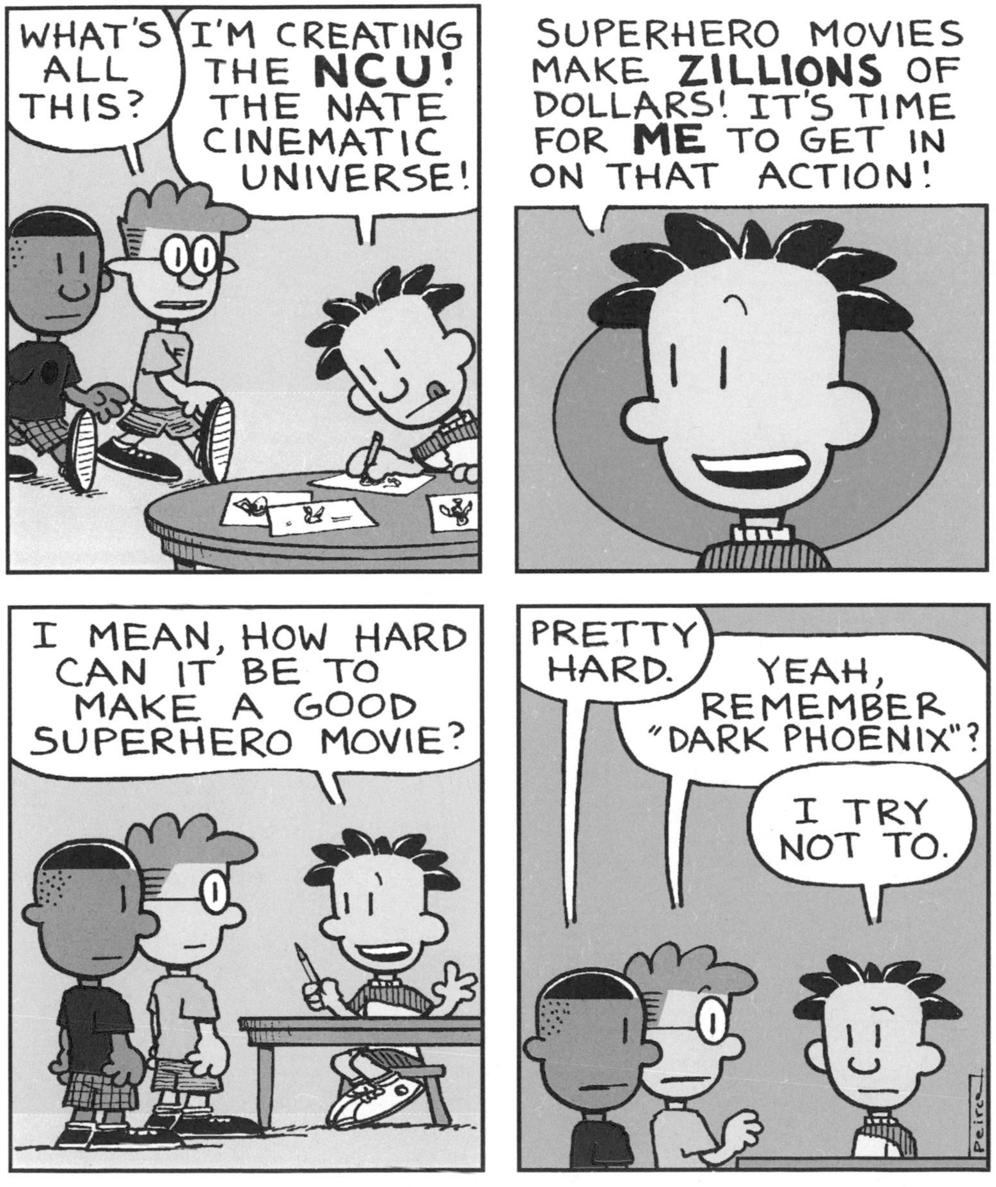
WHAT'S ALL THIS?
I'M CREATING THE NCU! THE NATE CINEMATIC UNIVERSE!
SUPERHERO MOVIES MAKE ZILLIONS OF DOLLARS! IT'S TIME FOR ME TO GET IN ON THAT ACTION!
I MEAN, HOW HARD CAN IT BE TO MAKE A GOOD SUPERHERO MOVIE?
PRETTY HARD.
YEAH, REMEMBER "DARK PHOENIX"?
I TRY NOT TO.
Peirce

THE NATE CINEMATIC UNIVERSE IS A COMPLEX WORLD FILLED WITH KICK-BUTT SUPERHEROES!

LIKE WHO?

LIKE THE **GNOME!** HE'S A LAWN GNOME WHO COMES TO LIFE DURING A WACKY DNA EXPERIMENT!

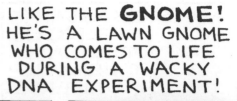

THEN HE DEVELOPS SUPERPOWERS AND—

HOLD IT! WHY IS A **LAWN GNOME** PART OF A **DNA EXPERIMENT?**

MAYBE HE'S A "**GENOME**"!

UH-HUH.

I'LL DEAL WITH THAT IN POST-PRODUCTION.

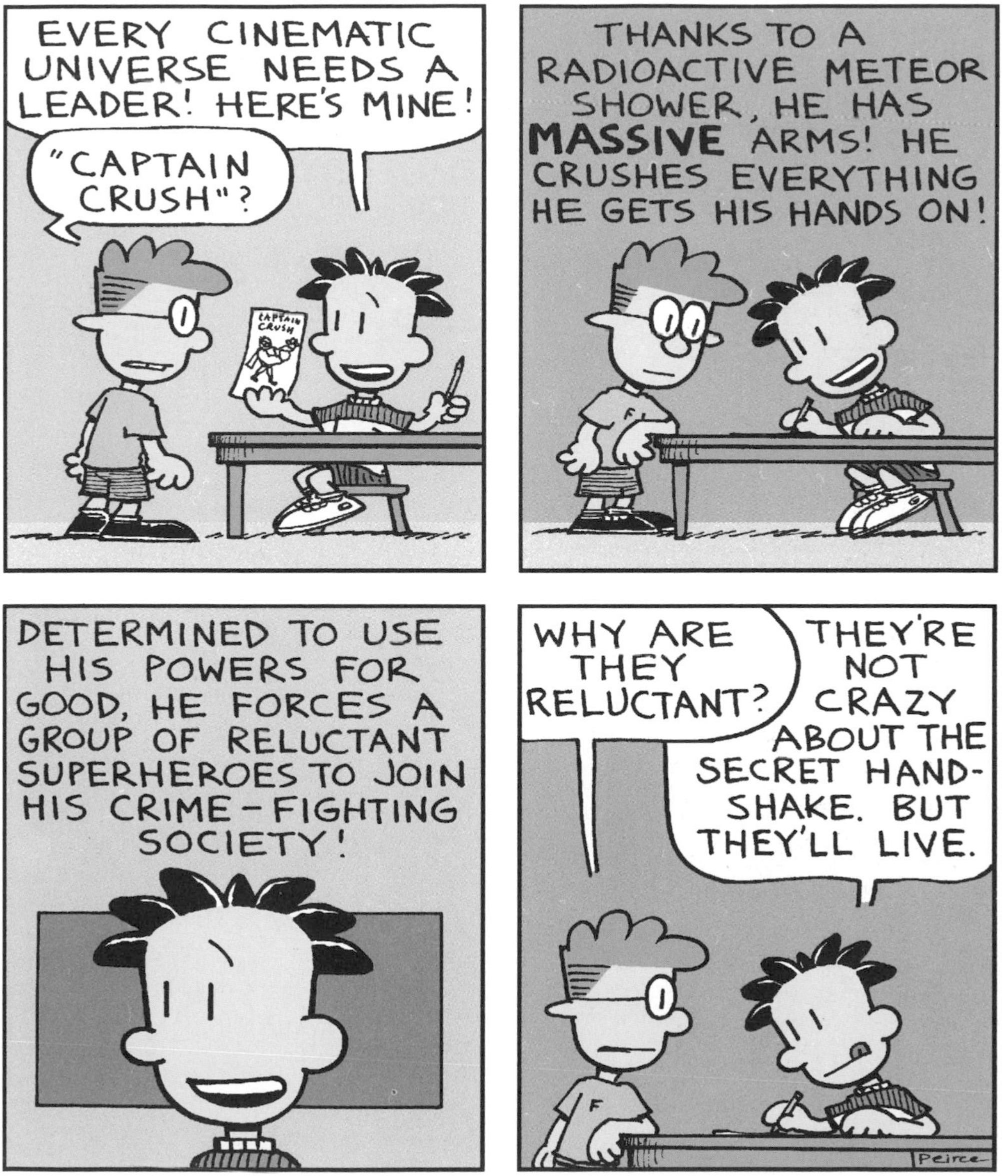

EVERY CINEMATIC UNIVERSE NEEDS A LEADER! HERE'S MINE!
"CAPTAIN CRUSH"?
CAPTAIN CRUSH
THANKS TO A RADIOACTIVE METEOR SHOWER, HE HAS **MASSIVE** ARMS! HE CRUSHES EVERYTHING HE GETS HIS HANDS ON!
DETERMINED TO USE HIS POWERS FOR GOOD, HE FORCES A GROUP OF RELUCTANT SUPERHEROES TO JOIN HIS CRIME-FIGHTING SOCIETY!
WHY ARE THEY RELUCTANT?
THEY'RE NOT CRAZY ABOUT THE SECRET HAND-SHAKE. BUT THEY'LL LIVE.
Peirce

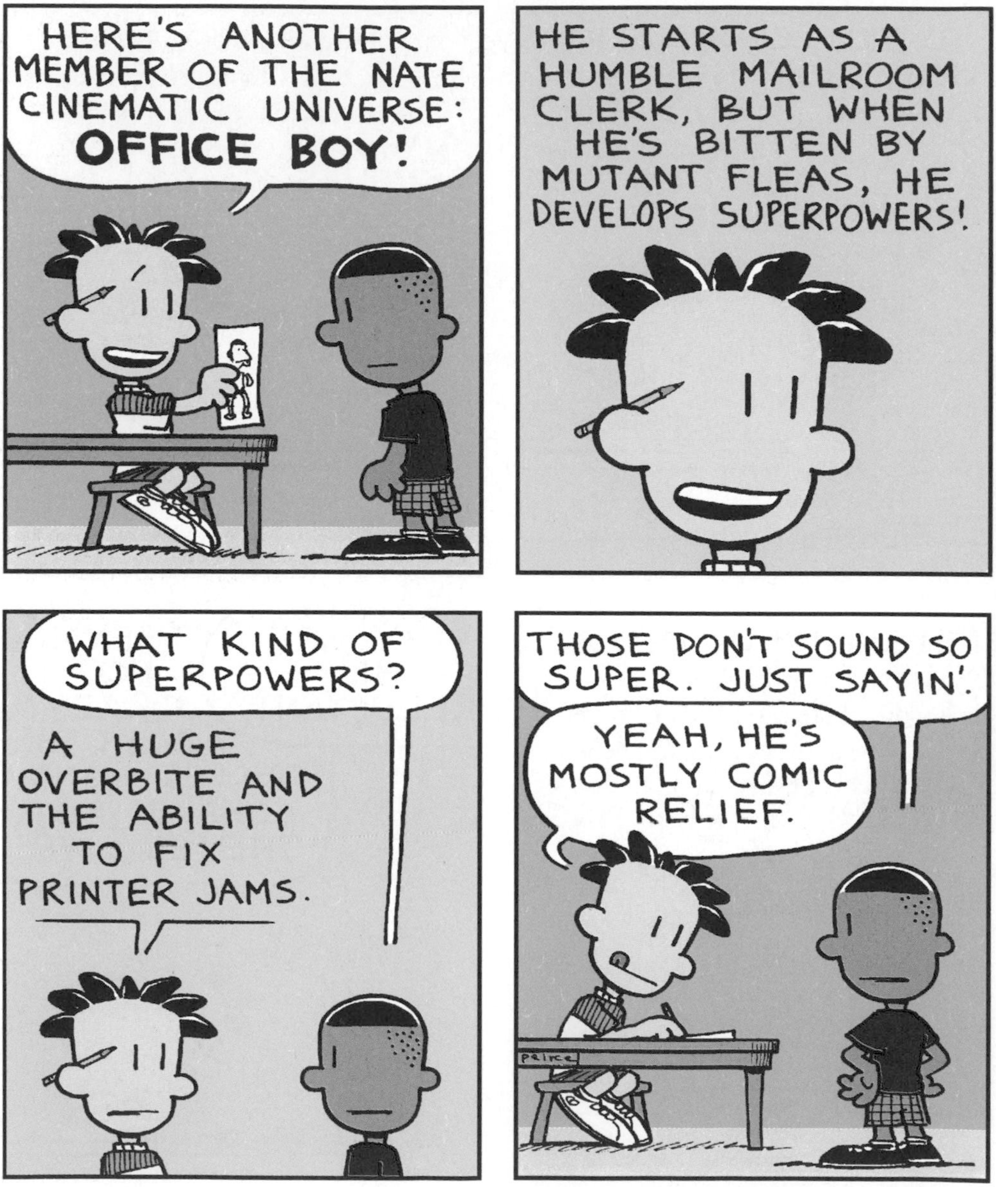
HERE'S ANOTHER MEMBER OF THE NATE CINEMATIC UNIVERSE: **OFFICE BOY!**
HE STARTS AS A HUMBLE MAILROOM CLERK, BUT WHEN HE'S BITTEN BY MUTANT FLEAS, HE DEVELOPS SUPERPOWERS!
WHAT KIND OF SUPERPOWERS?
A HUGE OVERBITE AND THE ABILITY TO FIX PRINTER JAMS.
THOSE DON'T SOUND SO SUPER. JUST SAYIN'.
YEAH, HE'S MOSTLY COMIC RELIEF.
peirce

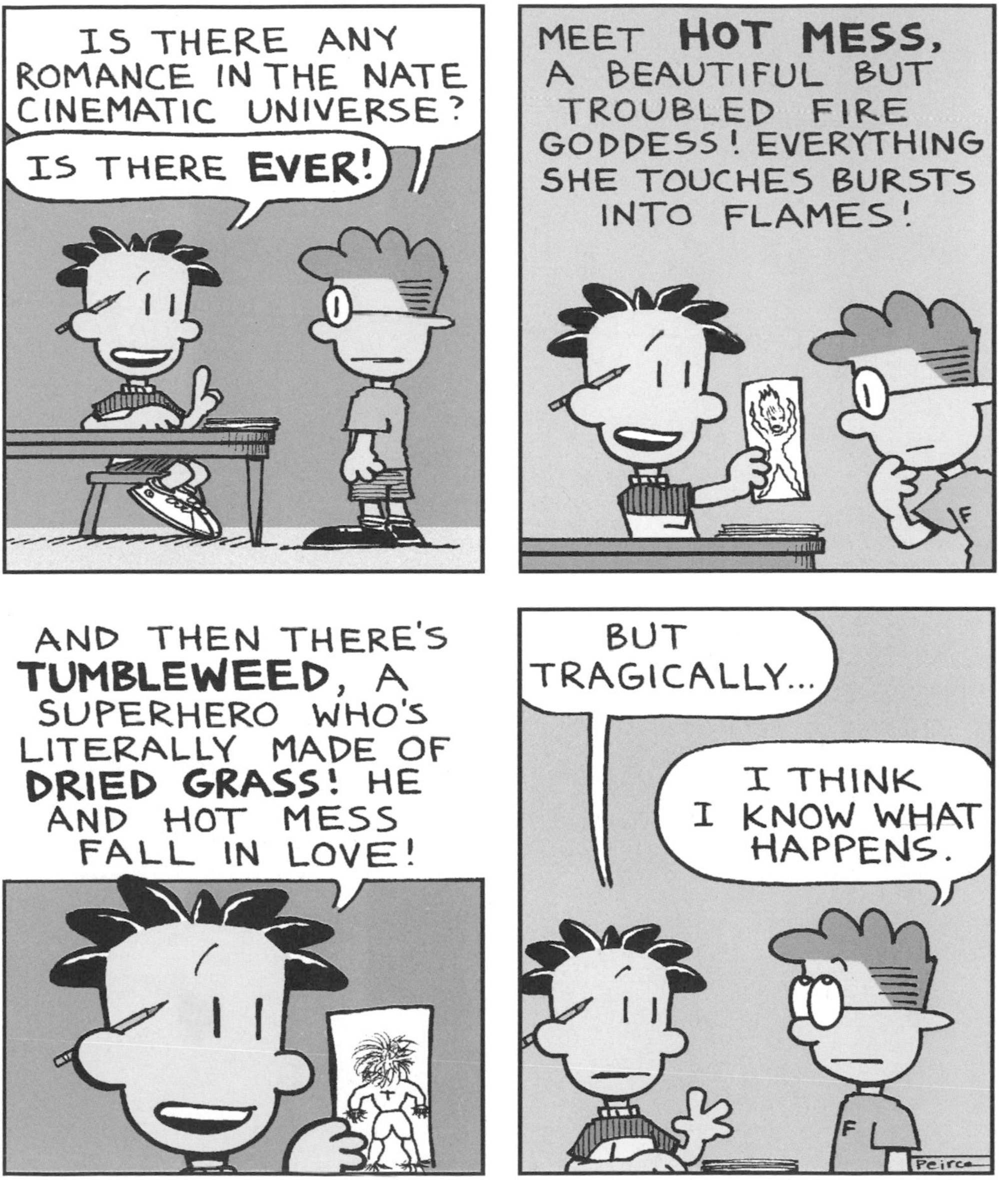
IS THERE ANY ROMANCE IN THE NATE CINEMATIC UNIVERSE?
IS THERE **EVER**!
MEET **HOT MESS,** A BEAUTIFUL BUT TROUBLED FIRE GODDESS! EVERYTHING SHE TOUCHES BURSTS INTO FLAMES!
F
AND THEN THERE'S **TUMBLEWEED,** A SUPERHERO WHO'S LITERALLY MADE OF **DRIED GRASS!** HE AND HOT MESS FALL IN LOVE!
BUT TRAGICALLY...
I THINK I KNOW WHAT HAPPENS.
F
Peirce

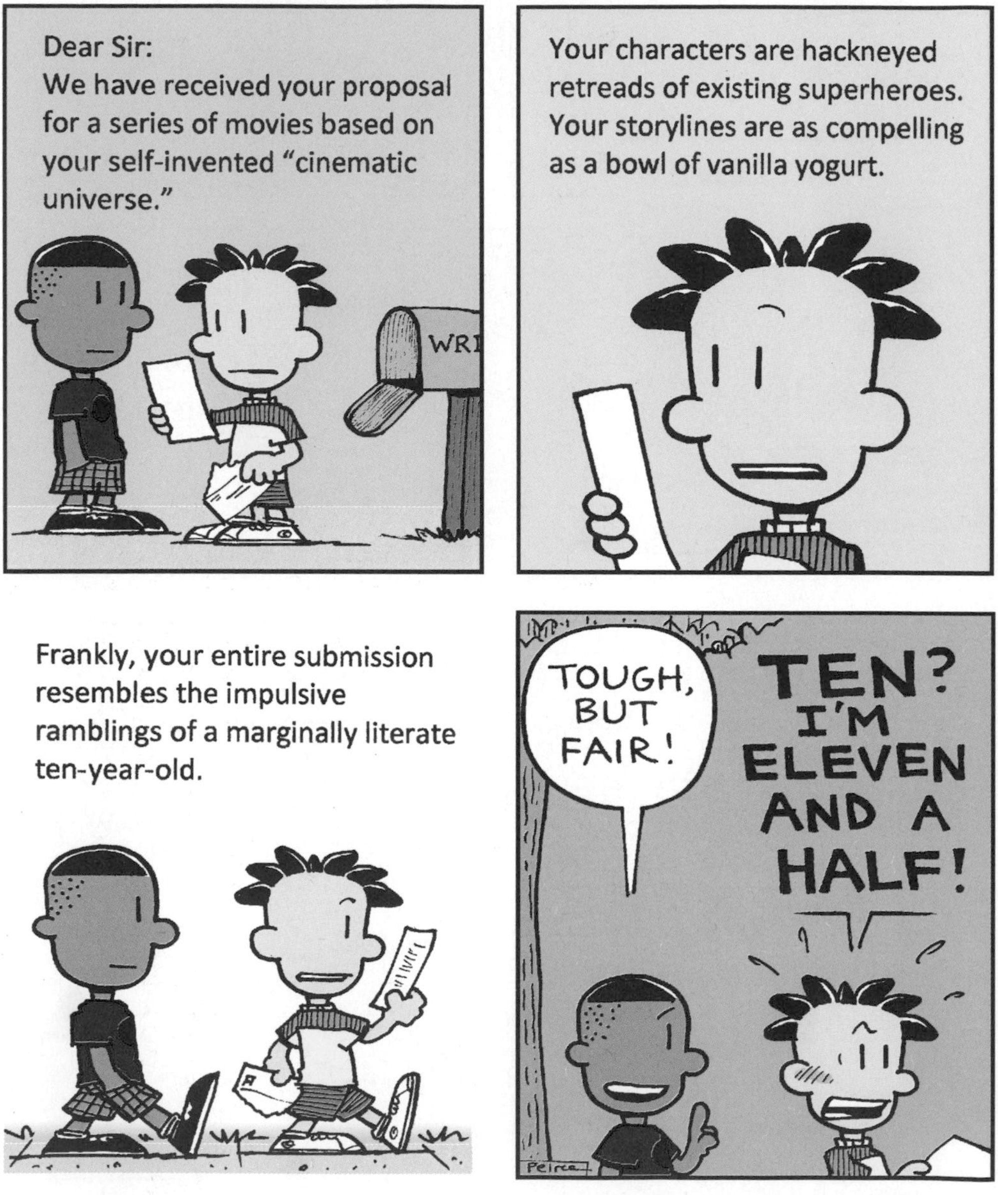
Dear Sir:
We have received your proposal for a series of movies based on your self-invented "cinematic universe."
WRI
Your characters are hackneyed retreads of existing superheroes. Your storylines are as compelling as a bowl of vanilla yogurt.
Frankly, your entire submission resembles the impulsive ramblings of a marginally literate ten-year-old.
TOUGH, BUT FAIR!
TEN? I'M ELEVEN AND A HALF!
Peirce

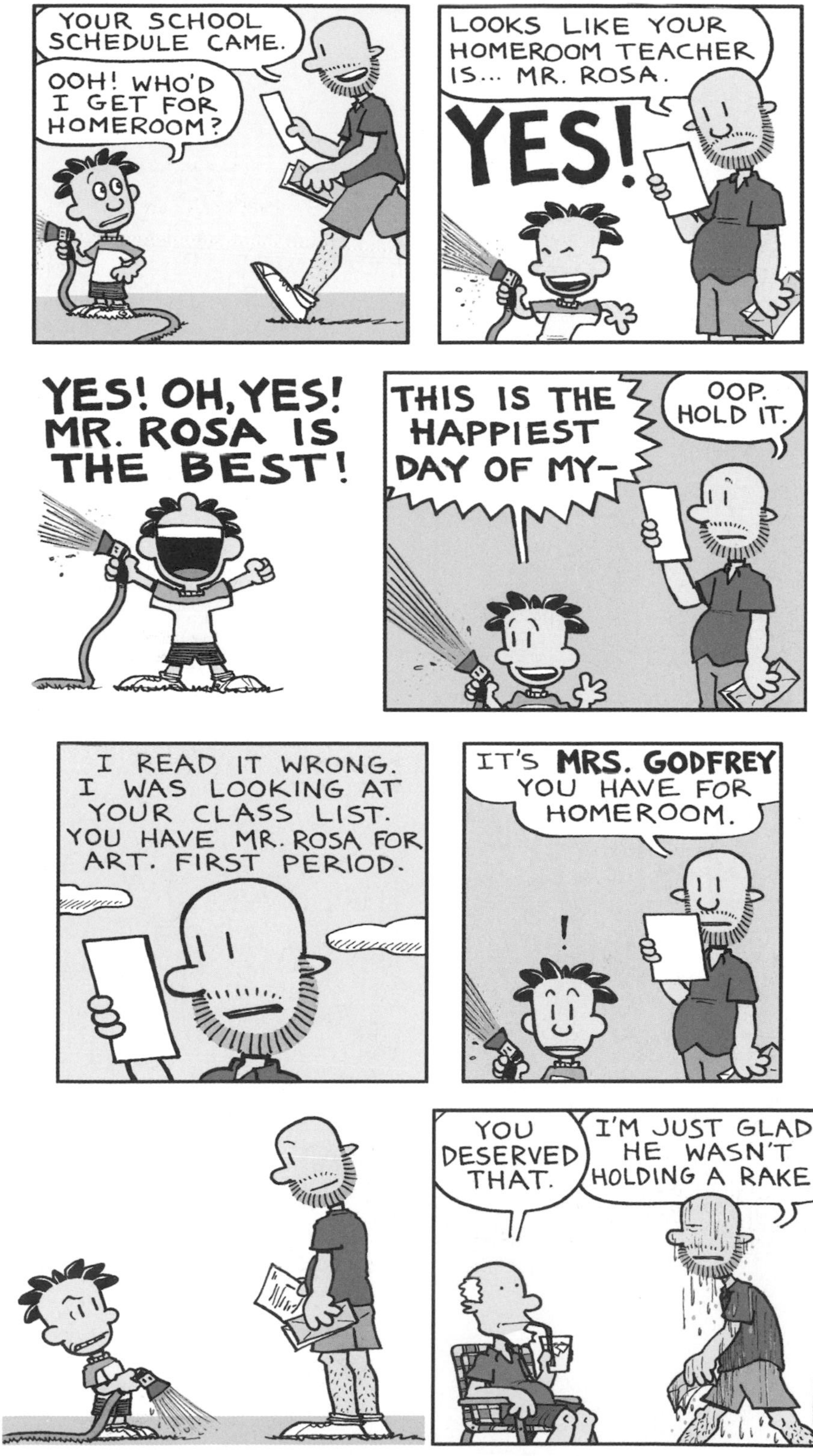
YOUR SCHOOL SCHEDULE CAME.
OOH! WHO'D I GET FOR HOMEROOM?
LOOKS LIKE YOUR HOMEROOM TEACHER IS... MR. ROSA.
YES!
YES! OH, YES! MR. ROSA IS THE BEST!
THIS IS THE HAPPIEST DAY OF MY–
OOP. HOLD IT.
I READ IT WRONG. I WAS LOOKING AT YOUR CLASS LIST. YOU HAVE MR. ROSA FOR ART. FIRST PERIOD.
IT'S MRS. GODFREY YOU HAVE FOR HOMEROOM.
!
YOU DESERVED THAT.
I'M JUST GLAD HE WASN'T HOLDING A RAKE.

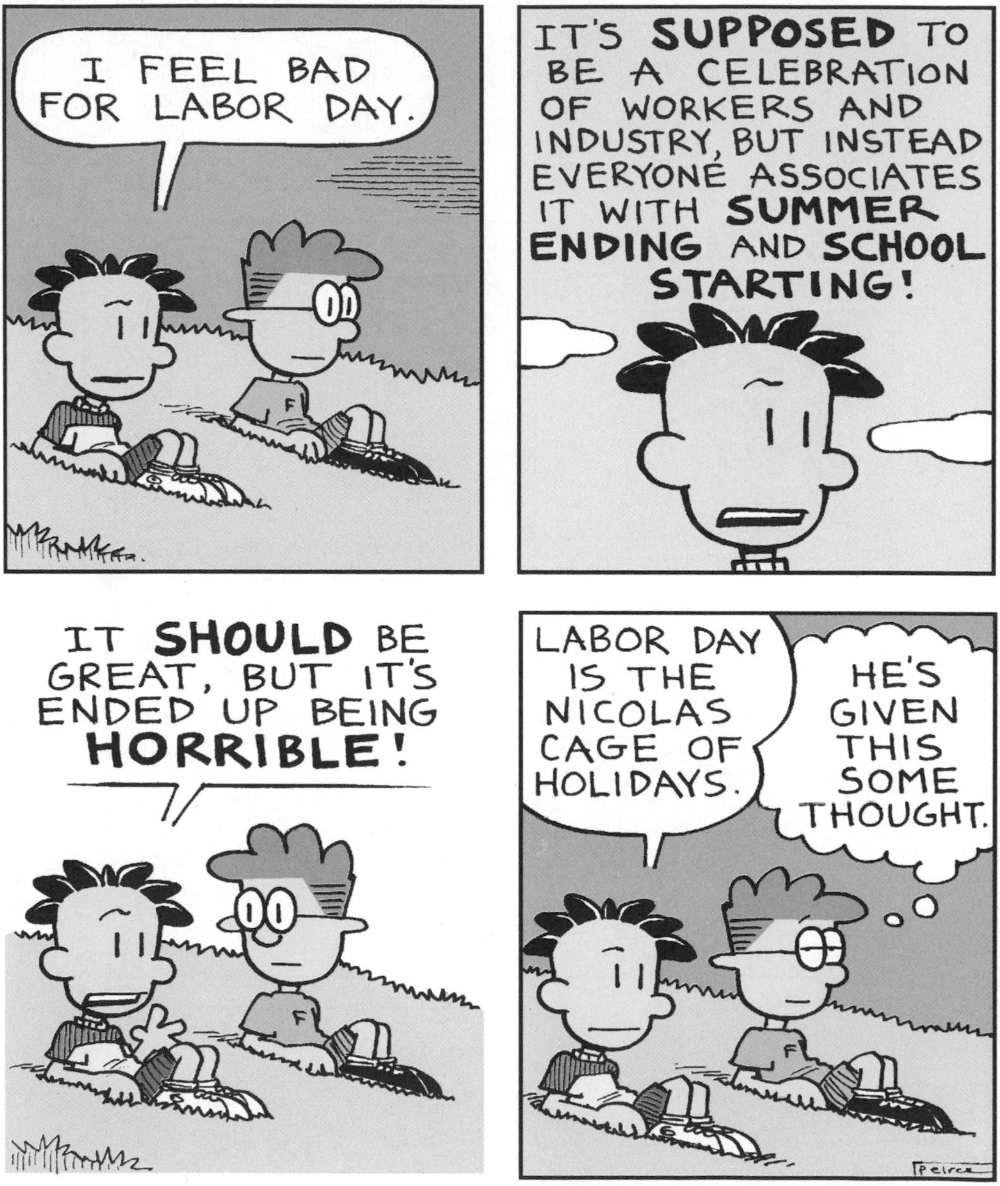
I FEEL BAD FOR LABOR DAY.
IT'S **SUPPOSED** TO BE A CELEBRATION OF WORKERS AND INDUSTRY, BUT INSTEAD EVERYONE ASSOCIATES IT WITH **SUMMER ENDING** AND **SCHOOL STARTING!**
IT **SHOULD** BE GREAT, BUT IT'S ENDED UP BEING **HORRIBLE!**
LABOR DAY IS THE NICOLAS CAGE OF HOLIDAYS.
HE'S GIVEN THIS SOME THOUGHT.
Peirce

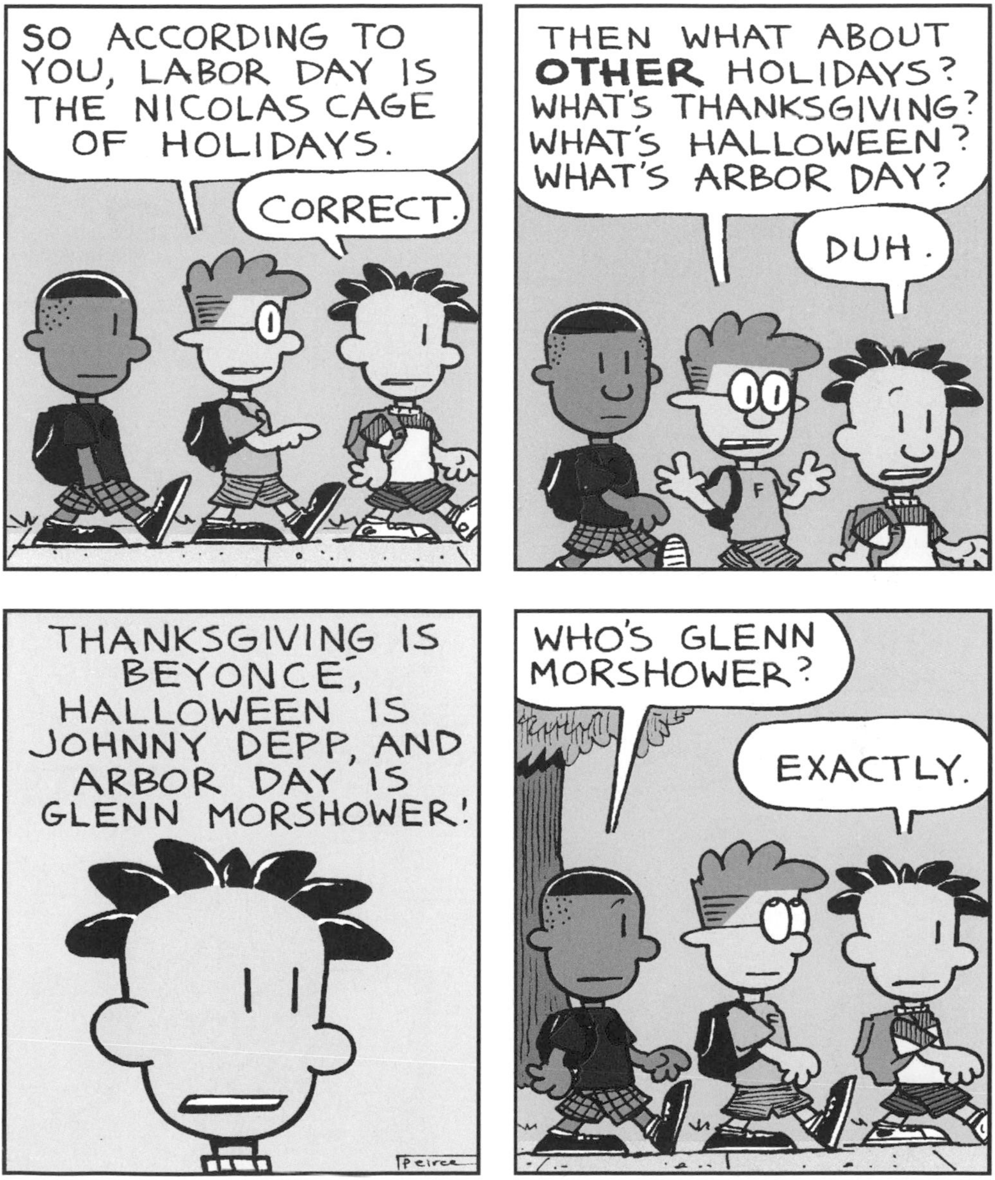
SO ACCORDING TO YOU, LABOR DAY IS THE NICOLAS CAGE OF HOLIDAYS.
CORRECT.
THEN WHAT ABOUT **OTHER** HOLIDAYS? WHAT'S THANKSGIVING? WHAT'S HALLOWEEN? WHAT'S ARBOR DAY?
DUH.
THANKSGIVING IS BEYONCÉ, HALLOWEEN IS JOHNNY DEPP, AND ARBOR DAY IS GLENN MORSHOWER!
Peirce
WHO'S GLENN MORSHOWER?
EXACTLY.

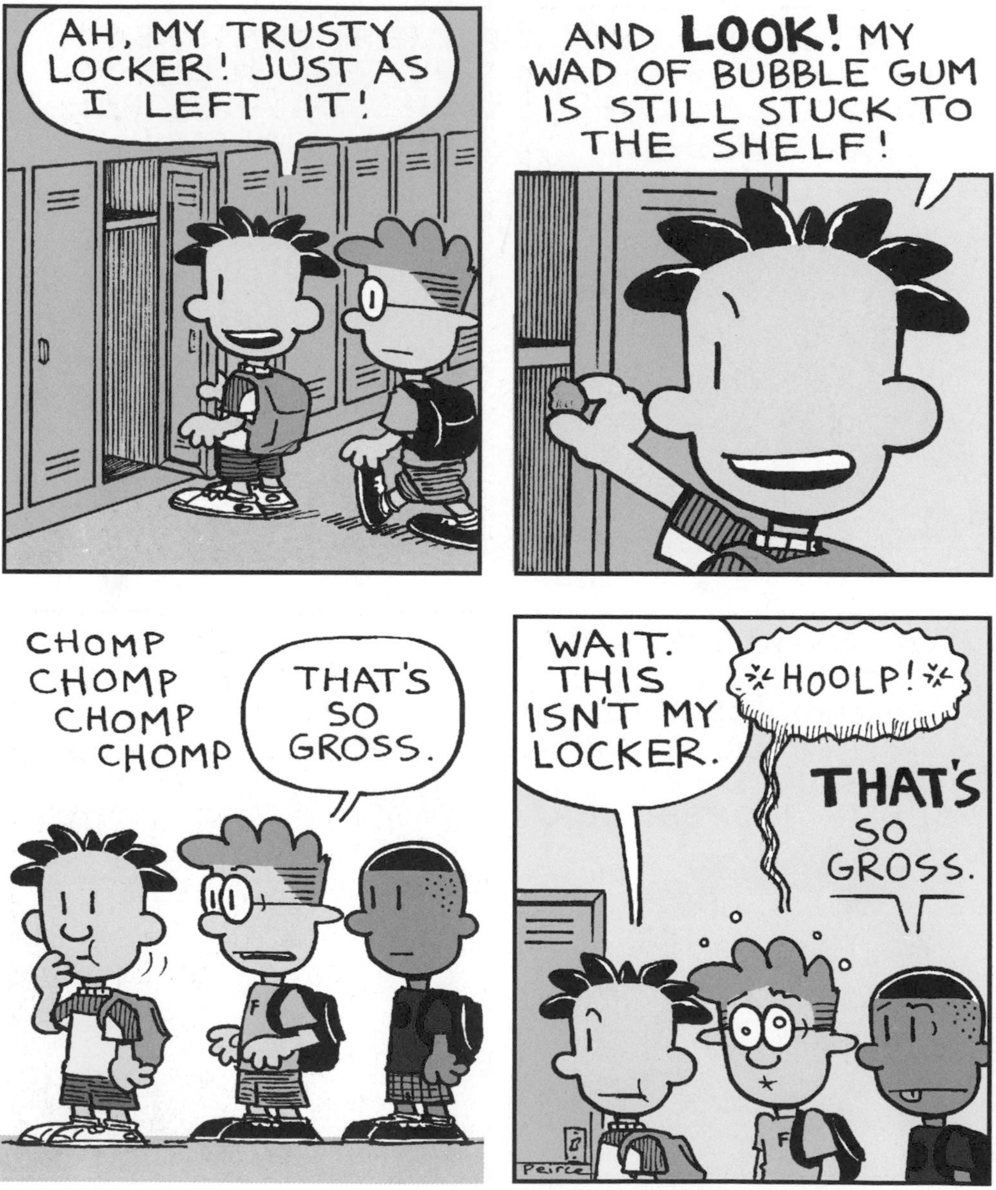
AH, MY TRUSTY LOCKER! JUST AS I LEFT IT!
AND LOOK! MY WAD OF BUBBLE GUM IS STILL STUCK TO THE SHELF!
CHOMP CHOMP CHOMP CHOMP
THAT'S SO GROSS.
WAIT. THIS ISN'T MY LOCKER.
HOOLP!
THAT'S SO GROSS.
Peirce

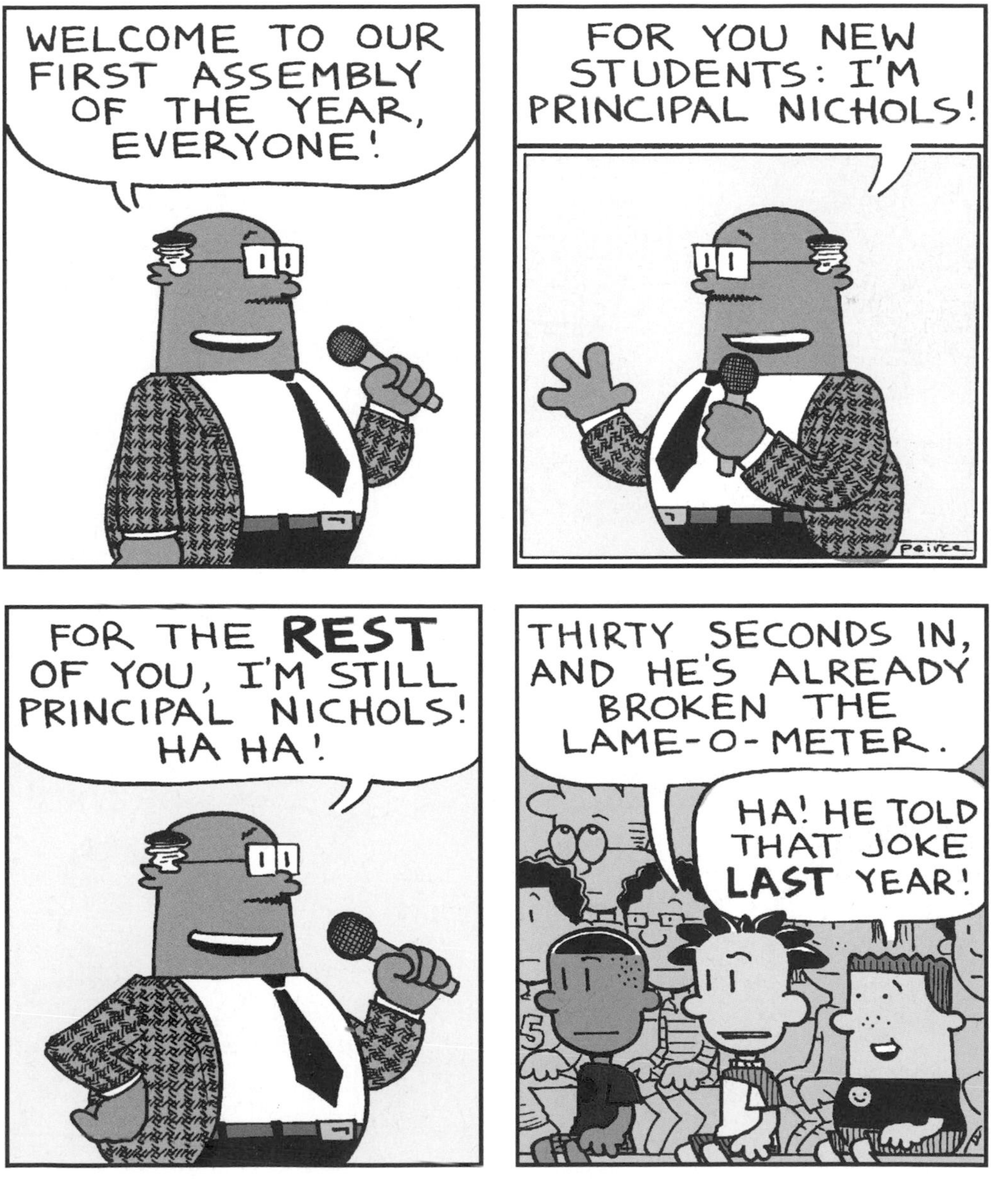
WELCOME TO OUR FIRST ASSEMBLY OF THE YEAR, EVERYONE!
FOR YOU NEW STUDENTS: I'M PRINCIPAL NICHOLS!
peirce
FOR THE **REST** OF YOU, I'M STILL PRINCIPAL NICHOLS! HA HA!
THIRTY SECONDS IN, AND HE'S ALREADY BROKEN THE LAME-O-METER.
HA! HE TOLD THAT JOKE **LAST** YEAR!

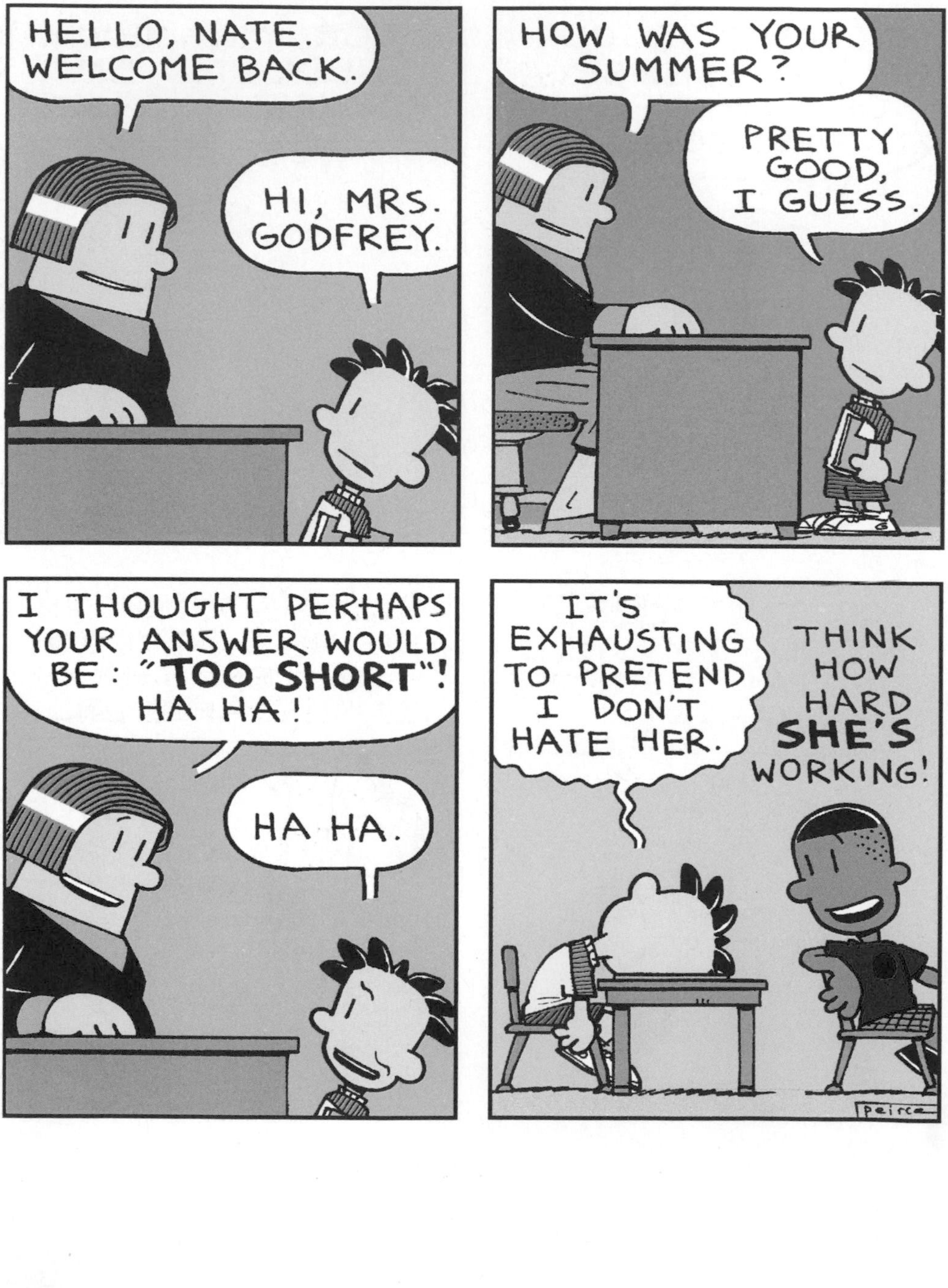
HELLO, NATE. WELCOME BACK.
HI, MRS. GODFREY.
HOW WAS YOUR SUMMER?
PRETTY GOOD, I GUESS.
I THOUGHT PERHAPS YOUR ANSWER WOULD BE: "**TOO SHORT**"! HA HA!
HA HA.
IT'S EXHAUSTING TO PRETEND I DON'T HATE HER.
THINK HOW HARD **SHE'S** WORKING!
peirce

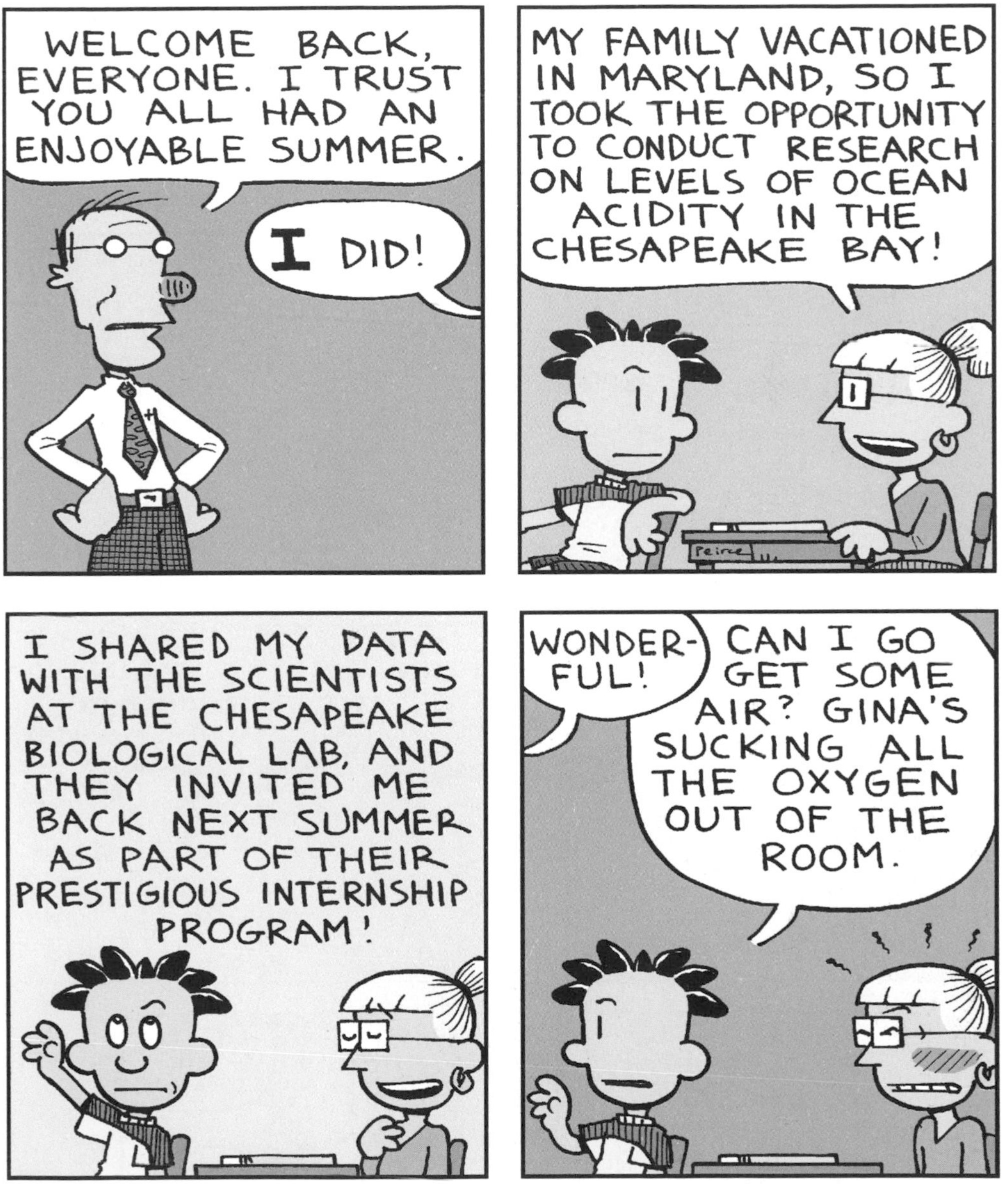
WELCOME BACK, EVERYONE. I TRUST YOU ALL HAD AN ENJOYABLE SUMMER.
I DID!
MY FAMILY VACATIONED IN MARYLAND, SO I TOOK THE OPPORTUNITY TO CONDUCT RESEARCH ON LEVELS OF OCEAN ACIDITY IN THE CHESAPEAKE BAY!
I SHARED MY DATA WITH THE SCIENTISTS AT THE CHESAPEAKE BIOLOGICAL LAB, AND THEY INVITED ME BACK NEXT SUMMER AS PART OF THEIR PRESTIGIOUS INTERNSHIP PROGRAM!
WONDER-FUL!
CAN I GO GET SOME AIR? GINA'S SUCKING ALL THE OXYGEN OUT OF THE ROOM.

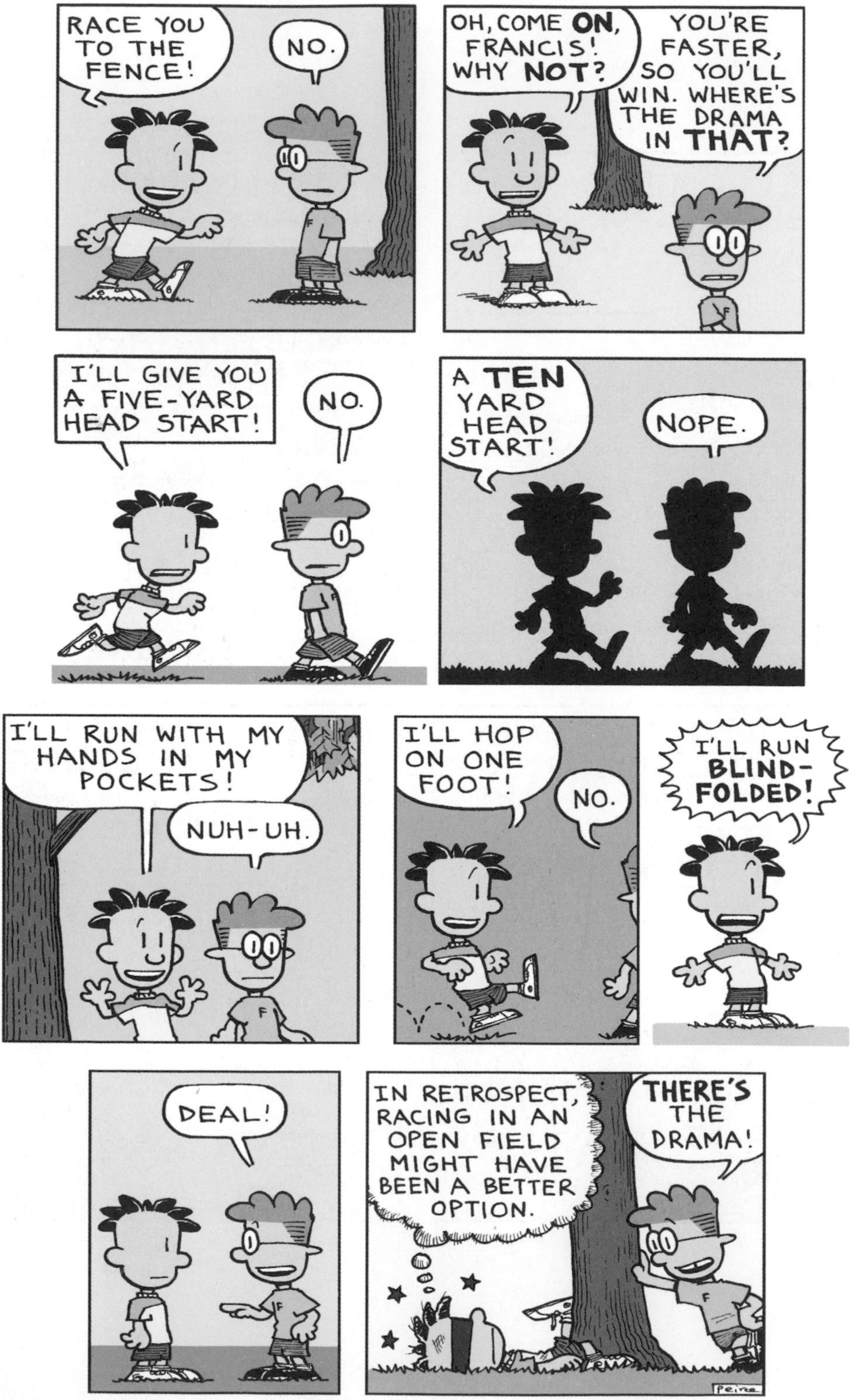
RACE YOU TO THE FENCE!
NO.
OH, COME ON, FRANCIS! WHY NOT?
YOU'RE FASTER, SO YOU'LL WIN. WHERE'S THE DRAMA IN THAT?
I'LL GIVE YOU A FIVE-YARD HEAD START!
NO.
A TEN YARD HEAD START!
NOPE.
I'LL RUN WITH MY HANDS IN MY POCKETS!
NUH-UH.
I'LL HOP ON ONE FOOT!
NO.
I'LL RUN BLIND-FOLDED!
DEAL!
IN RETROSPECT, RACING IN AN OPEN FIELD MIGHT HAVE BEEN A BETTER OPTION.
THERE'S THE DRAMA!
Peirce

HI, ALAN.

ACTUALLY, I'M NOT ALAN ANYMORE.

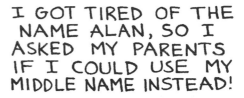

I GOT TIRED OF THE NAME ALAN, SO I ASKED MY PARENTS IF I COULD USE MY MIDDLE NAME INSTEAD!

THAT'S COOL. SO WHAT'S YOUR NEW NAME?

NATE!

WHAT?

JUST LIKE YOU!

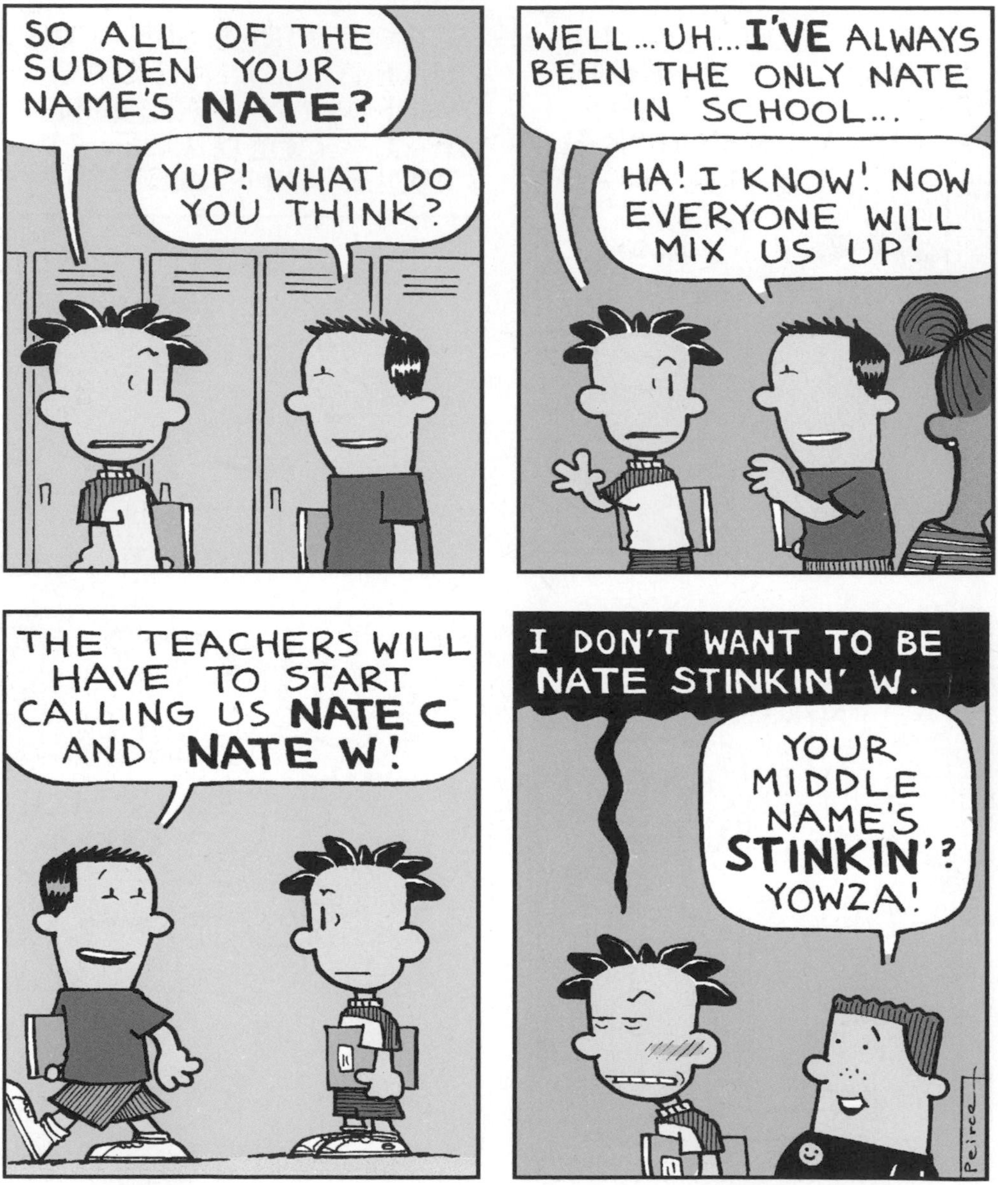
SO ALL OF THE SUDDEN YOUR NAME'S **NATE**?
YUP! WHAT DO YOU THINK?
WELL... UH... **I'VE** ALWAYS BEEN THE ONLY NATE IN SCHOOL...
HA! I KNOW! NOW EVERYONE WILL MIX US UP!
THE TEACHERS WILL HAVE TO START CALLING US **NATE C** AND **NATE W**!
I DON'T WANT TO BE NATE STINKIN' W.
YOUR MIDDLE NAME'S **STINKIN'**? YOWZA!
Peirce

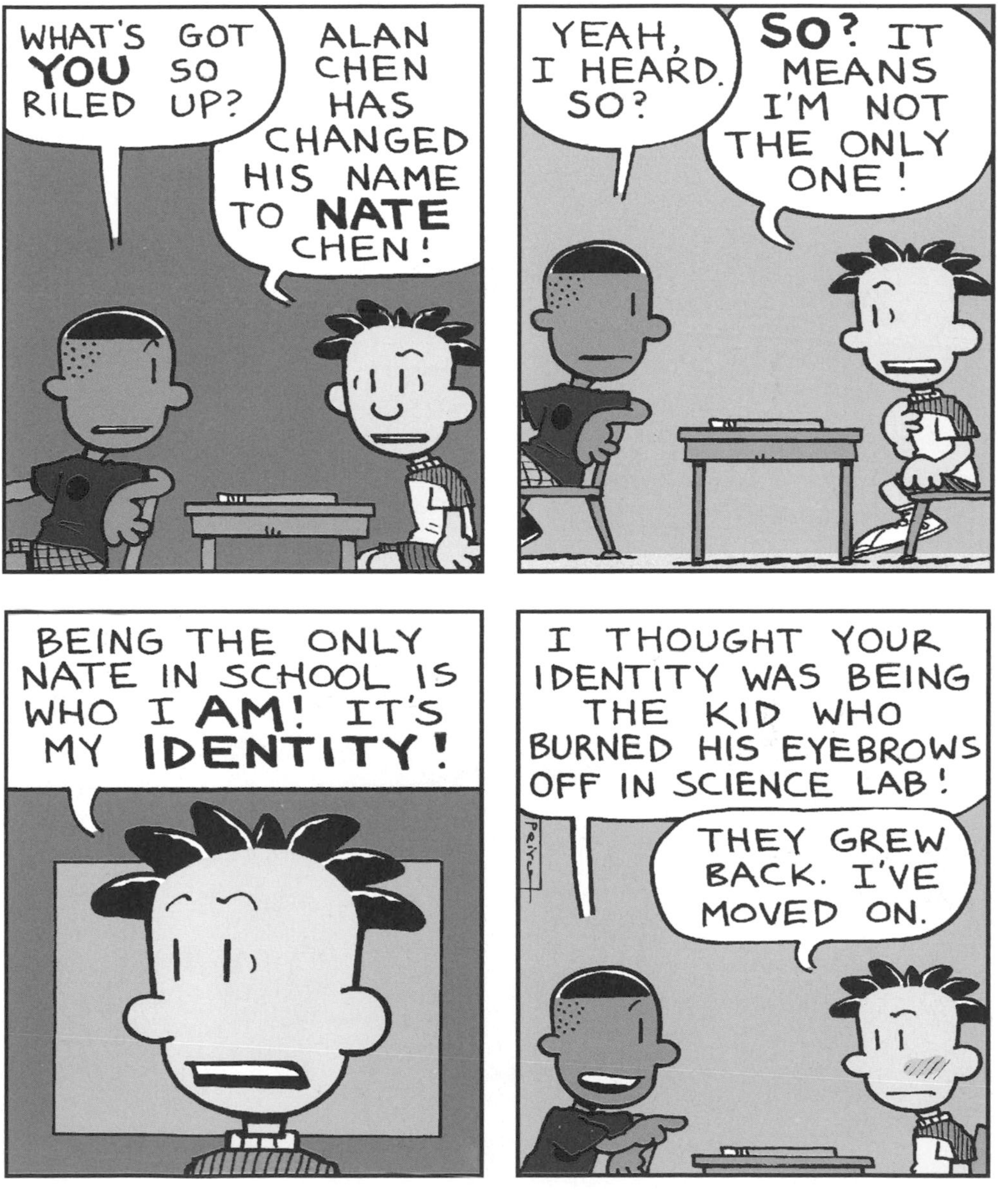
WHAT'S GOT **YOU** SO RILED UP?
ALAN CHEN HAS CHANGED HIS NAME TO **NATE** CHEN!
YEAH, I HEARD. SO?
SO? IT MEANS I'M NOT THE ONLY ONE!
BEING THE ONLY NATE IN SCHOOL IS WHO I **AM!** IT'S MY **IDENTITY!**
I THOUGHT YOUR IDENTITY WAS BEING THE KID WHO BURNED HIS EYEBROWS OFF IN SCIENCE LAB!
THEY GREW BACK. I'VE MOVED ON.
Peirce

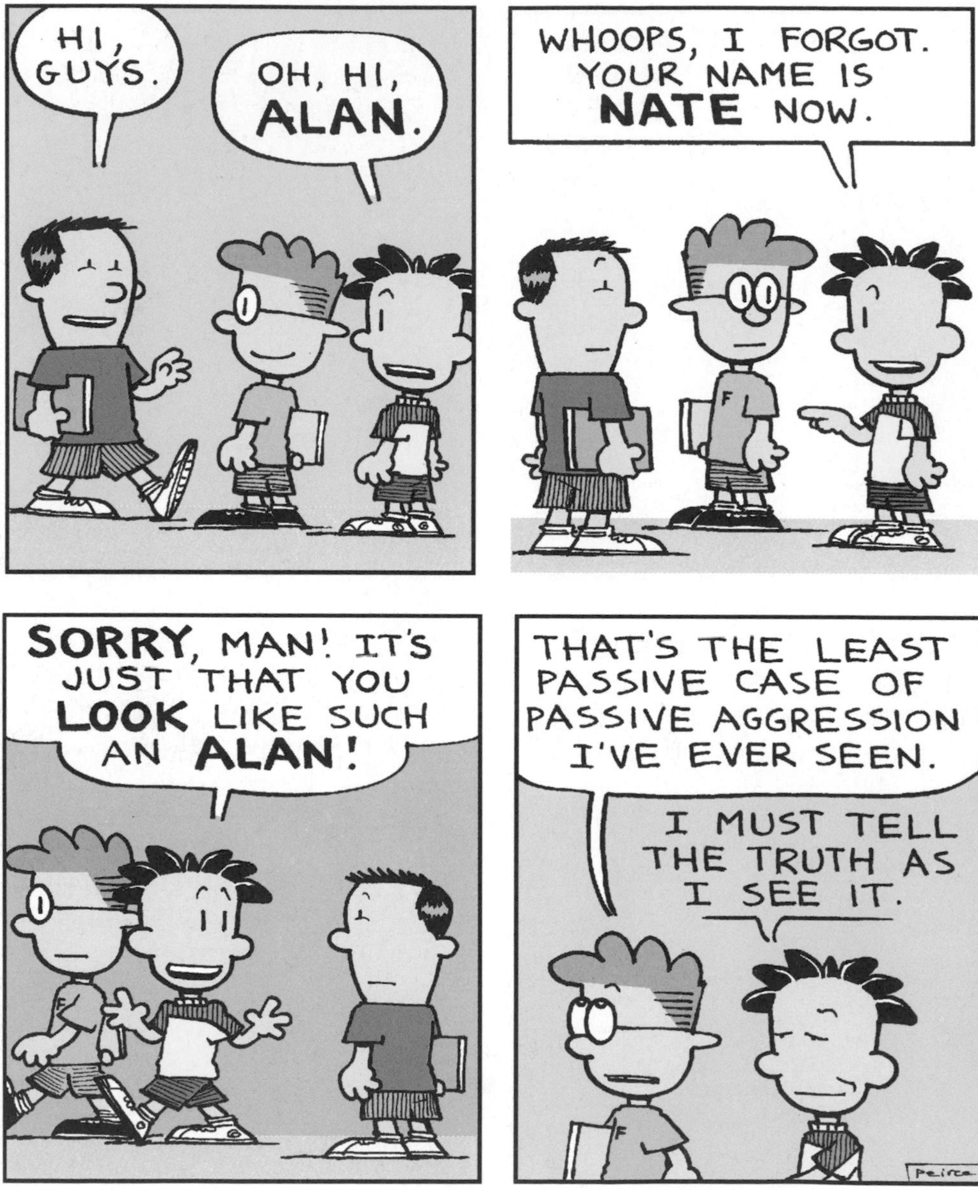
HI, GUYS.
OH, HI, **ALAN**.
WHOOPS, I FORGOT. YOUR NAME IS **NATE** NOW.
SORRY, MAN! IT'S JUST THAT YOU **LOOK** LIKE SUCH AN **ALAN**!
THAT'S THE LEAST PASSIVE CASE OF PASSIVE AGGRESSION I'VE EVER SEEN.
I MUST TELL THE TRUTH AS I SEE IT.
Peirce

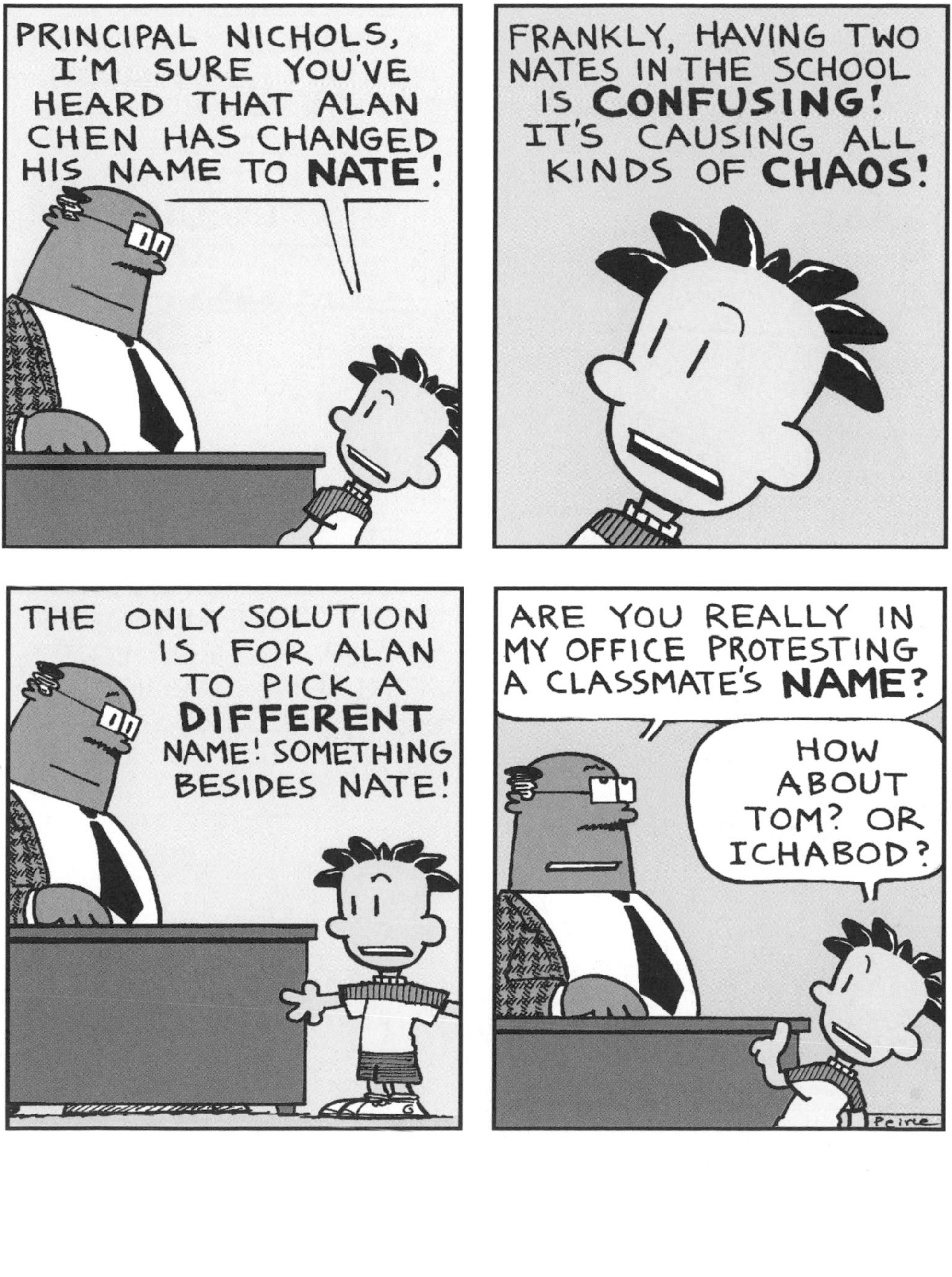
PRINCIPAL NICHOLS, I'M SURE YOU'VE HEARD THAT ALAN CHEN HAS CHANGED HIS NAME TO NATE!
FRANKLY, HAVING TWO NATES IN THE SCHOOL IS CONFUSING! IT'S CAUSING ALL KINDS OF CHAOS!
THE ONLY SOLUTION IS FOR ALAN TO PICK A DIFFERENT NAME! SOMETHING BESIDES NATE!
ARE YOU REALLY IN MY OFFICE PROTESTING A CLASSMATE'S NAME?
HOW ABOUT TOM? OR ICHABOD?
Peirce

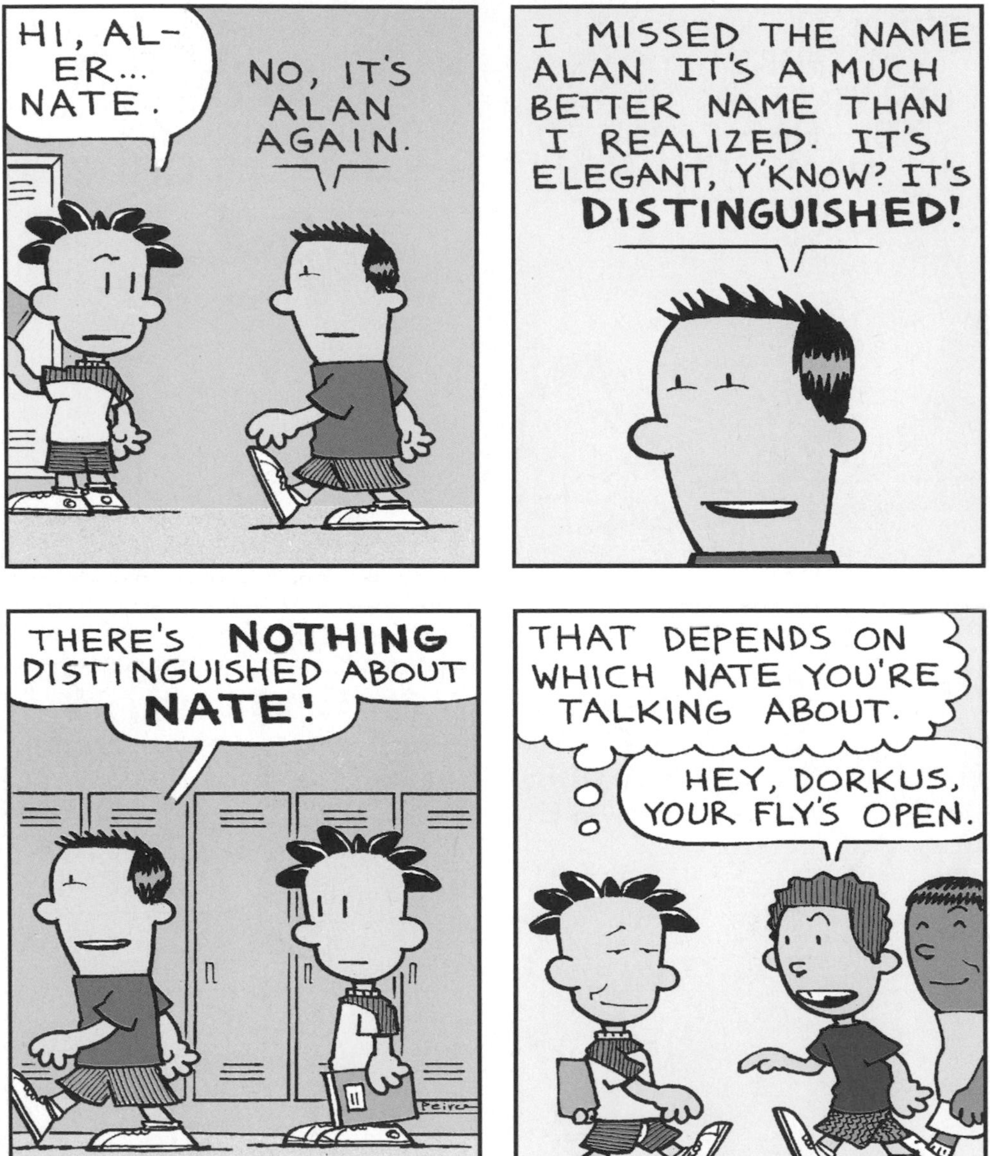
HI, AL- ER... NATE.
NO, IT'S ALAN AGAIN.
I MISSED THE NAME ALAN. IT'S A MUCH BETTER NAME THAN I REALIZED. IT'S ELEGANT, Y'KNOW? IT'S DISTINGUISHED!
THERE'S NOTHING DISTINGUISHED ABOUT NATE!
Peirce
THAT DEPENDS ON WHICH NATE YOU'RE TALKING ABOUT.
HEY, DORKUS, YOUR FLY'S OPEN.

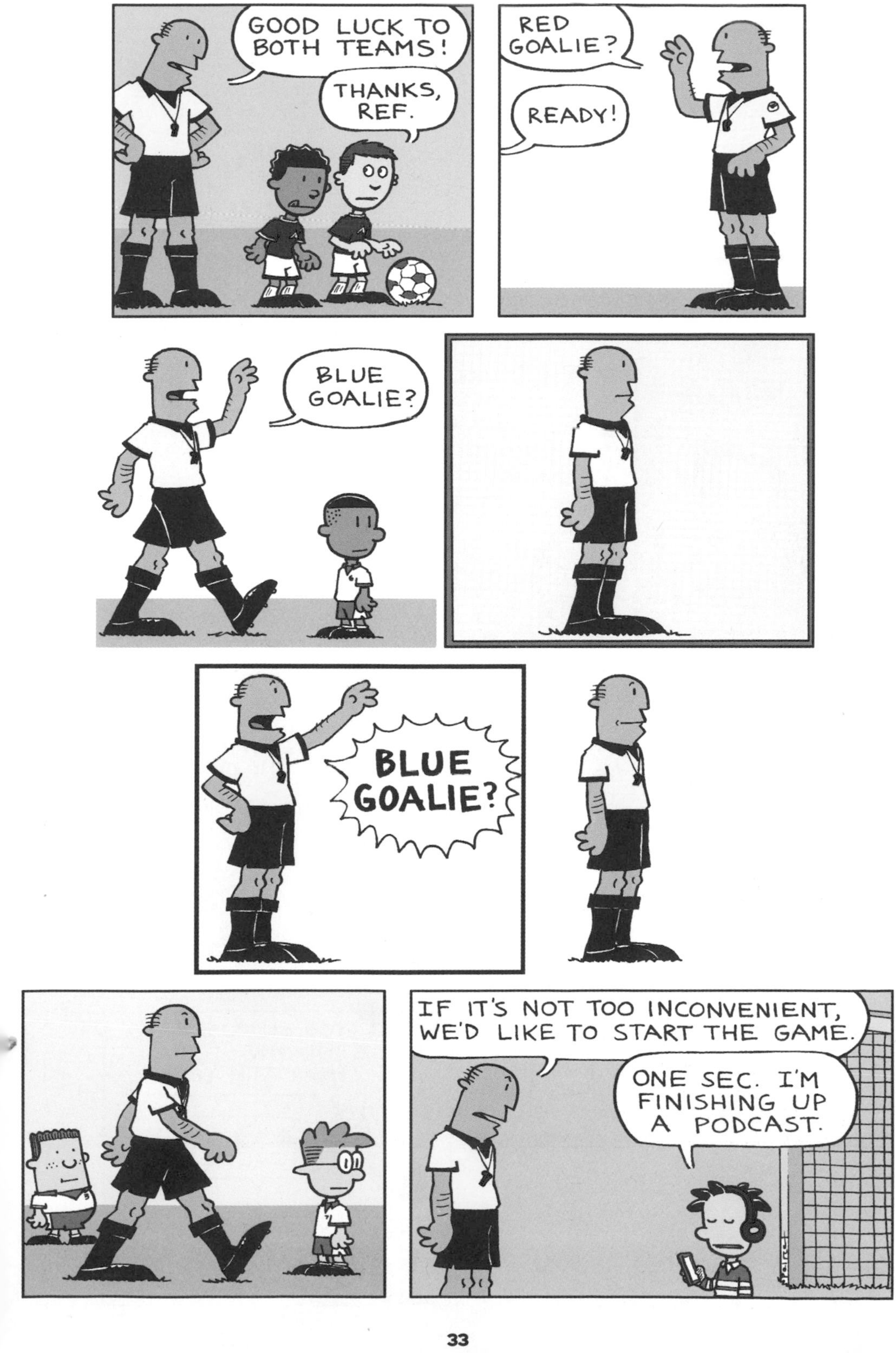
GOOD LUCK TO BOTH TEAMS!
THANKS, REF.
RED GOALIE?
READY!
BLUE GOALIE?
BLUE GOALIE?
IF IT'S NOT TOO INCONVENIENT, WE'D LIKE TO START THE GAME.
ONE SEC. I'M FINISHING UP A PODCAST.

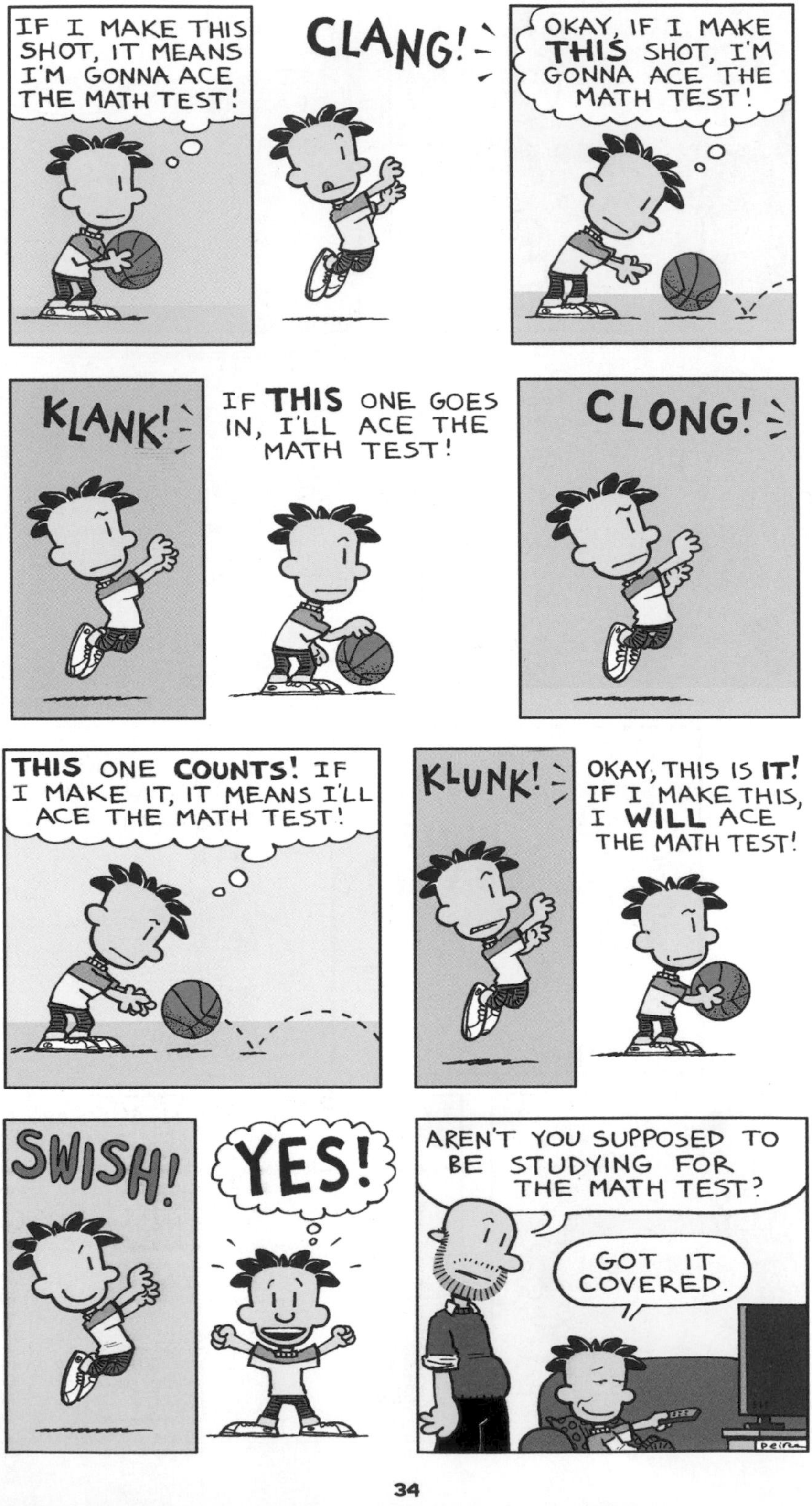
IF I MAKE THIS SHOT, IT MEANS I'M GONNA ACE THE MATH TEST!
CLANG!
OKAY, IF I MAKE THIS SHOT, I'M GONNA ACE THE MATH TEST!
KLANK!
IF THIS ONE GOES IN, I'LL ACE THE MATH TEST!
CLONG!
THIS ONE COUNTS! IF I MAKE IT, IT MEANS I'LL ACE THE MATH TEST!
KLUNK!
OKAY, THIS IS IT! IF I MAKE THIS, I WILL ACE THE MATH TEST!
SWISH!
YES!
AREN'T YOU SUPPOSED TO BE STUDYING FOR THE MATH TEST?
GOT IT COVERED.

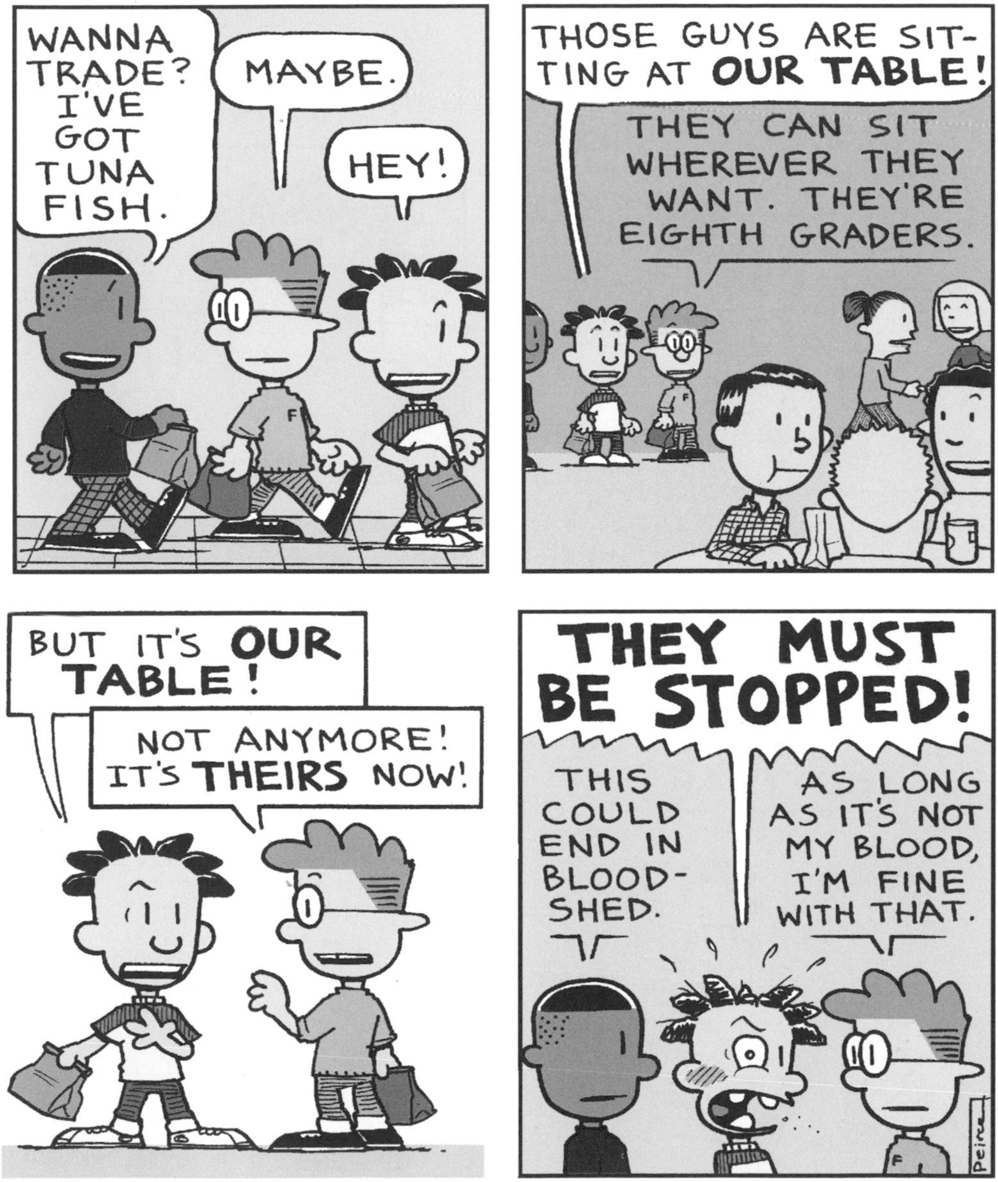

WANNA TRADE? I'VE GOT TUNA FISH.
MAYBE.
HEY!
THOSE GUYS ARE SIT-TING AT **OUR TABLE**!
THEY CAN SIT WHEREVER THEY WANT. THEY'RE EIGHTH GRADERS.
BUT IT'S **OUR TABLE**!
NOT ANYMORE! IT'S **THEIRS** NOW!
THEY MUST BE STOPPED!
THIS COULD END IN BLOOD-SHED.
AS LONG AS IT'S NOT MY BLOOD, I'M FINE WITH THAT.
Peirce

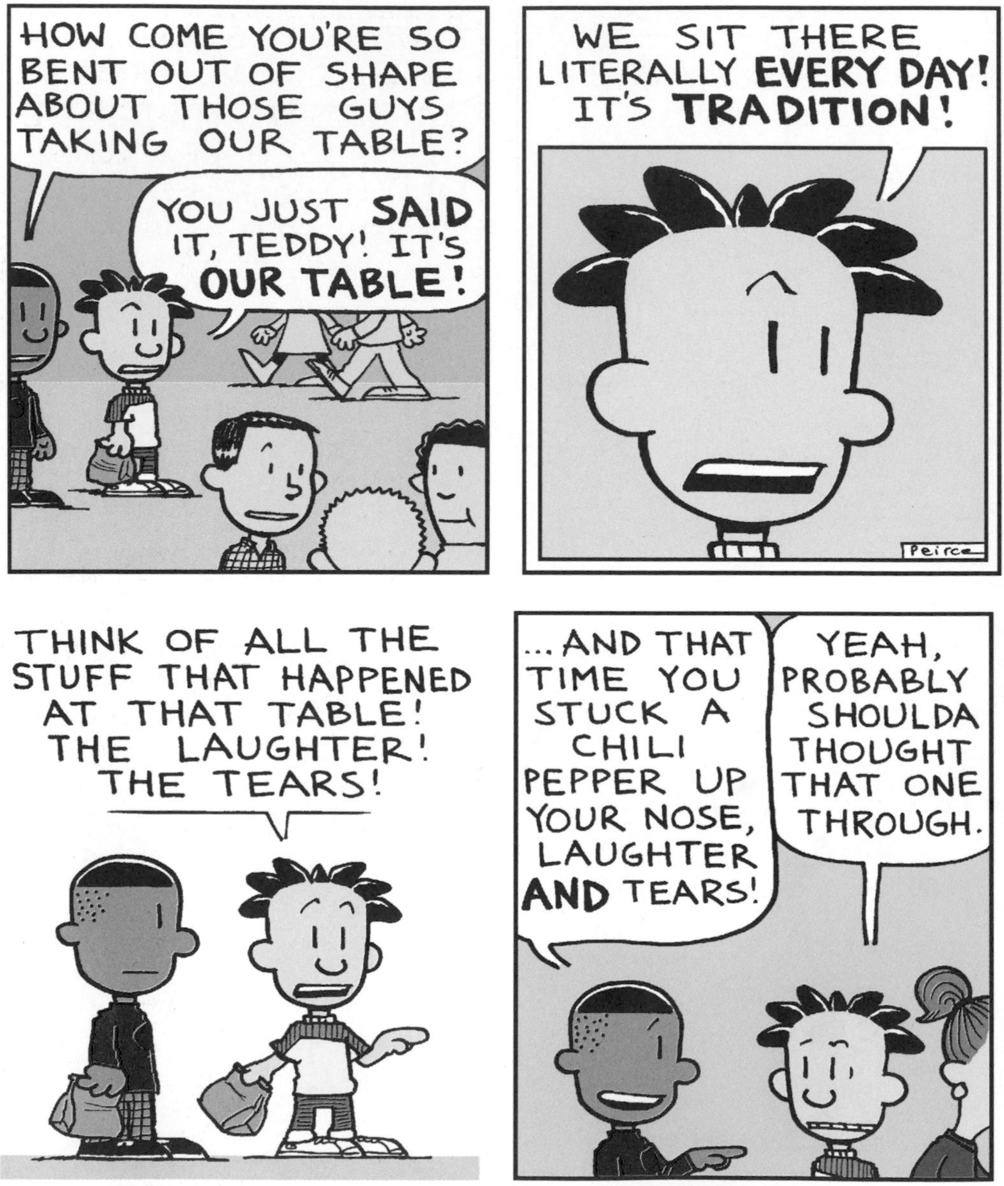
HOW COME YOU'RE SO BENT OUT OF SHAPE ABOUT THOSE GUYS TAKING OUR TABLE?
YOU JUST **SAID** IT, TEDDY! IT'S **OUR TABLE!**
WE SIT THERE LITERALLY **EVERY DAY!** IT'S **TRADITION!**
Peirce
THINK OF ALL THE STUFF THAT HAPPENED AT THAT TABLE! THE LAUGHTER! THE TEARS!
...AND THAT TIME YOU STUCK A CHILI PEPPER UP YOUR NOSE, LAUGHTER **AND** TEARS!
YEAH, PROBABLY SHOULDA THOUGHT THAT ONE THROUGH.

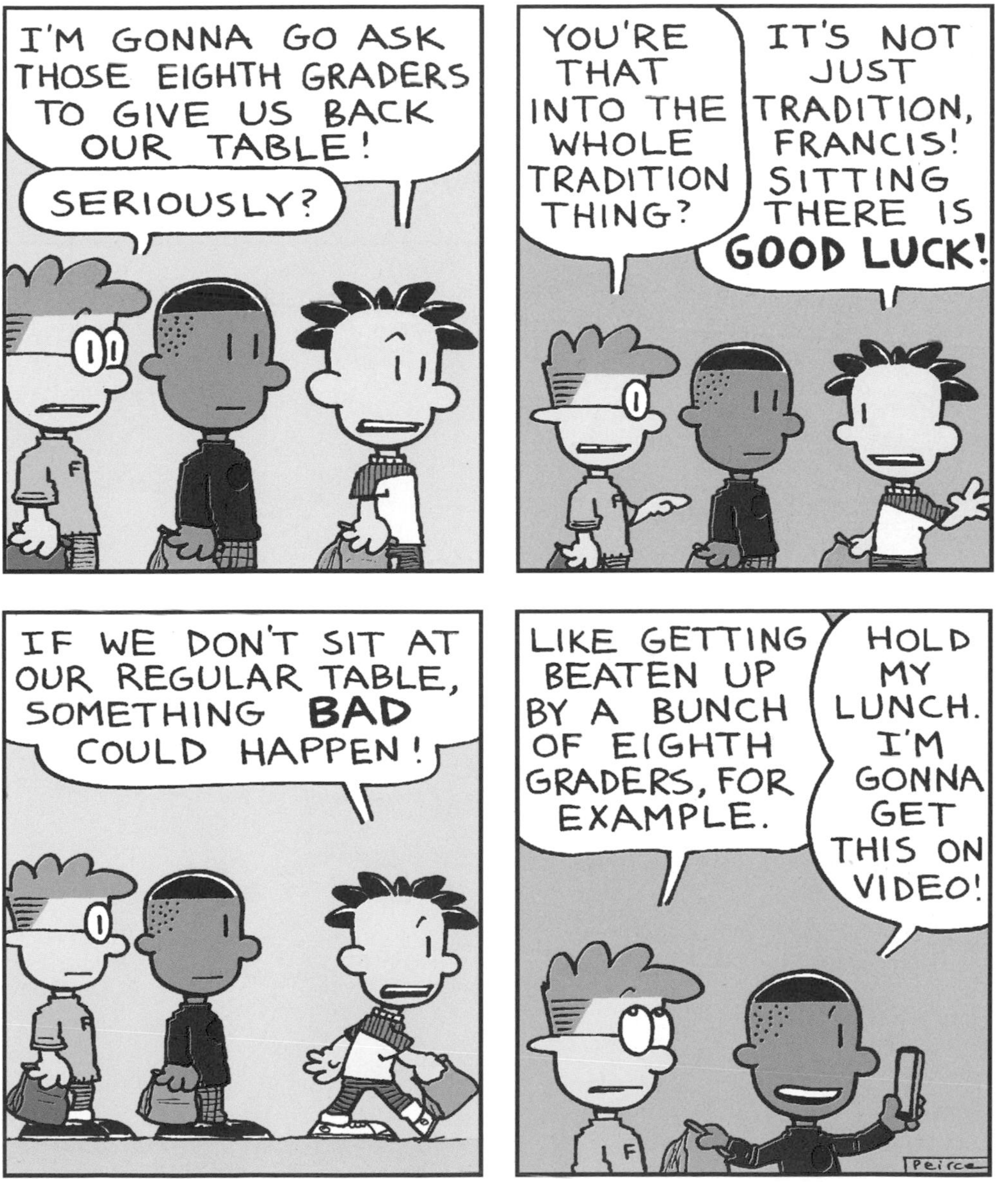
I'M GONNA GO ASK THOSE EIGHTH GRADERS TO GIVE US BACK OUR TABLE!
SERIOUSLY?
YOU'RE THAT INTO THE WHOLE TRADITION THING?
IT'S NOT JUST TRADITION, FRANCIS! SITTING THERE IS **GOOD LUCK!**
IF WE DON'T SIT AT OUR REGULAR TABLE, SOMETHING **BAD** COULD HAPPEN!
LIKE GETTING BEATEN UP BY A BUNCH OF EIGHTH GRADERS, FOR EXAMPLE.
HOLD MY LUNCH. I'M GONNA GET THIS ON VIDEO!
Peirce

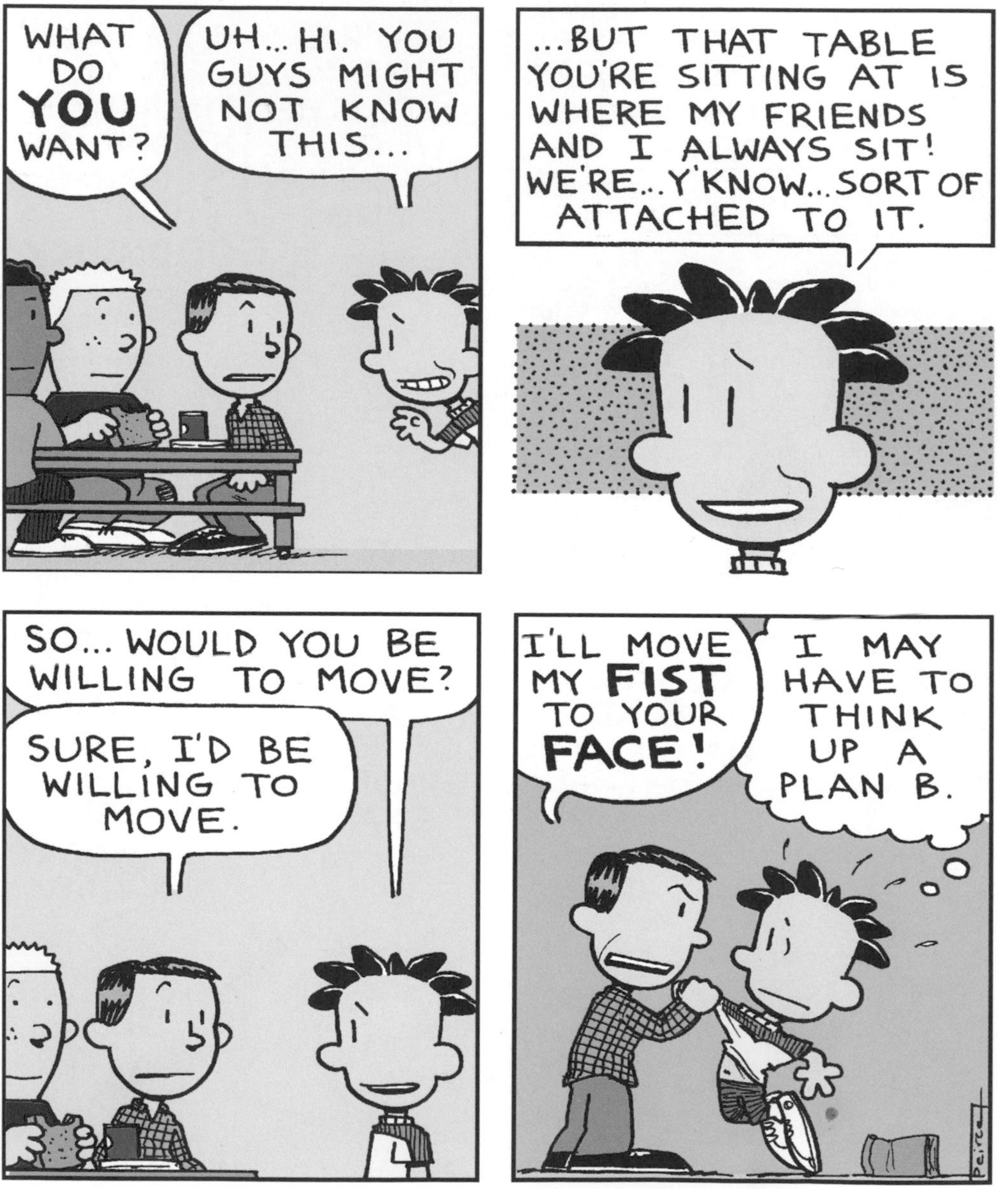
WHAT DO **YOU** WANT?
UH... HI. YOU GUYS MIGHT NOT KNOW THIS...
...BUT THAT TABLE YOU'RE SITTING AT IS WHERE MY FRIENDS AND I ALWAYS SIT! WE'RE... Y'KNOW... SORT OF ATTACHED TO IT.
SO... WOULD YOU BE WILLING TO MOVE?
SURE, I'D BE WILLING TO MOVE.
I'LL MOVE MY **FIST** TO YOUR **FACE**!
I MAY HAVE TO THINK UP A PLAN B.
Peirce

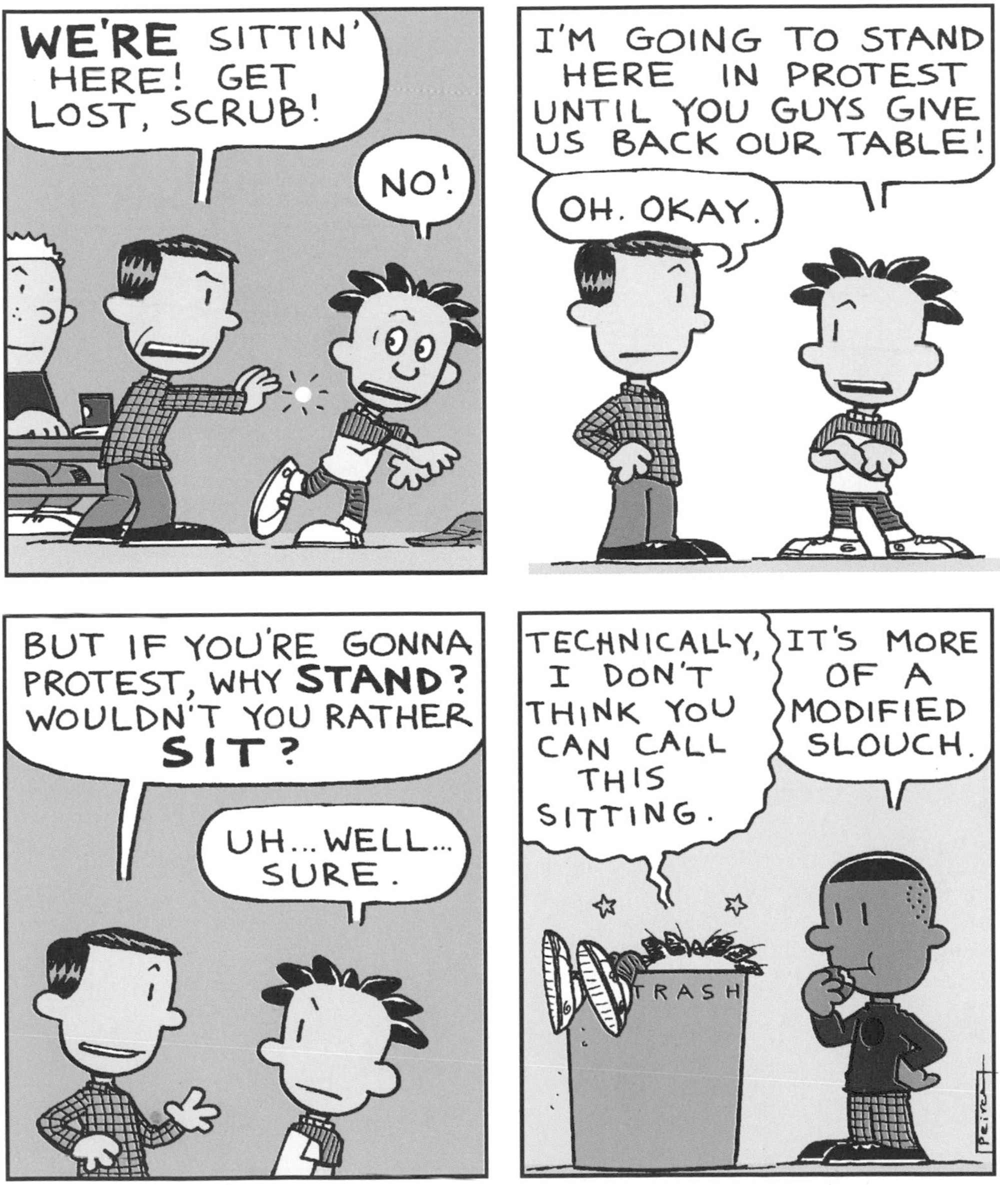
WE'RE SITTIN' HERE! GET LOST, SCRUB!
NO!
I'M GOING TO STAND HERE IN PROTEST UNTIL YOU GUYS GIVE US BACK OUR TABLE!
OH. OKAY.
BUT IF YOU'RE GONNA PROTEST, WHY STAND? WOULDN'T YOU RATHER SIT?
UH...WELL... SURE.
TECHNICALLY, I DON'T THINK YOU CAN CALL THIS SITTING.
IT'S MORE OF A MODIFIED SLOUCH.
TRASH
PEIRCE

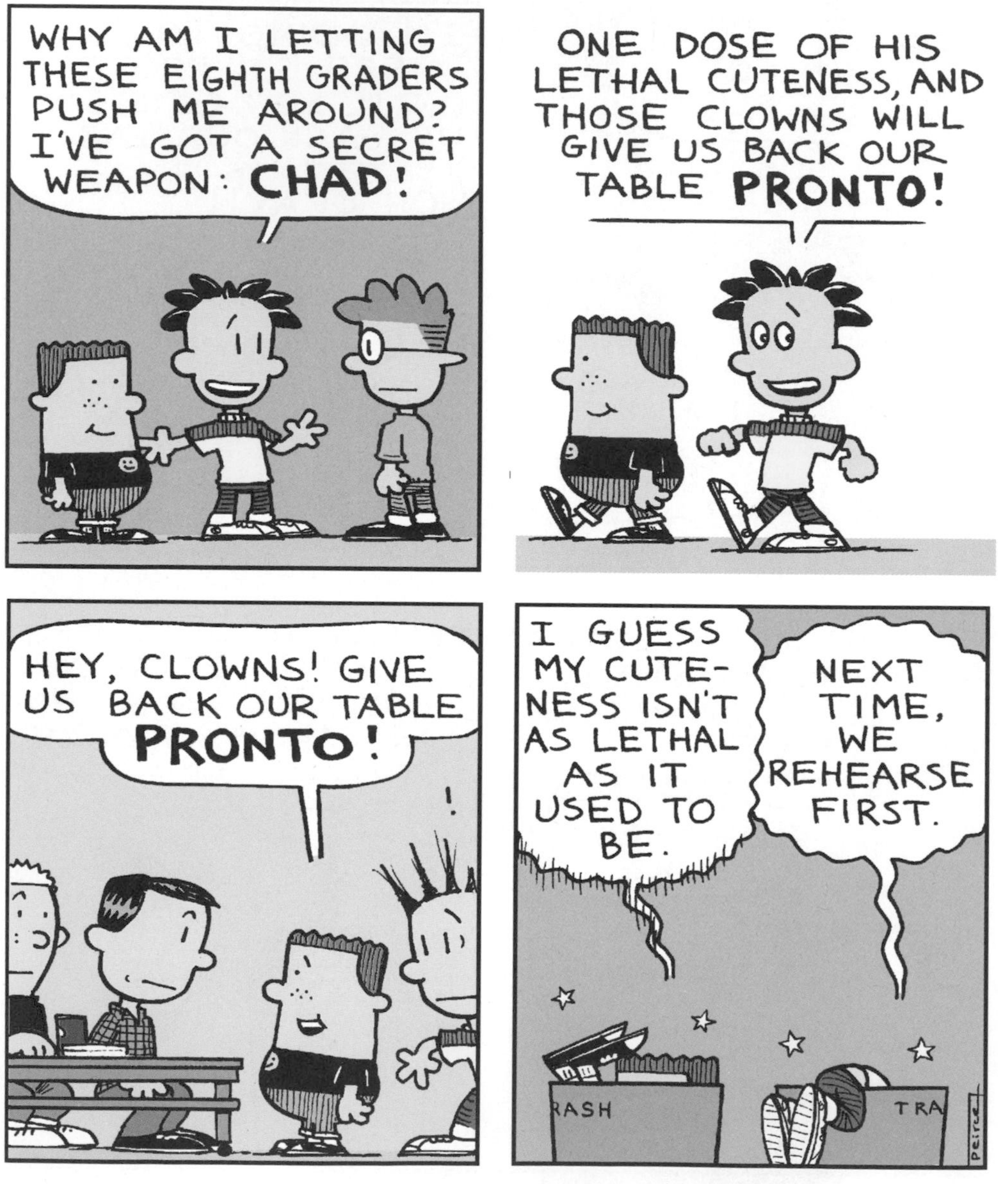
WHY AM I LETTING THESE EIGHTH GRADERS PUSH ME AROUND? I'VE GOT A SECRET WEAPON: CHAD!
ONE DOSE OF HIS LETHAL CUTENESS, AND THOSE CLOWNS WILL GIVE US BACK OUR TABLE PRONTO!
HEY, CLOWNS! GIVE US BACK OUR TABLE PRONTO!
!
I GUESS MY CUTENESS ISN'T AS LETHAL AS IT USED TO BE.
NEXT TIME, WE REHEARSE FIRST.
RASH
TRA
PEIRCE

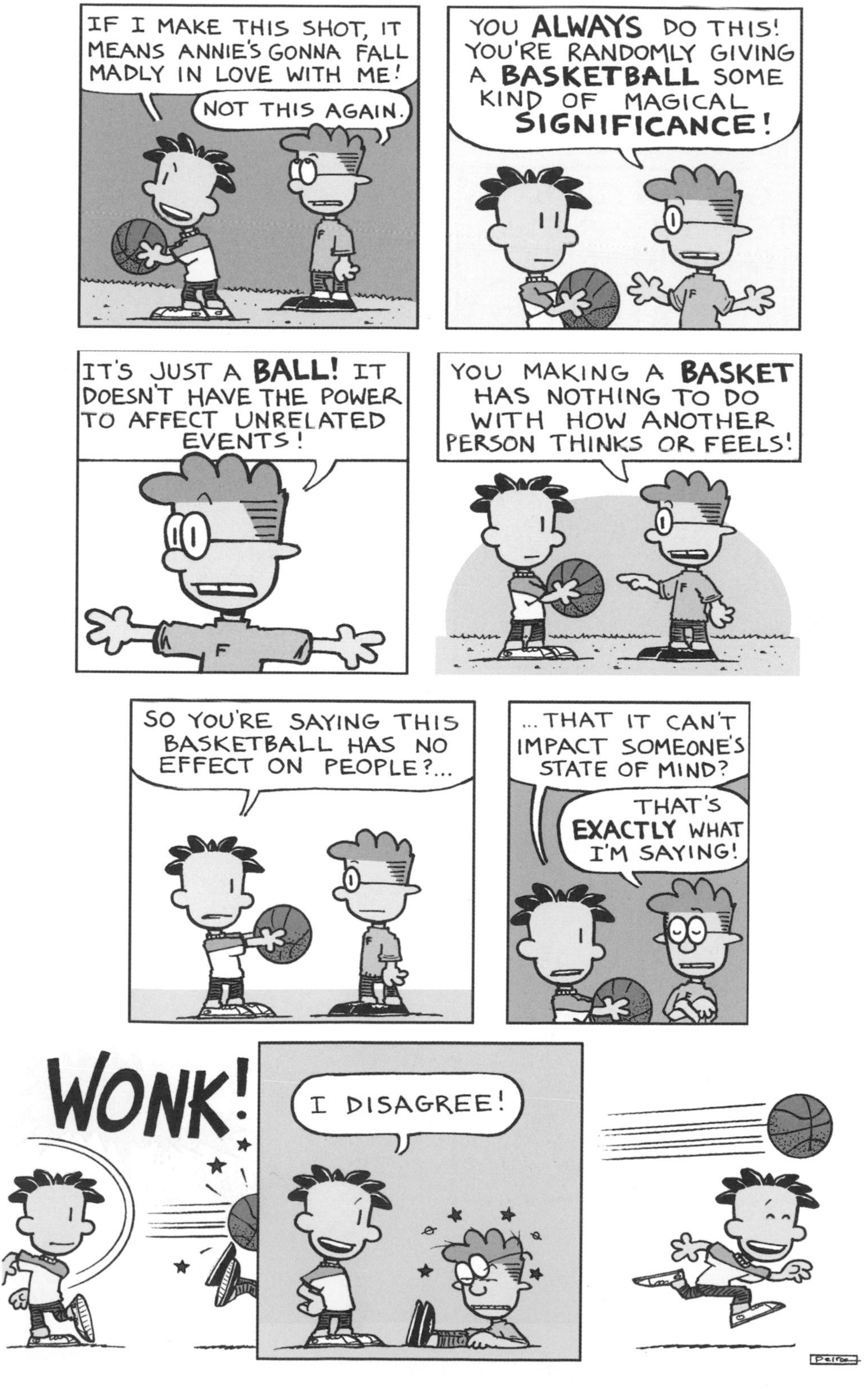
IF I MAKE THIS SHOT, IT MEANS ANNIE'S GONNA FALL MADLY IN LOVE WITH ME!
NOT THIS AGAIN.
YOU ALWAYS DO THIS! YOU'RE RANDOMLY GIVING A BASKETBALL SOME KIND OF MAGICAL SIGNIFICANCE!
IT'S JUST A BALL! IT DOESN'T HAVE THE POWER TO AFFECT UNRELATED EVENTS!
YOU MAKING A BASKET HAS NOTHING TO DO WITH HOW ANOTHER PERSON THINKS OR FEELS!
SO YOU'RE SAYING THIS BASKETBALL HAS NO EFFECT ON PEOPLE?...
...THAT IT CAN'T IMPACT SOMEONE'S STATE OF MIND?
THAT'S EXACTLY WHAT I'M SAYING!
WONK!
I DISAGREE!

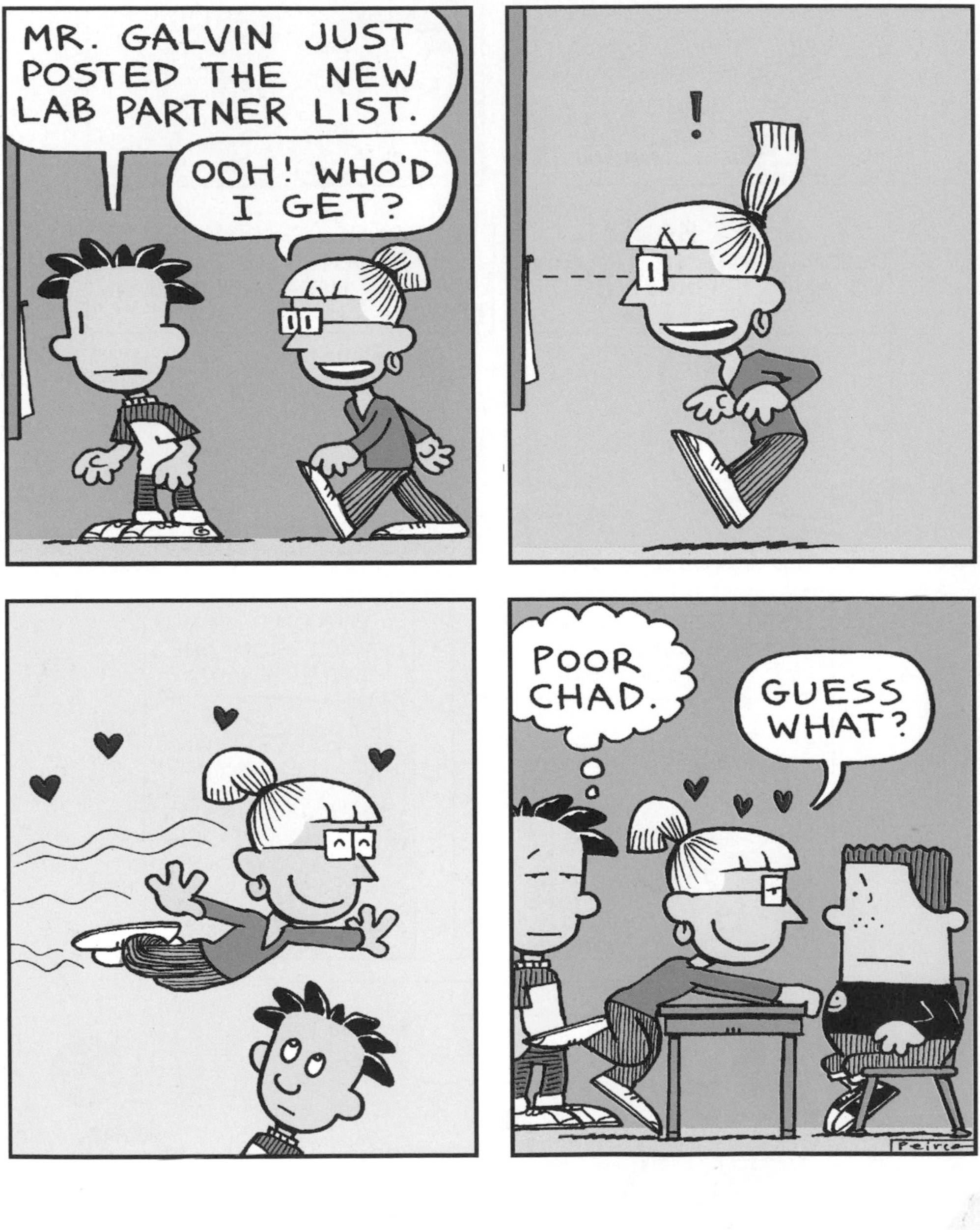
MR. GALVIN JUST POSTED THE NEW LAB PARTNER LIST.
OOH! WHO'D I GET?
!
POOR CHAD.
GUESS WHAT?
Peirce

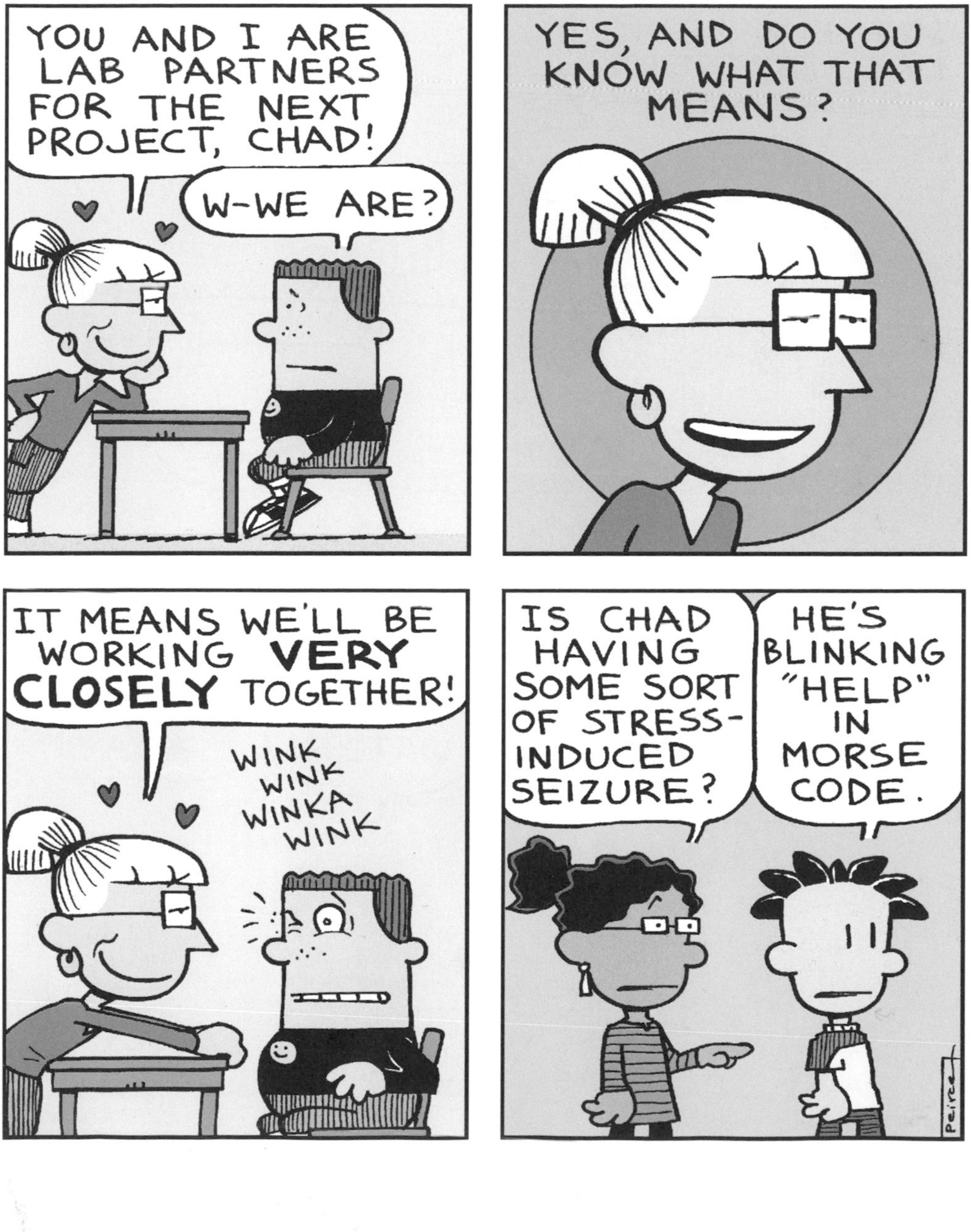
YOU AND I ARE LAB PARTNERS FOR THE NEXT PROJECT, CHAD!
W-WE ARE?
YES, AND DO YOU KNOW WHAT THAT MEANS?
IT MEANS WE'LL BE WORKING **VERY CLOSELY** TOGETHER!
WINK WINK WINKA WINK
IS CHAD HAVING SOME SORT OF STRESS-INDUCED SEIZURE?
HE'S BLINKING "HELP" IN MORSE CODE.
Peirce

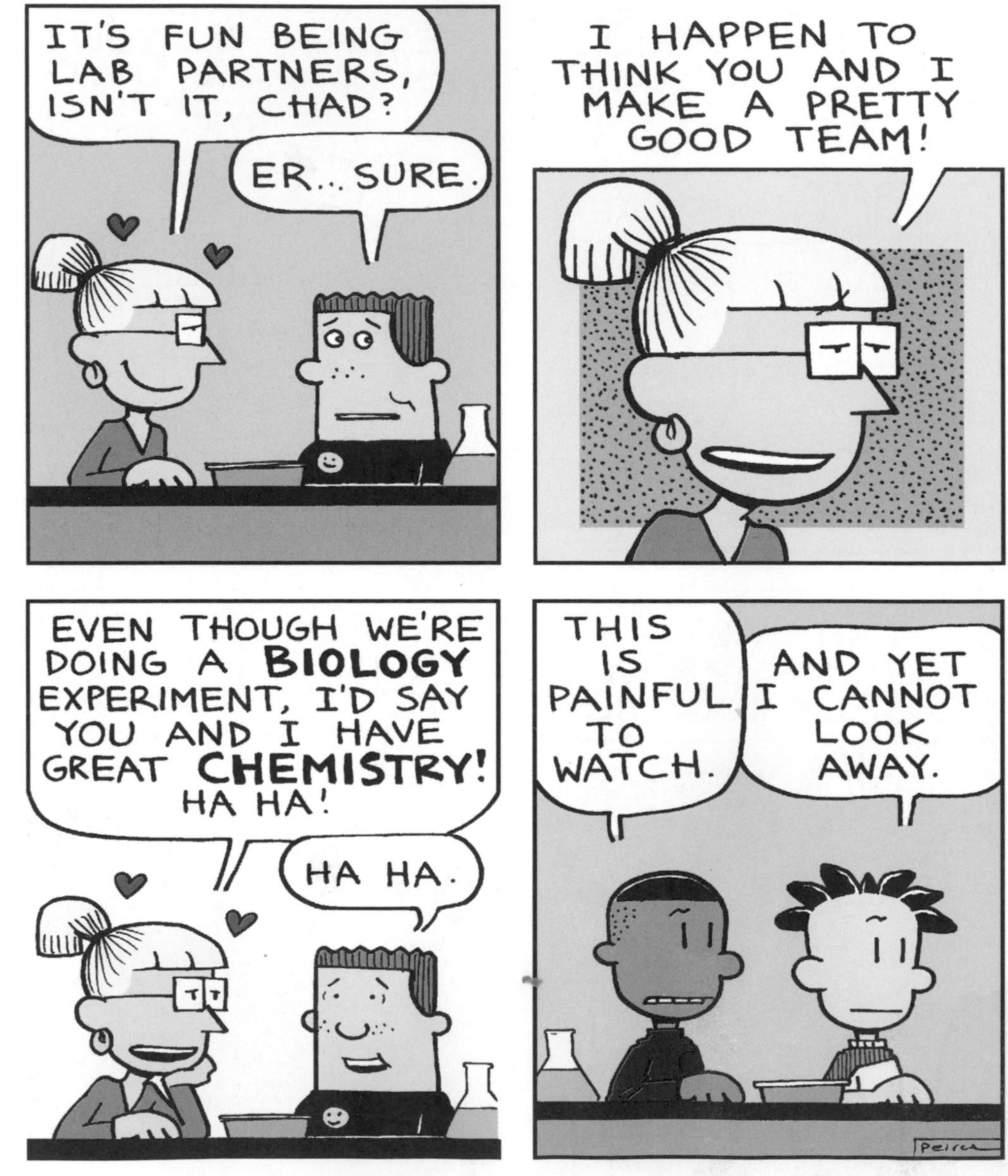
IT'S FUN BEING LAB PARTNERS, ISN'T IT, CHAD?
ER... SURE.
I HAPPEN TO THINK YOU AND I MAKE A PRETTY GOOD TEAM!
EVEN THOUGH WE'RE DOING A **BIOLOGY** EXPERIMENT, I'D SAY YOU AND I HAVE GREAT **CHEMISTRY!** HA HA!
HA HA.
THIS IS PAINFUL TO WATCH.
AND YET I CANNOT LOOK AWAY.
Peirce

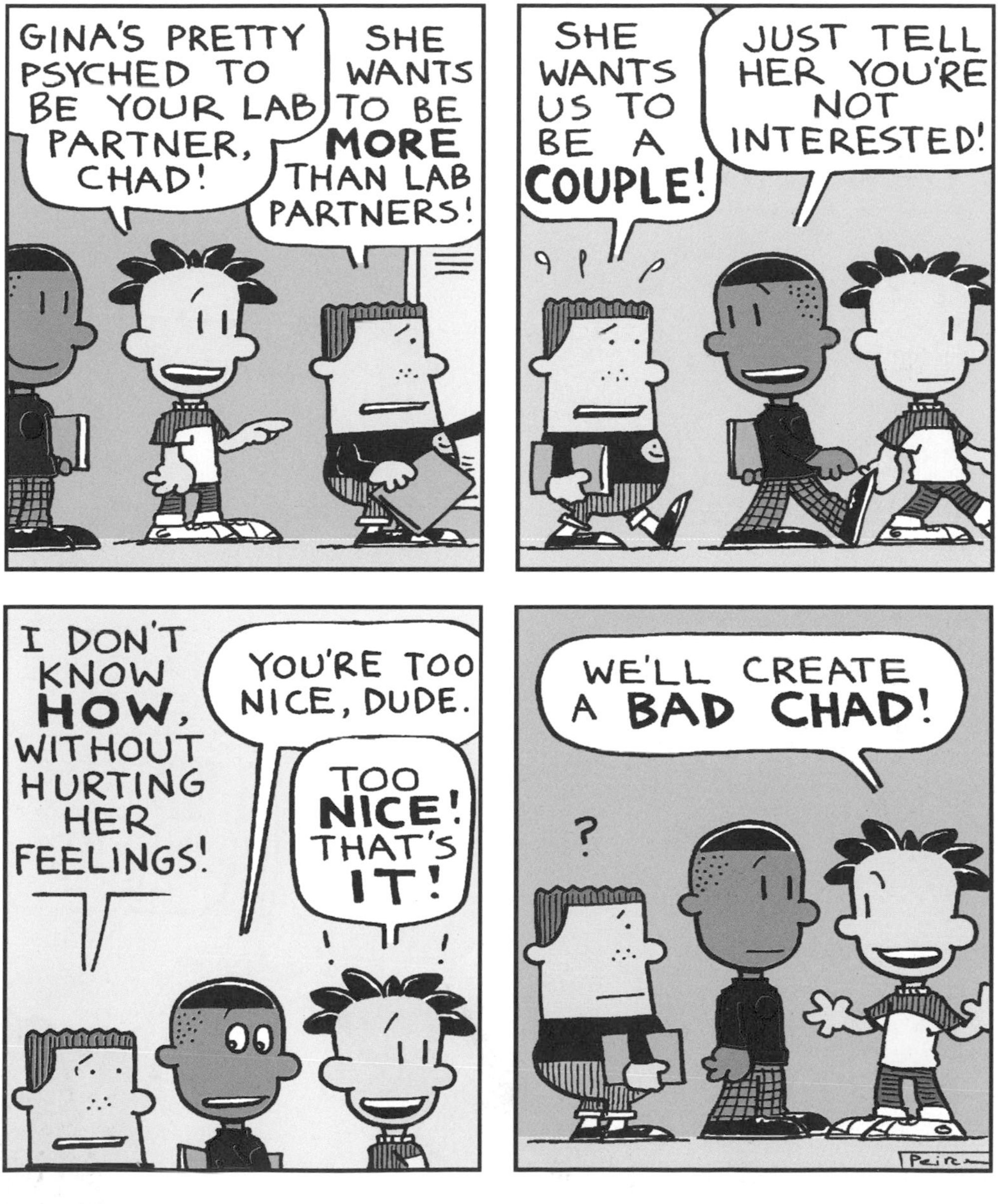
GINA'S PRETTY PSYCHED TO BE YOUR LAB PARTNER, CHAD!
SHE WANTS TO BE **MORE** THAN LAB PARTNERS!
SHE WANTS US TO BE A **COUPLE!**
JUST TELL HER YOU'RE NOT INTERESTED!
I DON'T KNOW **HOW**, WITHOUT HURTING HER FEELINGS!
YOU'RE TOO NICE, DUDE.
TOO **NICE!** THAT'S **IT!**
WE'LL CREATE A **BAD CHAD!**
?

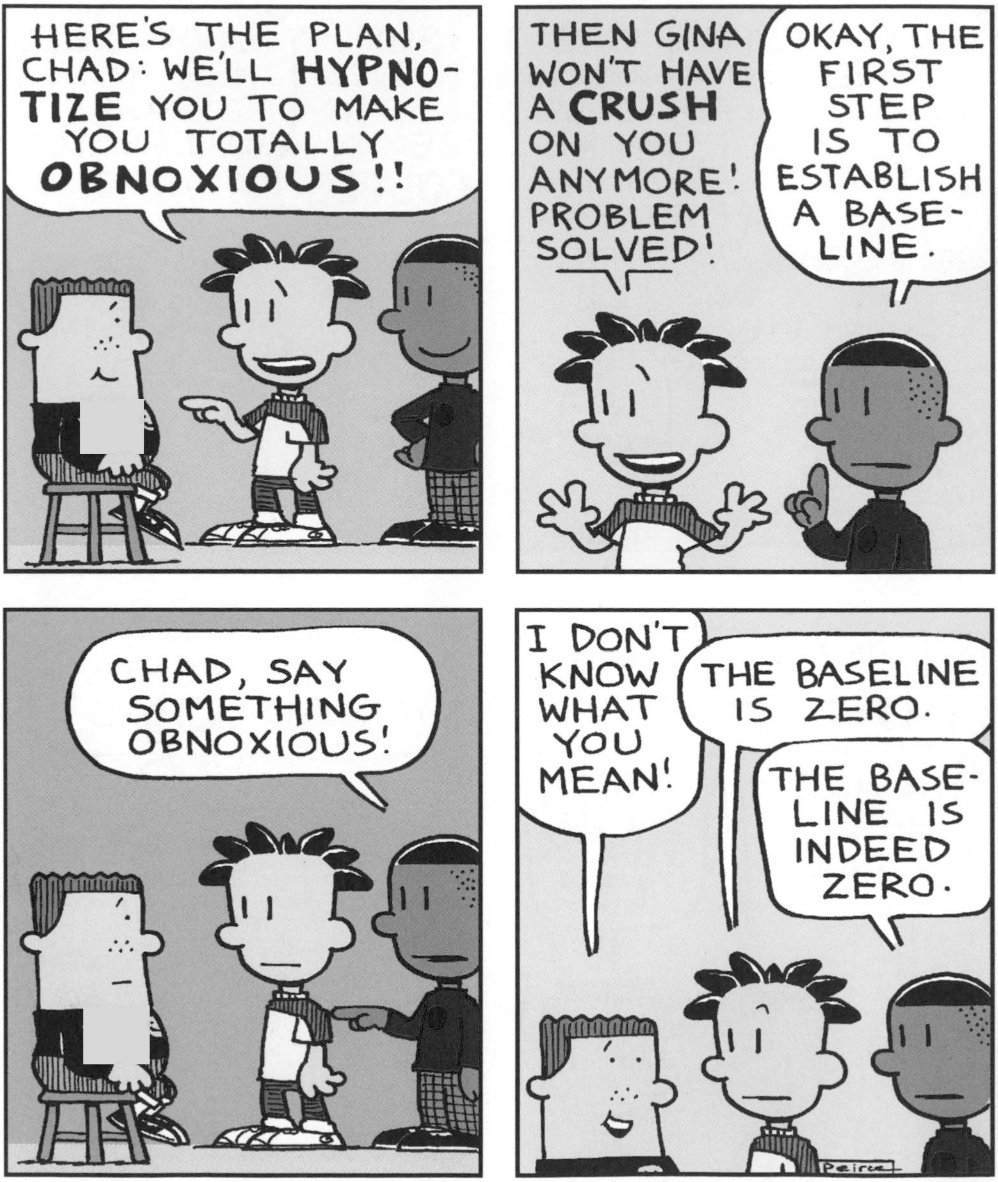
HERE'S THE PLAN, CHAD: WE'LL **HYPNOTIZE** YOU TO MAKE YOU TOTALLY **OBNOXIOUS**!!
THEN GINA WON'T HAVE A **CRUSH** ON YOU ANYMORE! PROBLEM SOLVED!
OKAY, THE FIRST STEP IS TO ESTABLISH A BASELINE.
CHAD, SAY SOMETHING OBNOXIOUS!
I DON'T KNOW WHAT YOU MEAN!
THE BASELINE IS ZERO.
THE BASELINE IS INDEED ZERO.
Peirce

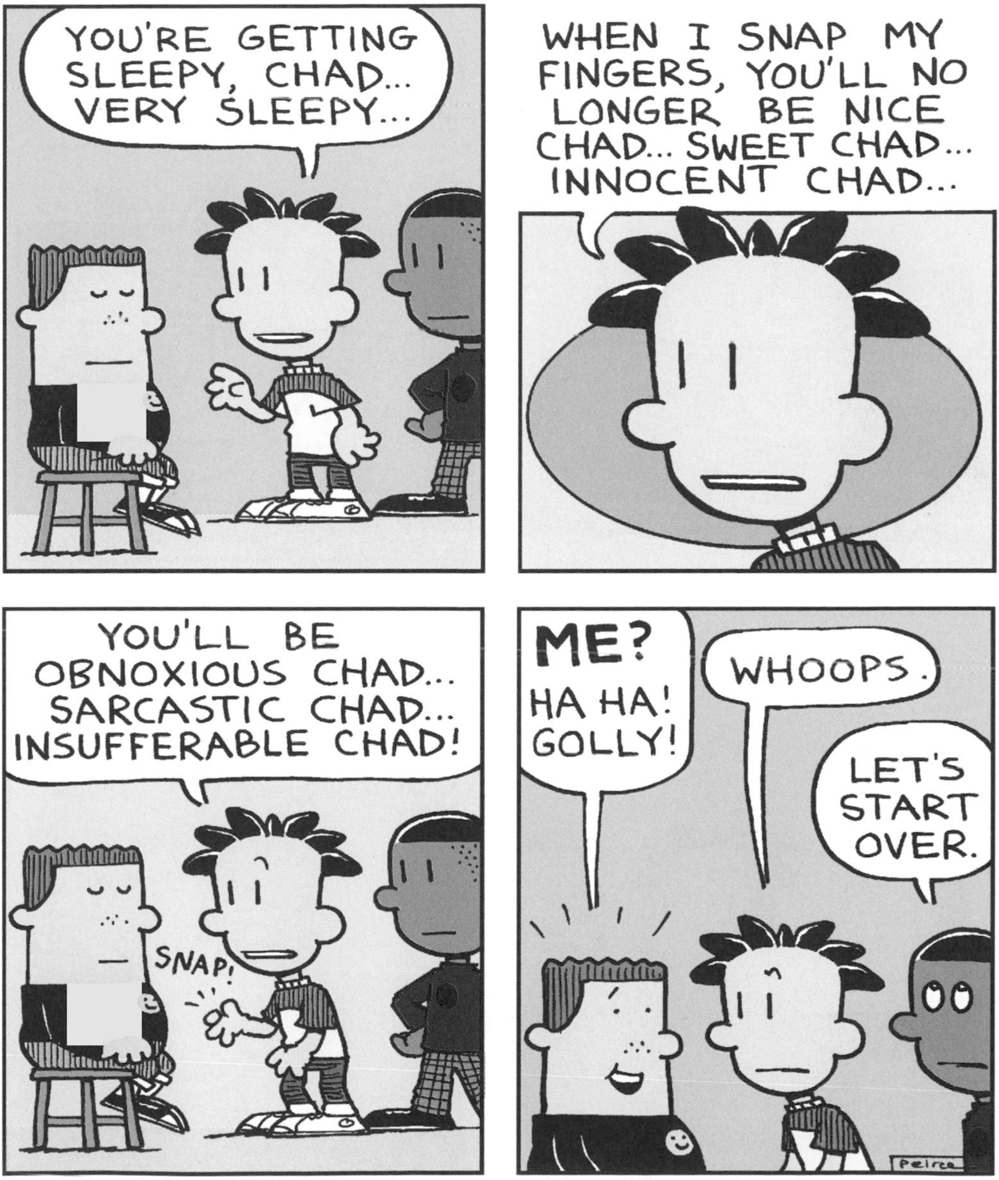
YOU'RE GETTING SLEEPY, CHAD... VERY SLEEPY...
WHEN I SNAP MY FINGERS, YOU'LL NO LONGER BE NICE CHAD... SWEET CHAD... INNOCENT CHAD...
YOU'LL BE OBNOXIOUS CHAD... SARCASTIC CHAD... INSUFFERABLE CHAD!
SNAP!
ME? HA HA! GOLLY!
WHOOPS.
LET'S START OVER.
Peirce

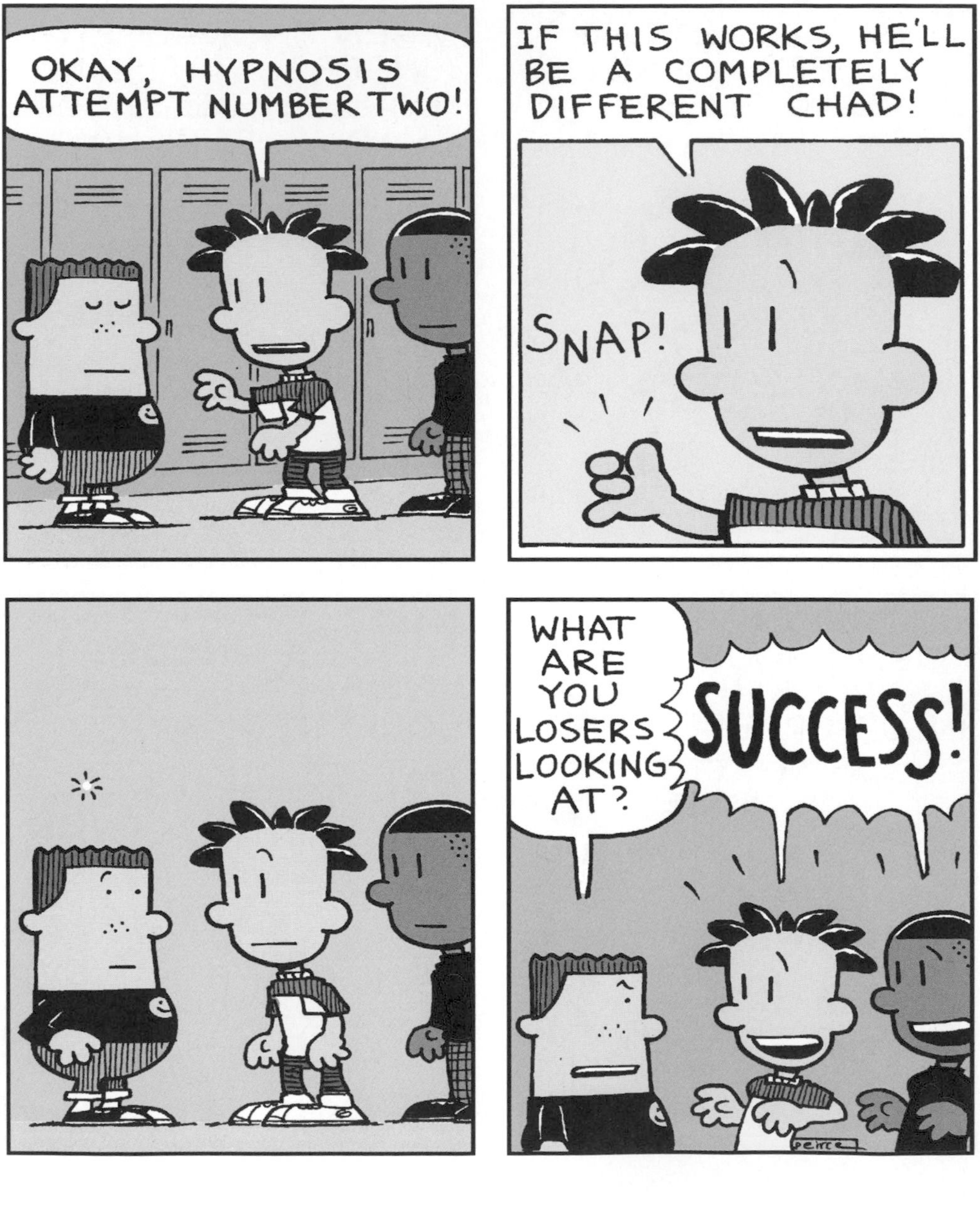
OKAY, HYPNOSIS ATTEMPT NUMBER TWO!
IF THIS WORKS, HE'LL BE A COMPLETELY DIFFERENT CHAD!
SNAP!
WHAT ARE YOU LOSERS LOOKING AT?
SUCCESS!

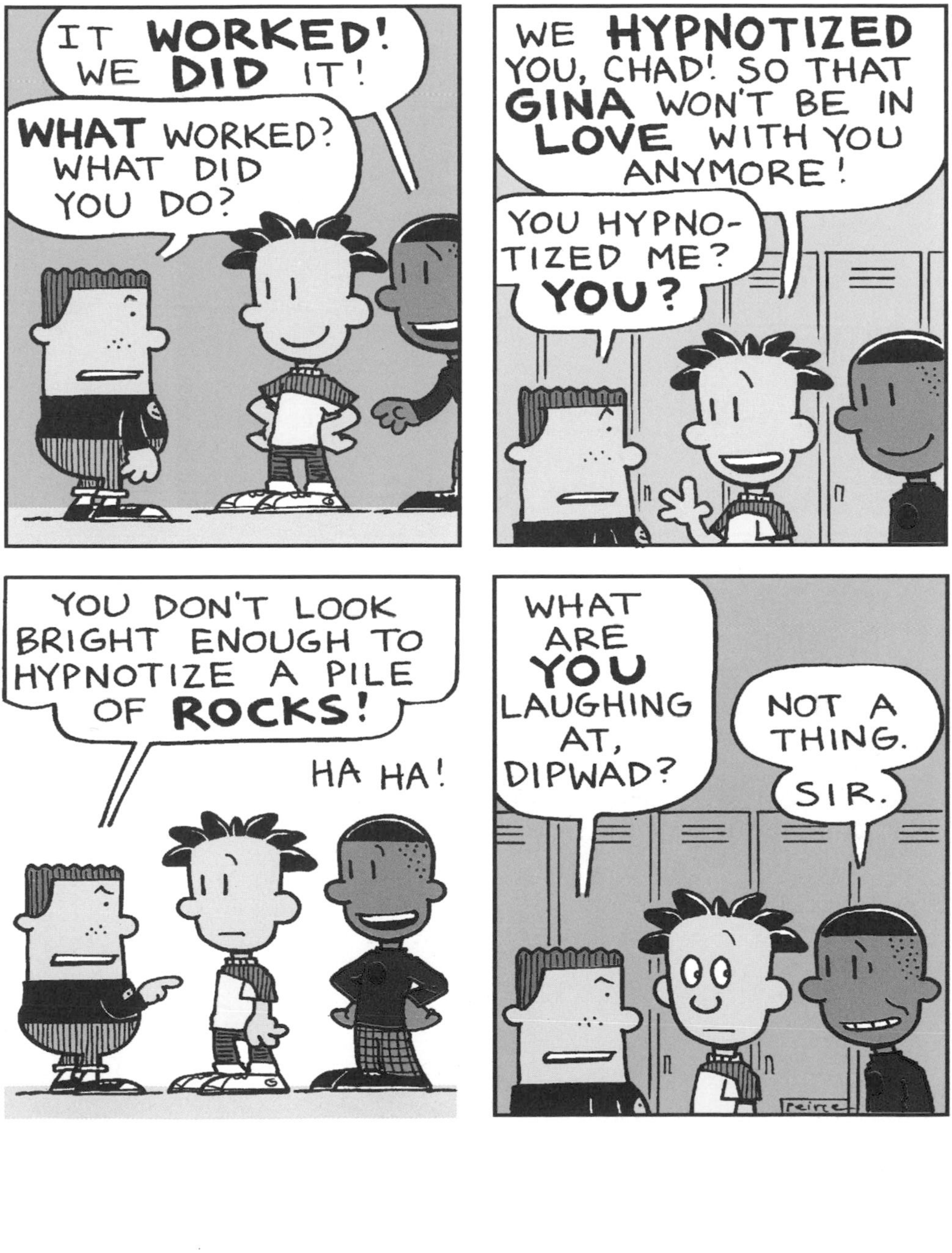
IT WORKED! WE DID IT!
WHAT WORKED? WHAT DID YOU DO?
WE HYPNOTIZED YOU, CHAD! SO THAT GINA WON'T BE IN LOVE WITH YOU ANYMORE!
YOU HYPNOTIZED ME? YOU?
YOU DON'T LOOK BRIGHT ENOUGH TO HYPNOTIZE A PILE OF ROCKS!
HA HA!
WHAT ARE YOU LAUGHING AT, DIPWAD?
NOT A THING.
SIR.
peirce

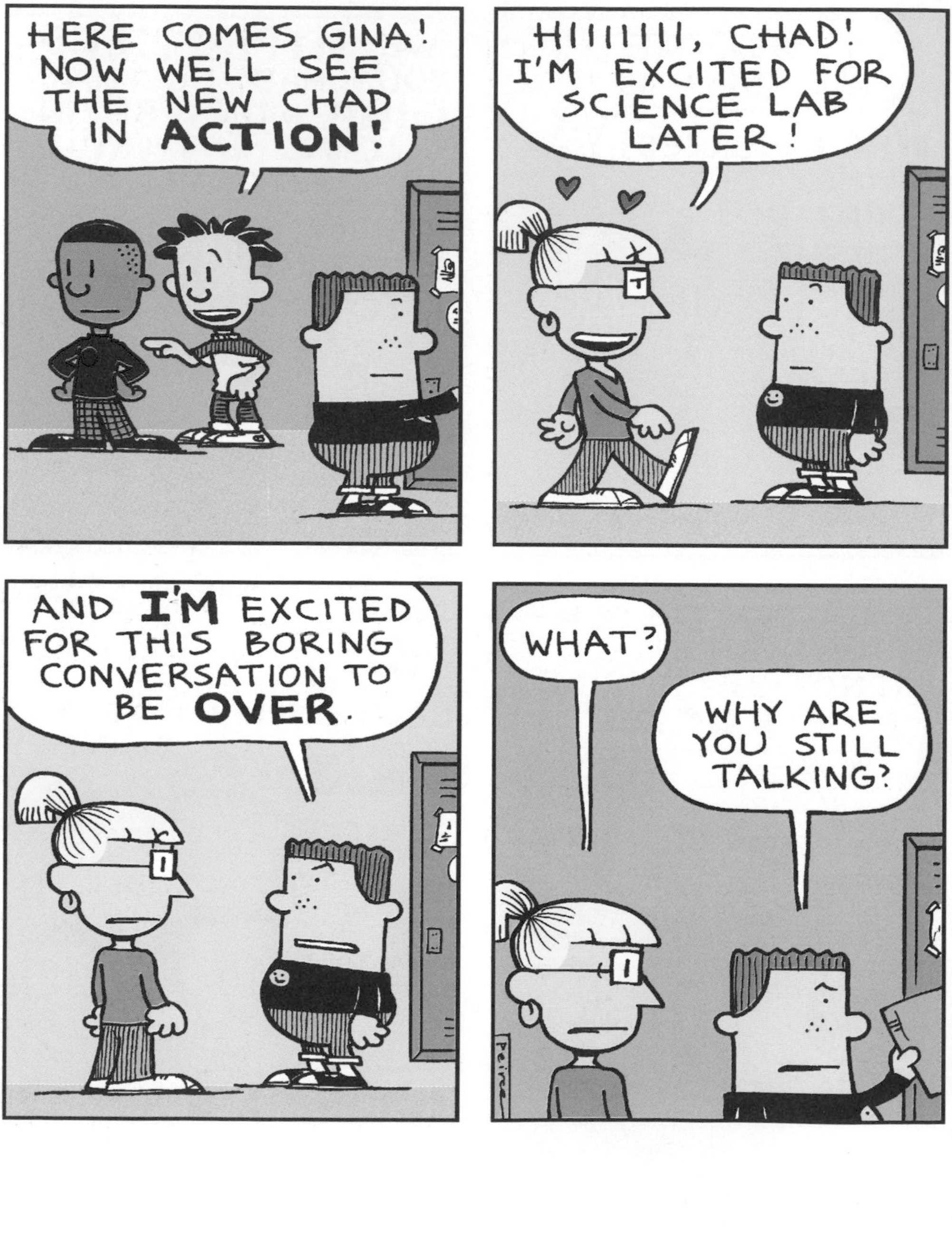
HERE COMES GINA! NOW WE'LL SEE THE NEW CHAD IN **ACTION**!
HIIIIIII, CHAD! I'M EXCITED FOR SCIENCE LAB LATER!
AND **I'M** EXCITED FOR THIS BORING CONVERSATION TO BE **OVER**.
WHAT?
WHY ARE YOU STILL TALKING?
Peirce

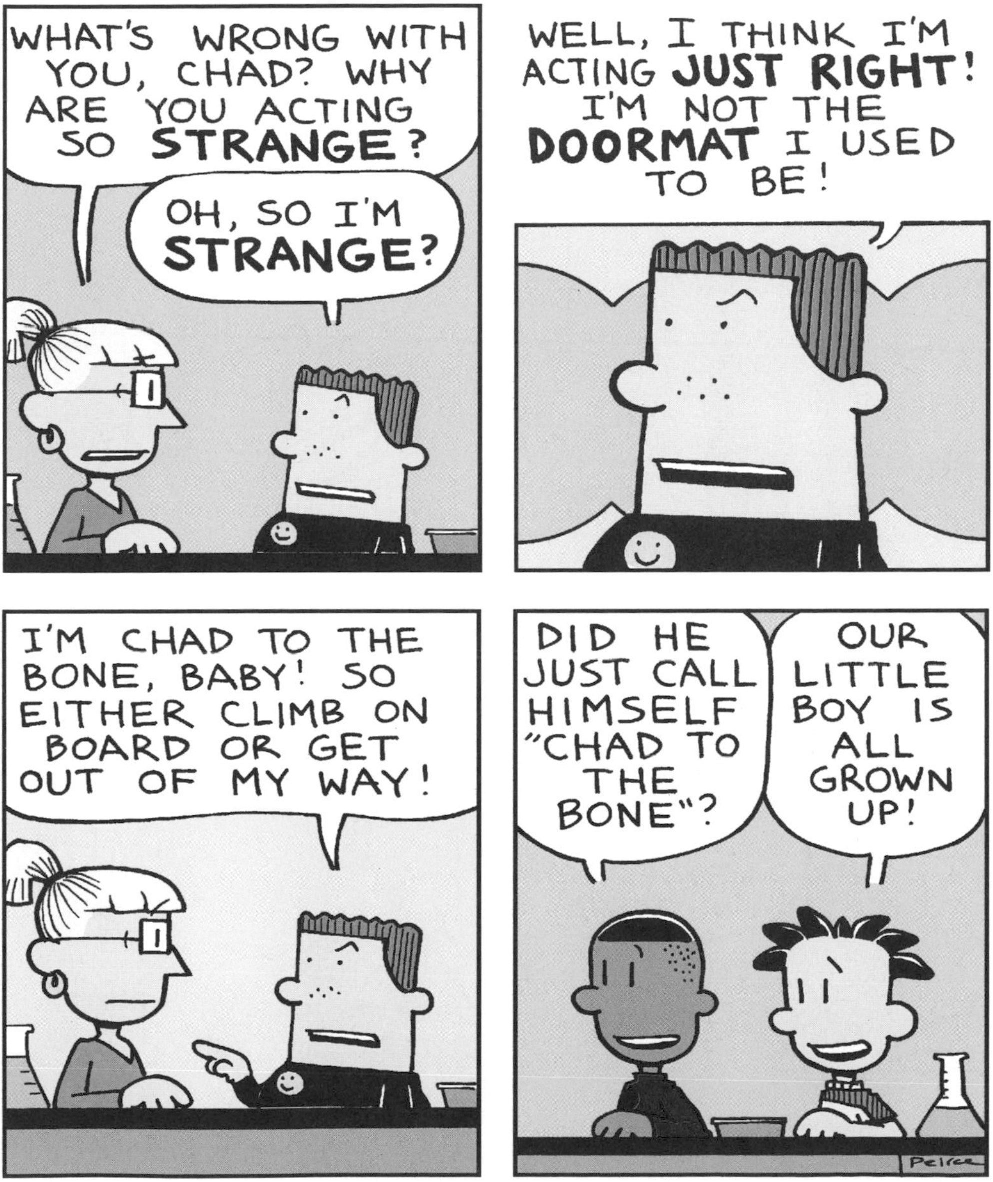
WHAT'S WRONG WITH YOU, CHAD? WHY ARE YOU ACTING SO STRANGE?
OH, SO I'M STRANGE?
WELL, I THINK I'M ACTING JUST RIGHT! I'M NOT THE DOORMAT I USED TO BE!
I'M CHAD TO THE BONE, BABY! SO EITHER CLIMB ON BOARD OR GET OUT OF MY WAY!
DID HE JUST CALL HIMSELF "CHAD TO THE BONE"?
OUR LITTLE BOY IS ALL GROWN UP!
Peirce

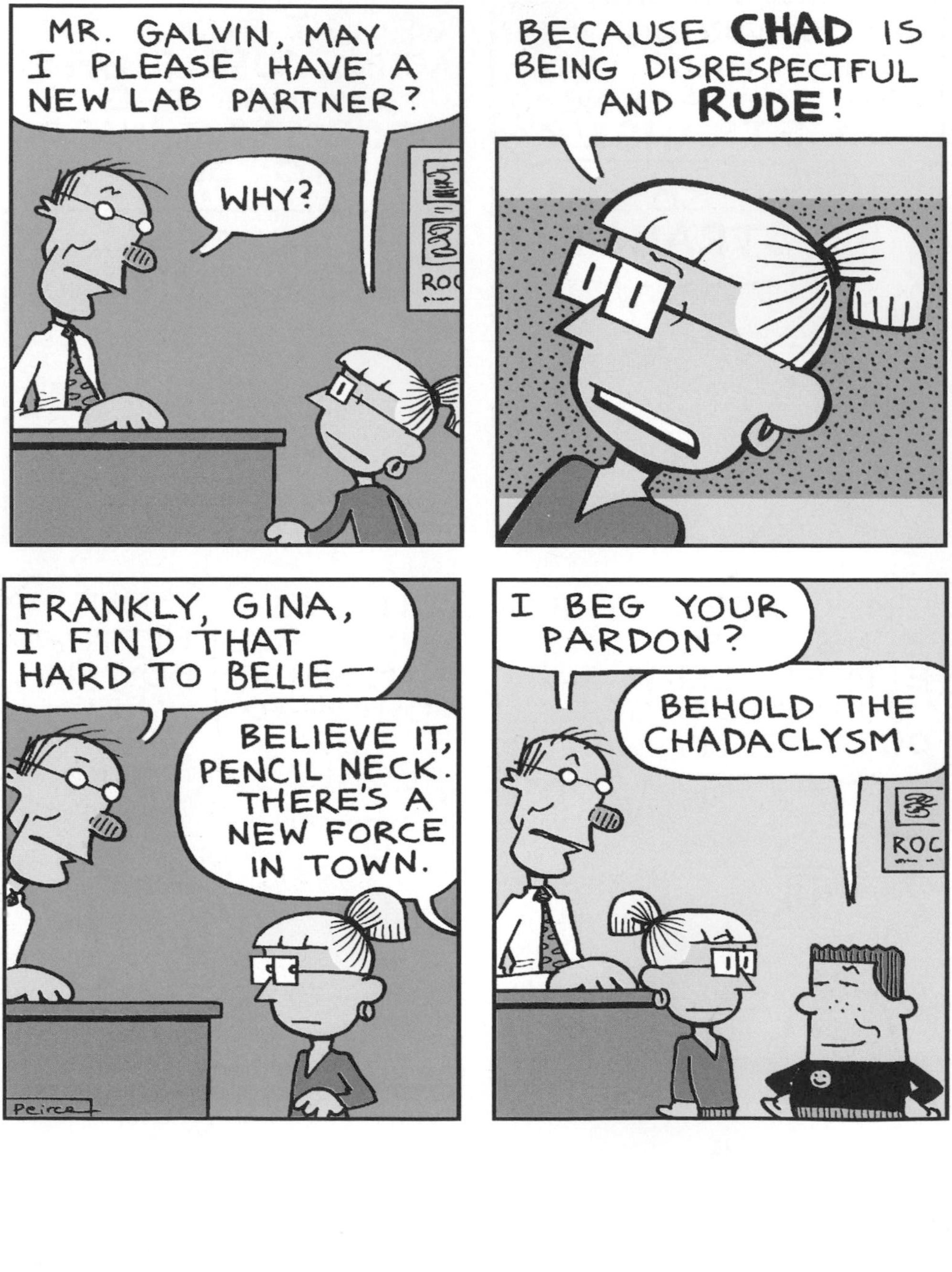
MR. GALVIN, MAY I PLEASE HAVE A NEW LAB PARTNER?
WHY?
BECAUSE CHAD IS BEING DISRESPECTFUL AND RUDE!
FRANKLY, GINA, I FIND THAT HARD TO BELIE—
BELIEVE IT, PENCIL NECK. THERE'S A NEW FORCE IN TOWN.
Peirce
I BEG YOUR PARDON?
BEHOLD THE CHADACLYSM.

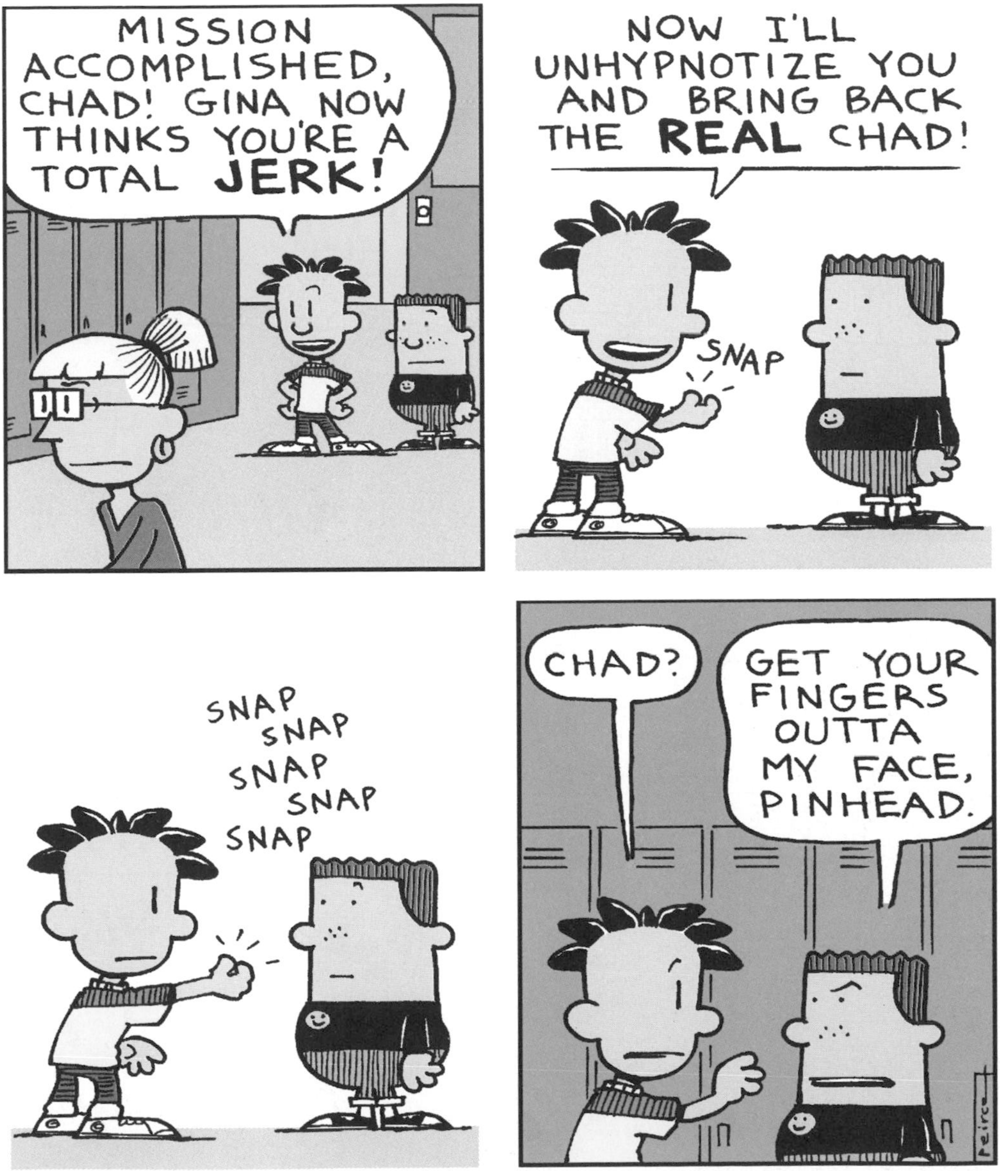
MISSION ACCOMPLISHED, CHAD! GINA NOW THINKS YOU'RE A TOTAL **JERK**!
NOW I'LL UNHYPNOTIZE YOU AND BRING BACK THE **REAL** CHAD!
SNAP
SNAP SNAP SNAP SNAP SNAP
CHAD?
GET YOUR FINGERS OUTTA MY FACE, PINHEAD.
Peirce

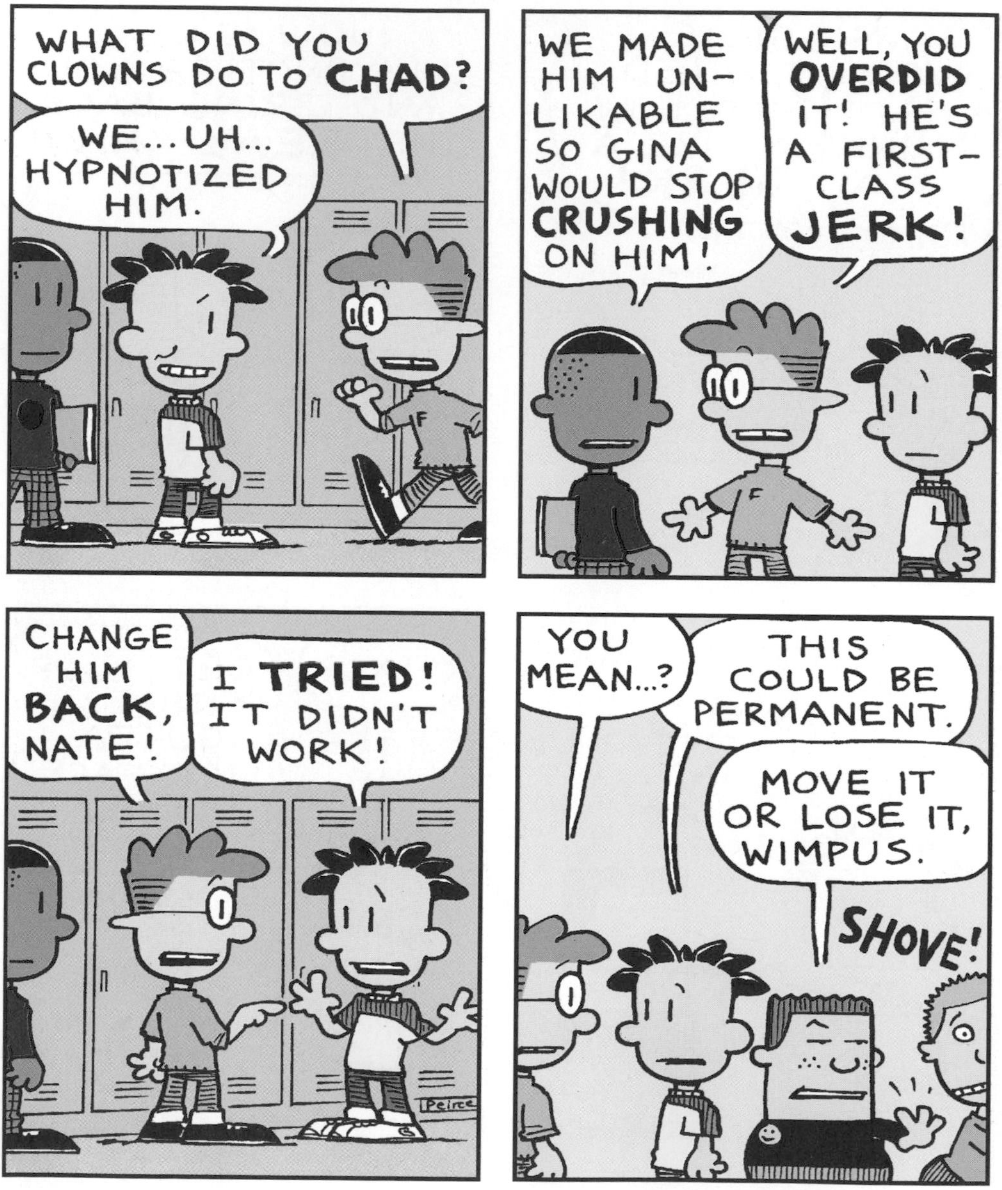
WHAT DID YOU CLOWNS DO TO CHAD?
WE... UH... HYPNOTIZED HIM.
WE MADE HIM UN-LIKABLE SO GINA WOULD STOP CRUSHING ON HIM!
WELL, YOU OVERDID IT! HE'S A FIRST-CLASS JERK!
CHANGE HIM BACK, NATE!
I TRIED! IT DIDN'T WORK!
Peirce
YOU MEAN...?
THIS COULD BE PERMANENT.
MOVE IT OR LOSE IT, WIMPUS.
SHOVE!

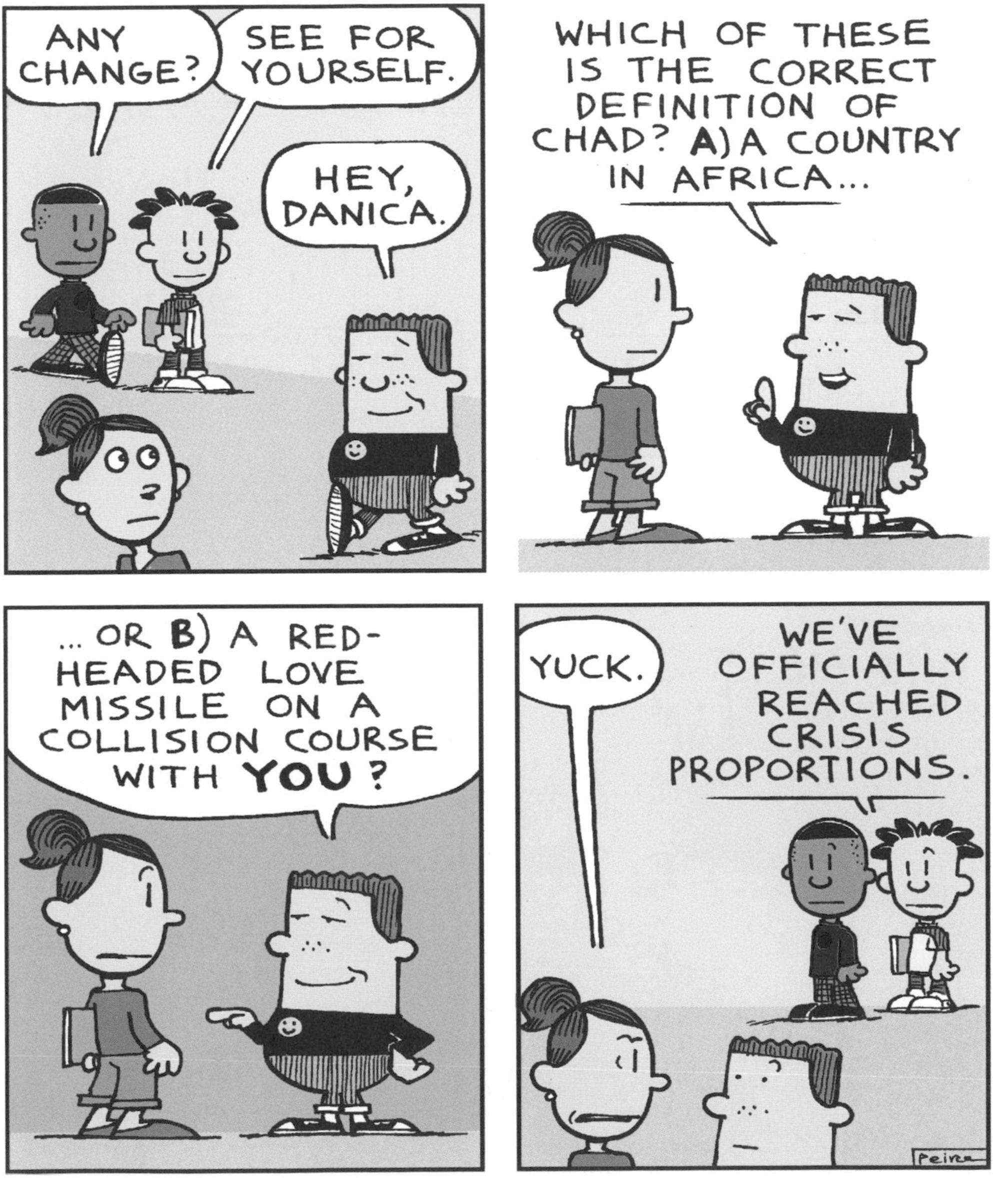
ANY CHANGE?
SEE FOR YOURSELF.
HEY, DANICA.
WHICH OF THESE IS THE CORRECT DEFINITION OF CHAD? **A)** A COUNTRY IN AFRICA...
... OR **B)** A RED-HEADED LOVE MISSILE ON A COLLISION COURSE WITH **YOU**?
YUCK.
WE'VE OFFICIALLY REACHED CRISIS PROPORTIONS.
peirce

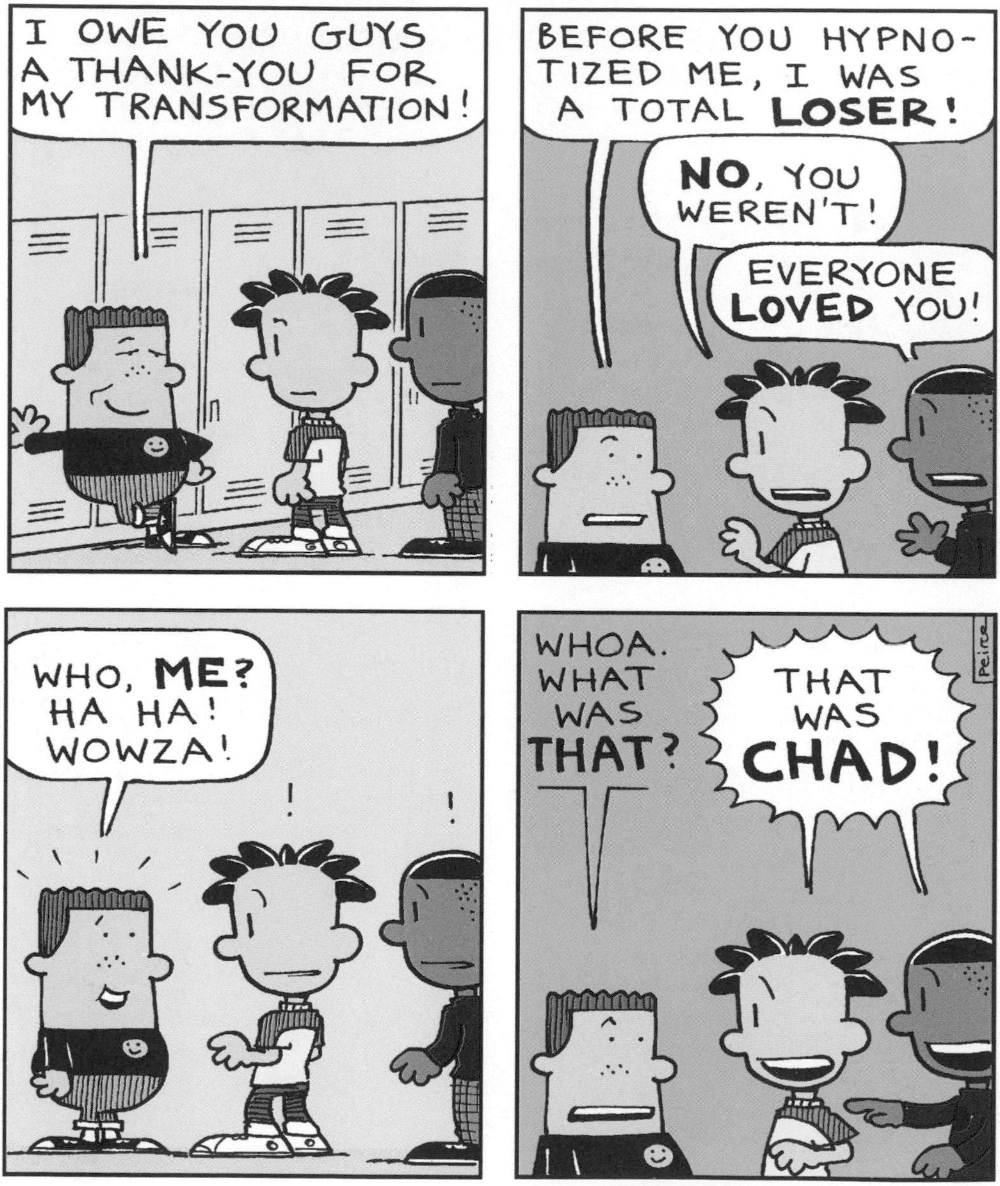
I OWE YOU GUYS A THANK-YOU FOR MY TRANSFORMATION!
BEFORE YOU HYPNOTIZED ME, I WAS A TOTAL **LOSER**!
NO, YOU WEREN'T!
EVERYONE **LOVED** YOU!
WHO, **ME**? HA HA! WOWZA!
!
!
WHOA. WHAT WAS **THAT**?
THAT WAS **CHAD**!
Peirce

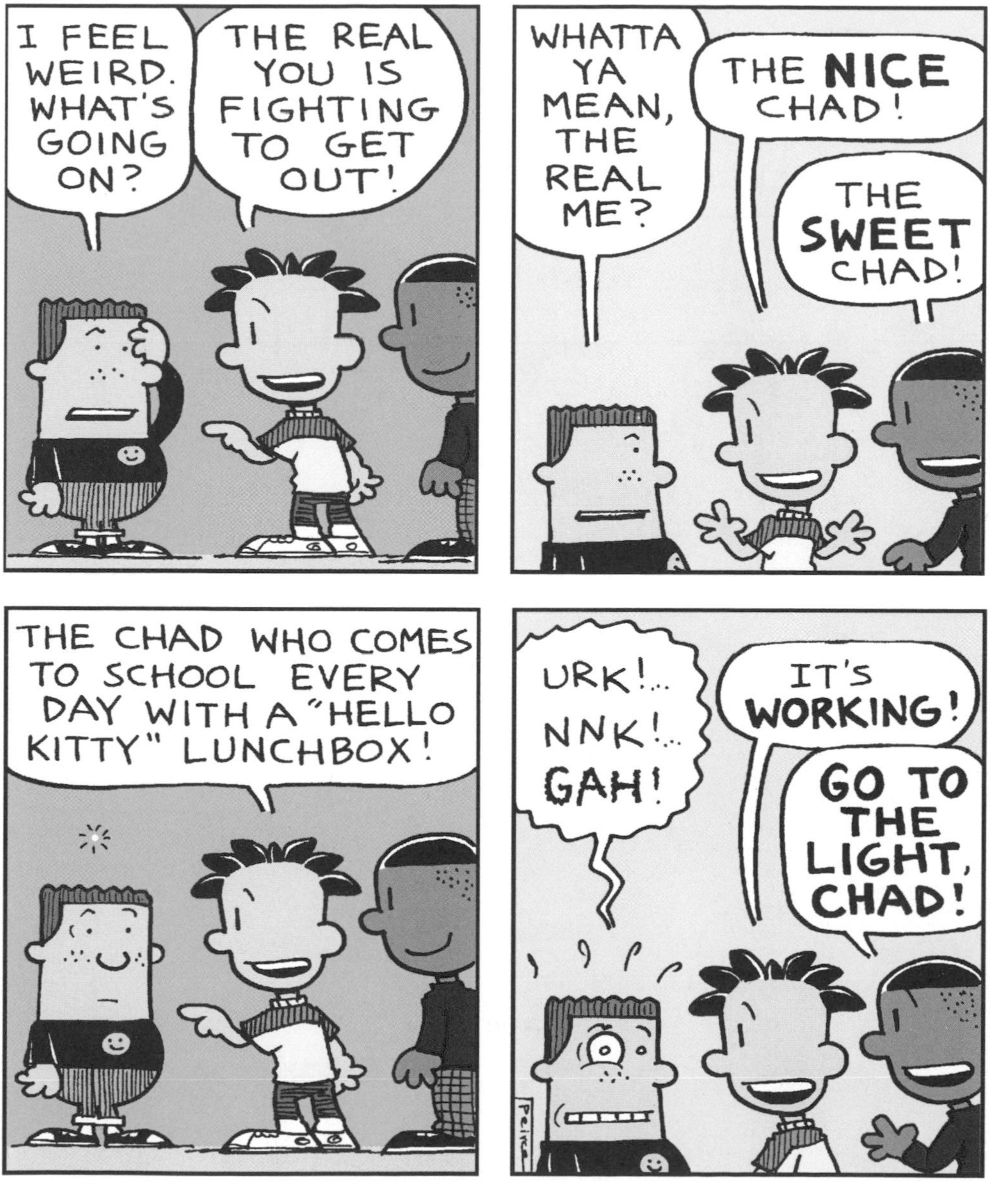
I FEEL WEIRD. WHAT'S GOING ON?
THE REAL YOU IS FIGHTING TO GET OUT!
WHATTA YA MEAN, THE REAL ME?
THE NICE CHAD!
THE SWEET CHAD!
THE CHAD WHO COMES TO SCHOOL EVERY DAY WITH A "HELLO KITTY" LUNCHBOX!
URK!... NNK!... GAH!
IT'S WORKING!
GO TO THE LIGHT, CHAD!
Peirce

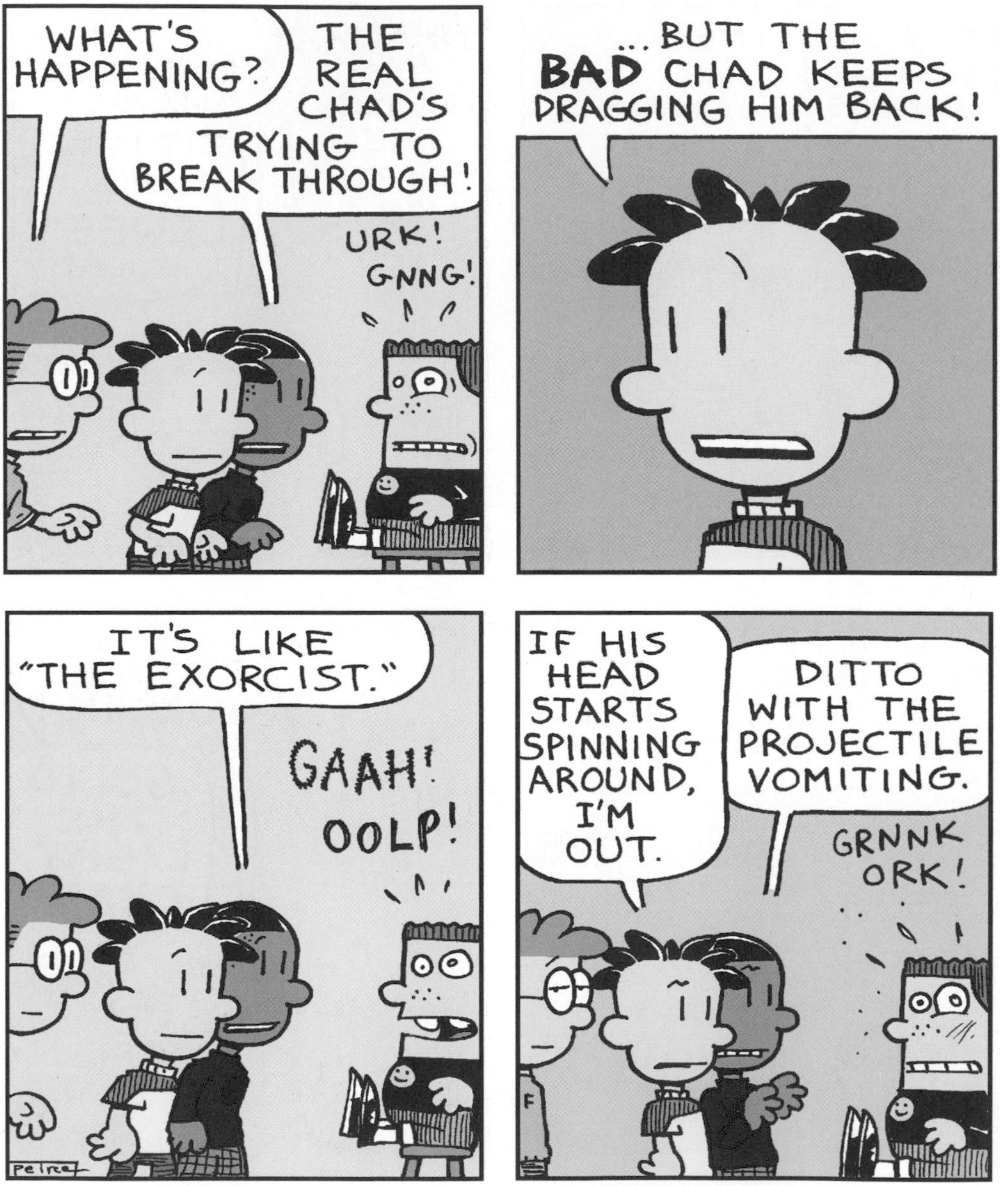
WHAT'S HAPPENING?
THE REAL CHAD'S TRYING TO BREAK THROUGH!
URK! GNNG!
...BUT THE BAD CHAD KEEPS DRAGGING HIM BACK!
IT'S LIKE "THE EXORCIST."
GAAH! OOLP!
IF HIS HEAD STARTS SPINNING AROUND, I'M OUT.
DITTO WITH THE PROJECTILE VOMITING.
GRNNK ORK!

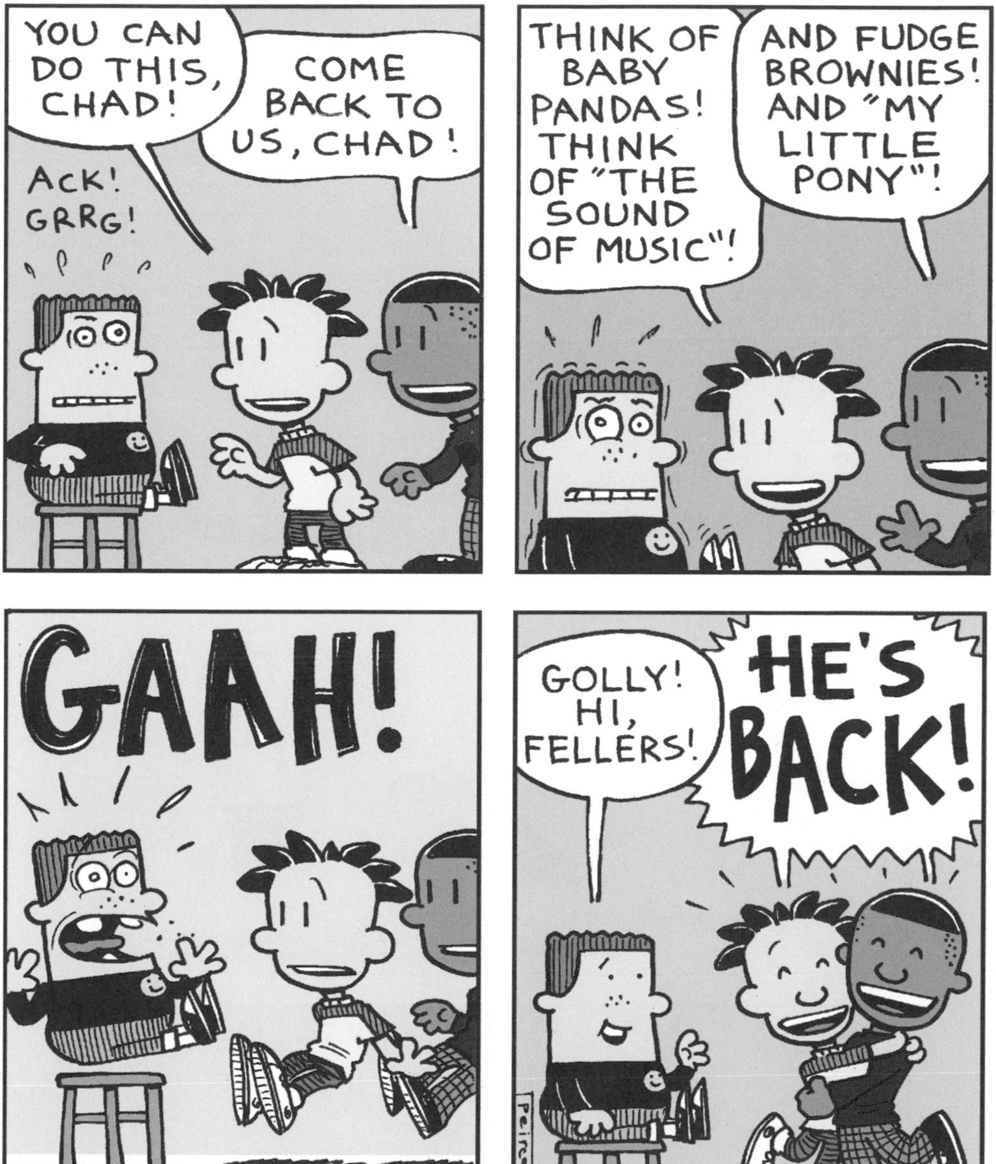
YOU CAN DO THIS, CHAD!
COME BACK TO US, CHAD!
ACK! GRRG!
THINK OF BABY PANDAS! THINK OF "THE SOUND OF MUSIC"!
AND FUDGE BROWNIES! AND "MY LITTLE PONY"!
GAAH!
GOLLY! HI, FELLERS!
HE'S BACK!
PEIRCE

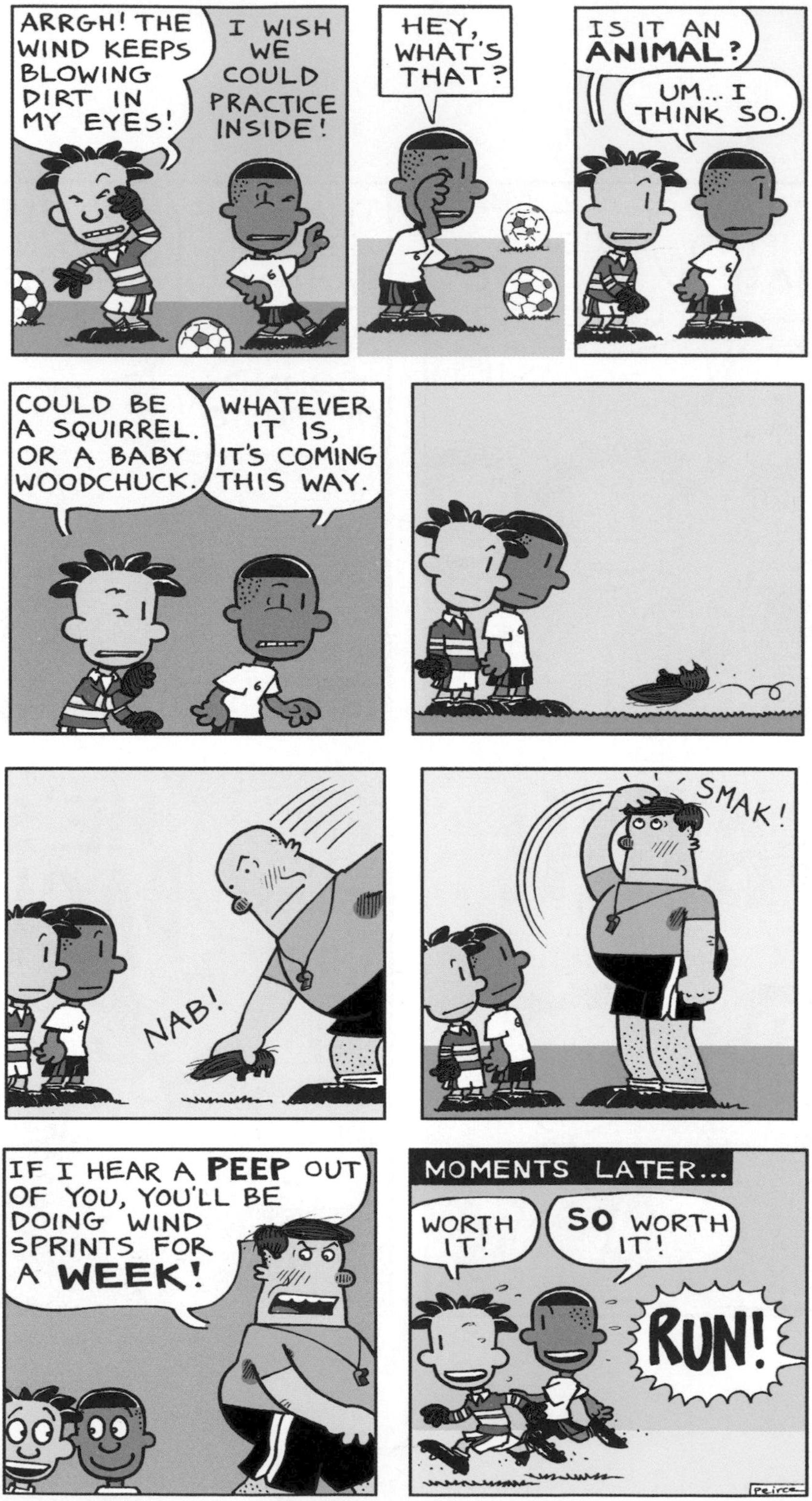
ARRGH! THE WIND KEEPS BLOWING DIRT IN MY EYES!
I WISH WE COULD PRACTICE INSIDE!
HEY, WHAT'S THAT?
IS IT AN **ANIMAL**?
UM... I THINK SO.
COULD BE A SQUIRREL. OR A BABY WOODCHUCK.
WHATEVER IT IS, IT'S COMING THIS WAY.
NAB!
SMAK!
IF I HEAR A **PEEP** OUT OF YOU, YOU'LL BE DOING WIND SPRINTS FOR A **WEEK**!
MOMENTS LATER...
WORTH IT!
SO WORTH IT!
RUN!
Peirce

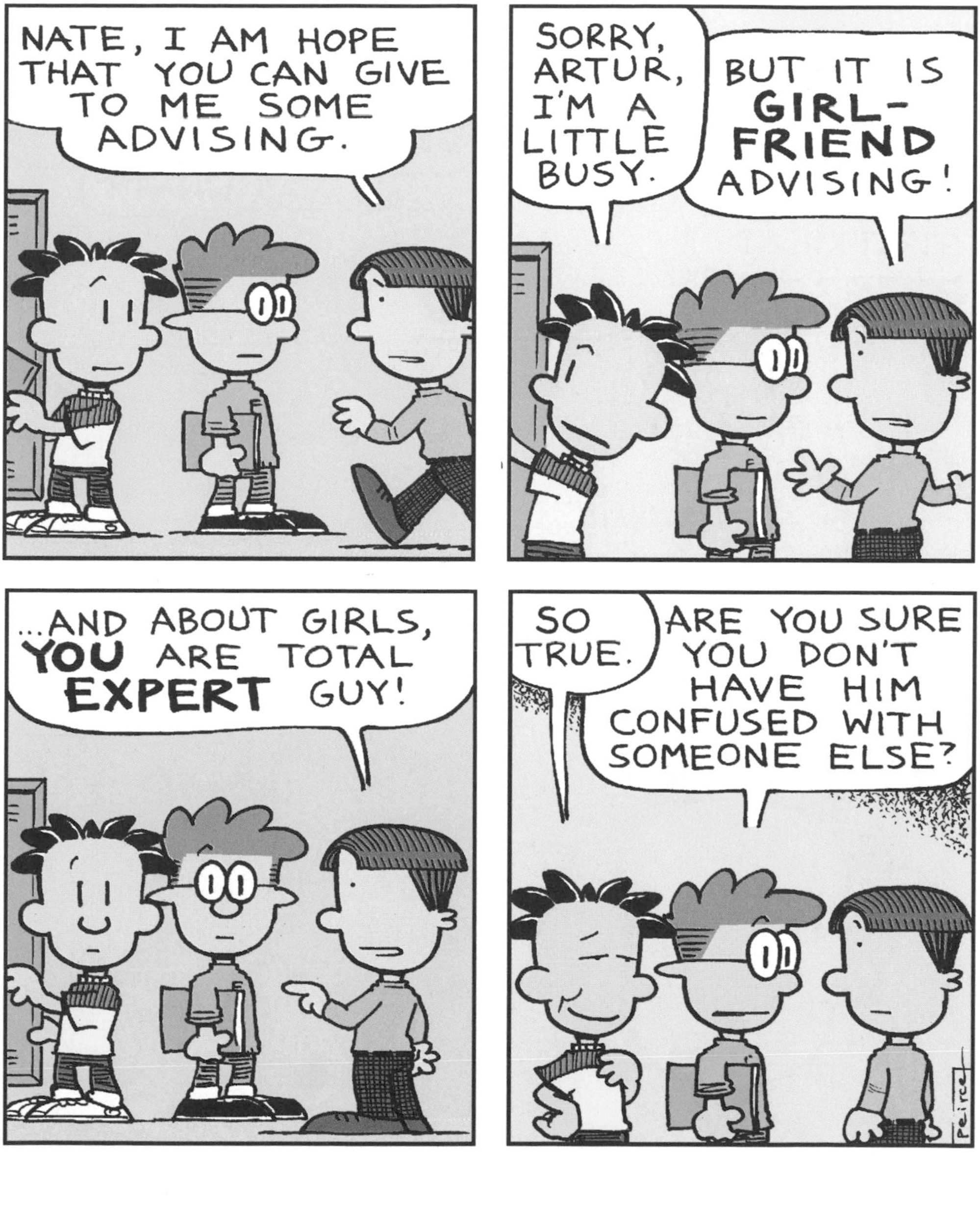
NATE, I AM HOPE THAT YOU CAN GIVE TO ME SOME ADVISING.
SORRY, ARTUR, I'M A LITTLE BUSY.
BUT IT IS **GIRL-FRIEND** ADVISING!
...AND ABOUT GIRLS, **YOU** ARE TOTAL **EXPERT** GUY!
SO TRUE.
ARE YOU SURE YOU DON'T HAVE HIM CONFUSED WITH SOMEONE ELSE?
peirce

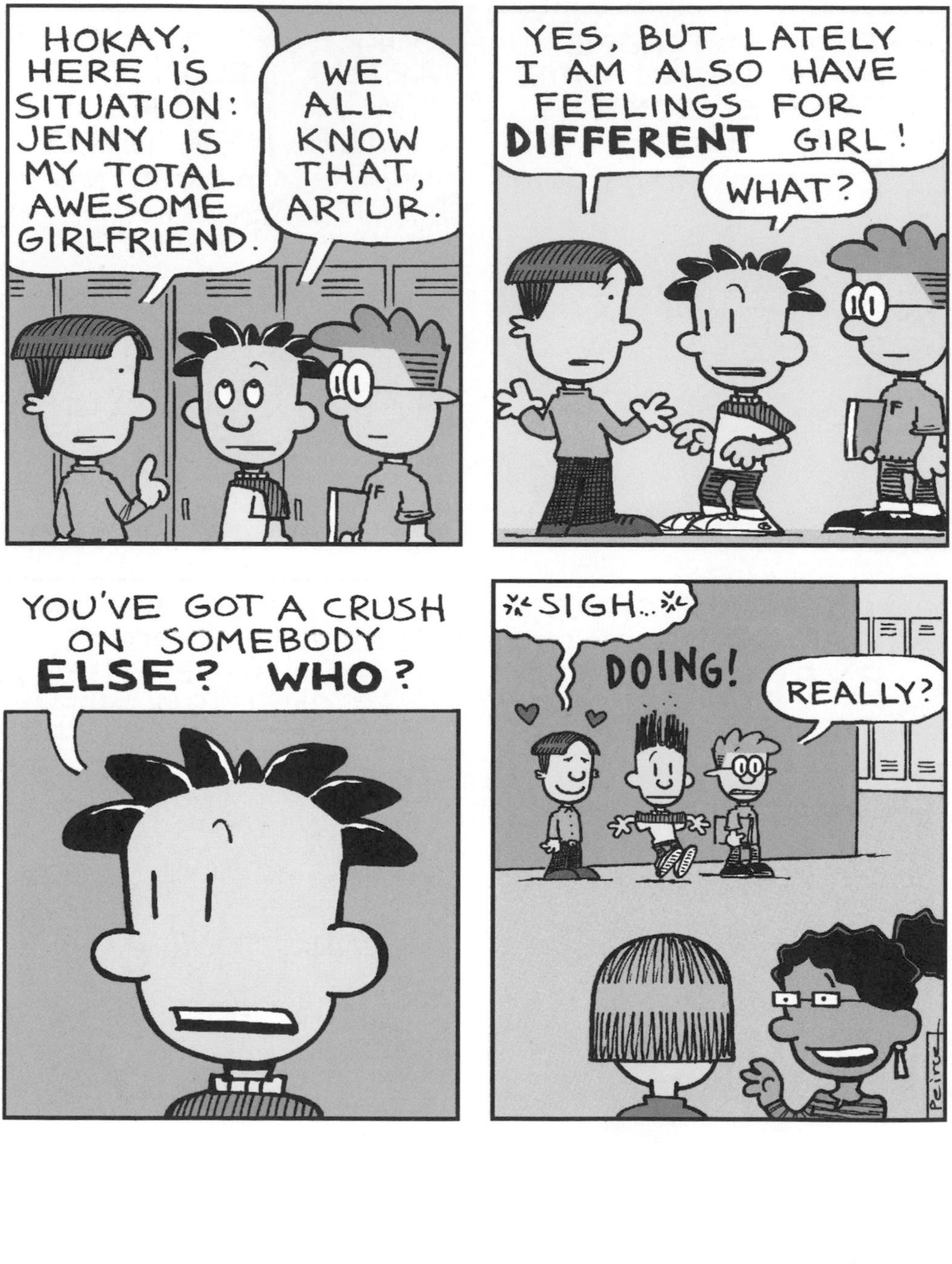

HOKAY, HERE IS SITUATION: JENNY IS MY TOTAL AWESOME GIRLFRIEND.
WE ALL KNOW THAT, ARTUR.
YES, BUT LATELY I AM ALSO HAVE FEELINGS FOR DIFFERENT GIRL!
WHAT?
YOU'VE GOT A CRUSH ON SOMEBODY ELSE? WHO?
SIGH...
DOING!
REALLY?
Peirce

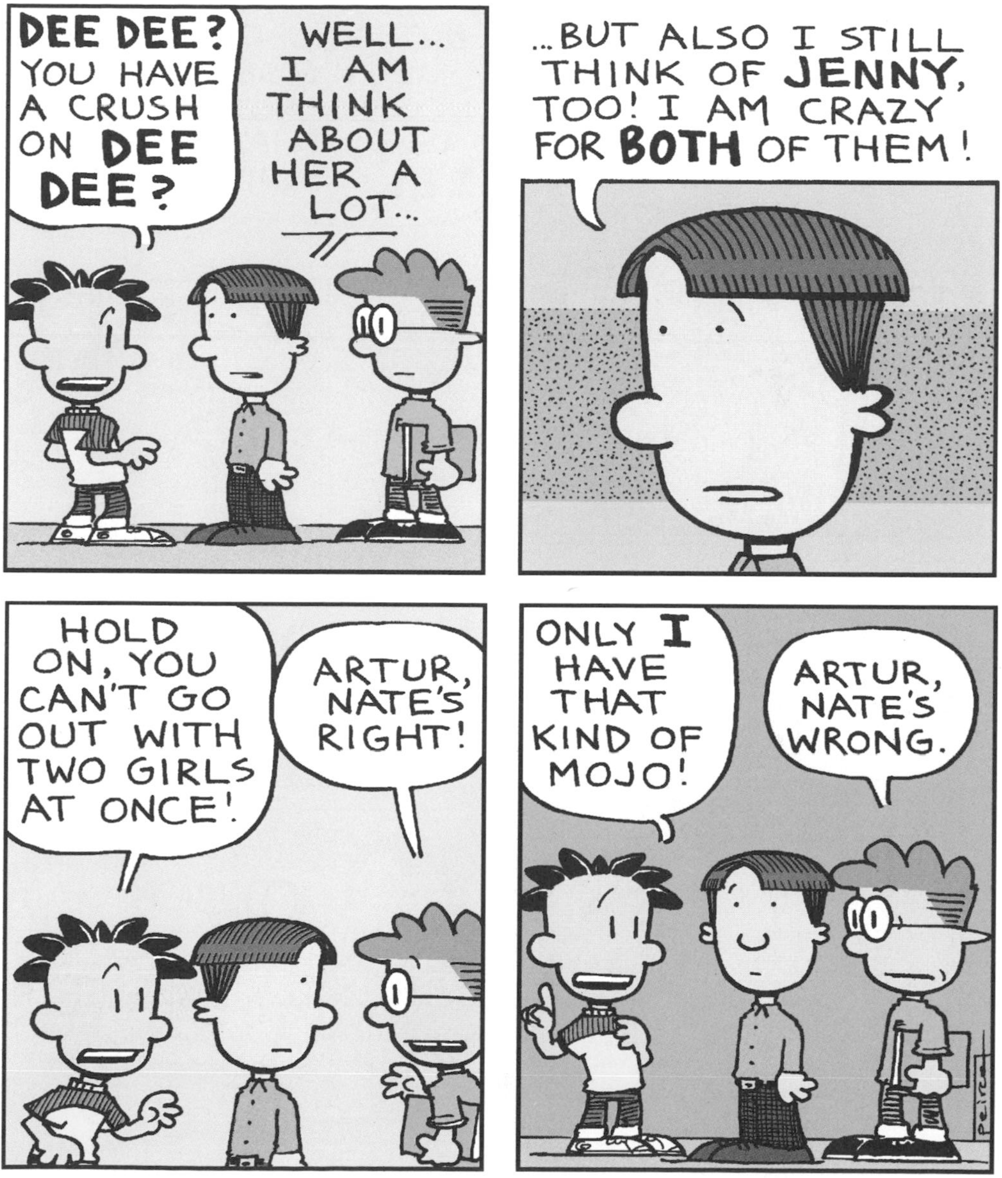
DEE DEE? YOU HAVE A CRUSH ON DEE DEE?
WELL... I AM THINK ABOUT HER A LOT...
...BUT ALSO I STILL THINK OF JENNY, TOO! I AM CRAZY FOR BOTH OF THEM!
HOLD ON, YOU CAN'T GO OUT WITH TWO GIRLS AT ONCE!
ARTUR, NATE'S RIGHT!
ONLY I HAVE THAT KIND OF MOJO!
ARTUR, NATE'S WRONG.
Peirce

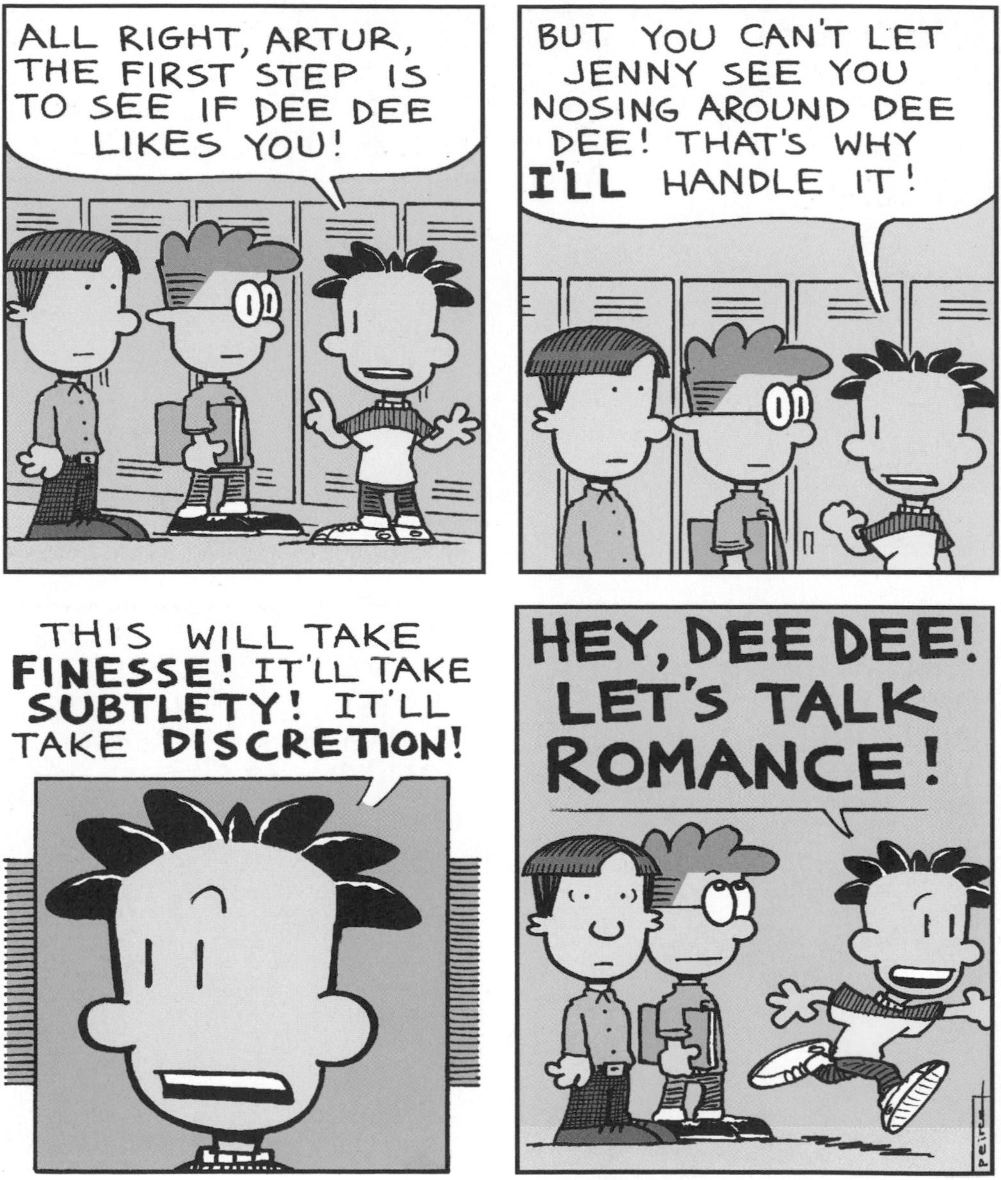
ALL RIGHT, ARTUR, THE FIRST STEP IS TO SEE IF DEE DEE LIKES YOU!
BUT YOU CAN'T LET JENNY SEE YOU NOSING AROUND DEE DEE! THAT'S WHY I'LL HANDLE IT!
THIS WILL TAKE FINESSE! IT'LL TAKE SUBTLETY! IT'LL TAKE DISCRETION!
HEY, DEE DEE! LET'S TALK ROMANCE!
PEIRCE

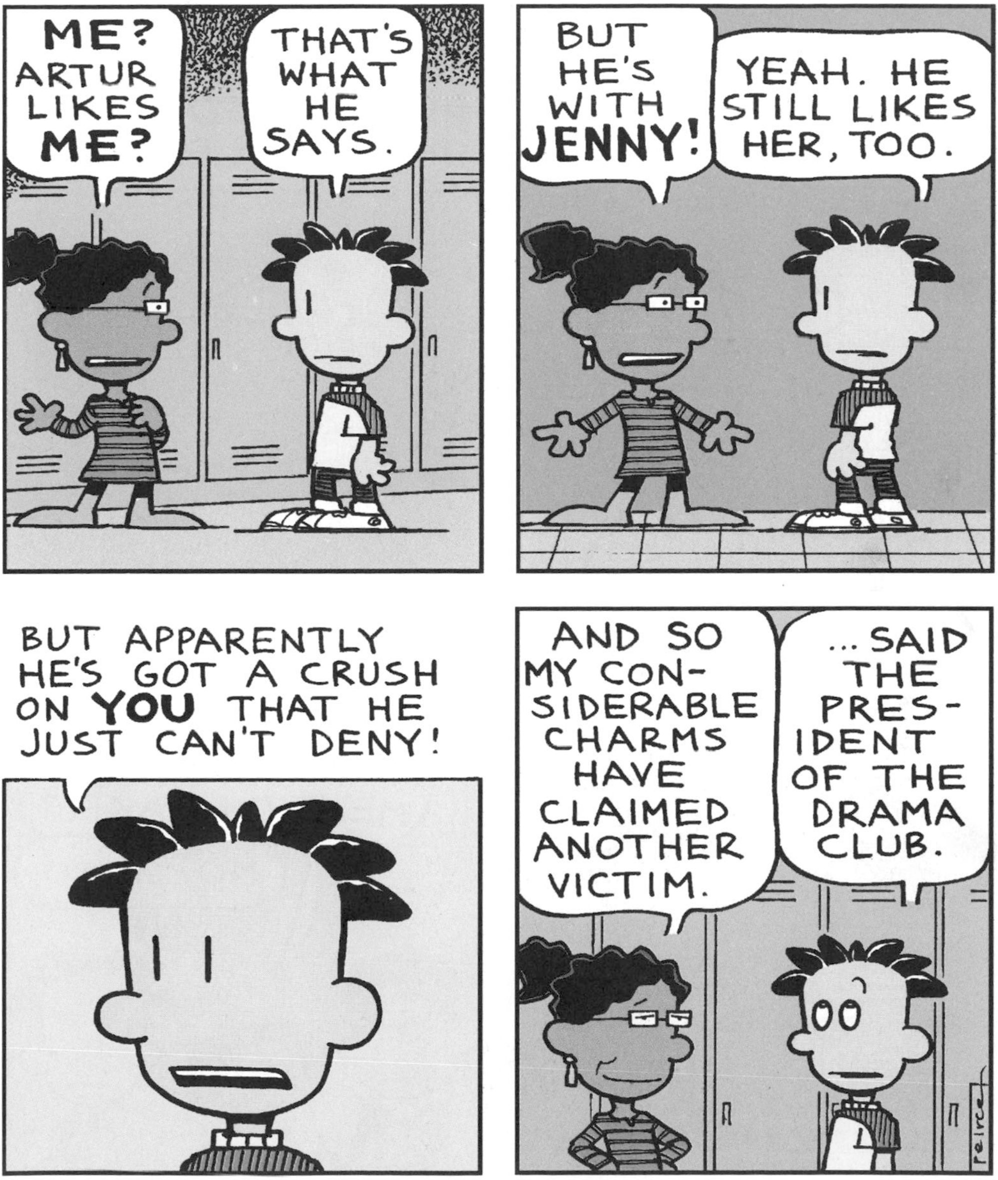

ME? ARTUR LIKES **ME?**
THAT'S WHAT HE SAYS.
BUT HE'S WITH **JENNY!**
YEAH. HE STILL LIKES HER, TOO.
BUT APPARENTLY HE'S GOT A CRUSH ON **YOU** THAT HE JUST CAN'T DENY!
AND SO MY CON-SIDERABLE CHARMS HAVE CLAIMED ANOTHER VICTIM.
...SAID THE PRES-IDENT OF THE DRAMA CLUB.
peirce

WHAT SHOULD I TELL ARTUR?

TELL HIM TO **GROW UP**, THAT'S WHAT!

"OOH, I LIKE JENNY, BUT I **ALSO** LIKE **DEE DEE**! POOR **ME**! WHAT A **DILEMMA**!"

HE'S JUST LOOKING FOR PERMISSION TO DATE TWO GIRLS AT THE SAME TIME!

HE WANTS TO HAVE HIS CAKE AND EAT IT, TOO.

DID SOMEBODY MENTION CAKE?

NO, CHAD.

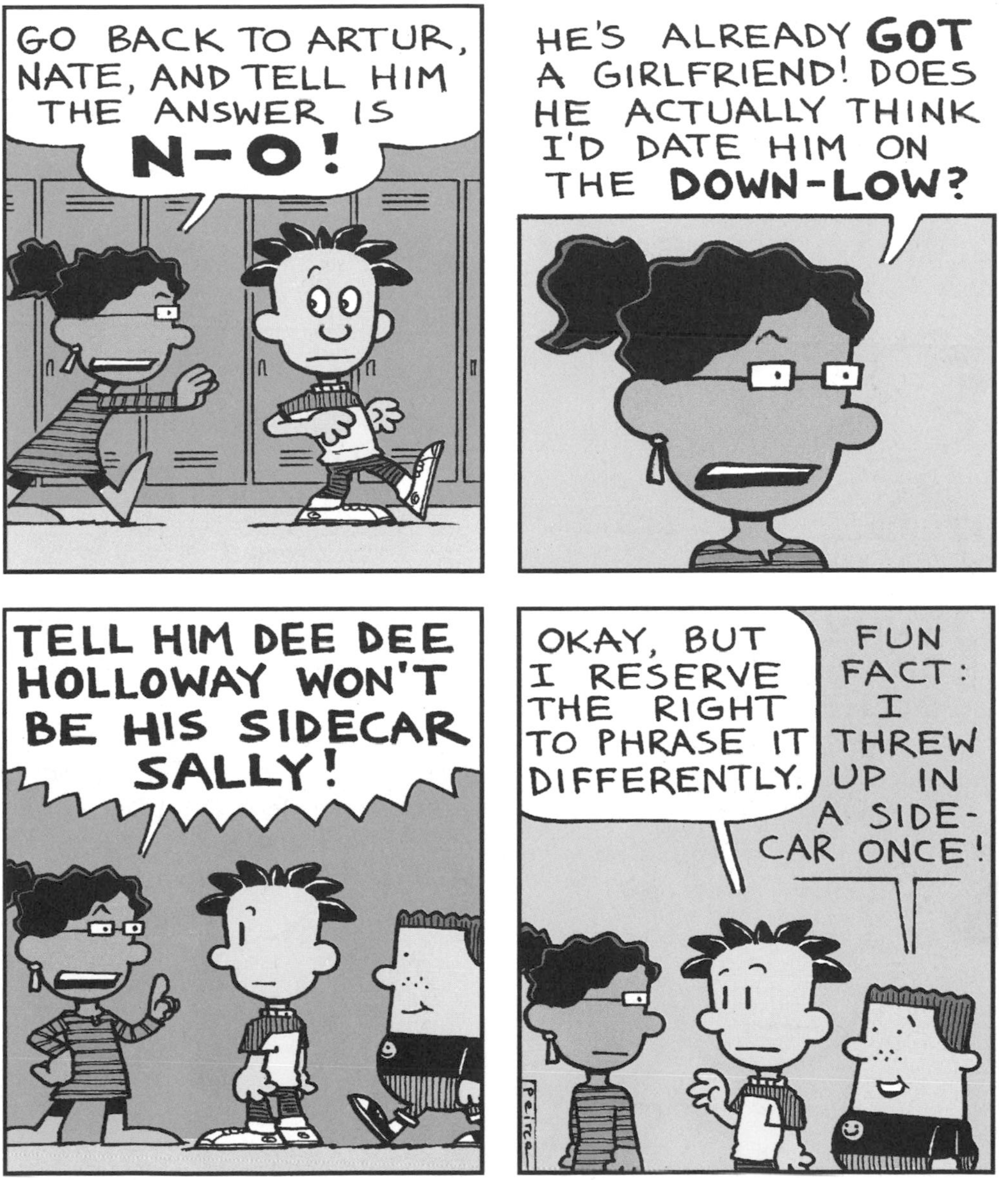
GO BACK TO ARTUR, NATE, AND TELL HIM THE ANSWER IS **N-O!**
HE'S ALREADY **GOT** A GIRLFRIEND! DOES HE ACTUALLY THINK I'D DATE HIM ON THE **DOWN-LOW?**
TELL HIM DEE DEE HOLLOWAY WON'T BE HIS SIDECAR SALLY!
OKAY, BUT I RESERVE THE RIGHT TO PHRASE IT DIFFERENTLY.
FUN FACT: I THREW UP IN A SIDE-CAR ONCE!
Peirce

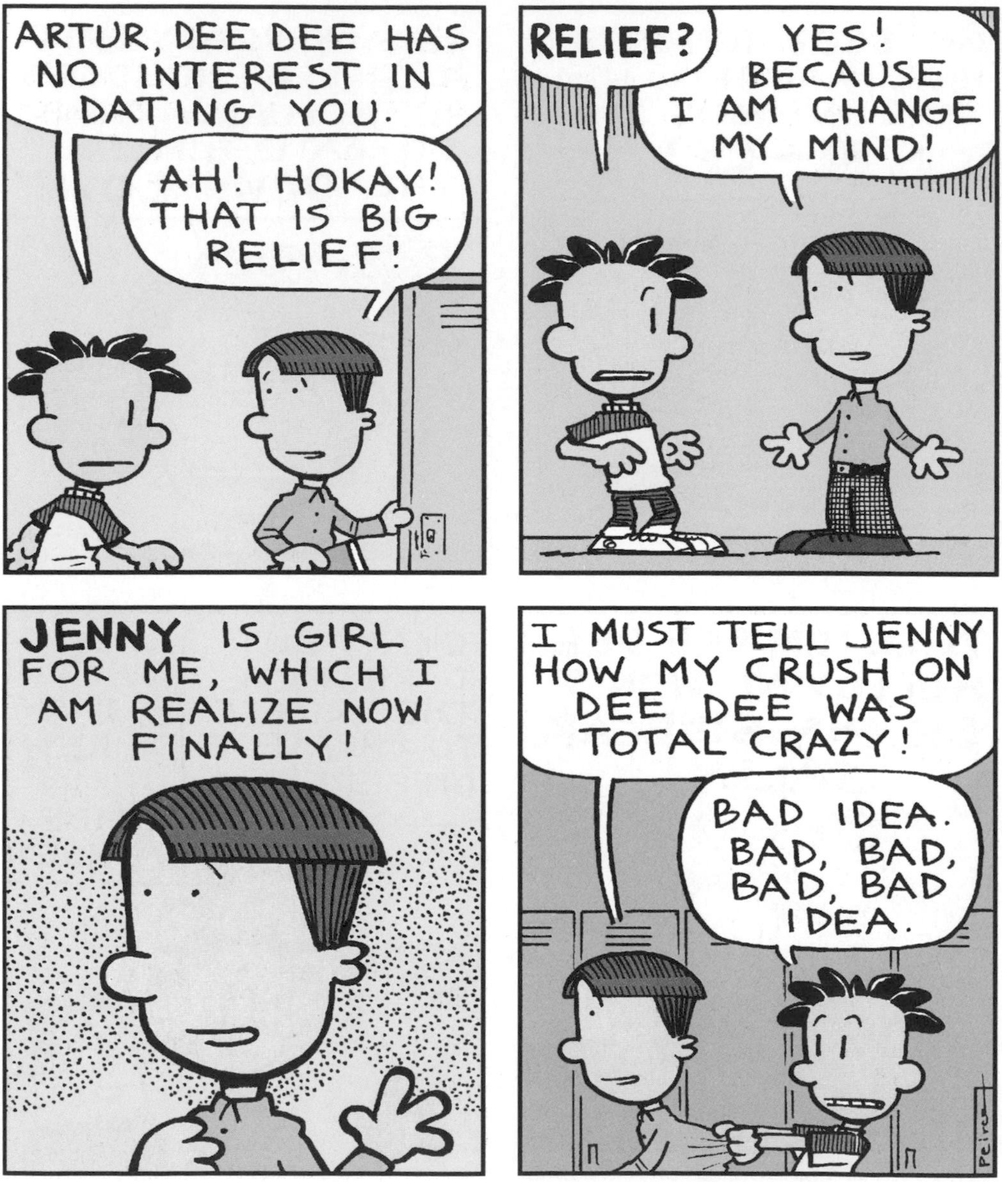
ARTUR, DEE DEE HAS NO INTEREST IN DATING YOU.
AH! HOKAY! THAT IS BIG RELIEF!
RELIEF?
YES! BECAUSE I AM CHANGE MY MIND!
JENNY IS GIRL FOR ME, WHICH I AM REALIZE NOW FINALLY!
I MUST TELL JENNY HOW MY CRUSH ON DEE DEE WAS TOTAL CRAZY!
BAD IDEA. BAD, BAD, BAD, BAD IDEA.
Peirce

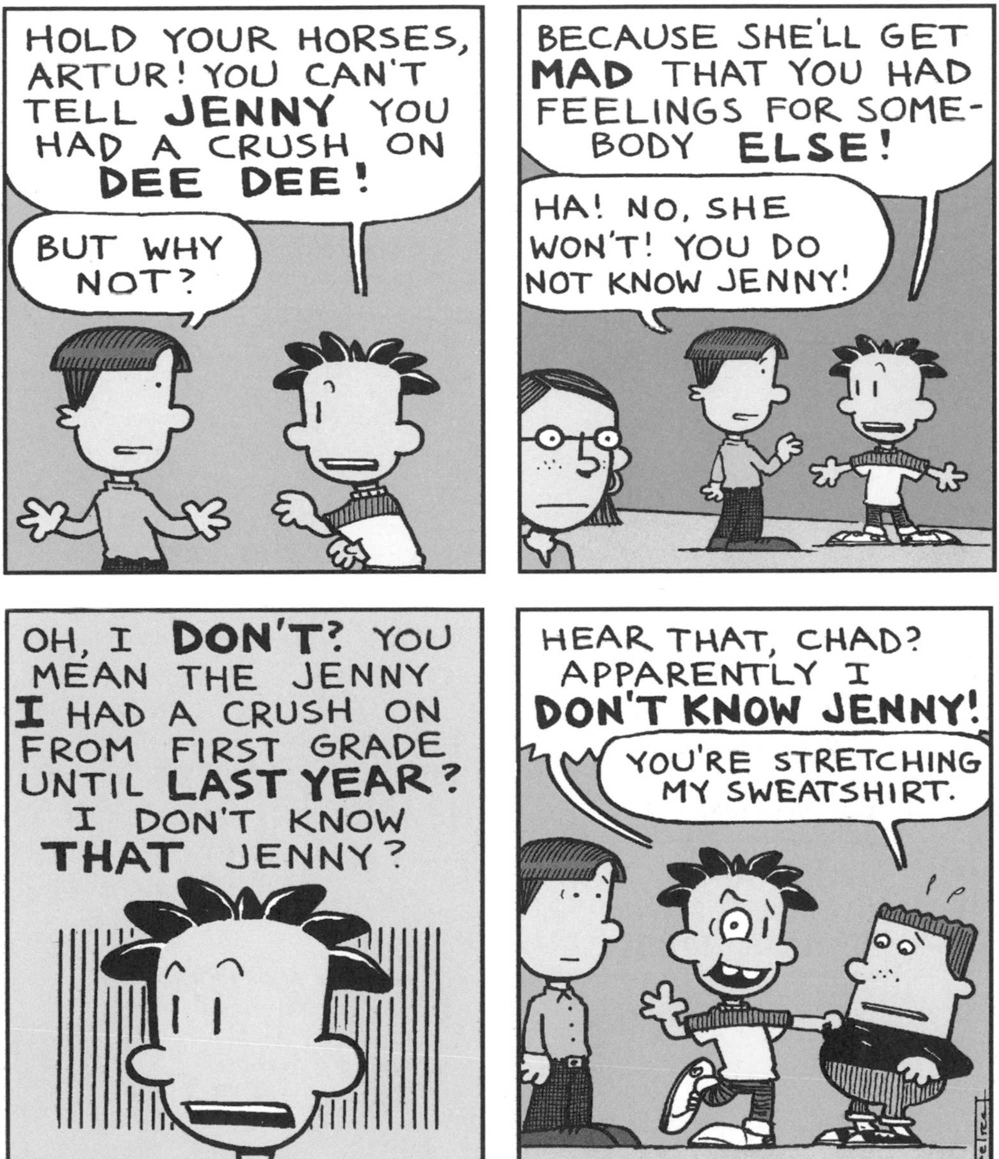
HOLD YOUR HORSES, ARTUR! YOU CAN'T TELL JENNY YOU HAD A CRUSH ON DEE DEE!
BUT WHY NOT?
BECAUSE SHE'LL GET MAD THAT YOU HAD FEELINGS FOR SOME-BODY ELSE!
HA! NO, SHE WON'T! YOU DO NOT KNOW JENNY!
OH, I DON'T? YOU MEAN THE JENNY I HAD A CRUSH ON FROM FIRST GRADE UNTIL LAST YEAR? I DON'T KNOW THAT JENNY?
HEAR THAT, CHAD? APPARENTLY I DON'T KNOW JENNY!
YOU'RE STRETCHING MY SWEATSHIRT.

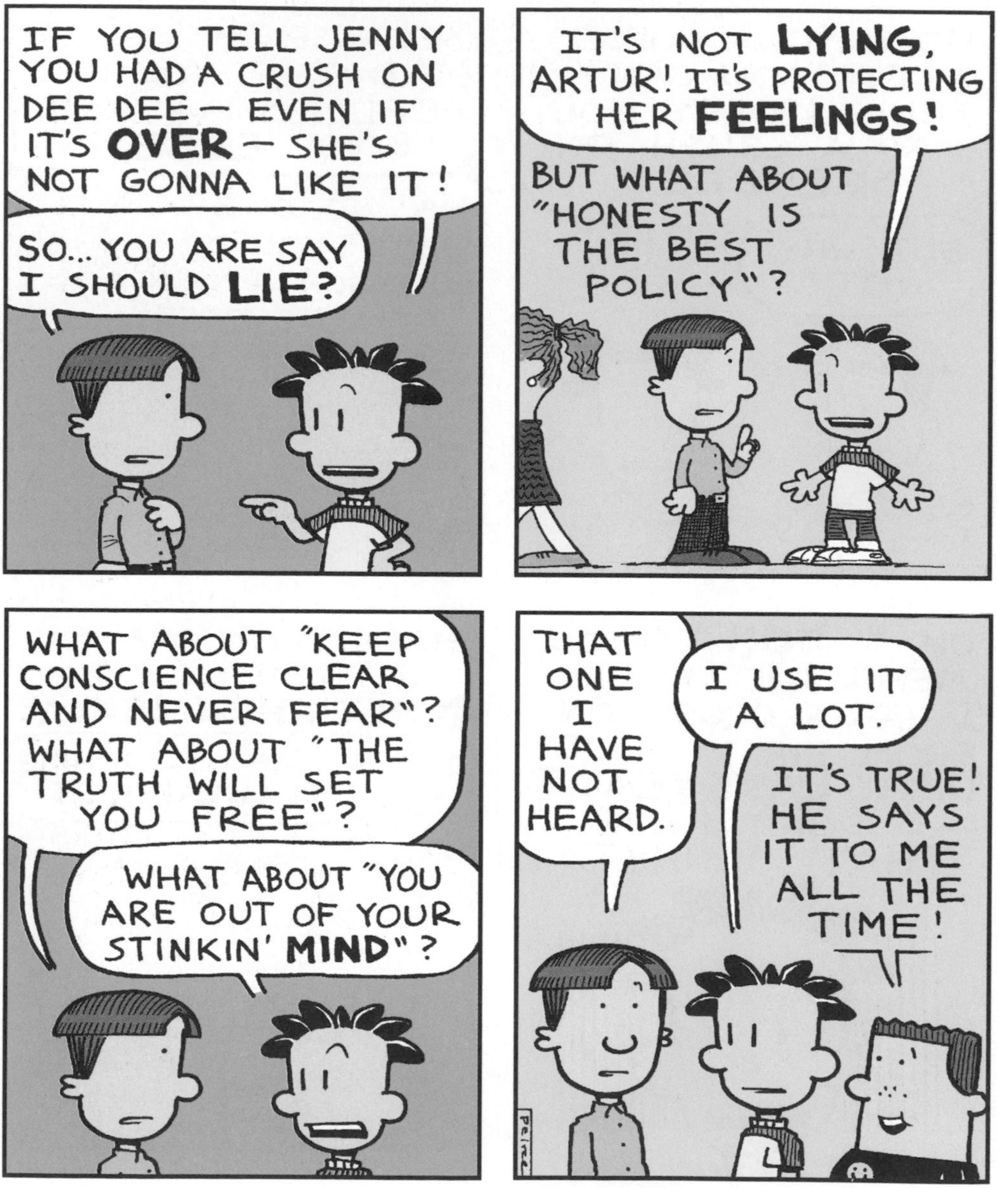
IF YOU TELL JENNY YOU HAD A CRUSH ON DEE DEE — EVEN IF IT'S **OVER** — SHE'S NOT GONNA LIKE IT!
SO... YOU ARE SAY I SHOULD **LIE?**
IT'S NOT **LYING**, ARTUR! IT'S PROTECTING HER **FEELINGS!**
BUT WHAT ABOUT "HONESTY IS THE BEST POLICY"?
WHAT ABOUT "KEEP CONSCIENCE CLEAR AND NEVER FEAR"? WHAT ABOUT "THE TRUTH WILL SET YOU FREE"?
WHAT ABOUT "YOU ARE OUT OF YOUR STINKIN' **MIND**"?
THAT ONE I HAVE NOT HEARD.
I USE IT A LOT.
IT'S TRUE! HE SAYS IT TO ME ALL THE TIME!
PEIRCE

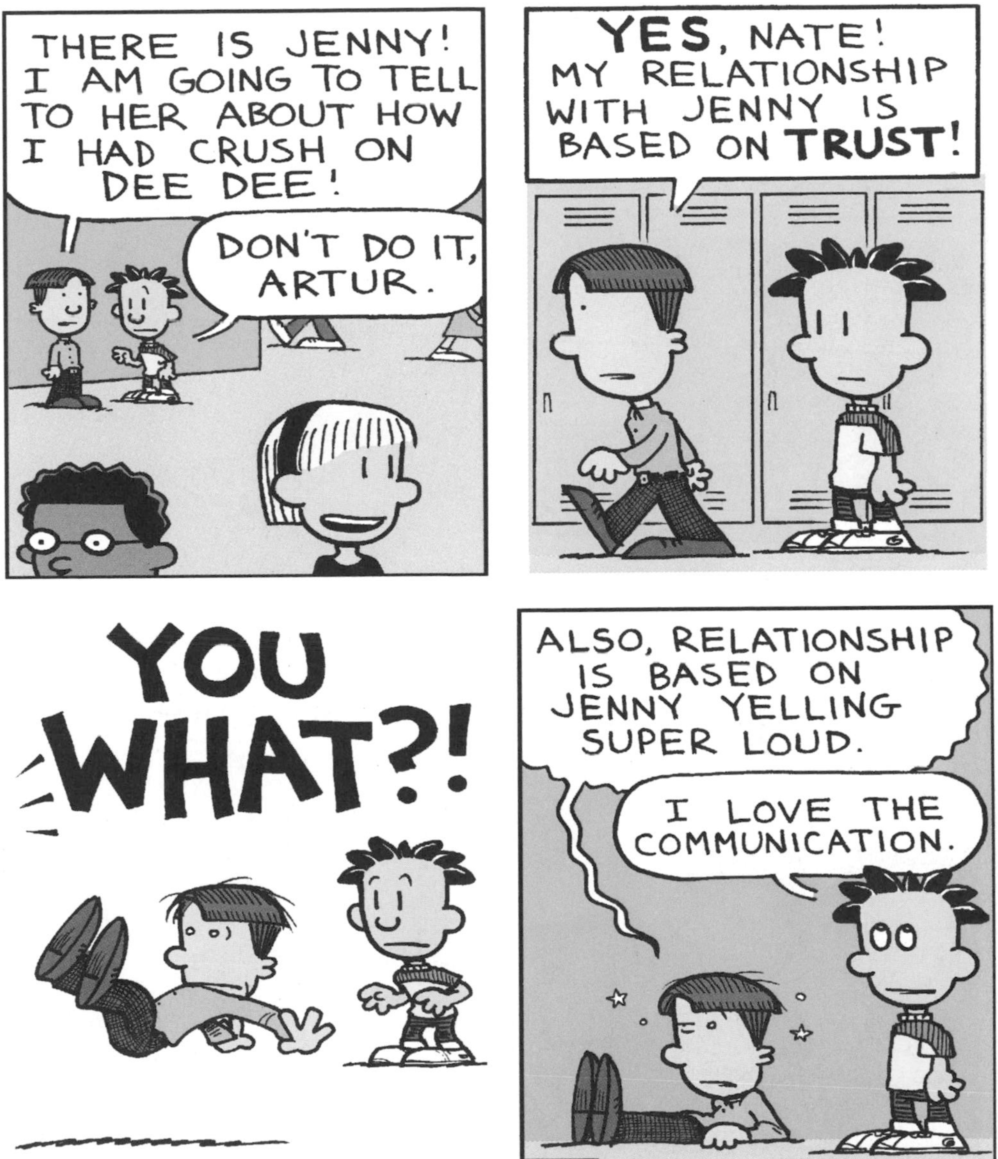
THERE IS JENNY! I AM GOING TO TELL TO HER ABOUT HOW I HAD CRUSH ON DEE DEE!
DON'T DO IT, ARTUR.
YES, NATE! MY RELATIONSHIP WITH JENNY IS BASED ON TRUST!
YOU WHAT?!
ALSO, RELATIONSHIP IS BASED ON JENNY YELLING SUPER LOUD.
I LOVE THE COMMUNICATION.
Peirce

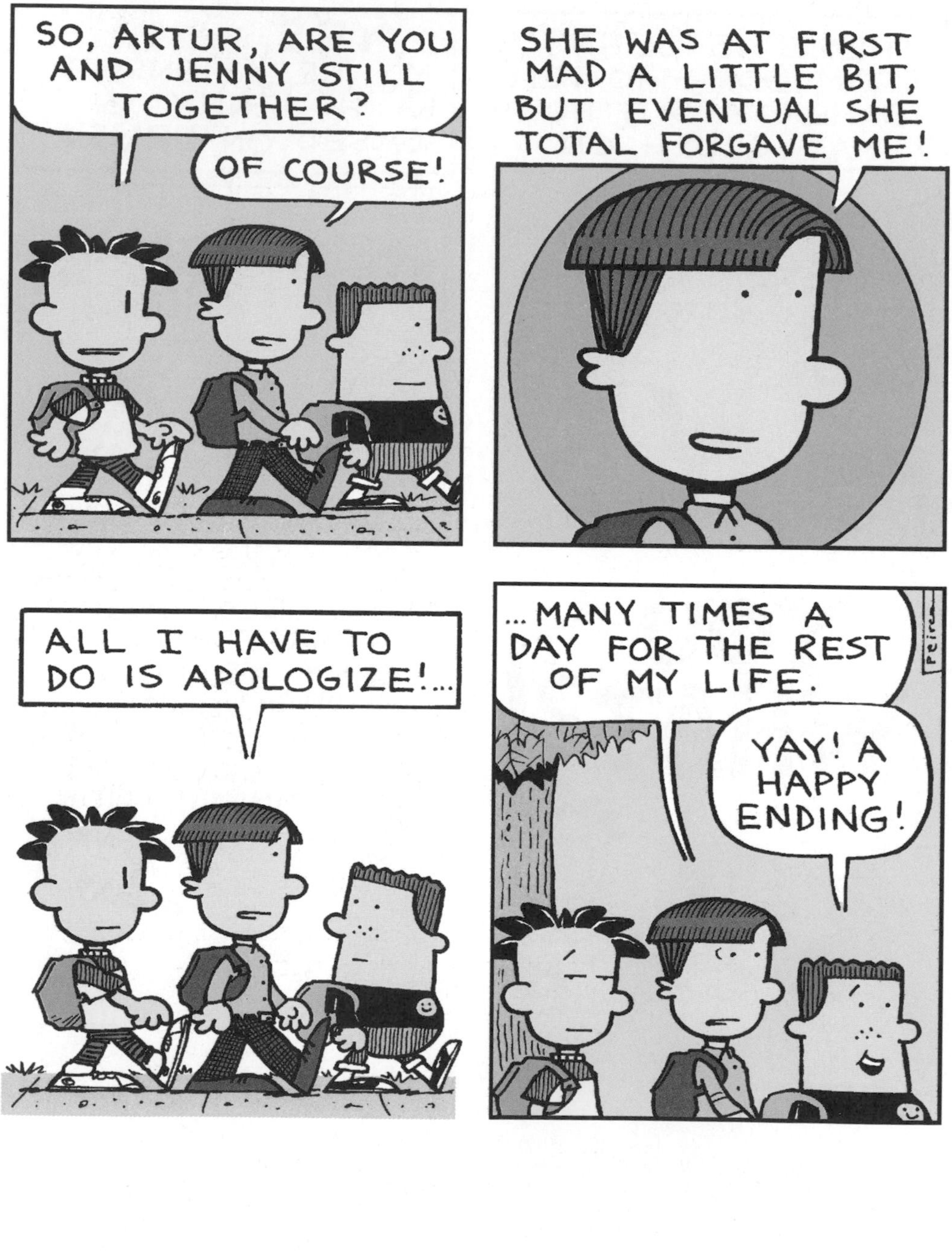
SO, ARTUR, ARE YOU AND JENNY STILL TOGETHER?
OF COURSE!
SHE WAS AT FIRST MAD A LITTLE BIT, BUT EVENTUAL SHE TOTAL FORGAVE ME!
ALL I HAVE TO DO IS APOLOGIZE!...
...MANY TIMES A DAY FOR THE REST OF MY LIFE.
YAY! A HAPPY ENDING!
Peirce

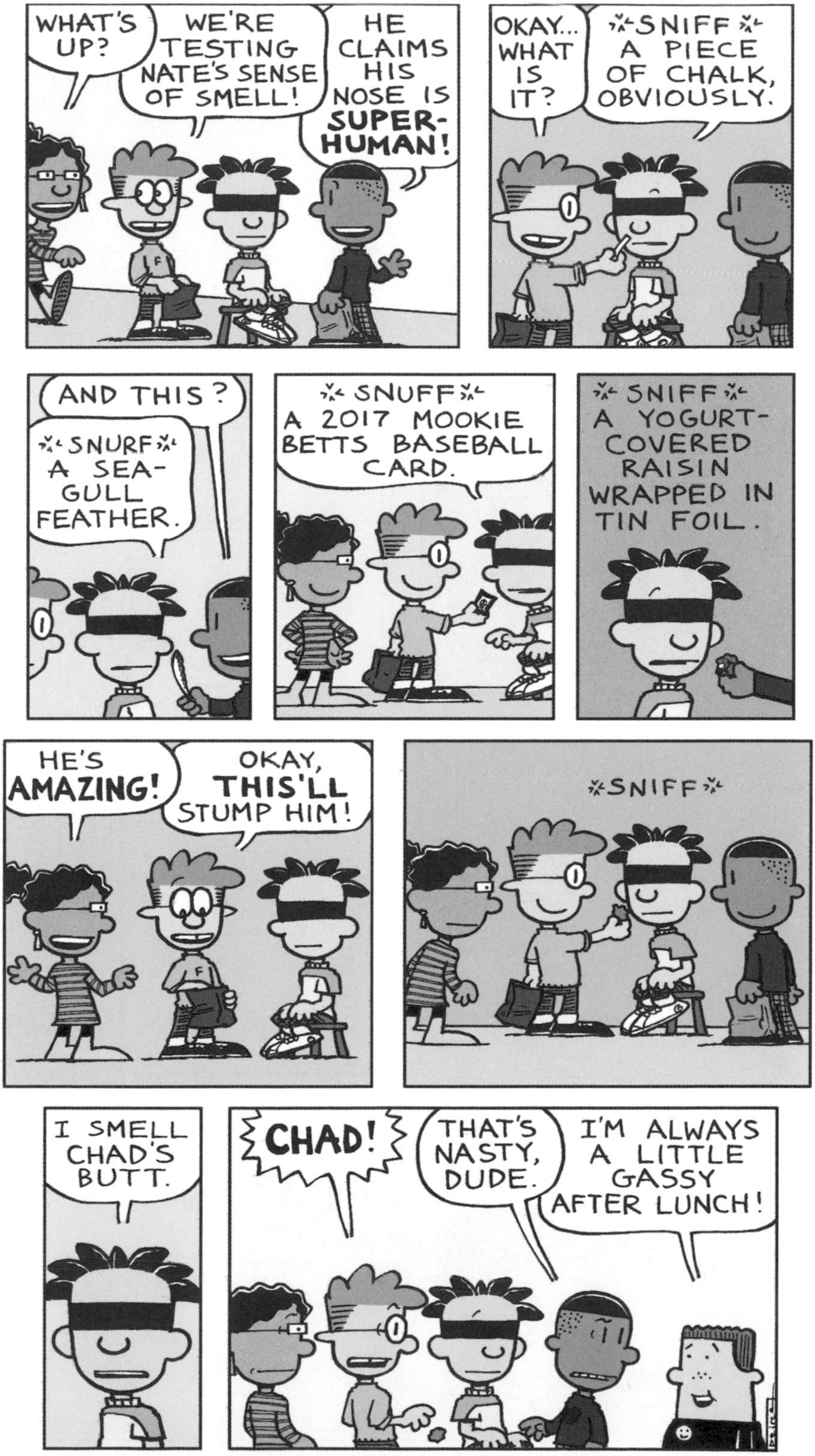

WHAT'S UP?
WE'RE TESTING NATE'S SENSE OF SMELL!
HE CLAIMS HIS NOSE IS **SUPER-HUMAN!**
OKAY... WHAT IS IT?
SNIFF A PIECE OF CHALK, OBVIOUSLY.
AND THIS?
SNURF A SEA-GULL FEATHER.
SNUFF A 2017 MOOKIE BETTS BASEBALL CARD.
SNIFF A YOGURT-COVERED RAISIN WRAPPED IN TIN FOIL.
HE'S **AMAZING!**
OKAY, **THIS'LL** STUMP HIM!
SNIFF
I SMELL CHAD'S BUTT.
CHAD!
THAT'S NASTY, DUDE.
I'M ALWAYS A LITTLE GASSY AFTER LUNCH!

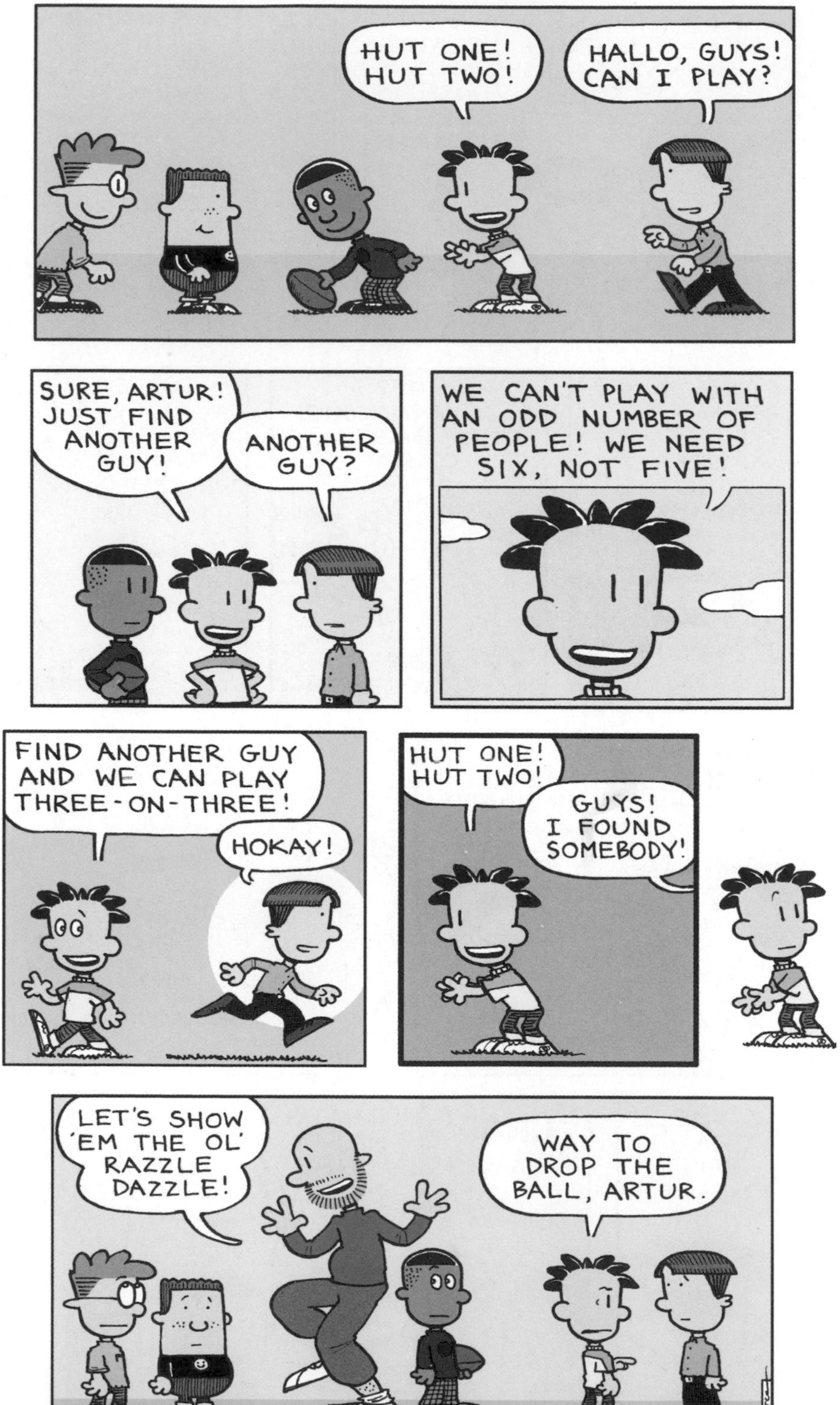
HUT ONE! HUT TWO!
HALLO, GUYS! CAN I PLAY?
SURE, ARTUR! JUST FIND ANOTHER GUY!
ANOTHER GUY?
WE CAN'T PLAY WITH AN ODD NUMBER OF PEOPLE! WE NEED SIX, NOT FIVE!
FIND ANOTHER GUY AND WE CAN PLAY THREE-ON-THREE!
HOKAY!
HUT ONE! HUT TWO!
GUYS! I FOUND SOMEBODY!
LET'S SHOW 'EM THE OL' RAZZLE DAZZLE!
WAY TO DROP THE BALL, ARTUR.

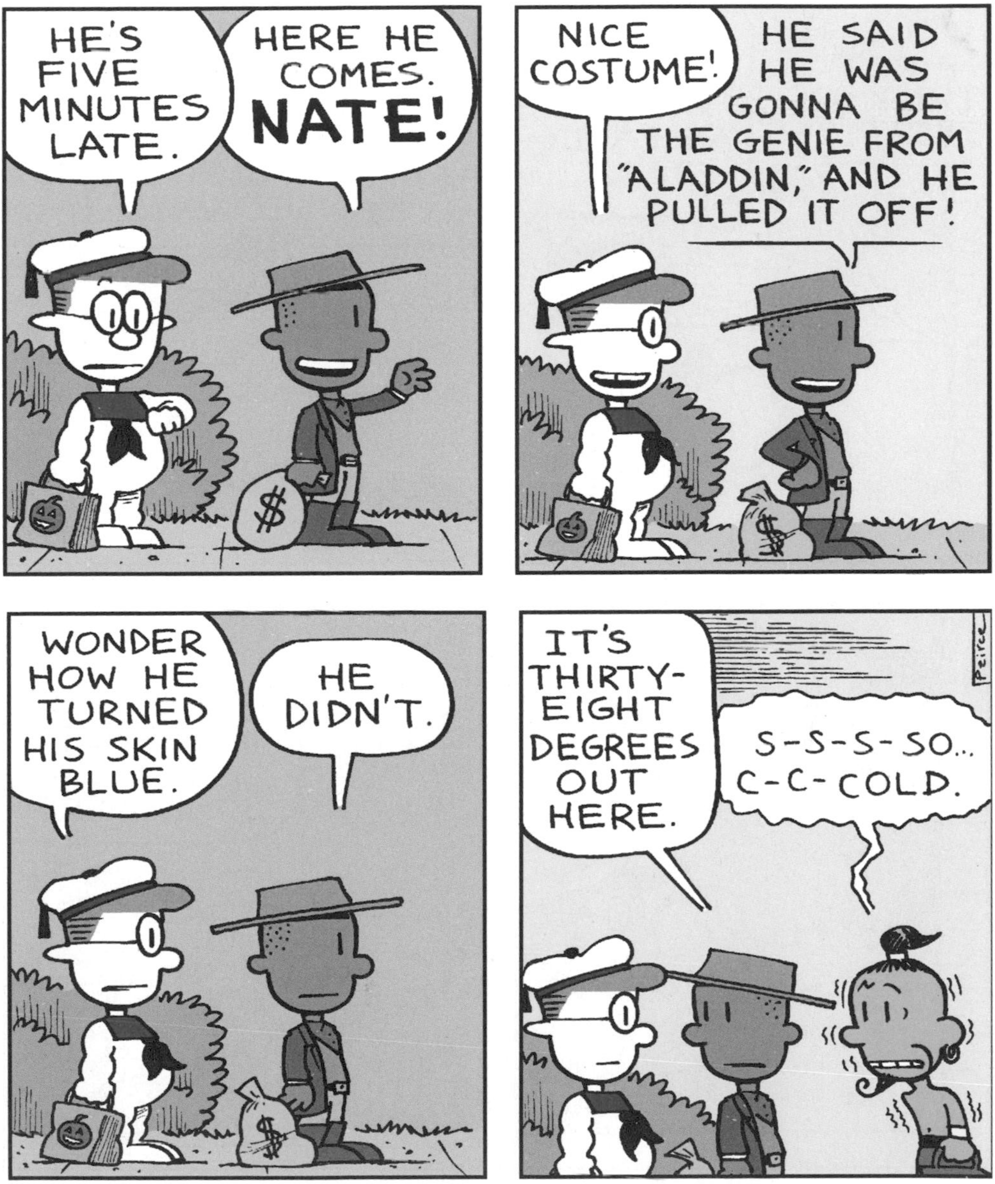
HE'S FIVE MINUTES LATE.
HERE HE COMES. NATE!
NICE COSTUME!
HE SAID HE WAS GONNA BE THE GENIE FROM "ALADDIN," AND HE PULLED IT OFF!
WONDER HOW HE TURNED HIS SKIN BLUE.
HE DIDN'T.
IT'S THIRTY-EIGHT DEGREES OUT HERE.
S-S-S-SO... C-C-COLD.
Peirce

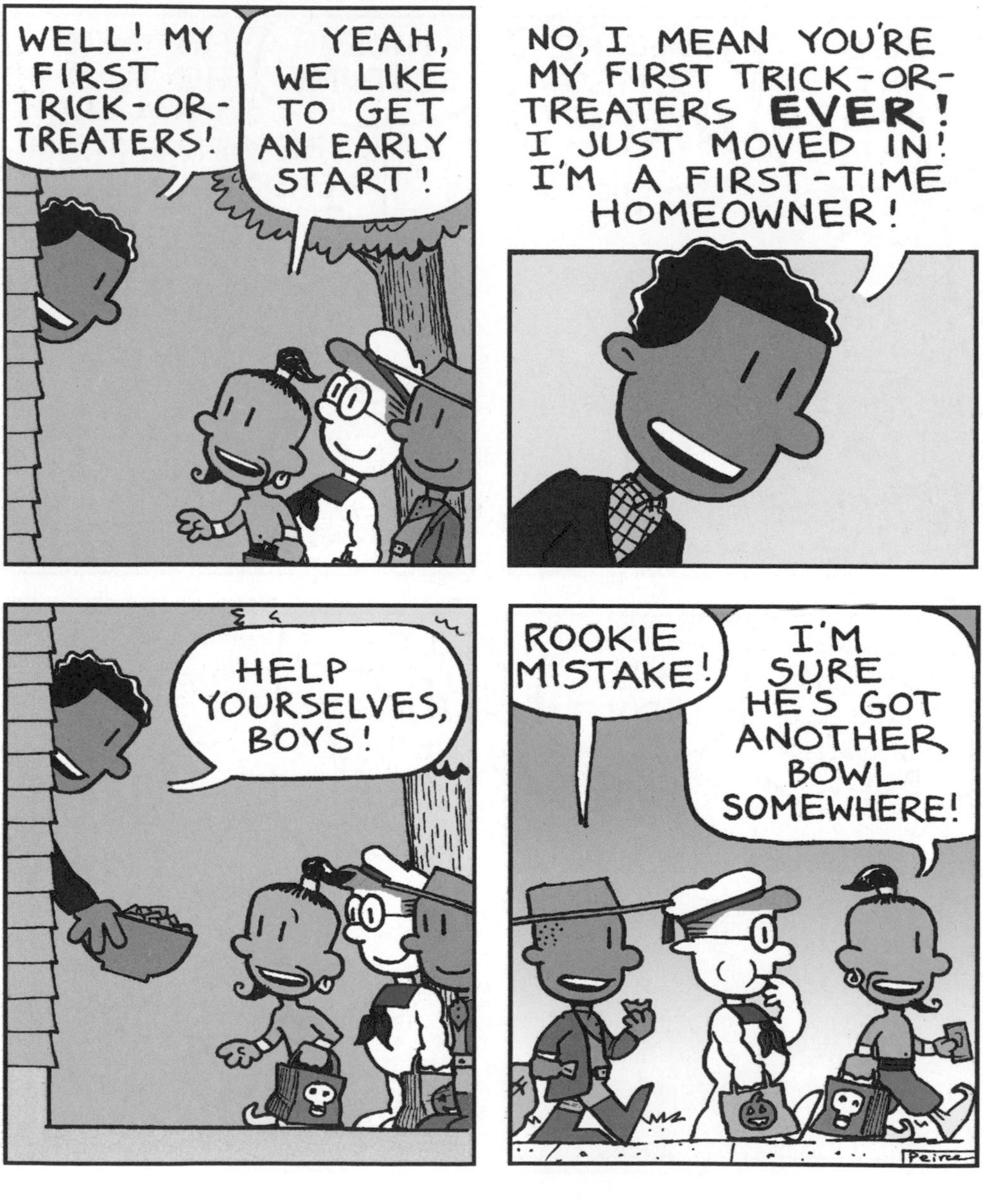
WELL! MY FIRST TRICK-OR-TREATERS!
YEAH, WE LIKE TO GET AN EARLY START!
NO, I MEAN YOU'RE MY FIRST TRICK-OR-TREATERS **EVER**! I JUST MOVED IN! I'M A FIRST-TIME HOMEOWNER!
HELP YOURSELVES, BOYS!
ROOKIE MISTAKE!
I'M SURE HE'S GOT ANOTHER BOWL SOMEWHERE!
Peirce

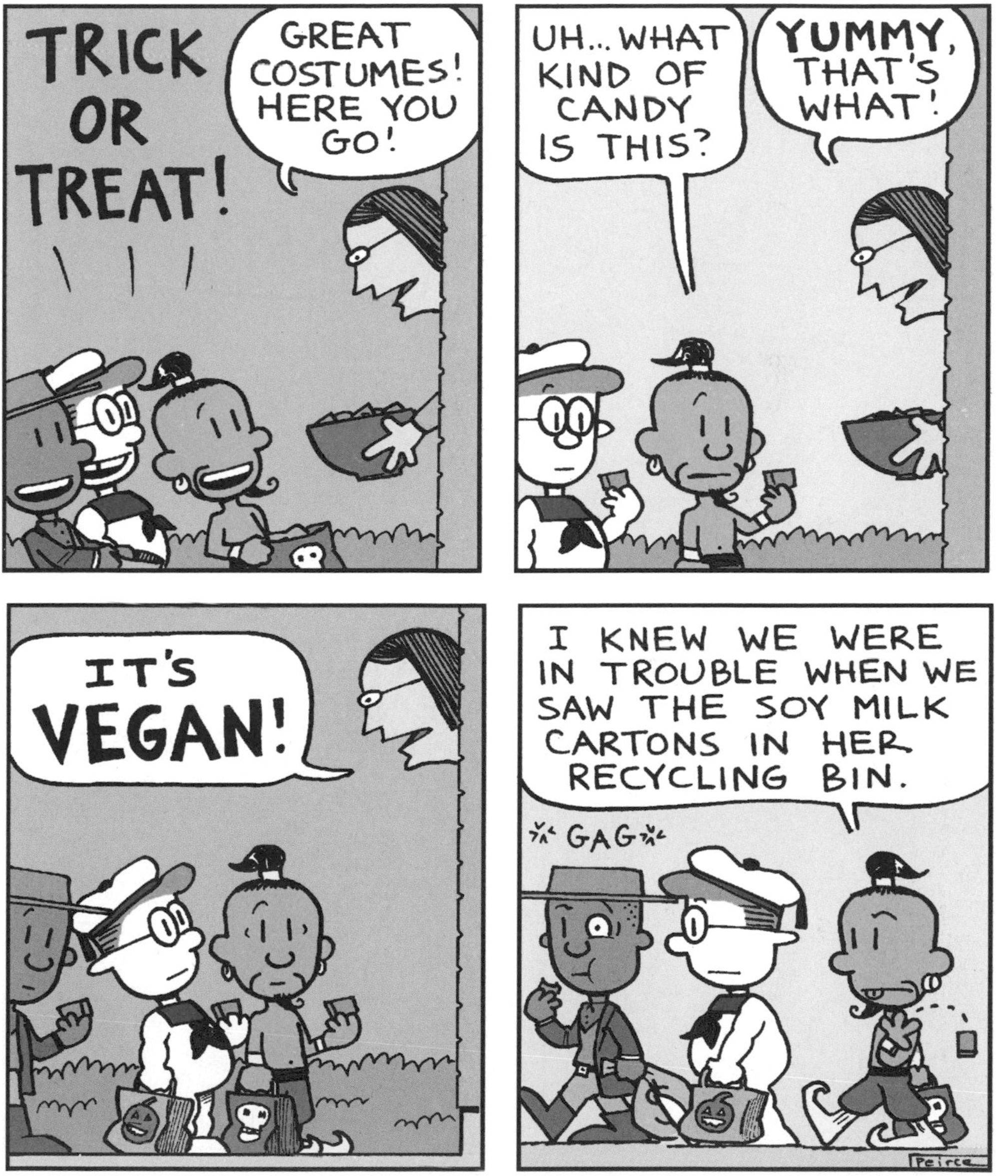

TRICK OR TREAT!
GREAT COSTUMES! HERE YOU GO!
UH... WHAT KIND OF CANDY IS THIS?
YUMMY, THAT'S WHAT!
IT'S VEGAN!
I KNEW WE WERE IN TROUBLE WHEN WE SAW THE SOY MILK CARTONS IN HER RECYCLING BIN.
GAG
Peirce

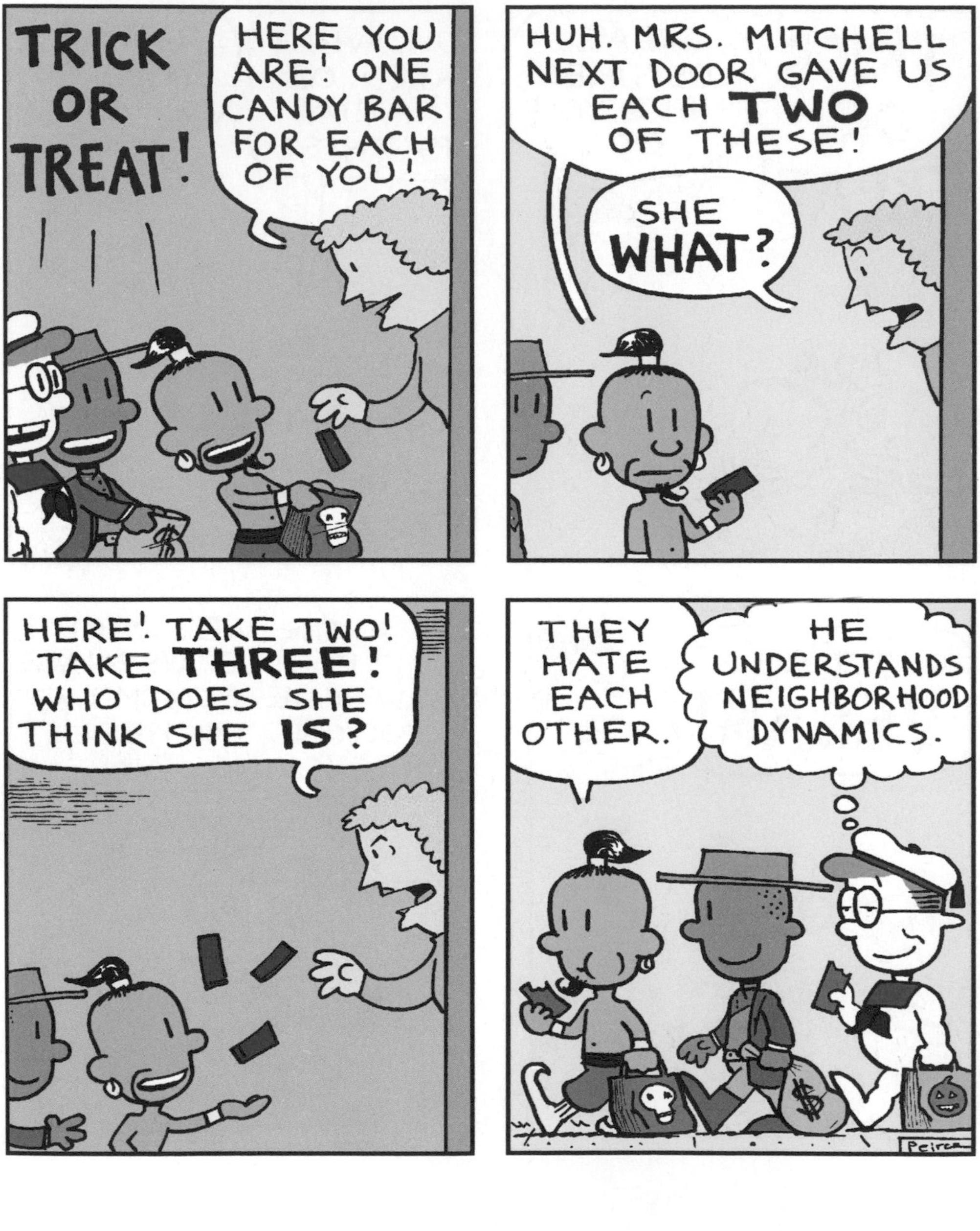
TRICK OR TREAT!
HERE YOU ARE! ONE CANDY BAR FOR EACH OF YOU!
HUH. MRS. MITCHELL NEXT DOOR GAVE US EACH TWO OF THESE!
SHE WHAT?
HERE! TAKE TWO! TAKE THREE! WHO DOES SHE THINK SHE IS?
THEY HATE EACH OTHER.
HE UNDERSTANDS NEIGHBORHOOD DYNAMICS.
Peirce

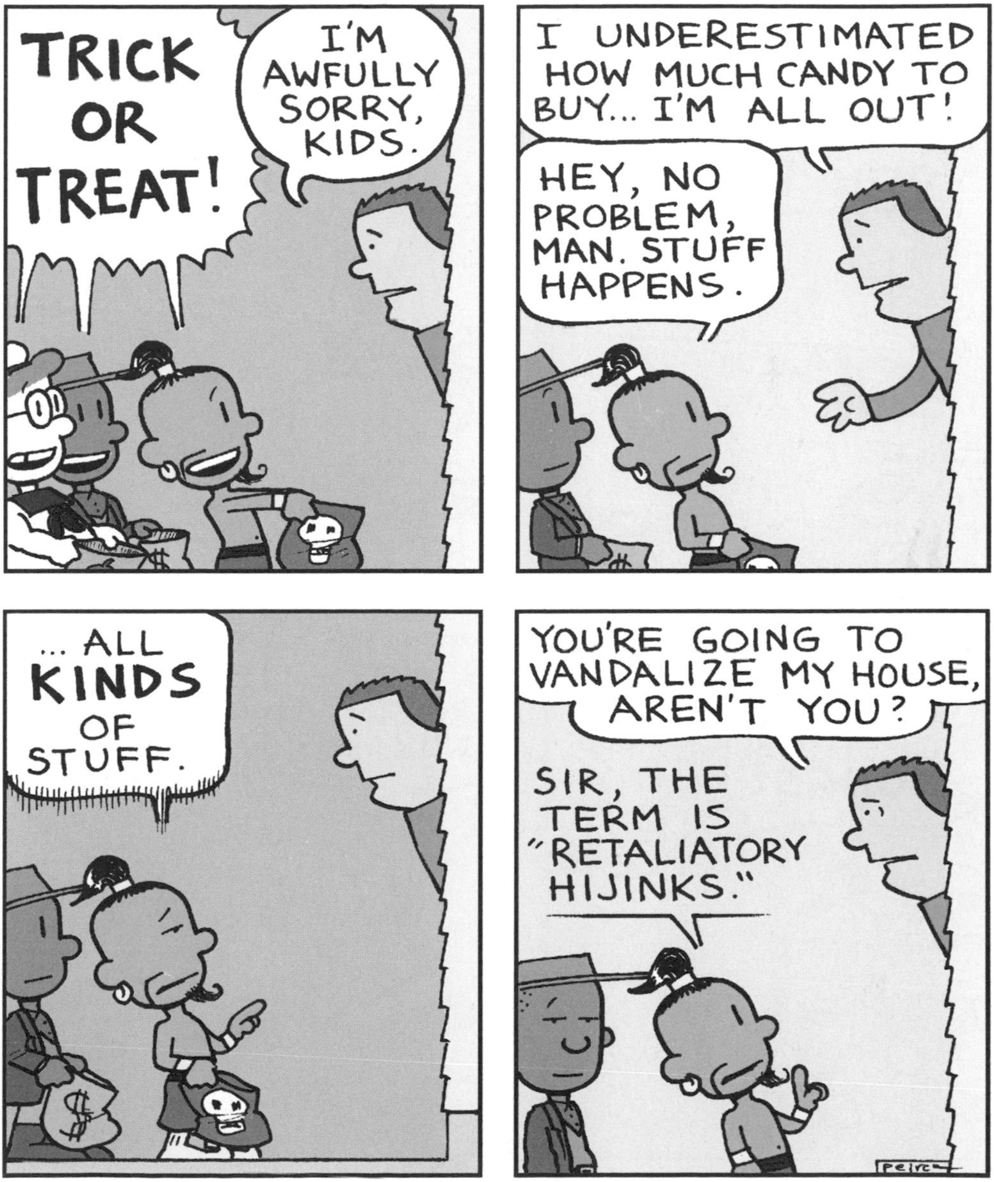
TRICK OR TREAT!
I'M AWFULLY SORRY, KIDS.
I UNDERESTIMATED HOW MUCH CANDY TO BUY... I'M ALL OUT!
HEY, NO PROBLEM, MAN. STUFF HAPPENS.
... ALL KINDS OF STUFF.
YOU'RE GOING TO VANDALIZE MY HOUSE, AREN'T YOU?
SIR, THE TERM IS "RETALIATORY HIJINKS."
PEIRCE

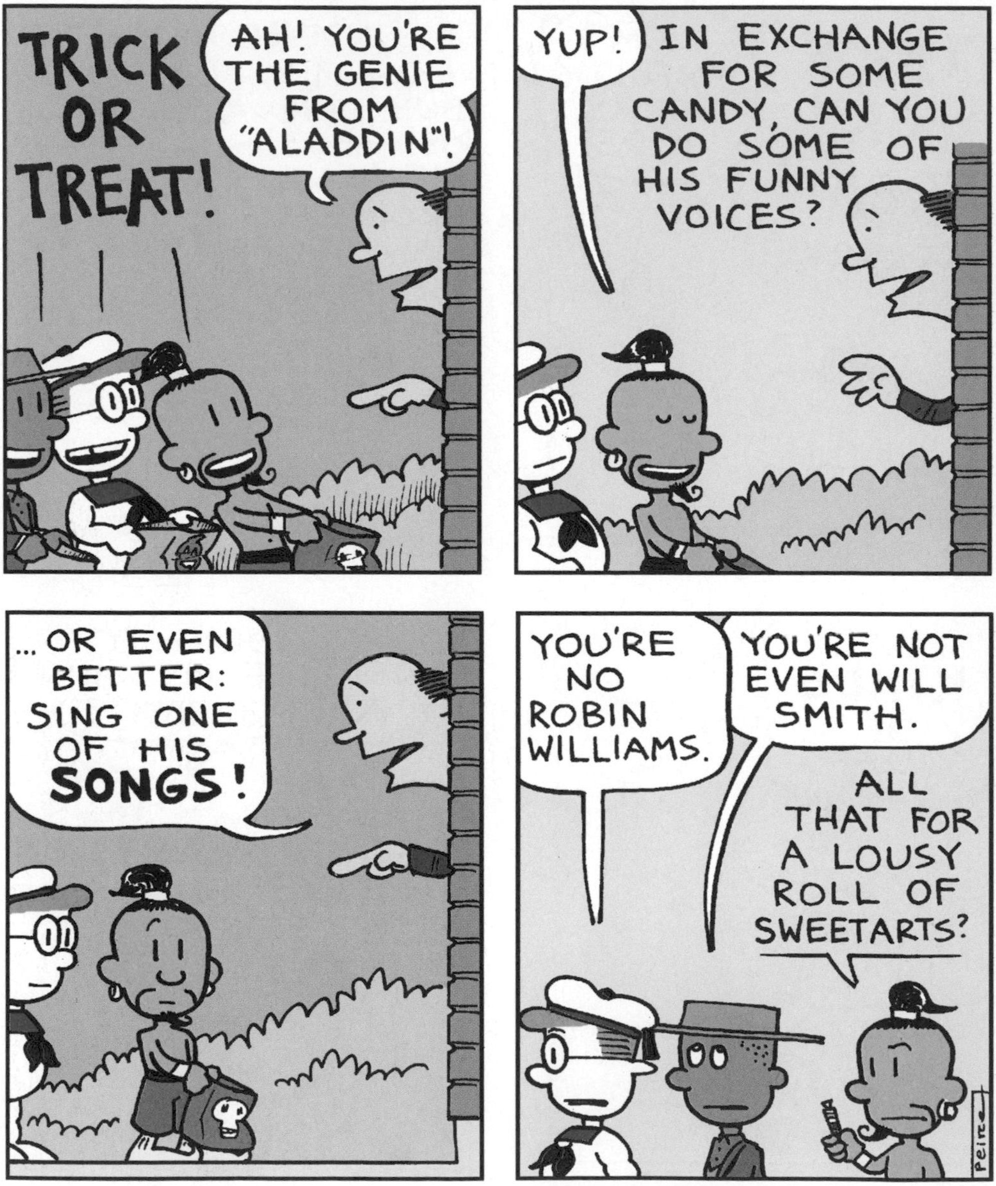
TRICK OR TREAT!
AH! YOU'RE THE GENIE FROM "ALADDIN"!
YUP!
IN EXCHANGE FOR SOME CANDY, CAN YOU DO SOME OF HIS FUNNY VOICES?
...OR EVEN BETTER: SING ONE OF HIS SONGS!
YOU'RE NO ROBIN WILLIAMS.
YOU'RE NOT EVEN WILL SMITH.
ALL THAT FOR A LOUSY ROLL OF SWEETARTS?
PEIRCE

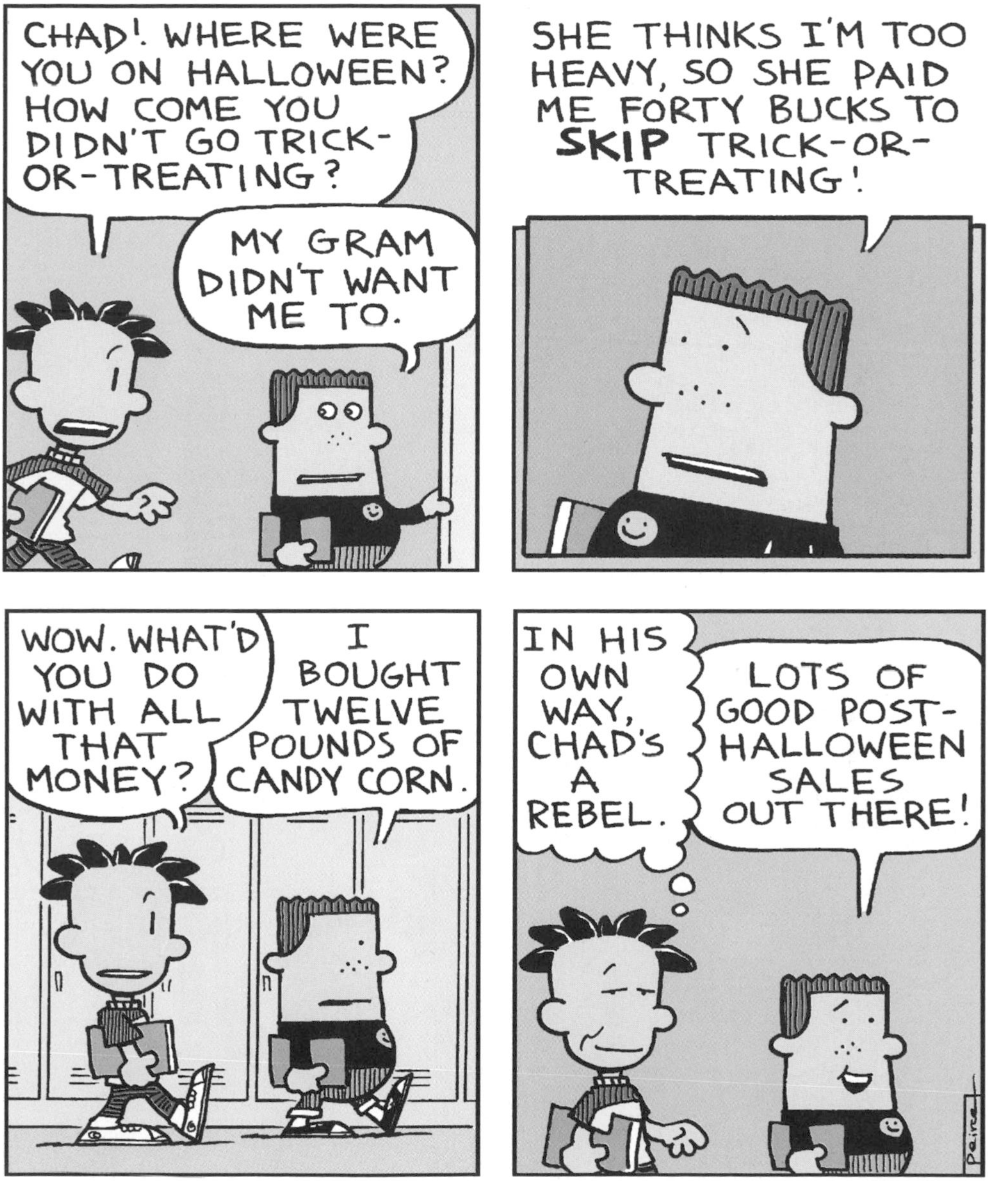
CHAD! WHERE WERE YOU ON HALLOWEEN? HOW COME YOU DIDN'T GO TRICK-OR-TREATING?
MY GRAM DIDN'T WANT ME TO.
SHE THINKS I'M TOO HEAVY, SO SHE PAID ME FORTY BUCKS TO **SKIP** TRICK-OR-TREATING!
WOW. WHAT'D YOU DO WITH ALL THAT MONEY?
I BOUGHT TWELVE POUNDS OF CANDY CORN.
IN HIS OWN WAY, CHAD'S A REBEL.
LOTS OF GOOD POST-HALLOWEEN SALES OUT THERE!
Peirce

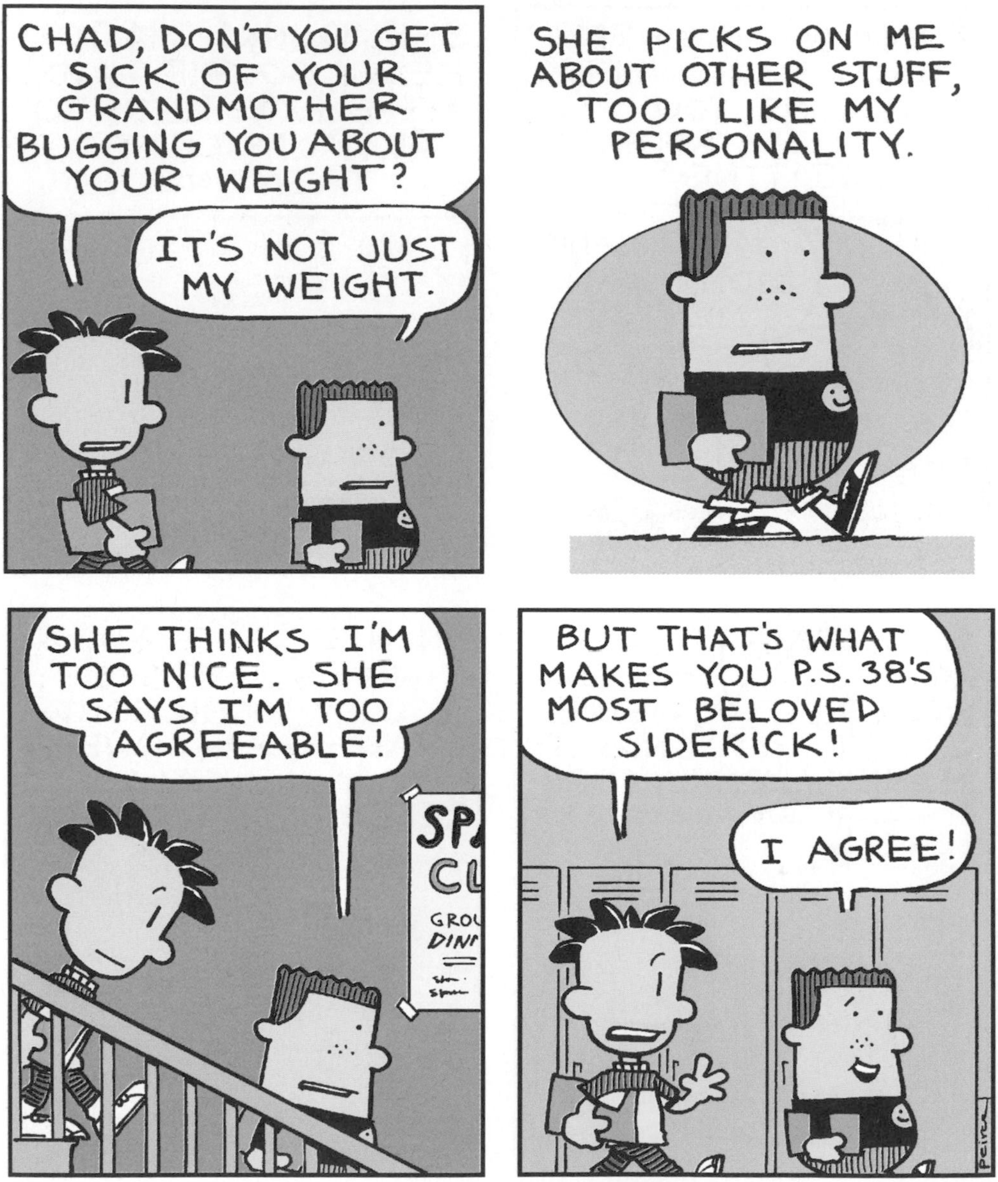
CHAD, DON'T YOU GET SICK OF YOUR GRANDMOTHER BUGGING YOU ABOUT YOUR WEIGHT?
IT'S NOT JUST MY WEIGHT.
SHE PICKS ON ME ABOUT OTHER STUFF, TOO. LIKE MY PERSONALITY.
SHE THINKS I'M TOO NICE. SHE SAYS I'M TOO AGREEABLE!
BUT THAT'S WHAT MAKES YOU P.S. 38'S MOST BELOVED SIDEKICK!
I AGREE!

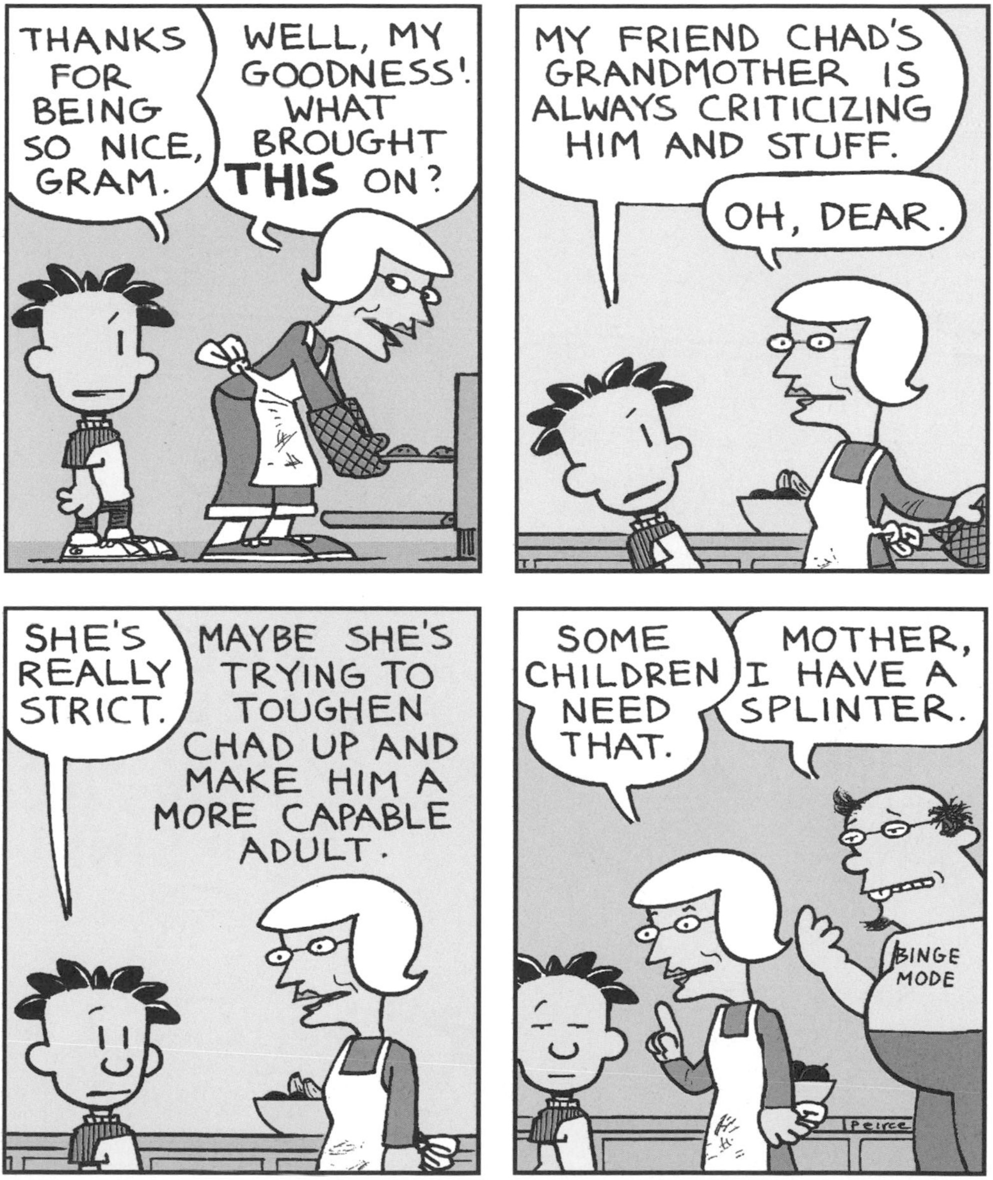
THANKS FOR BEING SO NICE, GRAM.
WELL, MY GOODNESS! WHAT BROUGHT **THIS** ON?
MY FRIEND CHAD'S GRANDMOTHER IS ALWAYS CRITICIZING HIM AND STUFF.
OH, DEAR.
SHE'S REALLY STRICT.
MAYBE SHE'S TRYING TO TOUGHEN CHAD UP AND MAKE HIM A MORE CAPABLE ADULT.
SOME CHILDREN NEED THAT.
MOTHER, I HAVE A SPLINTER.
BINGE MODE
Peirce

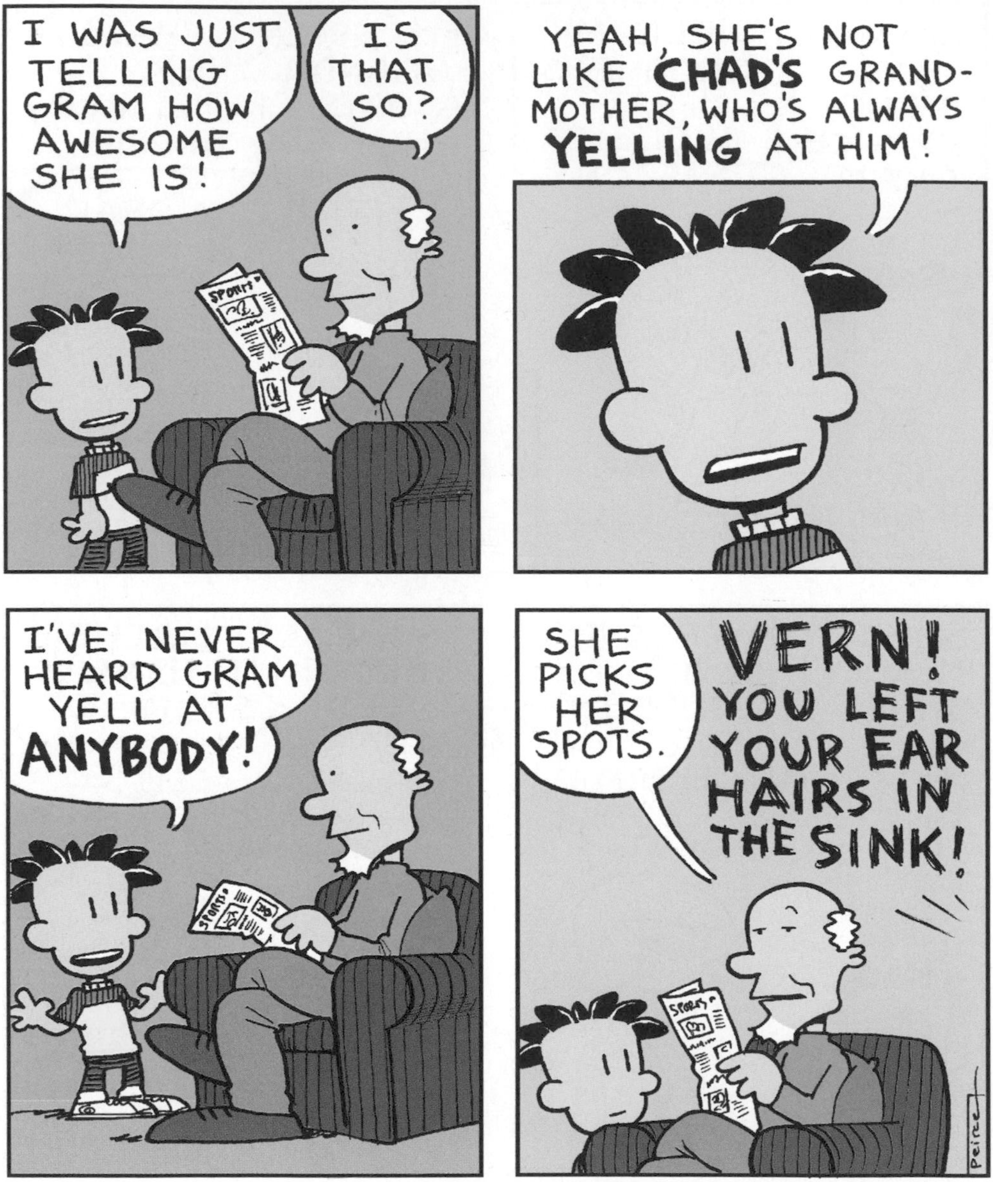
I WAS JUST TELLING GRAM HOW AWESOME SHE IS!
IS THAT SO?
SPORTS
YEAH, SHE'S NOT LIKE **CHAD'S** GRAND-MOTHER, WHO'S ALWAYS **YELLING** AT HIM!
I'VE NEVER HEARD GRAM YELL AT **ANYBODY!**
SPORTS
SHE PICKS HER SPOTS.
VERN! YOU LEFT YOUR EAR HAIRS IN THE SINK!
SPORTS
PEIRCE

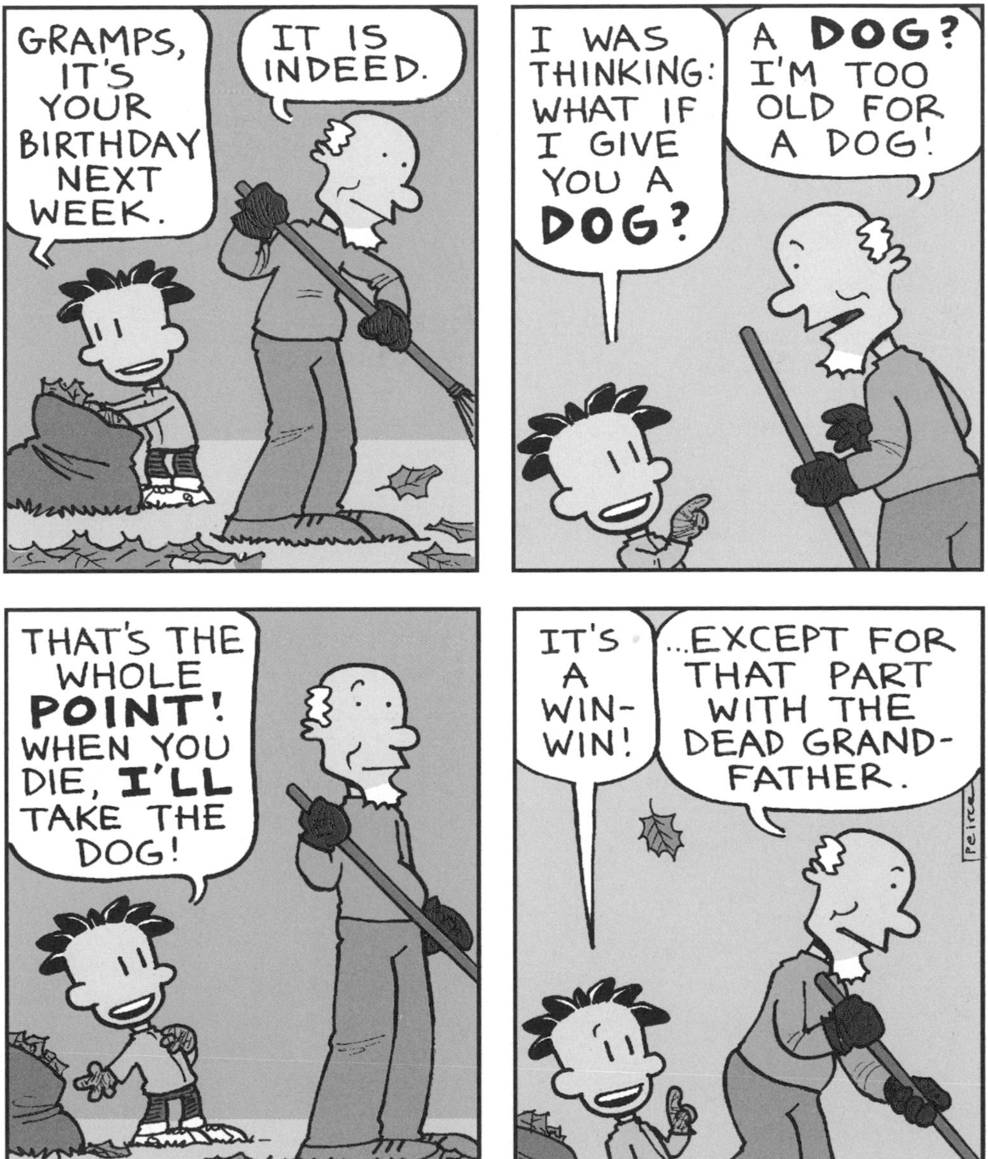
GRAMPS, IT'S YOUR BIRTHDAY NEXT WEEK.
IT IS INDEED.
I WAS THINKING: WHAT IF I GIVE YOU A **DOG**?
A **DOG**? I'M TOO OLD FOR A DOG!
THAT'S THE WHOLE **POINT**! WHEN YOU DIE, **I'LL** TAKE THE DOG!
IT'S A WIN-WIN!
...EXCEPT FOR THAT PART WITH THE DEAD GRAND-FATHER.
Peirce

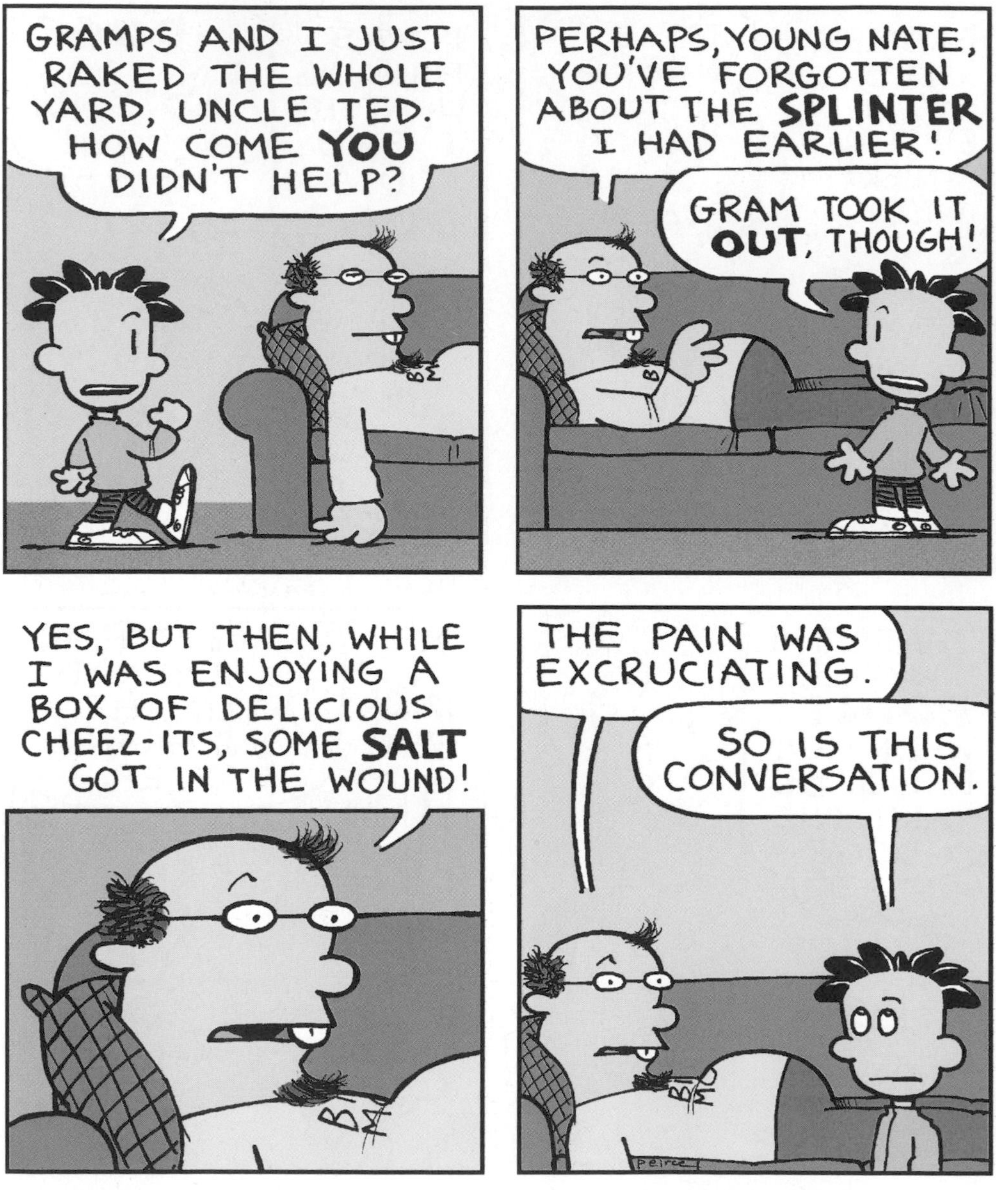
GRAMPS AND I JUST RAKED THE WHOLE YARD, UNCLE TED. HOW COME **YOU** DIDN'T HELP?
PERHAPS, YOUNG NATE, YOU'VE FORGOTTEN ABOUT THE **SPLINTER** I HAD EARLIER!
GRAM TOOK IT **OUT**, THOUGH!
YES, BUT THEN, WHILE I WAS ENJOYING A BOX OF DELICIOUS CHEEZ-ITS, SOME **SALT** GOT IN THE WOUND!
THE PAIN WAS EXCRUCIATING.
SO IS THIS CONVERSATION.
peirce

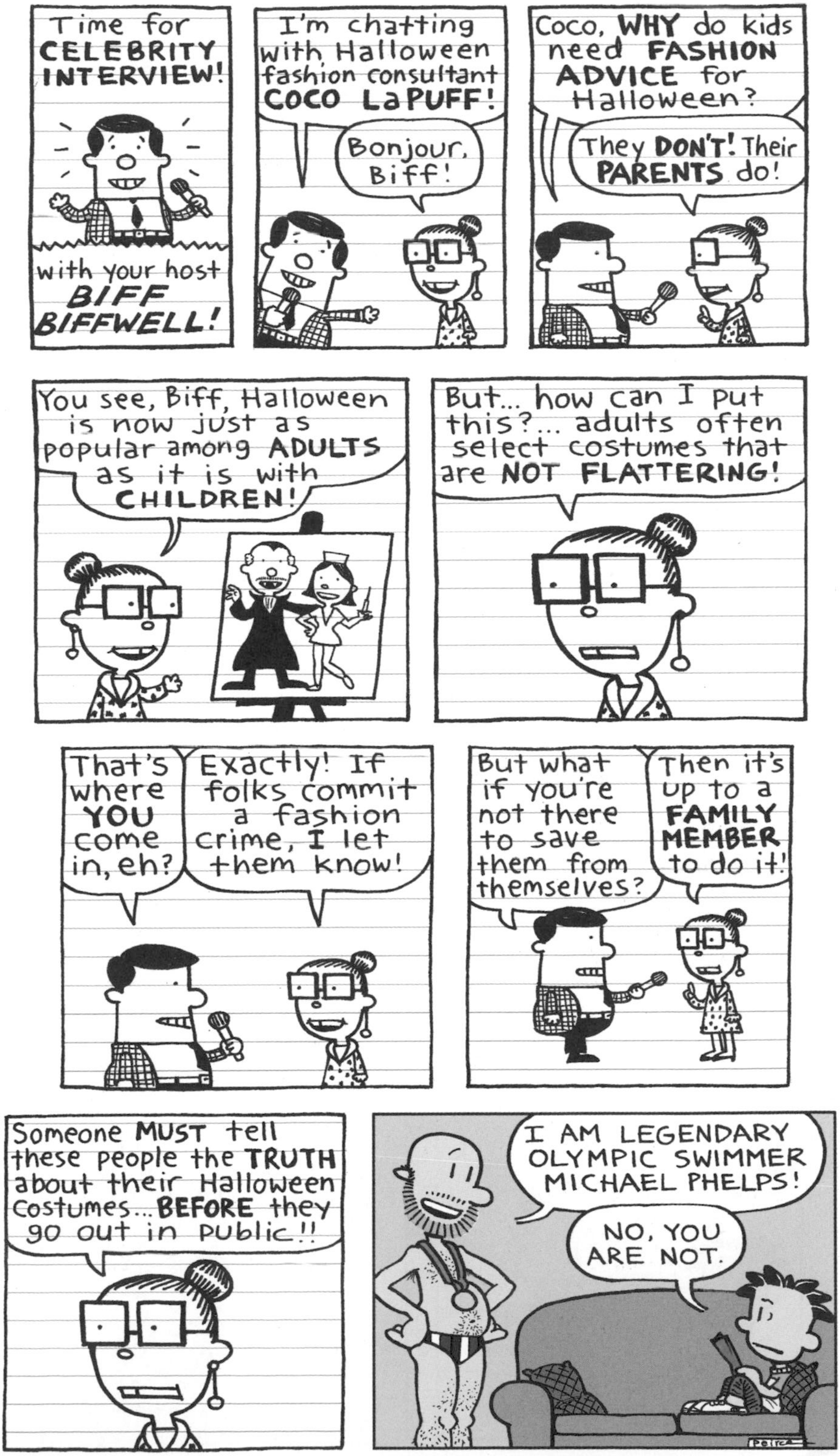
Time for CELEBRITY INTERVIEW!
with your host BIFF BIFFWELL!
I'm chatting with Halloween fashion consultant COCO LaPUFF!
Bonjour, Biff!
Coco, WHY do kids need FASHION ADVICE for Halloween?
They DON'T! Their PARENTS do!
You see, Biff, Halloween is now just as popular among ADULTS as it is with CHILDREN!
But... how can I put this?... adults often select costumes that are NOT FLATTERING!
That's where YOU come in, eh?
Exactly! If folks commit a fashion crime, I let them know!
But what if you're not there to save them from themselves?
Then it's up to a FAMILY MEMBER to do it!
Someone MUST tell these people the TRUTH about their Halloween costumes... BEFORE they go out in public!!
I AM LEGENDARY OLYMPIC SWIMMER MICHAEL PHELPS!
NO, YOU ARE NOT.
Peirce

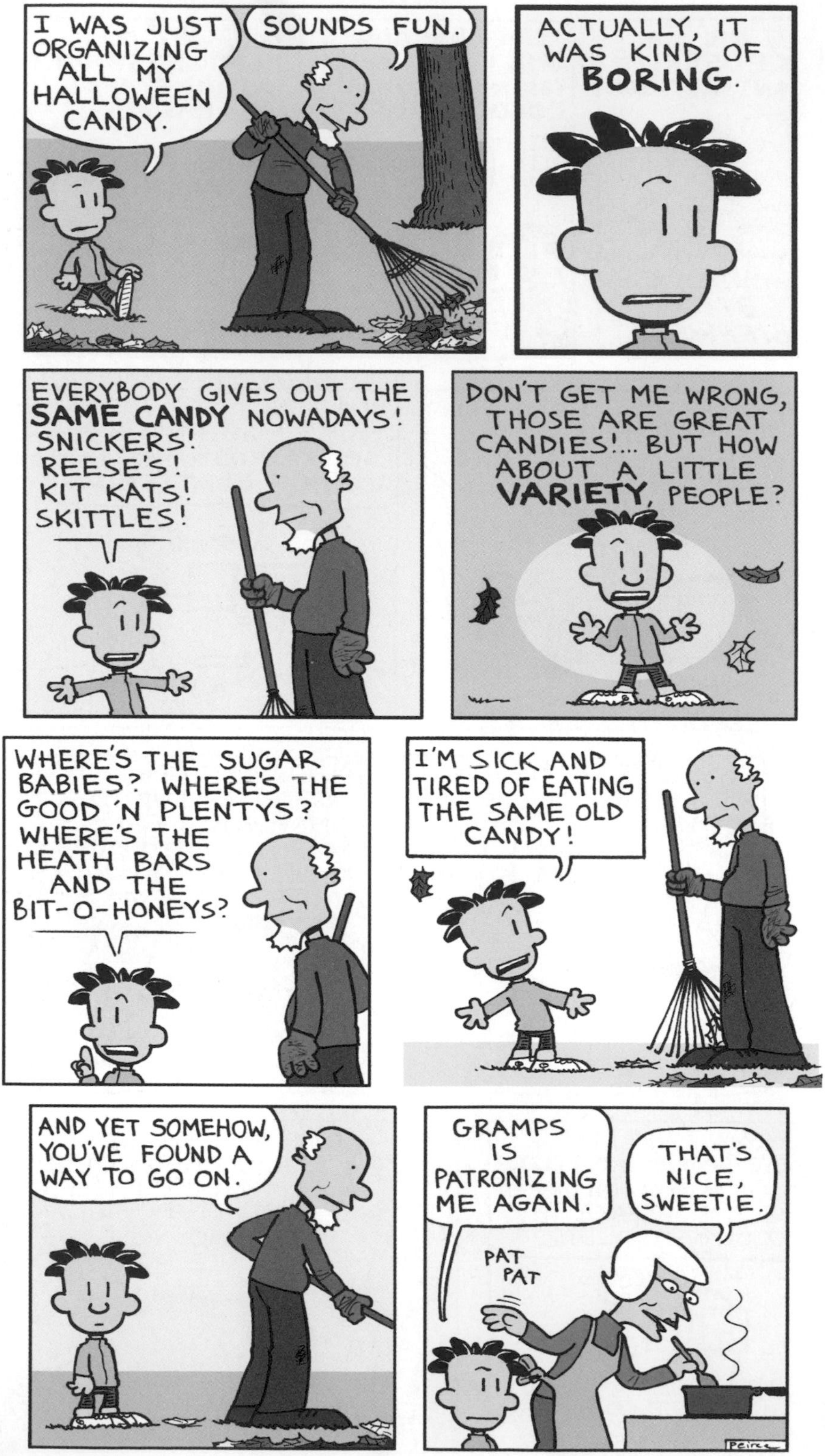
I WAS JUST ORGANIZING ALL MY HALLOWEEN CANDY.
SOUNDS FUN.
ACTUALLY, IT WAS KIND OF BORING.
EVERYBODY GIVES OUT THE SAME CANDY NOWADAYS! SNICKERS! REESE'S! KIT KATS! SKITTLES!
DON'T GET ME WRONG, THOSE ARE GREAT CANDIES!... BUT HOW ABOUT A LITTLE VARIETY, PEOPLE?
WHERE'S THE SUGAR BABIES? WHERE'S THE GOOD 'N PLENTYS? WHERE'S THE HEATH BARS AND THE BIT-O-HONEYS?
I'M SICK AND TIRED OF EATING THE SAME OLD CANDY!
AND YET SOMEHOW, YOU'VE FOUND A WAY TO GO ON.
GRAMPS IS PATRONIZING ME AGAIN.
THAT'S NICE, SWEETIE.
PAT PAT
Peirce

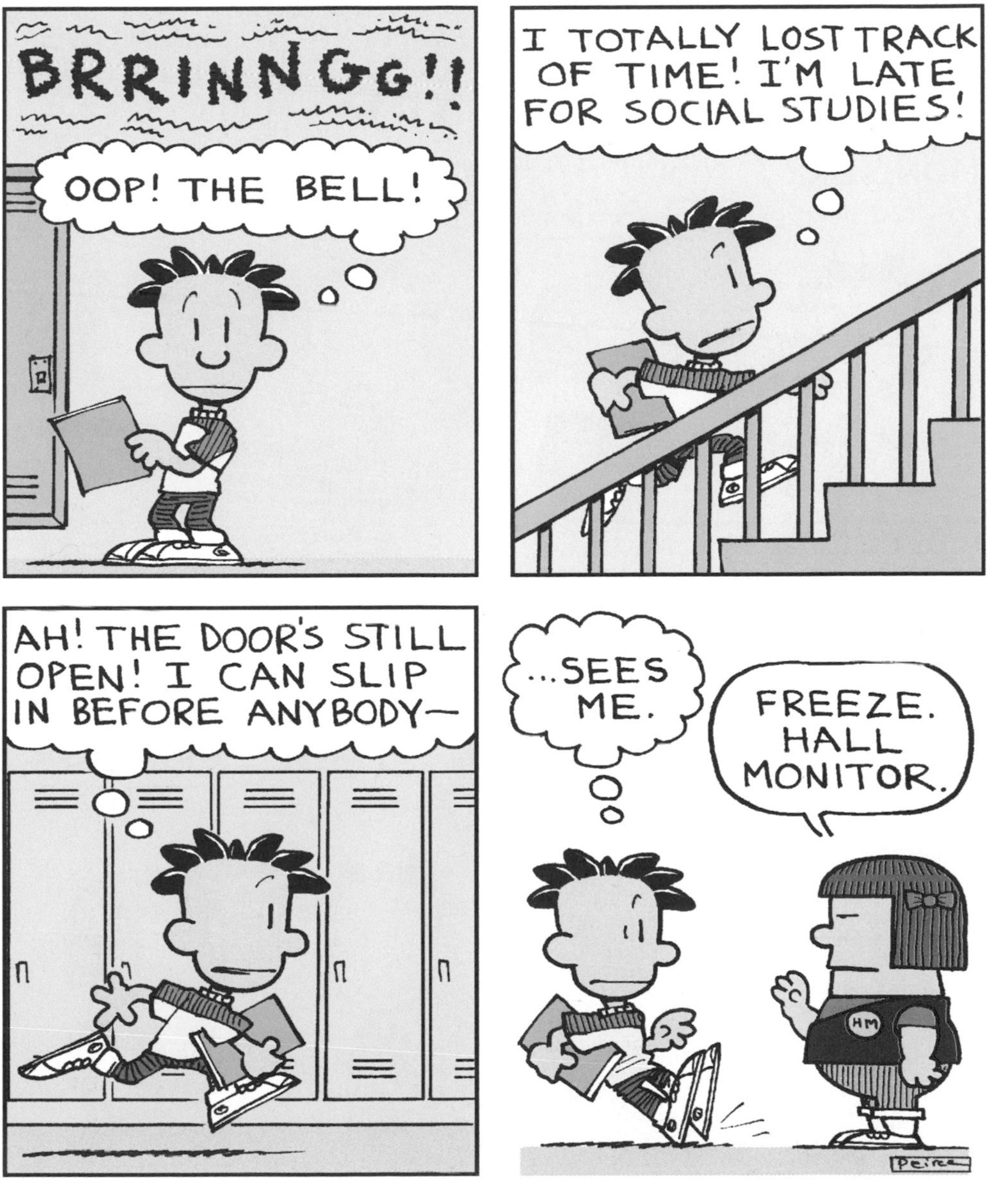
BRRINNGG!!
OOP! THE BELL!
I TOTALLY LOST TRACK OF TIME! I'M LATE FOR SOCIAL STUDIES!
AH! THE DOOR'S STILL OPEN! I CAN SLIP IN BEFORE ANYBODY—
...SEES ME.
FREEZE. HALL MONITOR.
HM
Peirce

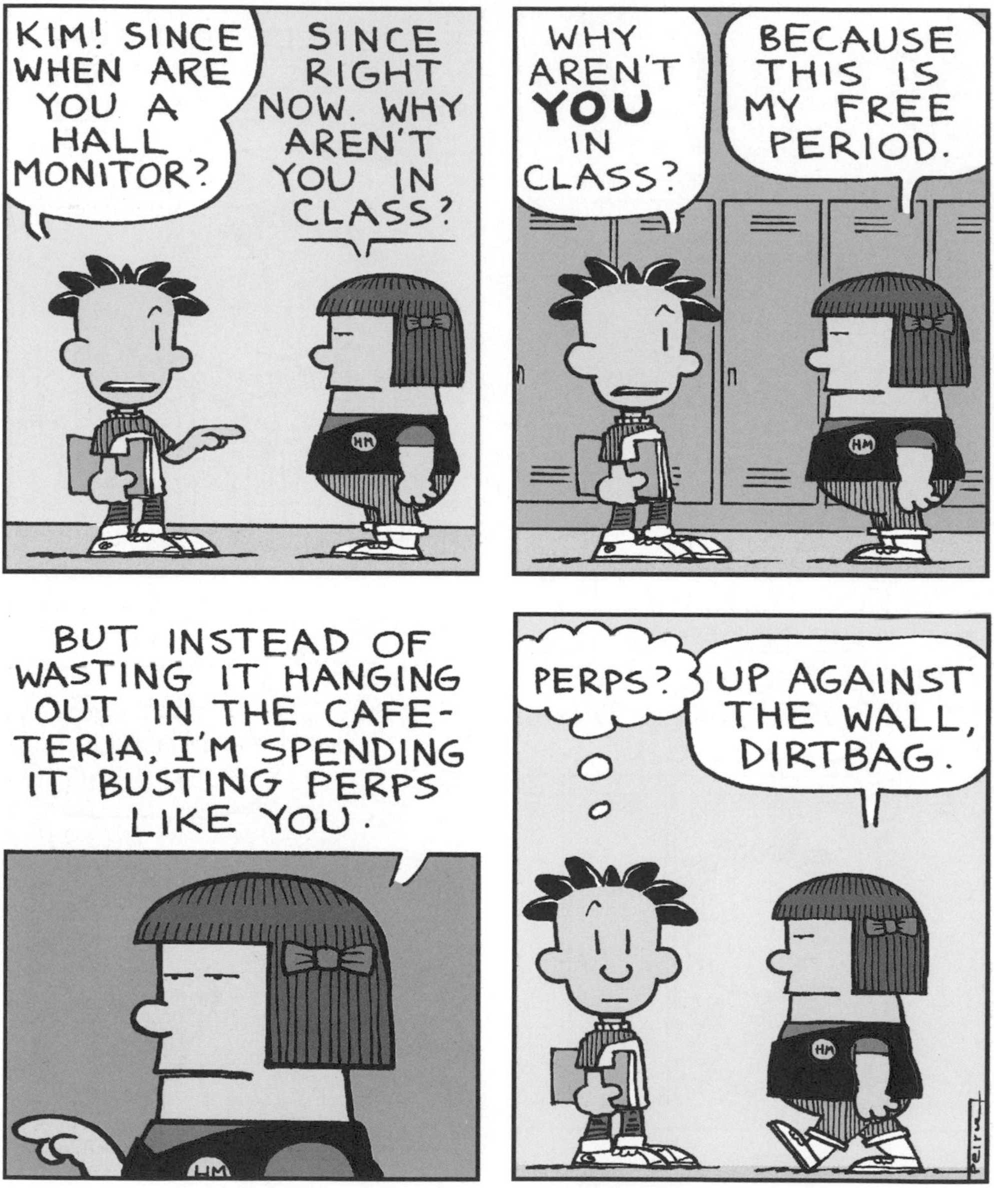
KIM! SINCE WHEN ARE YOU A HALL MONITOR?
SINCE RIGHT NOW. WHY AREN'T YOU IN CLASS?
WHY AREN'T **YOU** IN CLASS?
BECAUSE THIS IS MY FREE PERIOD.
BUT INSTEAD OF WASTING IT HANGING OUT IN THE CAFE-TERIA, I'M SPENDING IT BUSTING PERPS LIKE YOU.
PERPS?
UP AGAINST THE WALL, DIRTBAG.
HM

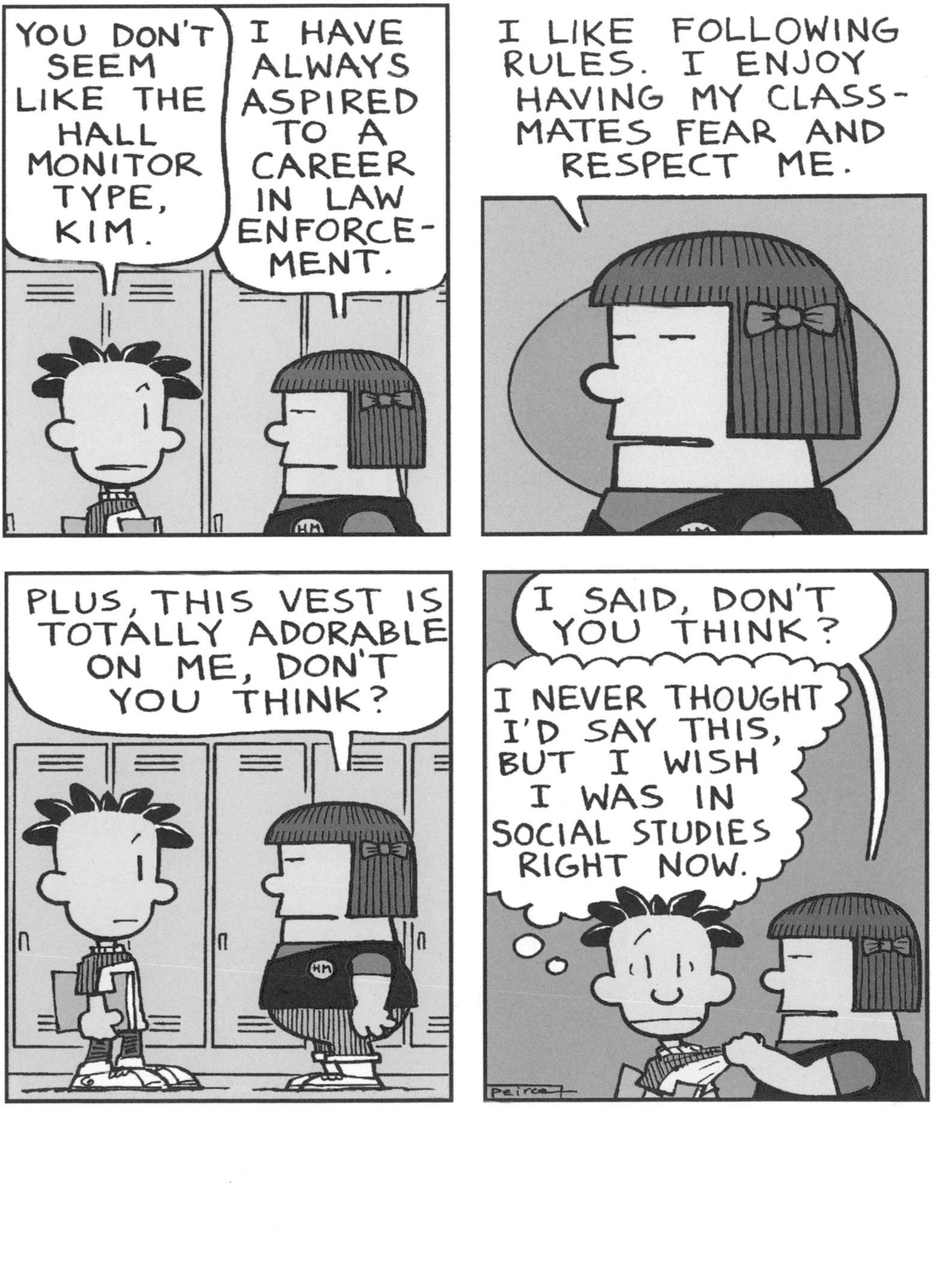

YOU DON'T SEEM LIKE THE HALL MONITOR TYPE, KIM.
I HAVE ALWAYS ASPIRED TO A CAREER IN LAW ENFORCEMENT.
I LIKE FOLLOWING RULES. I ENJOY HAVING MY CLASSMATES FEAR AND RESPECT ME.
PLUS, THIS VEST IS TOTALLY ADORABLE ON ME, DON'T YOU THINK?
I SAID, DON'T YOU THINK?
I NEVER THOUGHT I'D SAY THIS, BUT I WISH I WAS IN SOCIAL STUDIES RIGHT NOW.
Peirce

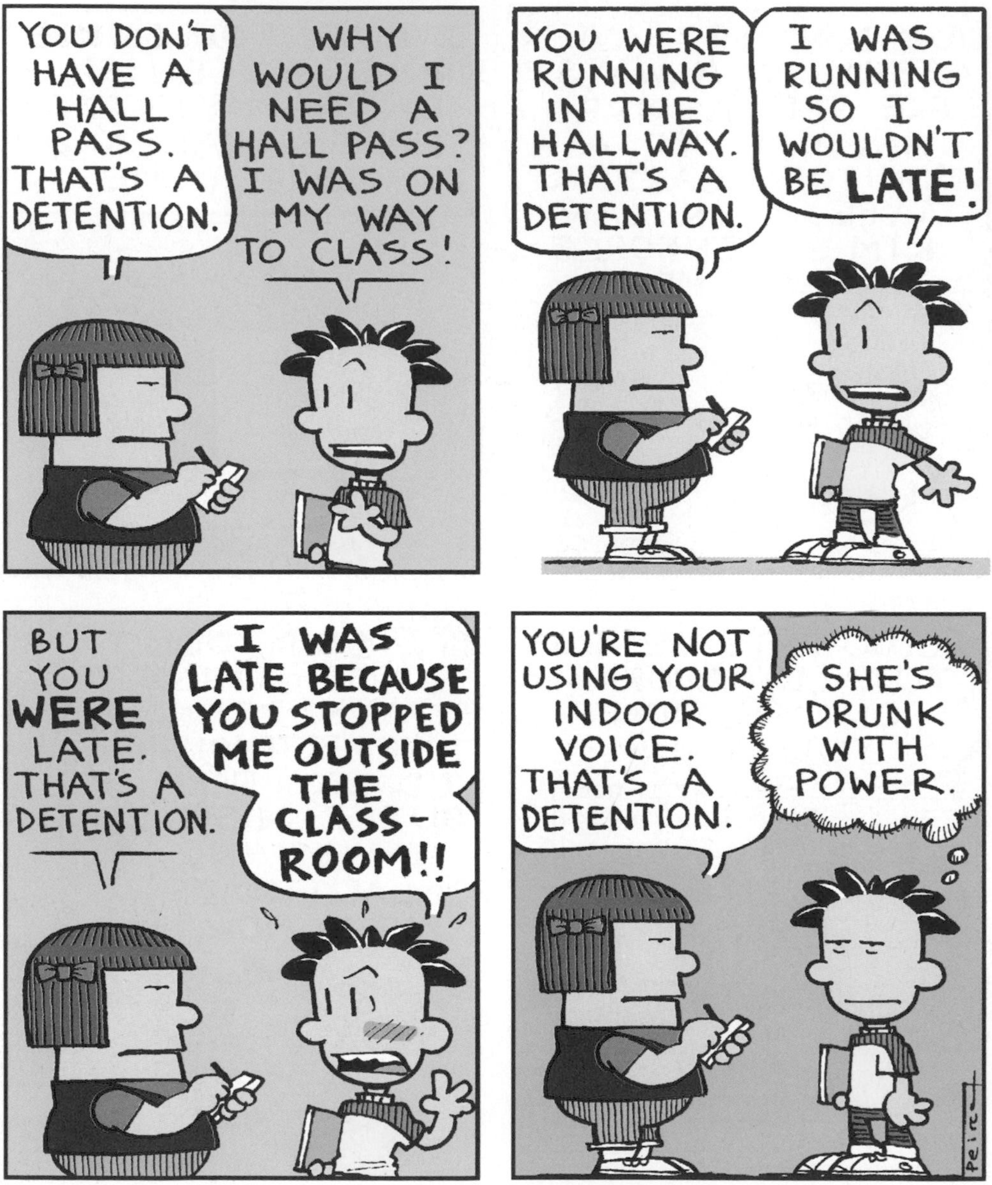
YOU DON'T HAVE A HALL PASS. THAT'S A DETENTION.
WHY WOULD I NEED A HALL PASS? I WAS ON MY WAY TO CLASS!
YOU WERE RUNNING IN THE HALLWAY. THAT'S A DETENTION.
I WAS RUNNING SO I WOULDN'T BE **LATE**!
BUT YOU **WERE** LATE. THAT'S A DETENTION.
I WAS LATE BECAUSE YOU STOPPED ME OUTSIDE THE CLASS-ROOM!!
YOU'RE NOT USING YOUR INDOOR VOICE. THAT'S A DETENTION.
SHE'S DRUNK WITH POWER.
Peirce

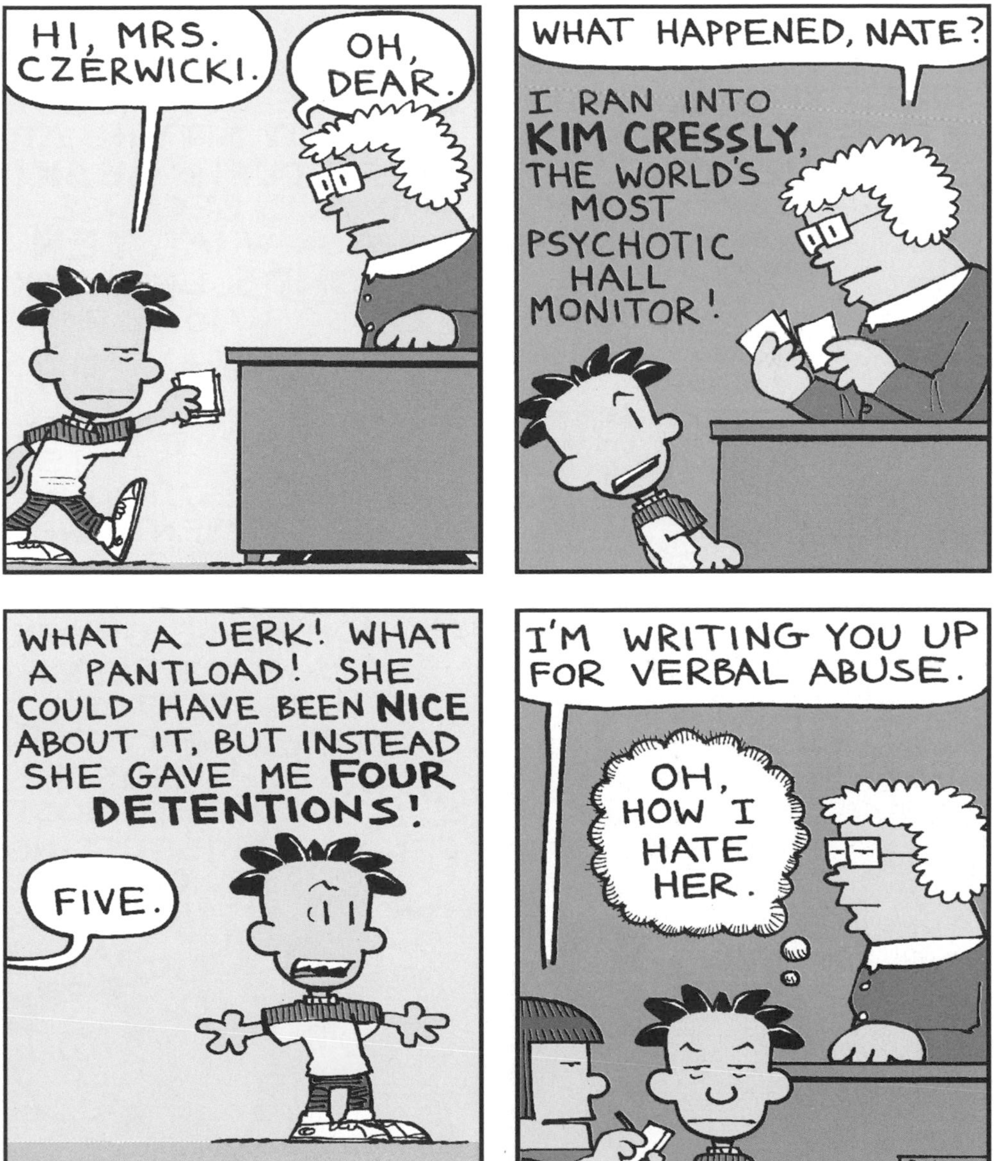
HI, MRS. CZERWICKI.
OH, DEAR.
WHAT HAPPENED, NATE?
I RAN INTO **KIM CRESSLY**, THE WORLD'S MOST PSYCHOTIC HALL MONITOR!
WHAT A JERK! WHAT A PANTLOAD! SHE COULD HAVE BEEN **NICE** ABOUT IT, BUT INSTEAD SHE GAVE ME **FOUR DETENTIONS**!
FIVE.
I'M WRITING YOU UP FOR VERBAL ABUSE.
OH, HOW I HATE HER.
Peirce

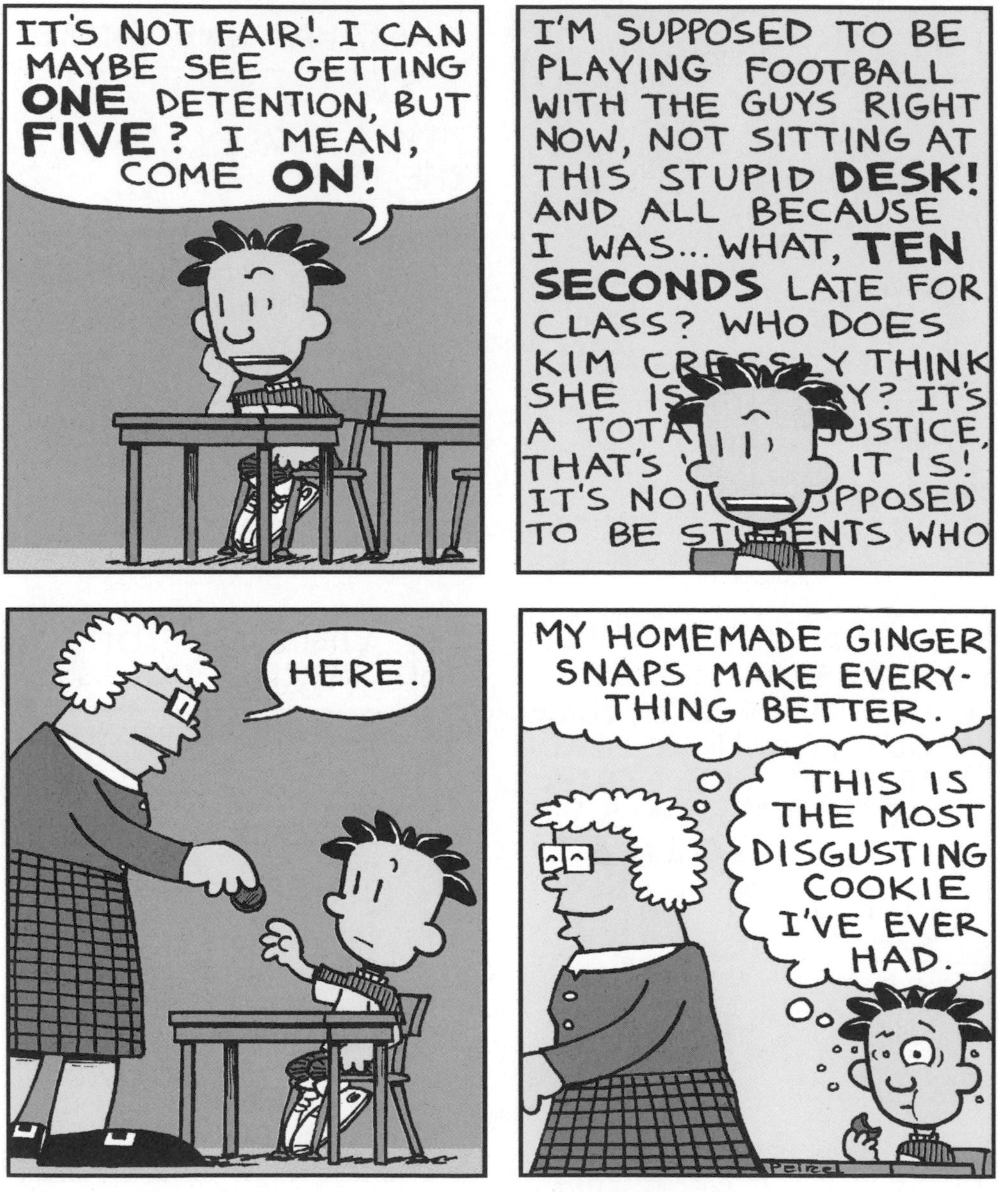
IT'S NOT FAIR! I CAN MAYBE SEE GETTING **ONE** DETENTION, BUT **FIVE**? I MEAN, COME **ON**!
I'M SUPPOSED TO BE PLAYING FOOTBALL WITH THE GUYS RIGHT NOW, NOT SITTING AT THIS STUPID **DESK!** AND ALL BECAUSE I WAS... WHAT, **TEN SECONDS** LATE FOR CLASS? WHO DOES KIM CR SLY THINK SHE IS Y? IT'S A TOTA JUSTICE, THAT'S IT IS! IT'S NO PPOSED TO BE ST ENTS WHO
HERE.
MY HOMEMADE GINGER SNAPS MAKE EVERY-THING BETTER.
THIS IS THE MOST DISGUSTING COOKIE I'VE EVER HAD.
Peirce

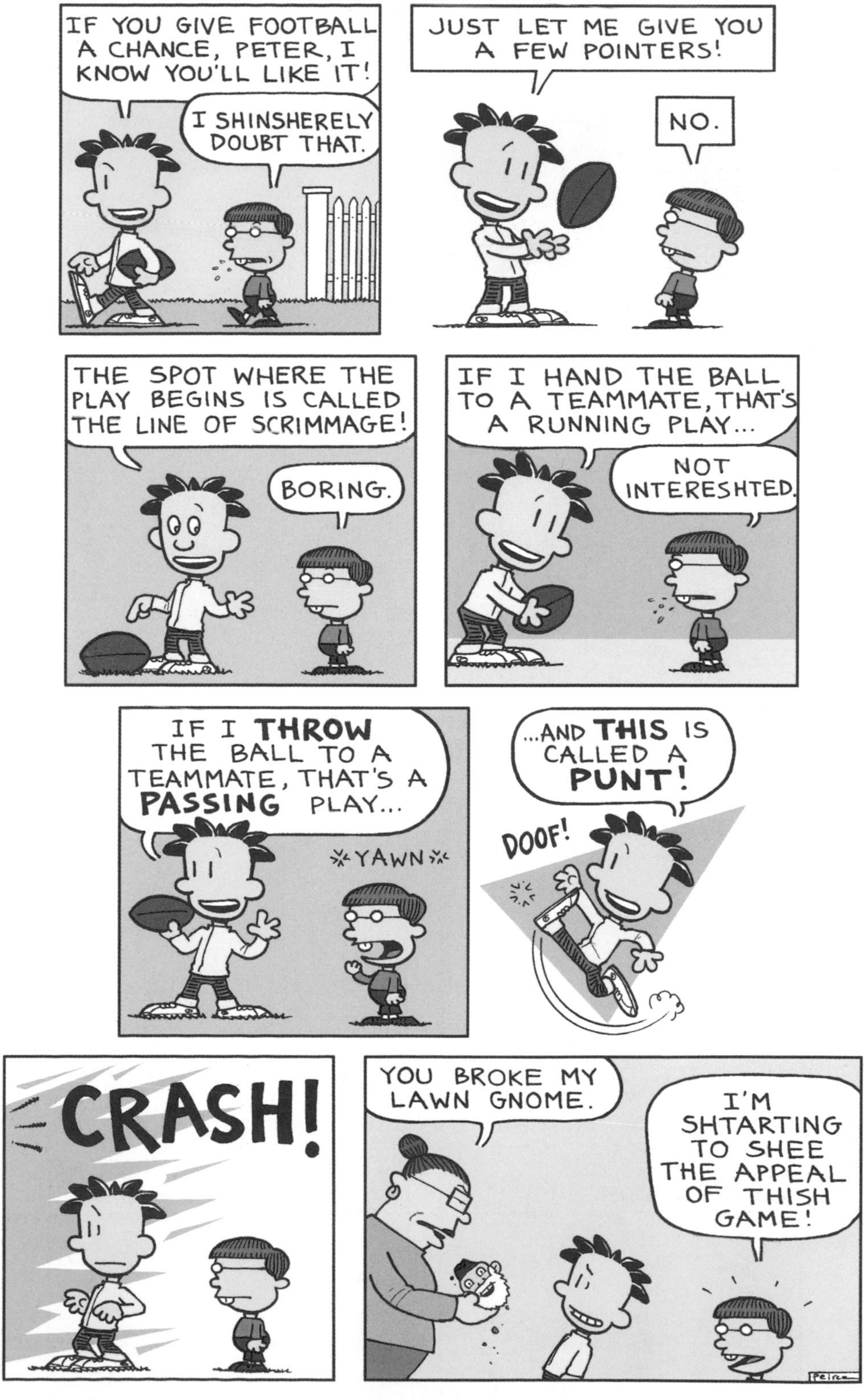
IF YOU GIVE FOOTBALL A CHANCE, PETER, I KNOW YOU'LL LIKE IT!
I SHINSHERELY DOUBT THAT.
JUST LET ME GIVE YOU A FEW POINTERS!
NO.
THE SPOT WHERE THE PLAY BEGINS IS CALLED THE LINE OF SCRIMMAGE!
BORING.
IF I HAND THE BALL TO A TEAMMATE, THAT'S A RUNNING PLAY...
NOT INTERESHTED.
IF I THROW THE BALL TO A TEAMMATE, THAT'S A PASSING PLAY...
YAWN
...AND THIS IS CALLED A PUNT!
DOOF!
CRASH!
YOU BROKE MY LAWN GNOME.
I'M SHTARTING TO SHEE THE APPEAL OF THISH GAME!
Peirce

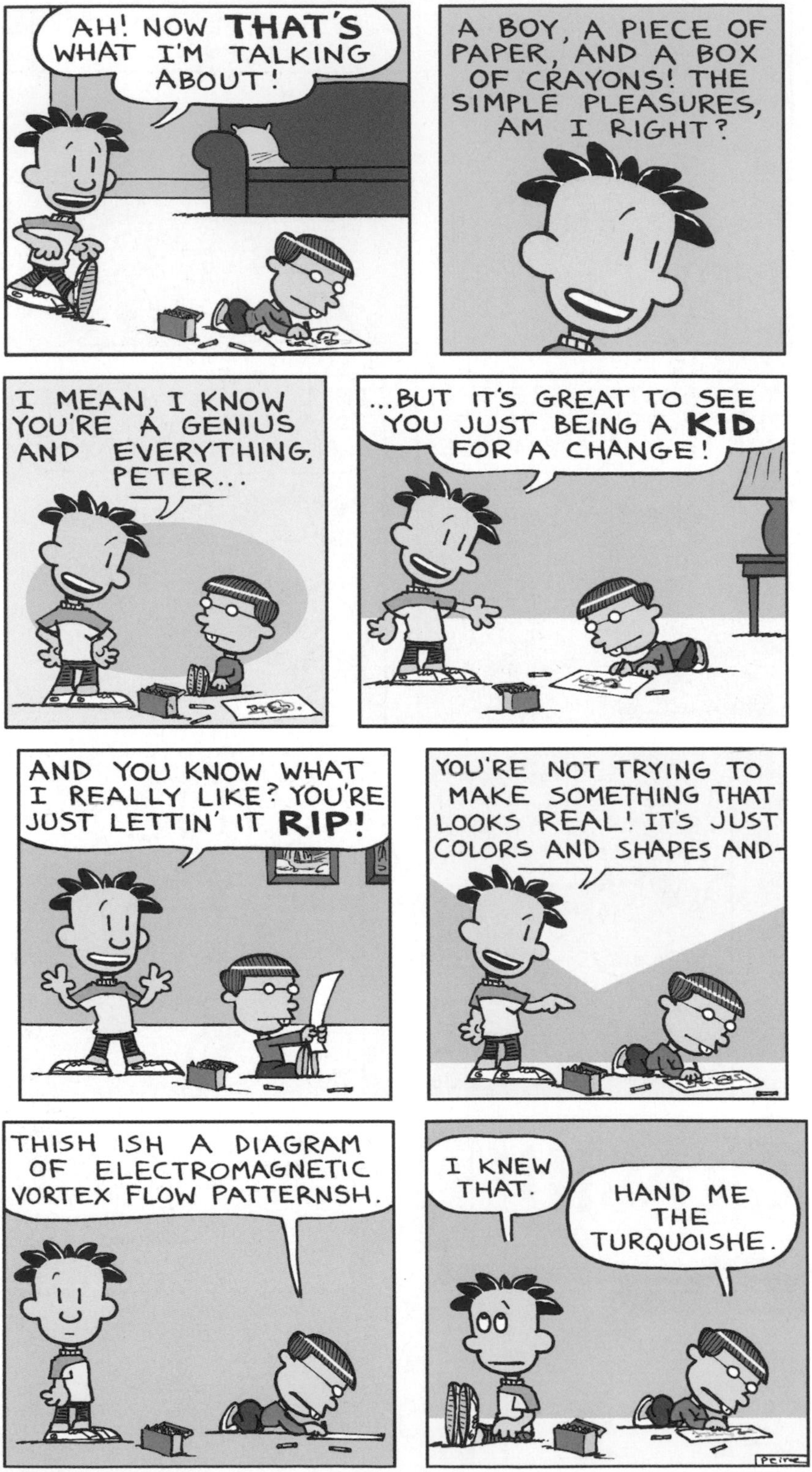

AH! NOW THAT'S WHAT I'M TALKING ABOUT!
A BOY, A PIECE OF PAPER, AND A BOX OF CRAYONS! THE SIMPLE PLEASURES, AM I RIGHT?
I MEAN, I KNOW YOU'RE A GENIUS AND EVERYTHING, PETER...
...BUT IT'S GREAT TO SEE YOU JUST BEING A KID FOR A CHANGE!
AND YOU KNOW WHAT I REALLY LIKE? YOU'RE JUST LETTIN' IT RIP!
YOU'RE NOT TRYING TO MAKE SOMETHING THAT LOOKS REAL! IT'S JUST COLORS AND SHAPES AND-
THISH ISH A DIAGRAM OF ELECTROMAGNETIC VORTEX FLOW PATTERNSH.
I KNEW THAT.
HAND ME THE TURQUOISHE.
Peirce

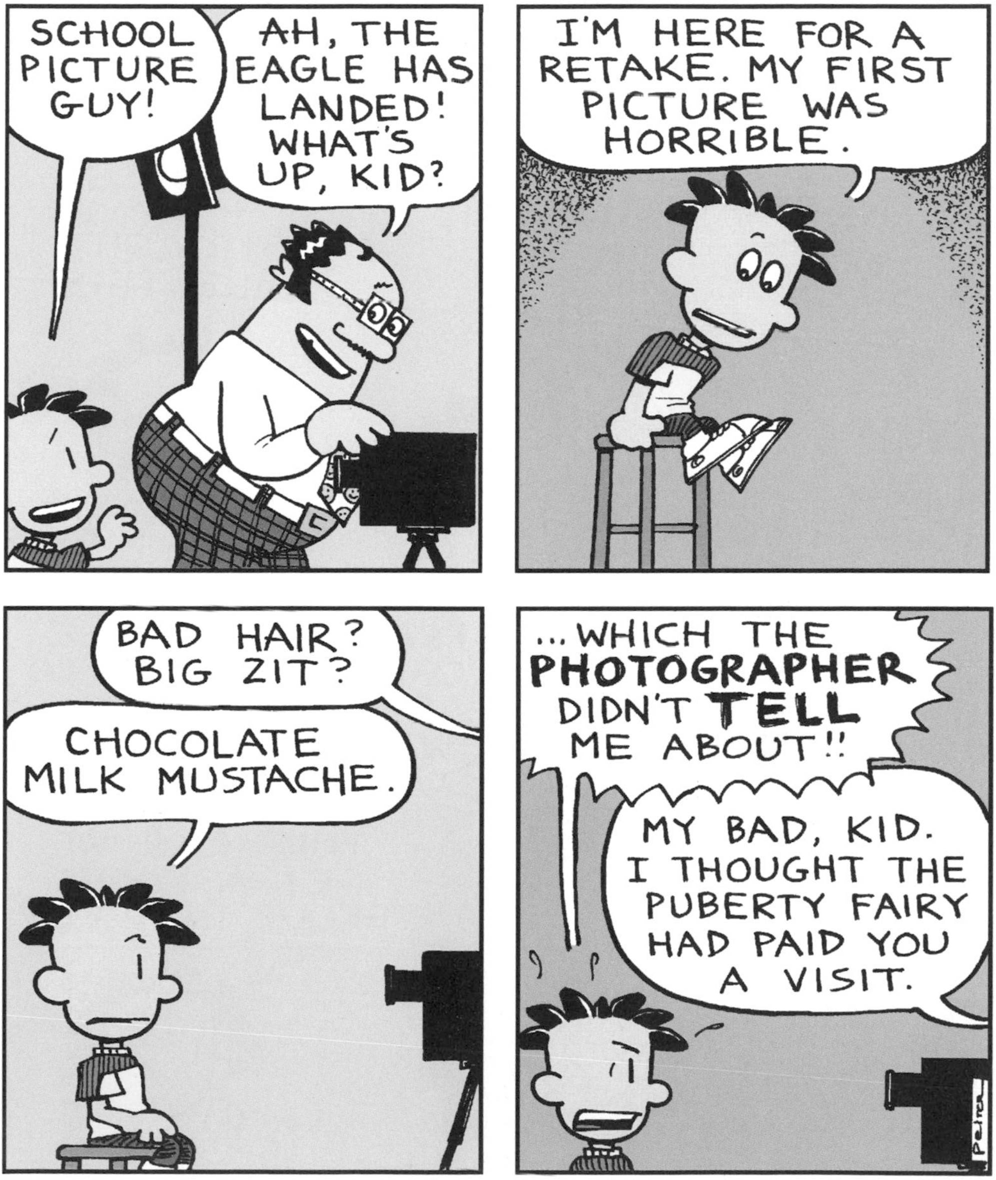
SCHOOL PICTURE GUY!
AH, THE EAGLE HAS LANDED! WHAT'S UP, KID?
I'M HERE FOR A RETAKE. MY FIRST PICTURE WAS HORRIBLE.
BAD HAIR? BIG ZIT?
CHOCOLATE MILK MUSTACHE.
...WHICH THE PHOTOGRAPHER DIDN'T TELL ME ABOUT!!
MY BAD, KID. I THOUGHT THE PUBERTY FAIRY HAD PAID YOU A VISIT.
Peirce

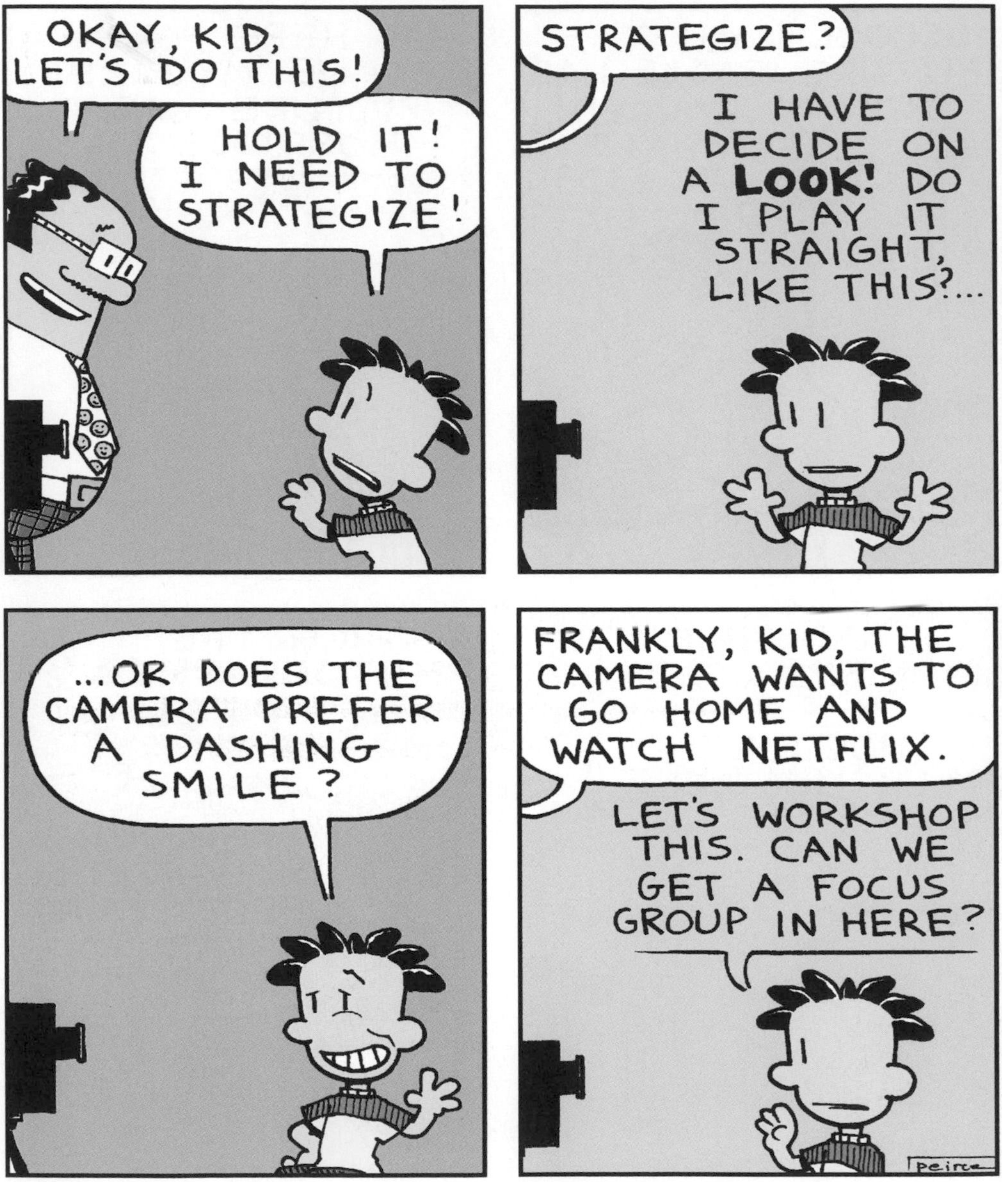
OKAY, KID, LET'S DO THIS!
HOLD IT! I NEED TO STRATEGIZE!
STRATEGIZE?
I HAVE TO DECIDE ON A **LOOK!** DO I PLAY IT STRAIGHT, LIKE THIS?...
...OR DOES THE CAMERA PREFER A DASHING SMILE?
FRANKLY, KID, THE CAMERA WANTS TO GO HOME AND WATCH NETFLIX.
LET'S WORKSHOP THIS. CAN WE GET A FOCUS GROUP IN HERE?
peirce

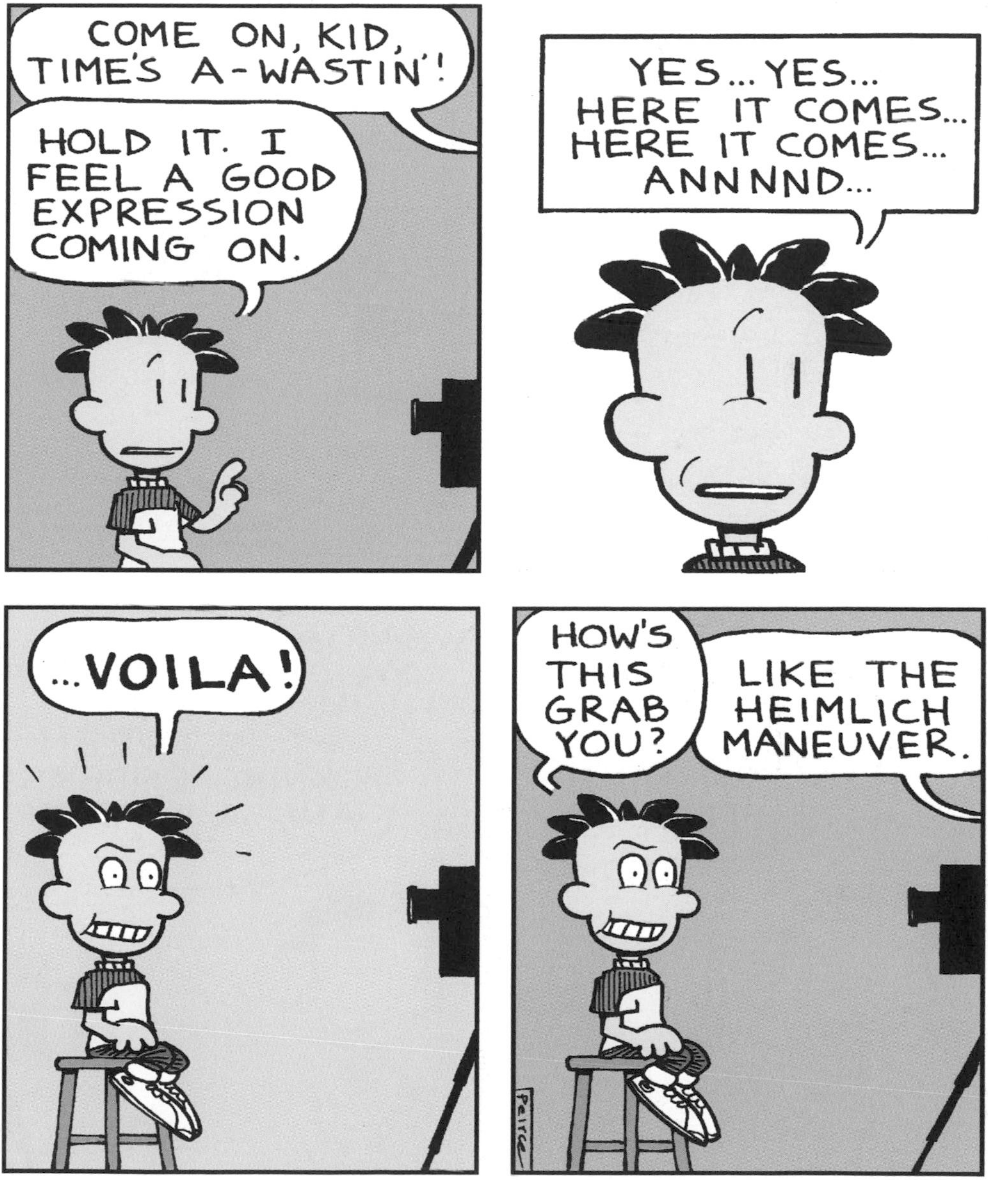
COME ON, KID, TIME'S A-WASTIN'!
HOLD IT. I FEEL A GOOD EXPRESSION COMING ON.
YES... YES... HERE IT COMES... HERE IT COMES... ANNNND...
...VOILA!
HOW'S THIS GRAB YOU?
LIKE THE HEIMLICH MANEUVER.
PEIRCE

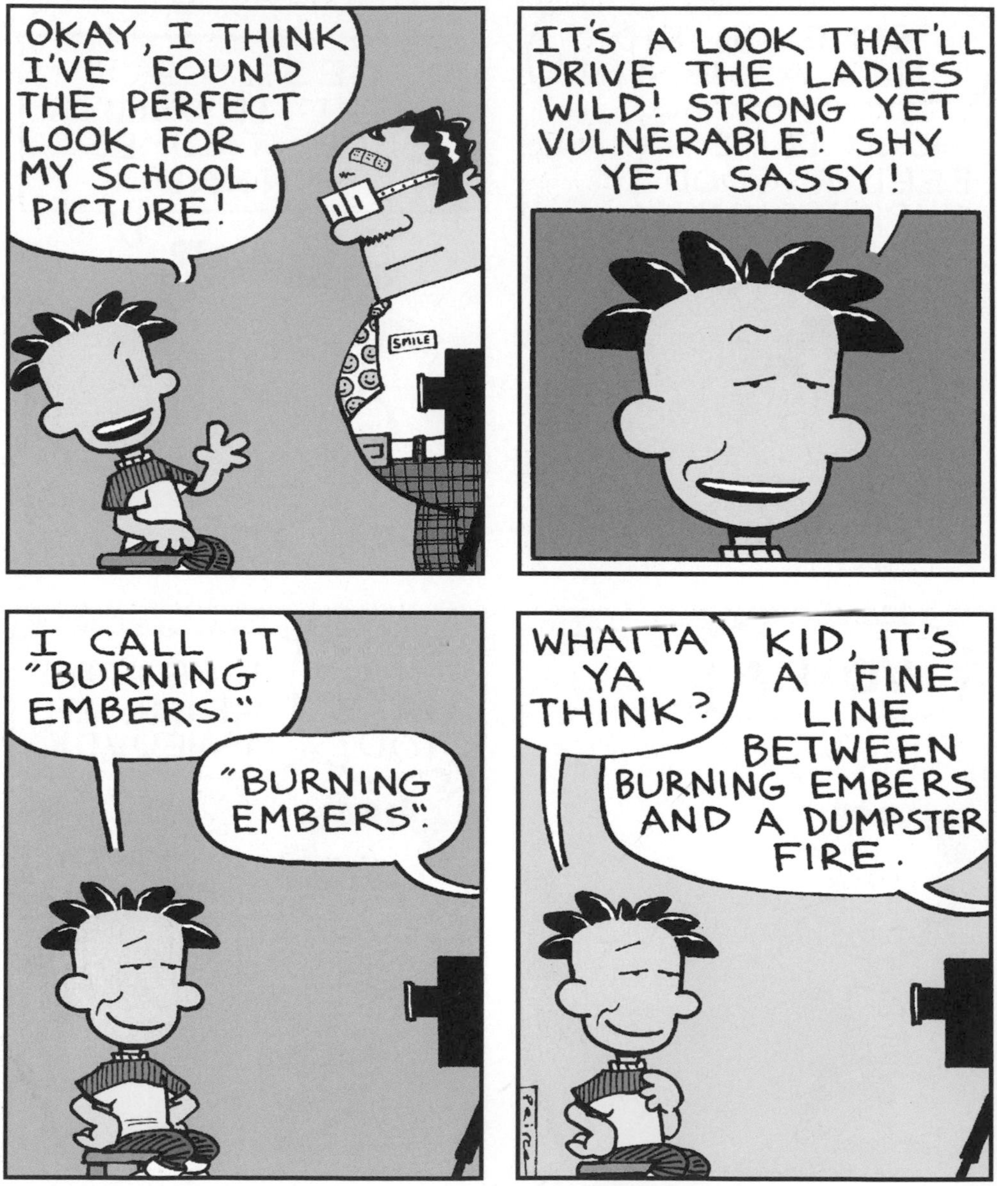
OKAY, I THINK I'VE FOUND THE PERFECT LOOK FOR MY SCHOOL PICTURE!
SMILE
IT'S A LOOK THAT'LL DRIVE THE LADIES WILD! STRONG YET VULNERABLE! SHY YET SASSY!
I CALL IT "BURNING EMBERS."
"BURNING EMBERS".
WHATTA YA THINK?
KID, IT'S A FINE LINE BETWEEN BURNING EMBERS AND A DUMPSTER FIRE.
PEIRCE

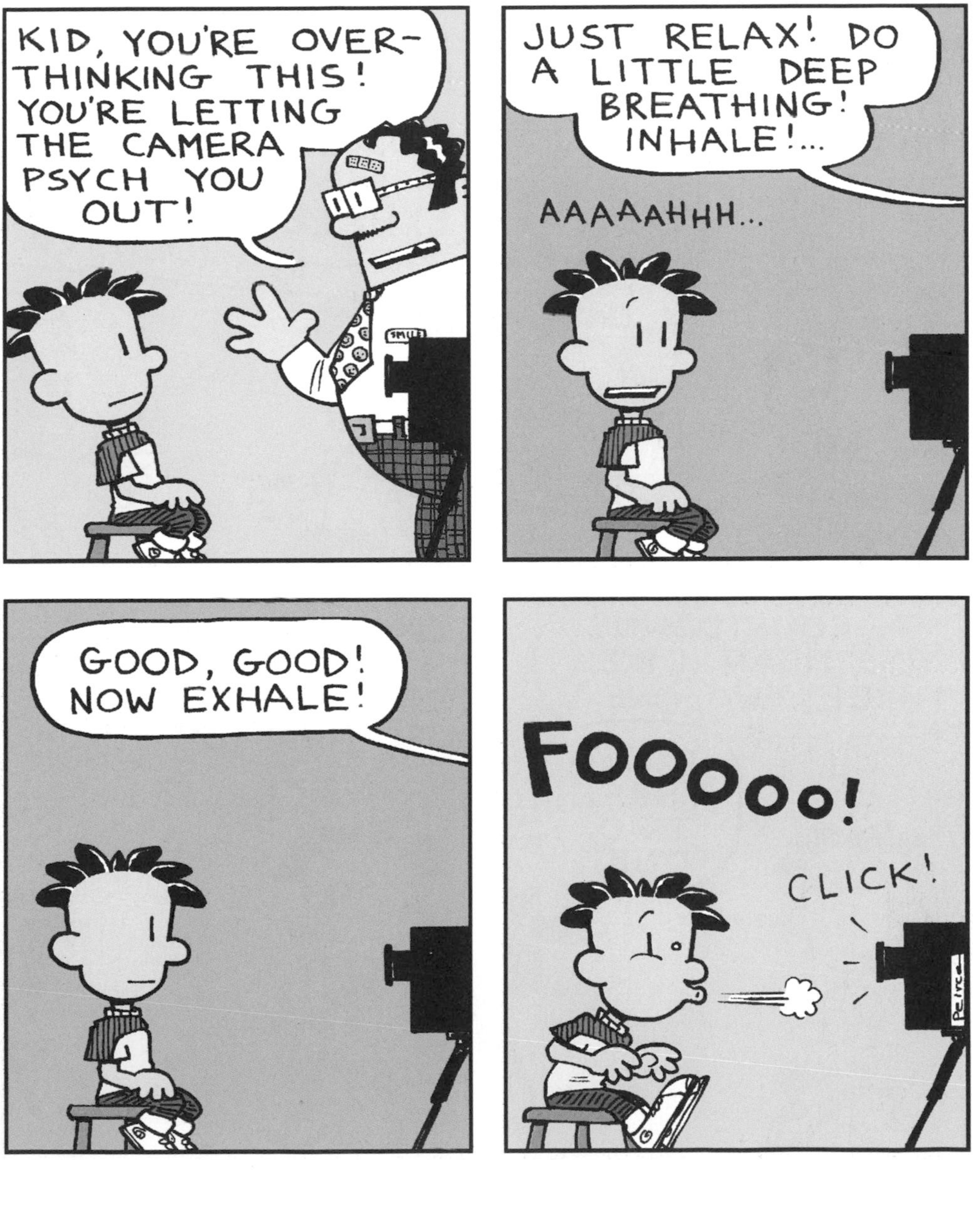
KID, YOU'RE OVER-THINKING THIS! YOU'RE LETTING THE CAMERA PSYCH YOU OUT!
JUST RELAX! DO A LITTLE DEEP BREATHING! INHALE!...
AAAAAHHH...
GOOD, GOOD! NOW EXHALE!
FOOOOO!
CLICK!
Peirce

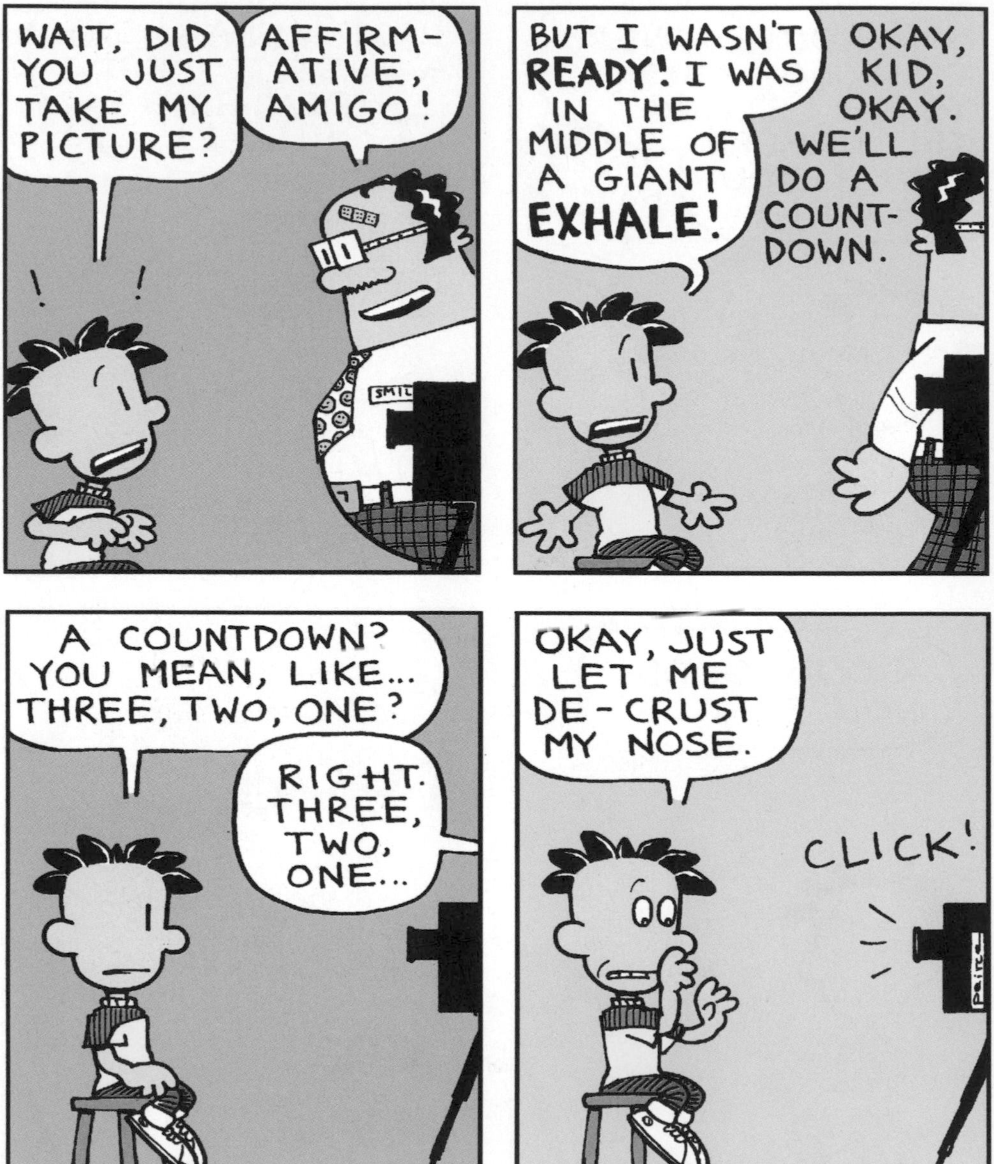
WAIT, DID YOU JUST TAKE MY PICTURE?
AFFIRM-ATIVE, AMIGO!
BUT I WASN'T READY! I WAS IN THE MIDDLE OF A GIANT EXHALE!
OKAY, KID, OKAY. WE'LL DO A COUNT-DOWN.
A COUNTDOWN? YOU MEAN, LIKE... THREE, TWO, ONE?
RIGHT. THREE, TWO, ONE...
OKAY, JUST LET ME DE-CRUST MY NOSE.
CLICK!

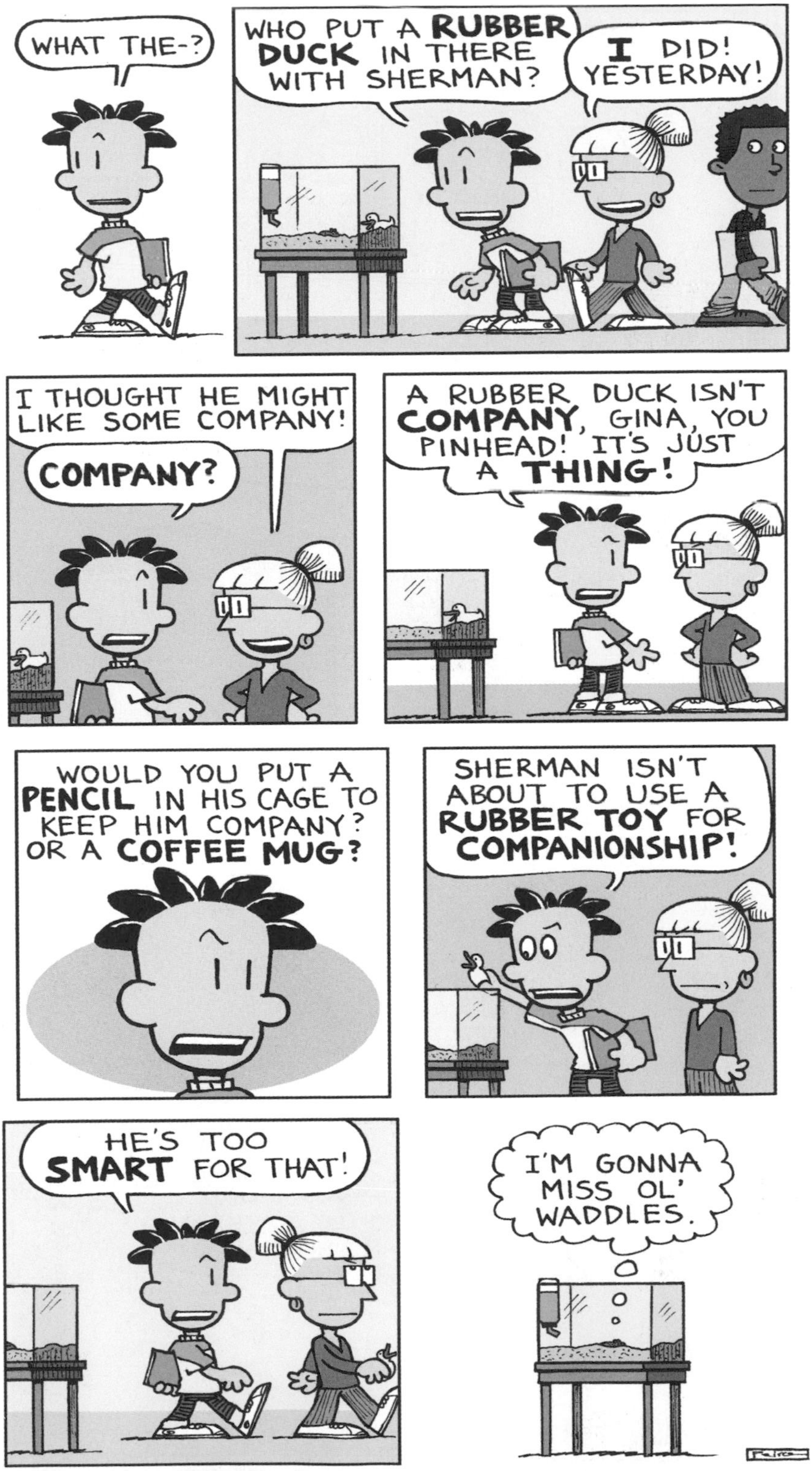

WHAT THE-?
WHO PUT A RUBBER DUCK IN THERE WITH SHERMAN?
I DID! YESTERDAY!
I THOUGHT HE MIGHT LIKE SOME COMPANY!
COMPANY?
A RUBBER DUCK ISN'T COMPANY, GINA, YOU PINHEAD! IT'S JUST A THING!
WOULD YOU PUT A PENCIL IN HIS CAGE TO KEEP HIM COMPANY? OR A COFFEE MUG?
SHERMAN ISN'T ABOUT TO USE A RUBBER TOY FOR COMPANIONSHIP!
HE'S TOO SMART FOR THAT!
I'M GONNA MISS OL' WADDLES.

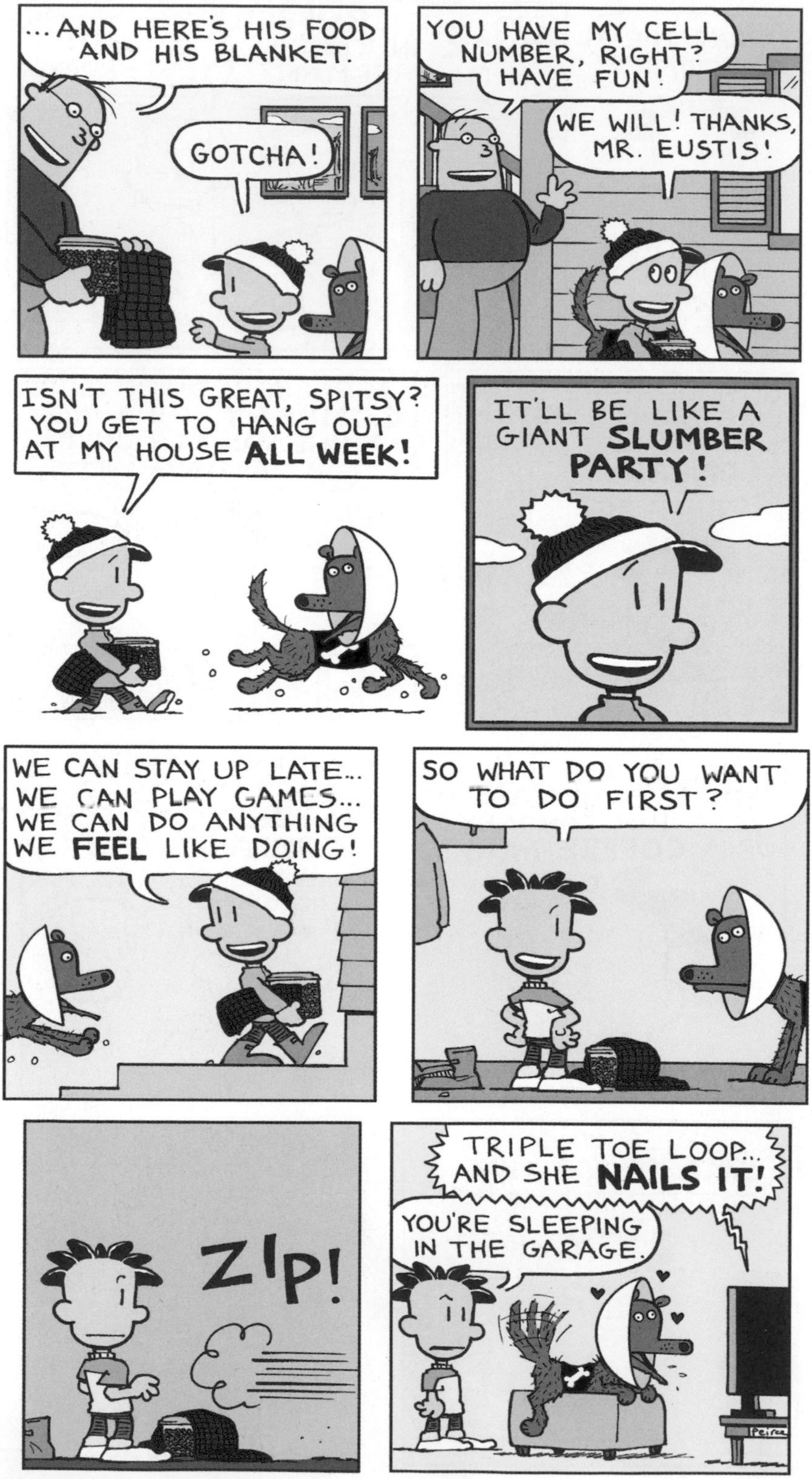
...AND HERE'S HIS FOOD AND HIS BLANKET.
GOTCHA!
YOU HAVE MY CELL NUMBER, RIGHT? HAVE FUN!
WE WILL! THANKS, MR. EUSTIS!
ISN'T THIS GREAT, SPITSY? YOU GET TO HANG OUT AT MY HOUSE ALL WEEK!
IT'LL BE LIKE A GIANT SLUMBER PARTY!
WE CAN STAY UP LATE... WE CAN PLAY GAMES... WE CAN DO ANYTHING WE FEEL LIKE DOING!
SO WHAT DO YOU WANT TO DO FIRST?
ZIP!
TRIPLE TOE LOOP... AND SHE NAILS IT!
YOU'RE SLEEPING IN THE GARAGE.
Peirce

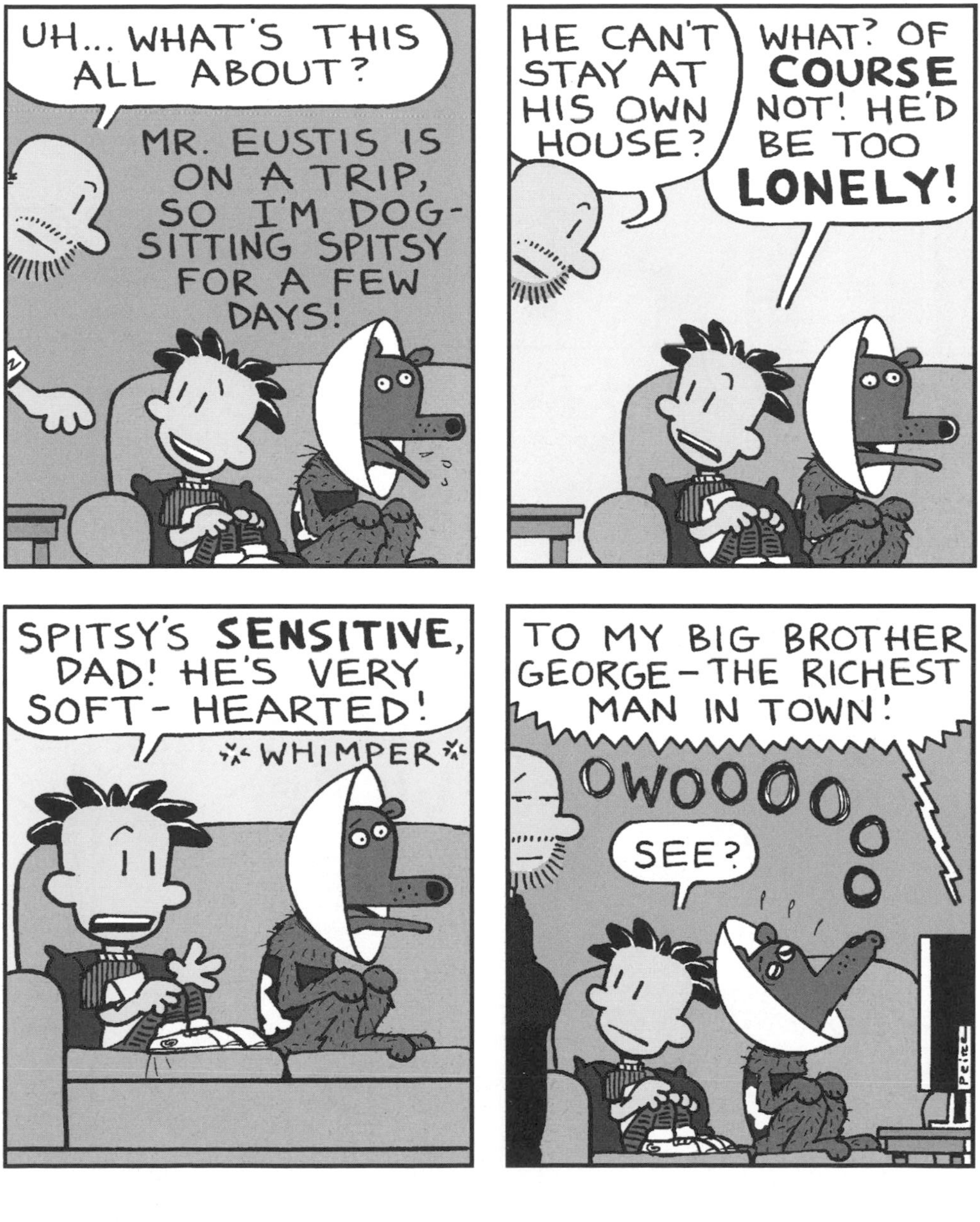
UH... WHAT'S THIS ALL ABOUT?
MR. EUSTIS IS ON A TRIP, SO I'M DOG-SITTING SPITSY FOR A FEW DAYS!
HE CAN'T STAY AT HIS OWN HOUSE?
WHAT? OF **COURSE** NOT! HE'D BE TOO **LONELY**!
SPITSY'S **SENSITIVE**, DAD! HE'S VERY SOFT-HEARTED!
WHIMPER
TO MY BIG BROTHER GEORGE – THE RICHEST MAN IN TOWN!
OWOOOOOOO
SEE?
PEIRCE

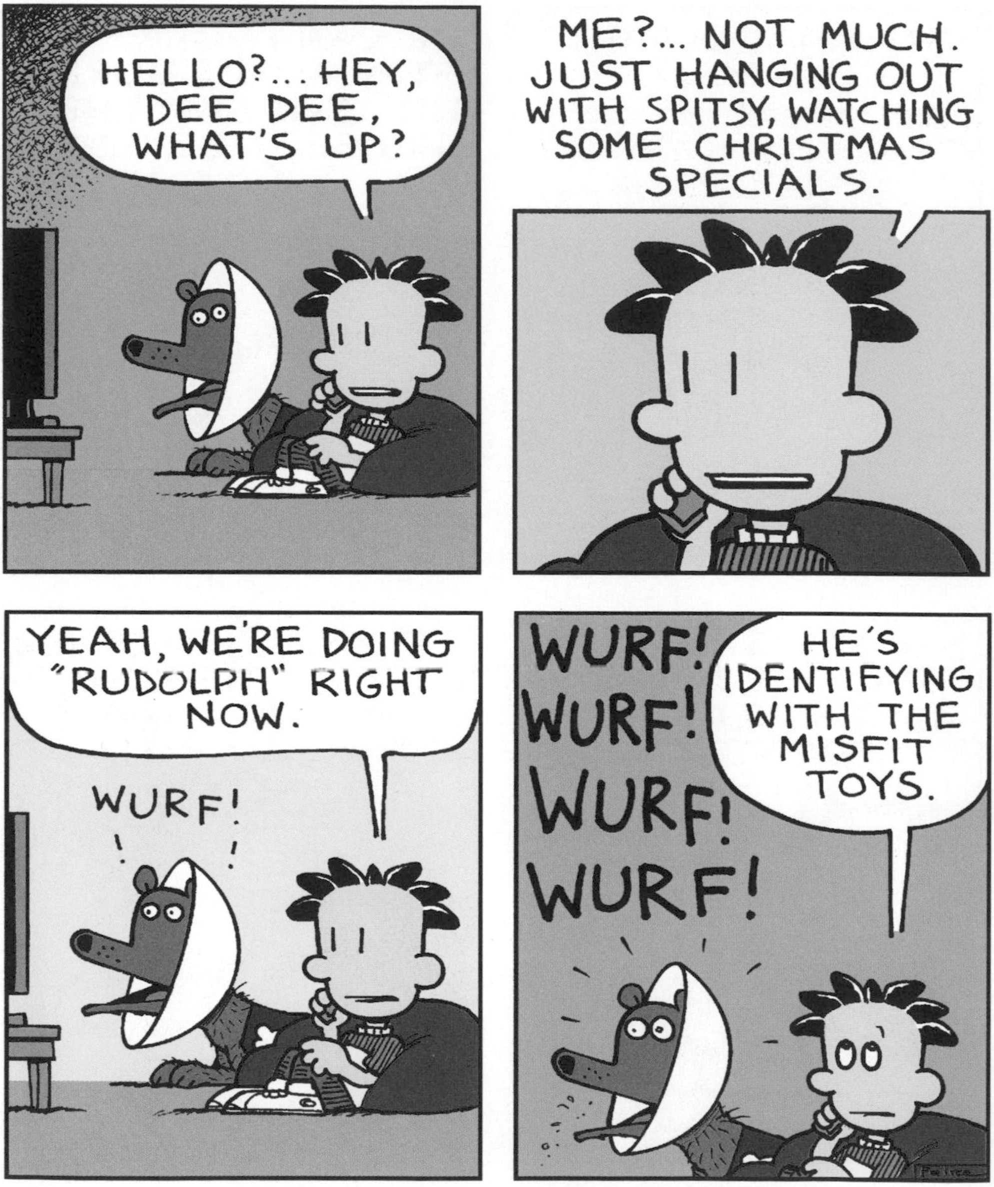
HELLO?... HEY, DEE DEE, WHAT'S UP?
ME?... NOT MUCH. JUST HANGING OUT WITH SPITSY, WATCHING SOME CHRISTMAS SPECIALS.
YEAH, WE'RE DOING "RUDOLPH" RIGHT NOW.
WURF!
WURF! WURF! WURF! WURF!
HE'S IDENTIFYING WITH THE MISFIT TOYS.

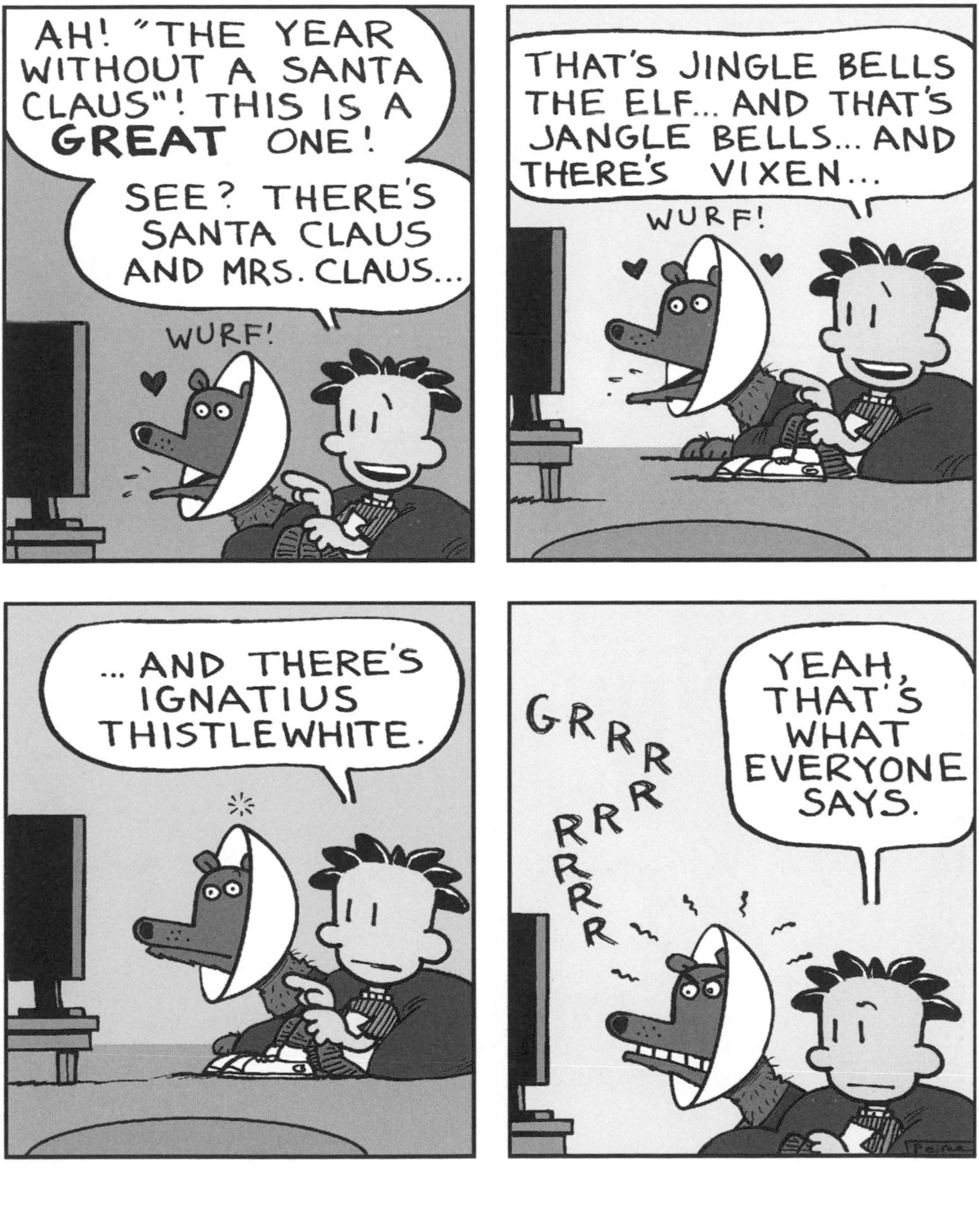

AH! "THE YEAR WITHOUT A SANTA CLAUS"! THIS IS A **GREAT** ONE!
SEE? THERE'S SANTA CLAUS AND MRS. CLAUS...
WURF!
THAT'S JINGLE BELLS THE ELF... AND THAT'S JANGLE BELLS... AND THERE'S VIXEN...
WURF!
... AND THERE'S IGNATIUS THISTLEWHITE.
GRRRRRRRRRR
YEAH, THAT'S WHAT EVERYONE SAYS.

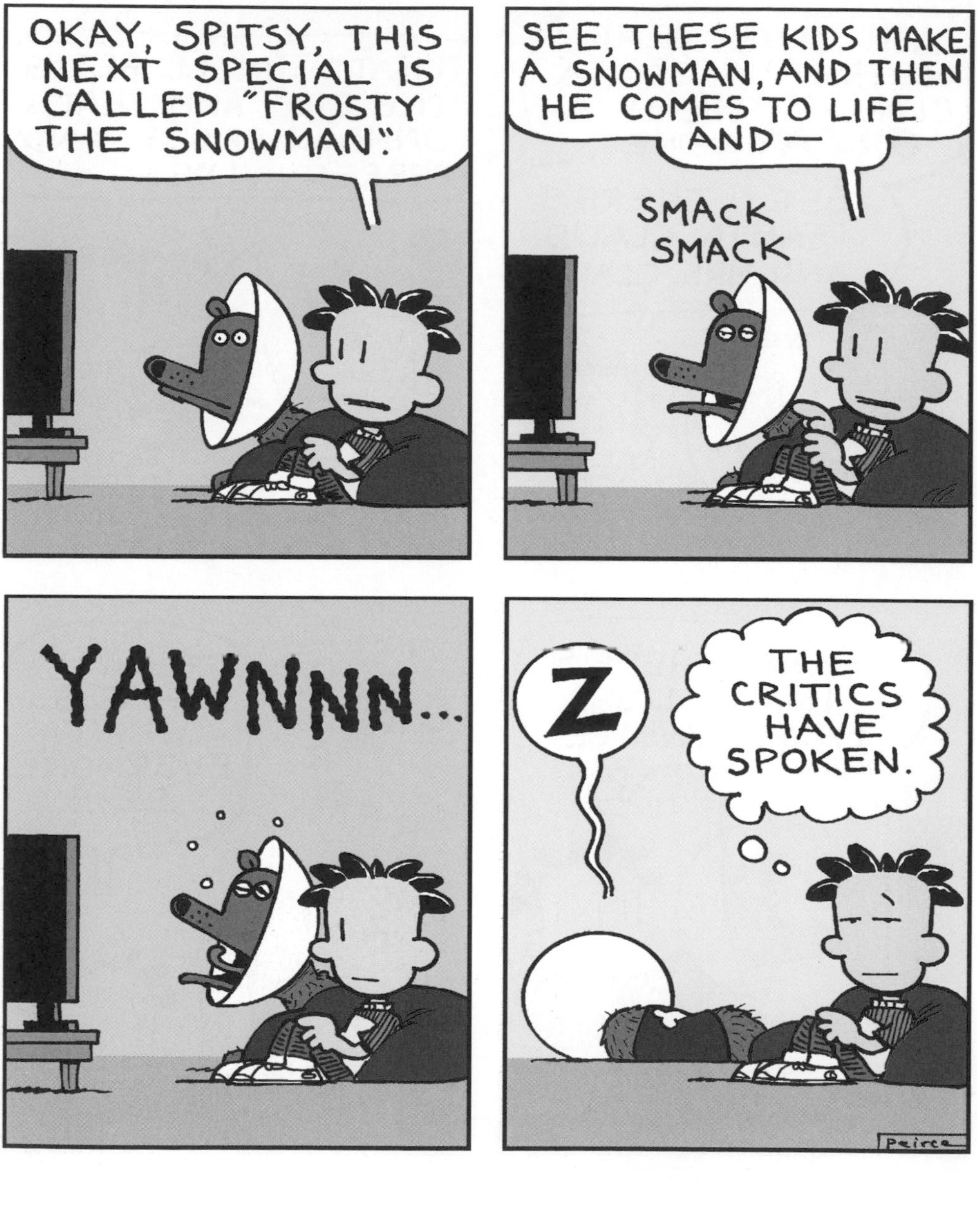
OKAY, SPITSY, THIS NEXT SPECIAL IS CALLED "FROSTY THE SNOWMAN."
SEE, THESE KIDS MAKE A SNOWMAN, AND THEN HE COMES TO LIFE AND—
SMACK SMACK
YAWNNN...
Z
THE CRITICS HAVE SPOKEN.
Peirce

THIS ONE'S A **CLASSIC**, SPITSY!
"A CHARLIE BROWN CHRISTMAS"!

WURF?

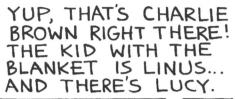

YUP, THAT'S CHARLIE BROWN RIGHT THERE! THE KID WITH THE BLANKET IS LINUS... AND THERE'S LUCY.

AND THAT'S SNOOPY!

WURF?

NO, HE'S NOT A **CAT**!

WURF.

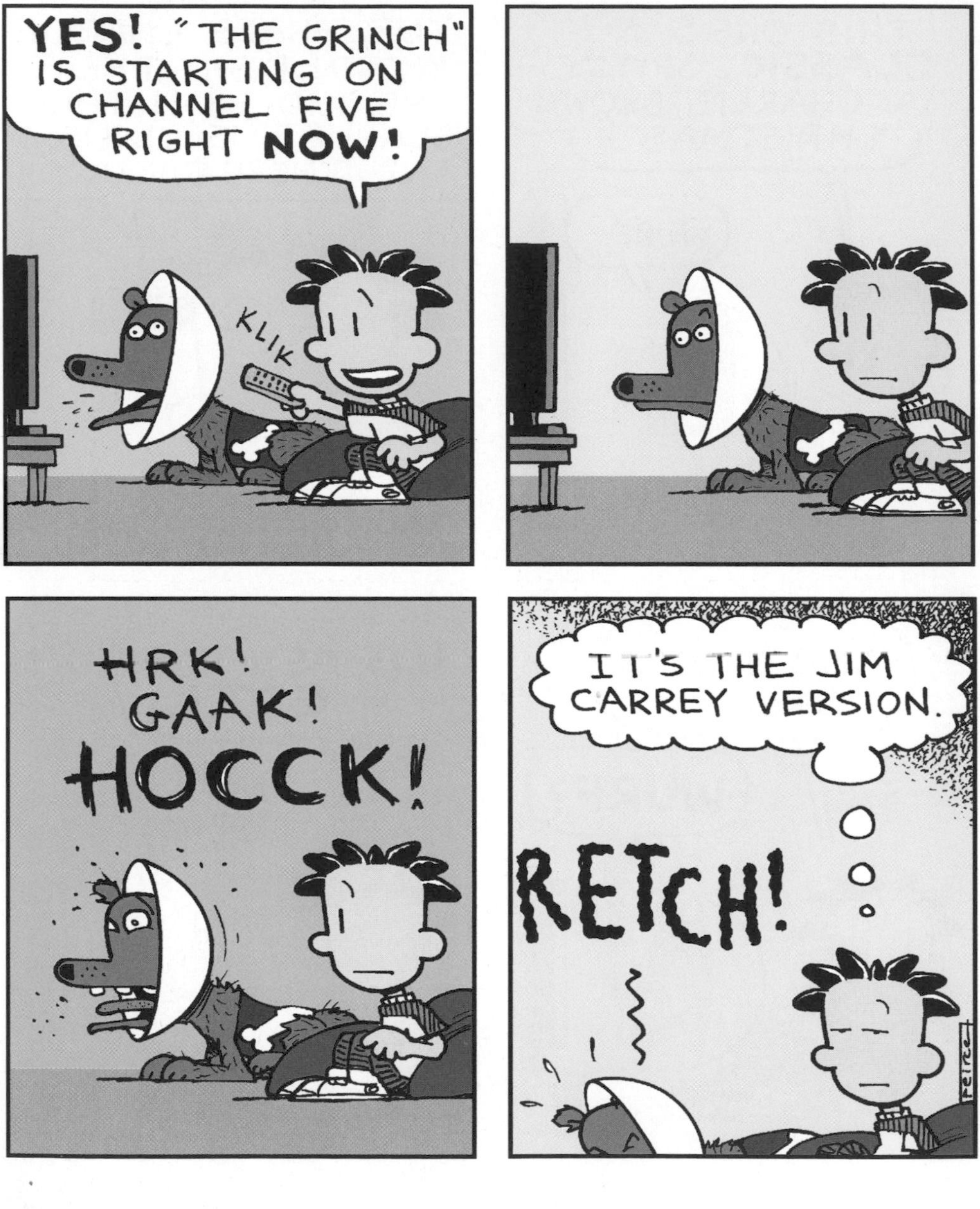
YES! "THE GRINCH" IS STARTING ON CHANNEL FIVE RIGHT NOW!
KLIK
HRK! GAAK! HOCCK!
IT'S THE JIM CARREY VERSION.
RETCH!
peirce

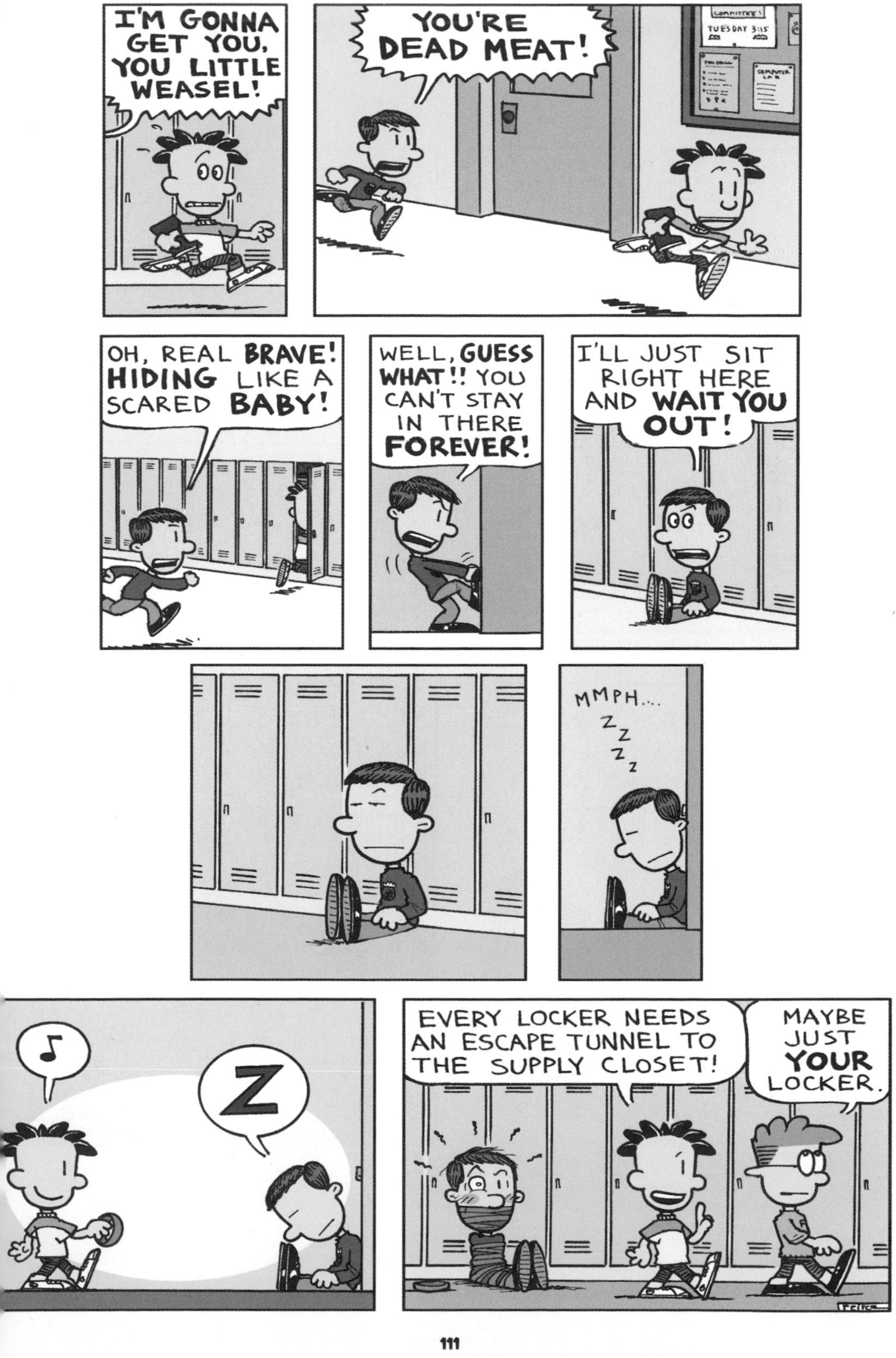
I'M GONNA GET YOU, YOU LITTLE WEASEL!
YOU'RE DEAD MEAT!
COMMITTEE! TUESDAY 3:15
COMPUTER LAB
OH, REAL BRAVE! HIDING LIKE A SCARED BABY!
WELL, GUESS WHAT!! YOU CAN'T STAY IN THERE FOREVER!
I'LL JUST SIT RIGHT HERE AND WAIT YOU OUT!
MMPH....
Z Z Z Z
Z
EVERY LOCKER NEEDS AN ESCAPE TUNNEL TO THE SUPPLY CLOSET!
MAYBE JUST YOUR LOCKER.

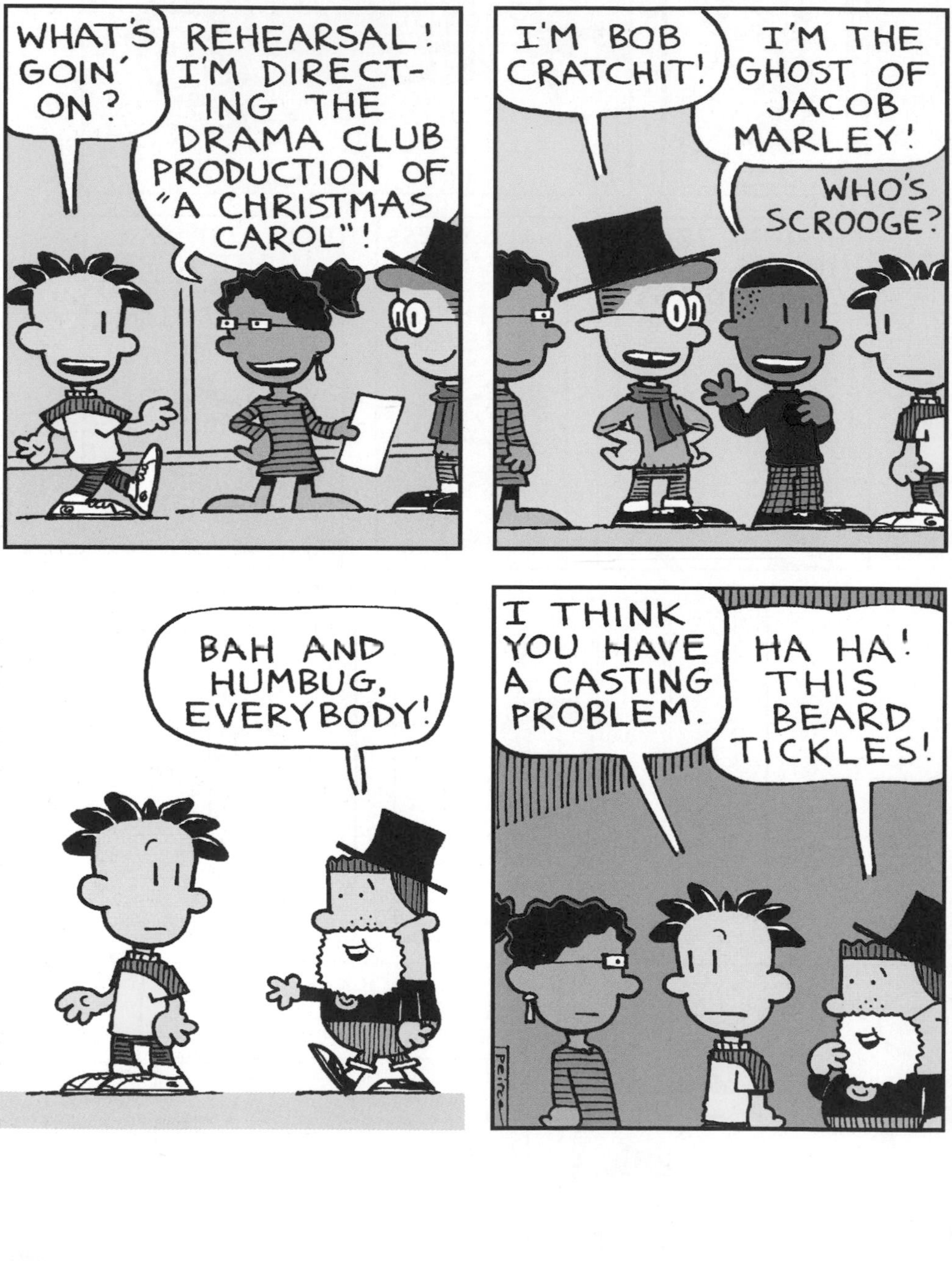
WHAT'S GOIN' ON?
REHEARSAL! I'M DIRECTING THE DRAMA CLUB PRODUCTION OF "A CHRISTMAS CAROL"!
I'M BOB CRATCHIT!
I'M THE GHOST OF JACOB MARLEY!
WHO'S SCROOGE?
BAH AND HUMBUG, EVERYBODY!
I THINK YOU HAVE A CASTING PROBLEM.
HA HA! THIS BEARD TICKLES!
Peirce

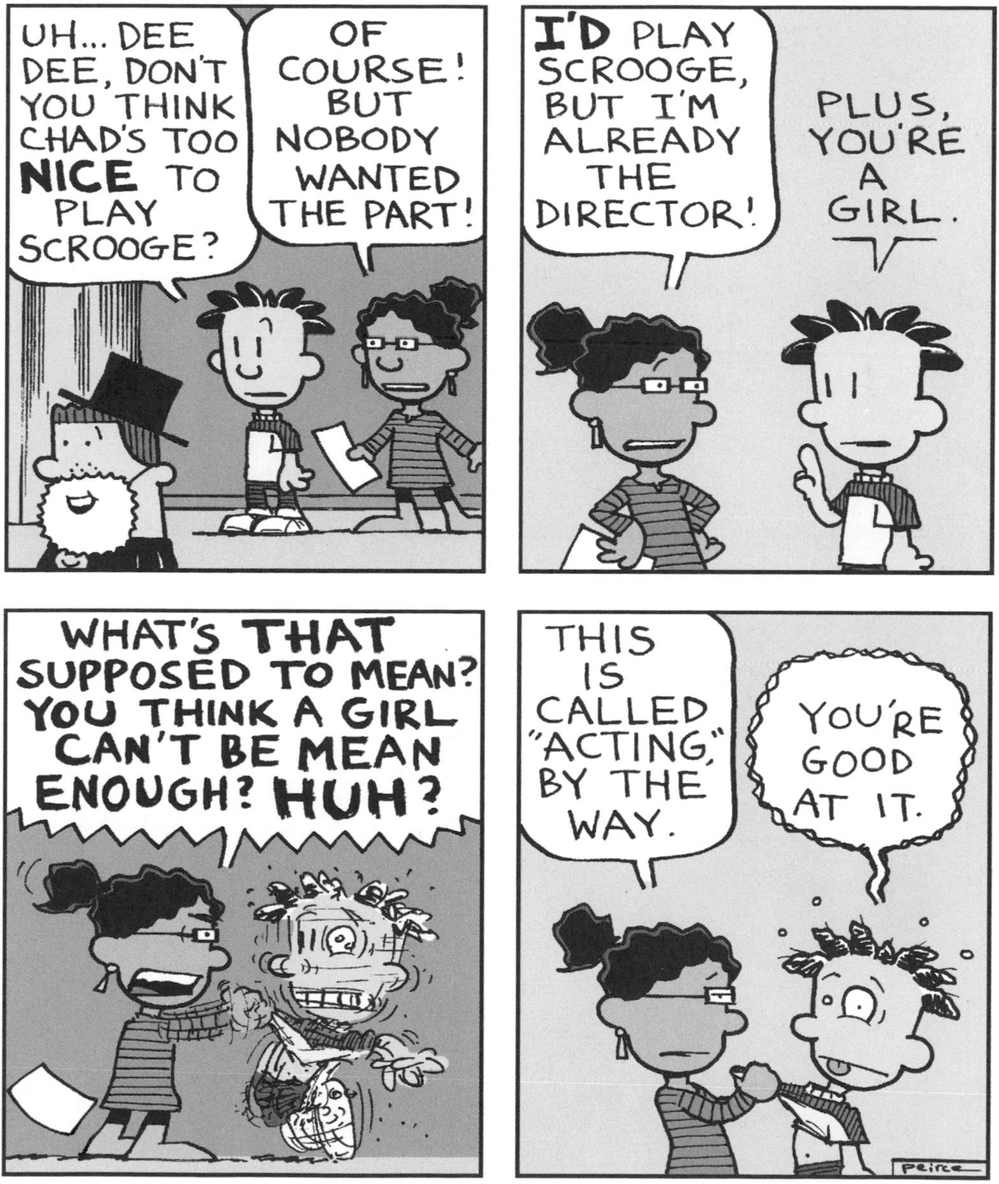
UH... DEE DEE, DON'T YOU THINK CHAD'S TOO **NICE** TO PLAY SCROOGE?
OF COURSE! BUT NOBODY WANTED THE PART!
I'D PLAY SCROOGE, BUT I'M ALREADY THE DIRECTOR!
PLUS, YOU'RE A GIRL.
WHAT'S **THAT** SUPPOSED TO MEAN? YOU THINK A GIRL CAN'T BE MEAN ENOUGH? **HUH?**
THIS IS CALLED "ACTING," BY THE WAY.
YOU'RE GOOD AT IT.
peirce

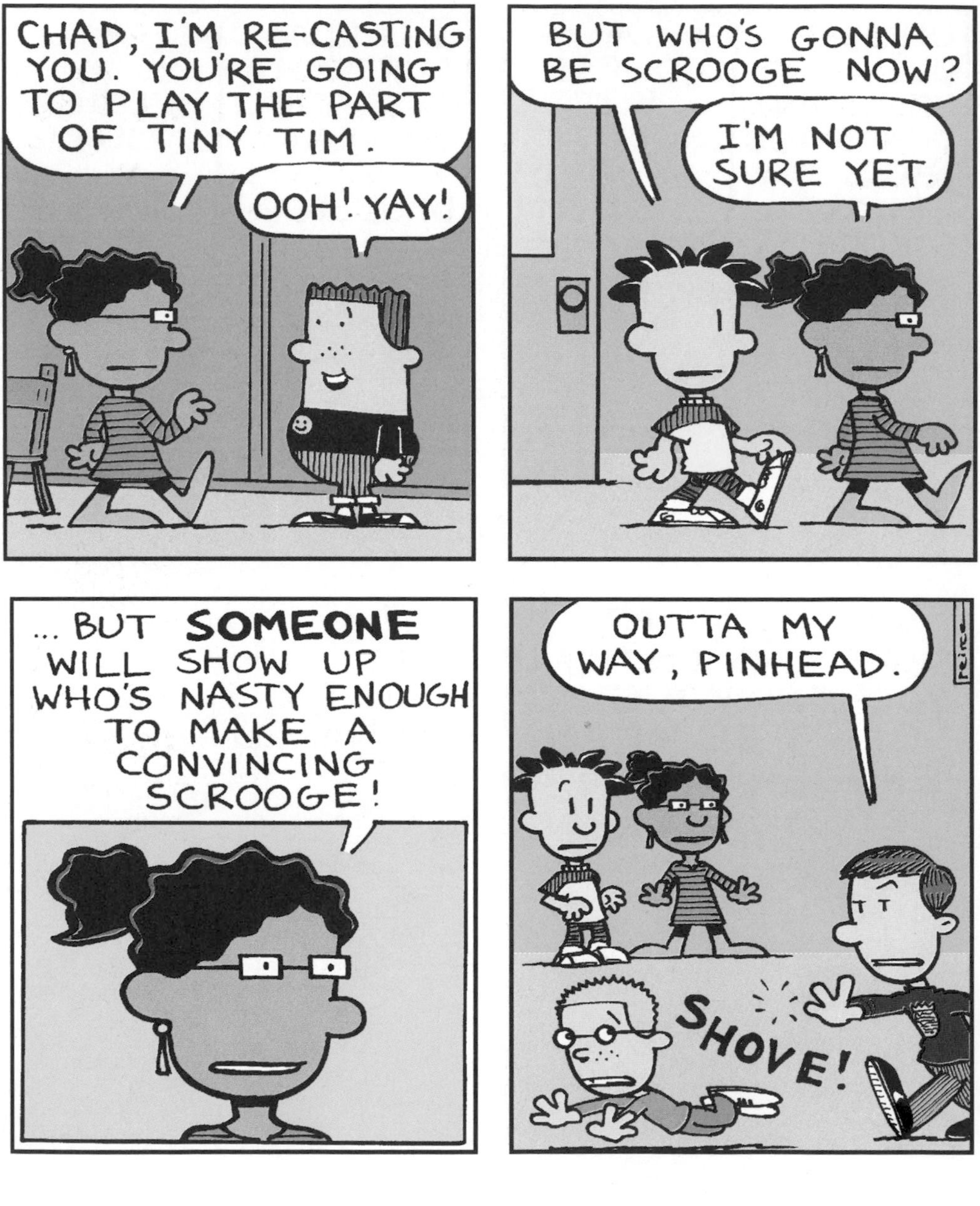

CHAD, I'M RE-CASTING YOU. YOU'RE GOING TO PLAY THE PART OF TINY TIM.
OOH! YAY!
BUT WHO'S GONNA BE SCROOGE NOW?
I'M NOT SURE YET.
... BUT SOMEONE WILL SHOW UP WHO'S NASTY ENOUGH TO MAKE A CONVINCING SCROOGE!
OUTTA MY WAY, PINHEAD.
SHOVE!
peirce

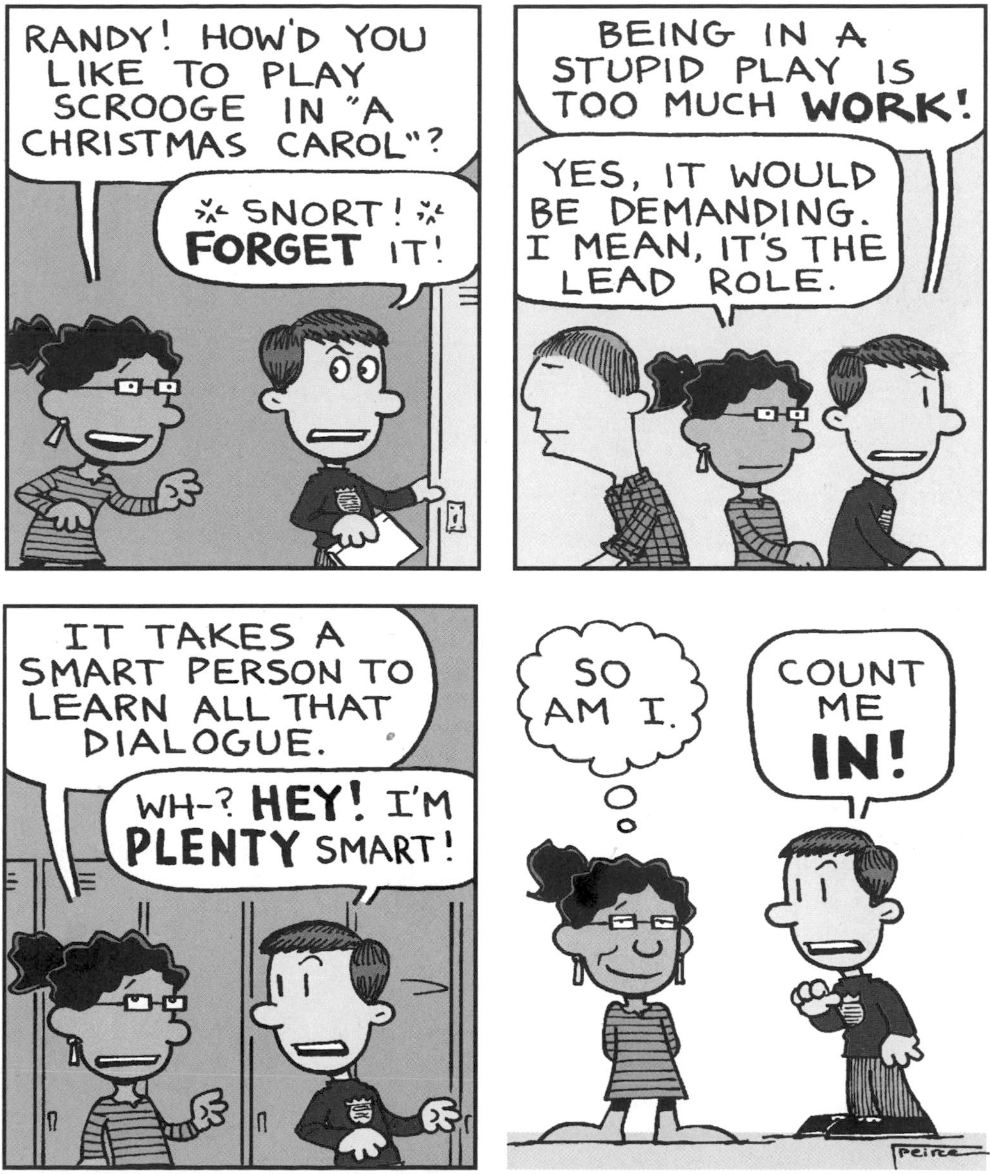
RANDY! HOW'D YOU LIKE TO PLAY SCROOGE IN "A CHRISTMAS CAROL"?
SNORT! **FORGET** IT!
BEING IN A STUPID PLAY IS TOO MUCH **WORK**!
YES, IT WOULD BE DEMANDING. I MEAN, IT'S THE LEAD ROLE.
IT TAKES A SMART PERSON TO LEARN ALL THAT DIALOGUE.
WH-? **HEY!** I'M **PLENTY** SMART!
SO AM I.
COUNT ME **IN!**
PEIRCE

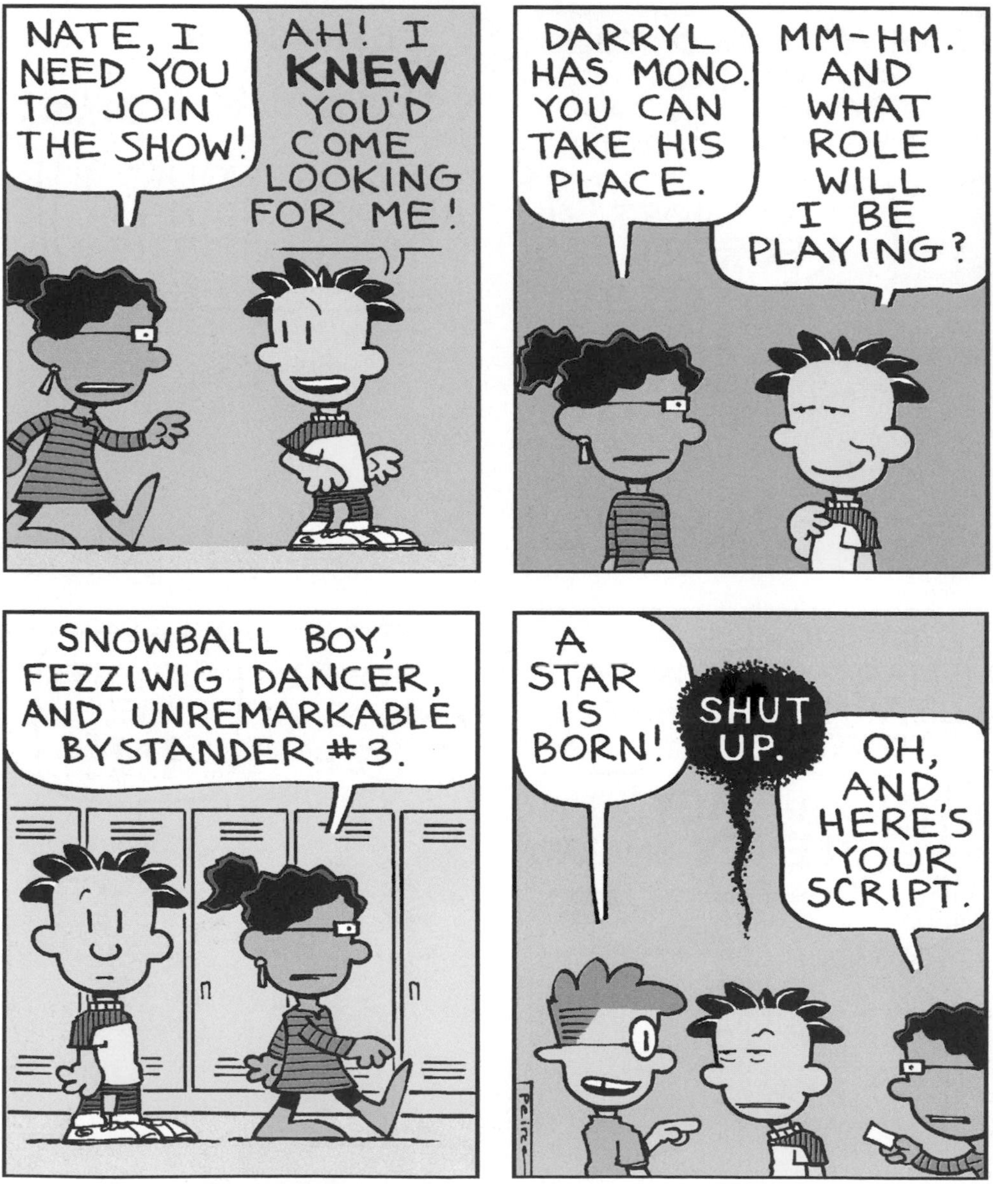
NATE, I NEED YOU TO JOIN THE SHOW!
AH! I **KNEW** YOU'D COME LOOKING FOR ME!
DARRYL HAS MONO. YOU CAN TAKE HIS PLACE.
MM-HM. AND WHAT ROLE WILL I BE PLAYING?
SNOWBALL BOY, FEZZIWIG DANCER, AND UNREMARKABLE BYSTANDER #3.
A STAR IS BORN!
SHUT UP.
OH, AND HERE'S YOUR SCRIPT.
Peirce

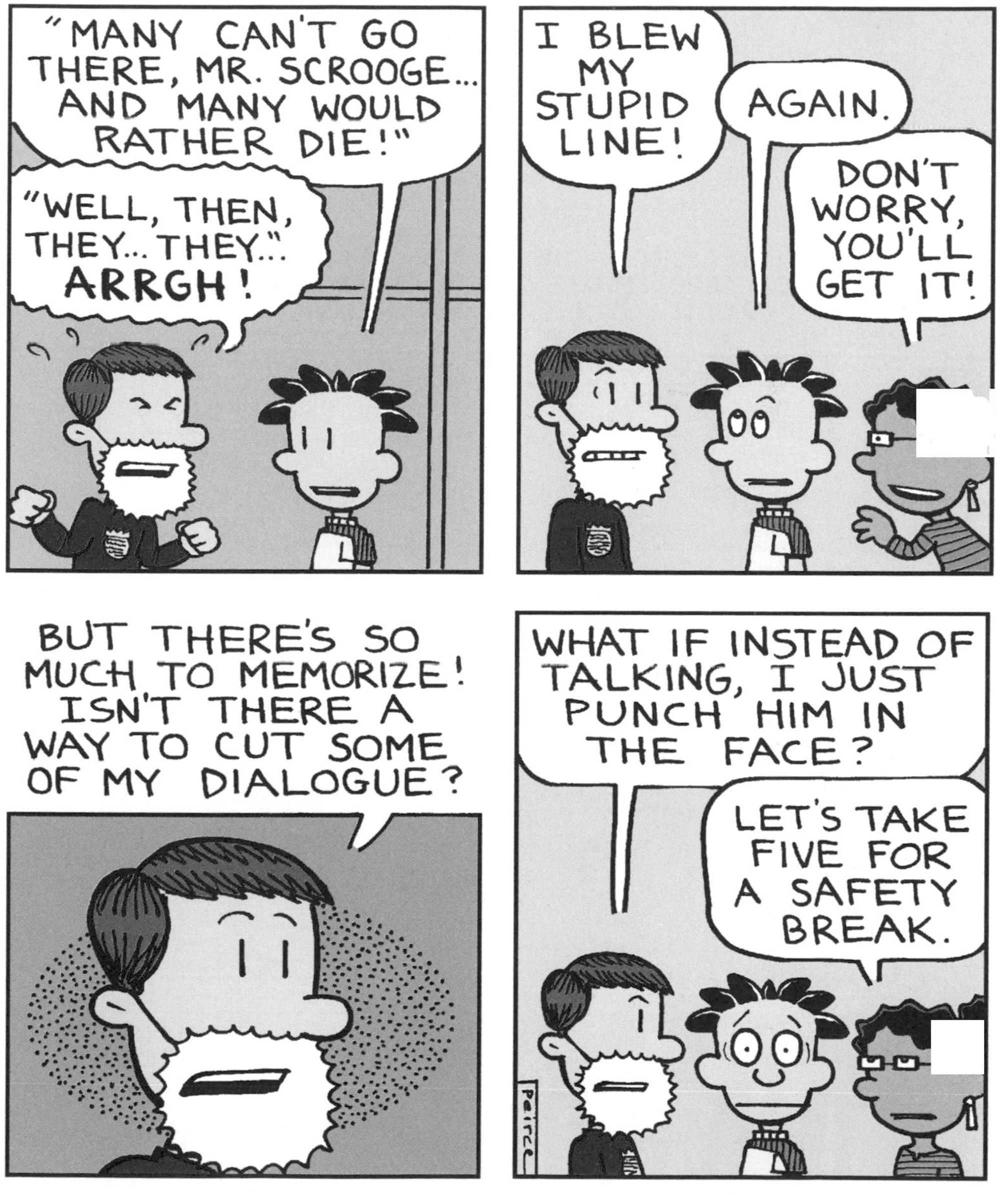
"MANY CAN'T GO THERE, MR. SCROOGE... AND MANY WOULD RATHER DIE!"
"WELL, THEN, THEY... THEY..." ARRGH!
I BLEW MY STUPID LINE!
AGAIN.
DON'T WORRY, YOU'LL GET IT!
BUT THERE'S SO MUCH TO MEMORIZE! ISN'T THERE A WAY TO CUT SOME OF MY DIALOGUE?
WHAT IF INSTEAD OF TALKING, I JUST PUNCH HIM IN THE FACE?
LET'S TAKE FIVE FOR A SAFETY BREAK.
PEIRCE

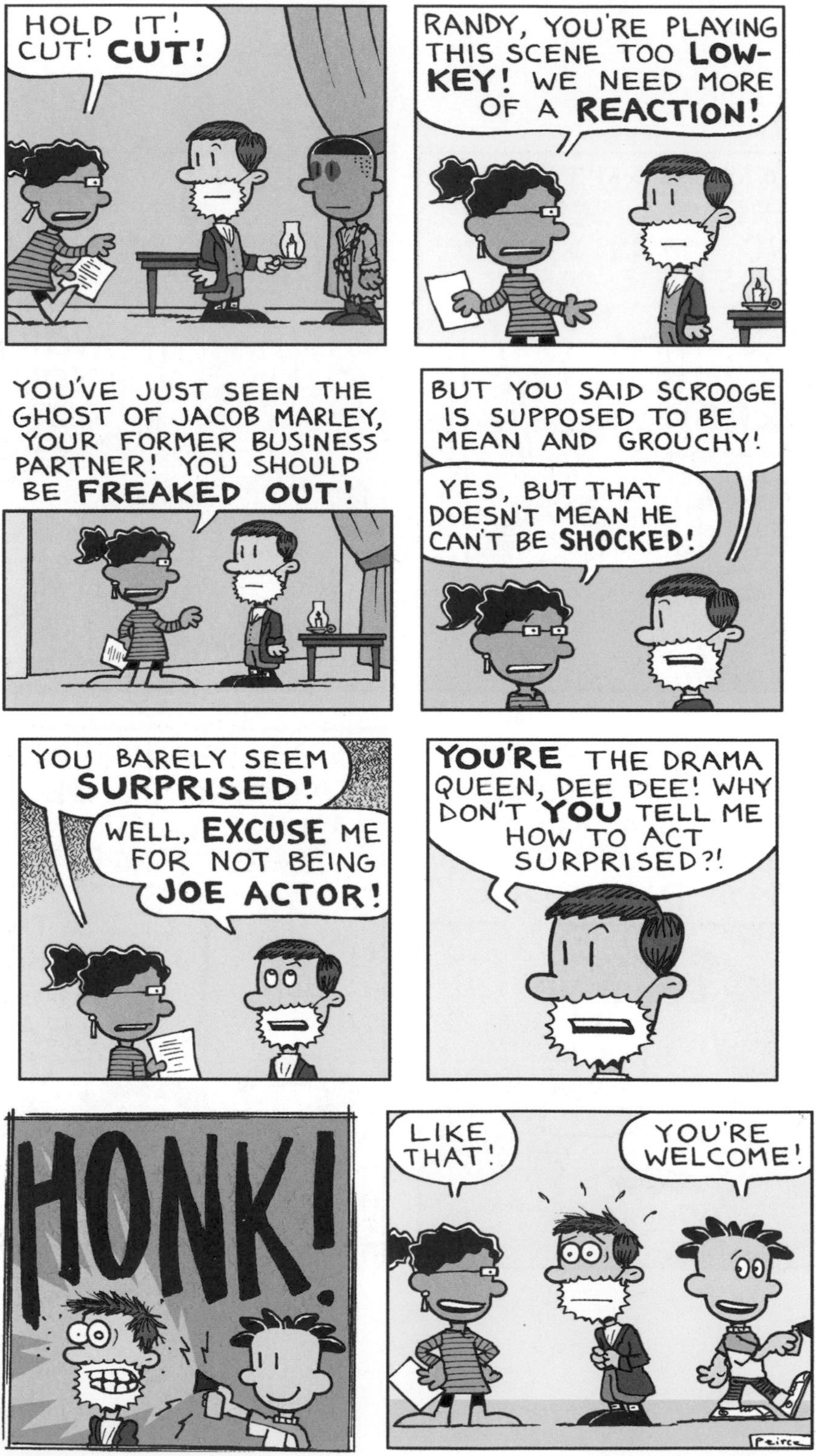
HOLD IT! CUT! CUT!
RANDY, YOU'RE PLAYING THIS SCENE TOO LOW-KEY! WE NEED MORE OF A REACTION!
YOU'VE JUST SEEN THE GHOST OF JACOB MARLEY, YOUR FORMER BUSINESS PARTNER! YOU SHOULD BE FREAKED OUT!
BUT YOU SAID SCROOGE IS SUPPOSED TO BE MEAN AND GROUCHY!
YES, BUT THAT DOESN'T MEAN HE CAN'T BE SHOCKED!
YOU BARELY SEEM SURPRISED!
WELL, EXCUSE ME FOR NOT BEING JOE ACTOR!
YOU'RE THE DRAMA QUEEN, DEE DEE! WHY DON'T YOU TELL ME HOW TO ACT SURPRISED?!
HONK!
LIKE THAT!
YOU'RE WELCOME!
Peirce

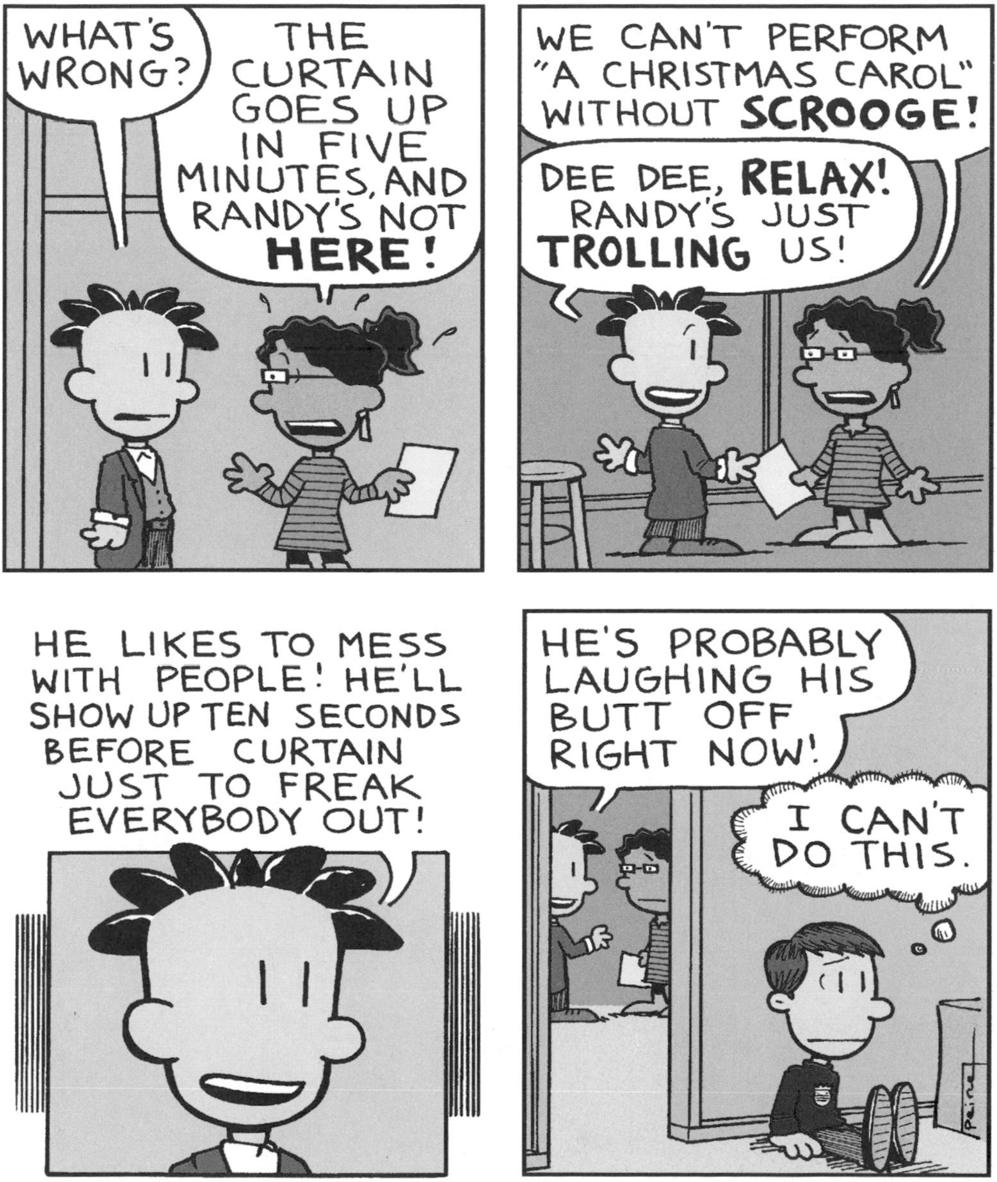
WHAT'S WRONG?
THE CURTAIN GOES UP IN FIVE MINUTES, AND RANDY'S NOT **HERE**!
WE CAN'T PERFORM "A CHRISTMAS CAROL" WITHOUT **SCROOGE**!
DEE DEE, **RELAX**! RANDY'S JUST **TROLLING** US!
HE LIKES TO MESS WITH PEOPLE! HE'LL SHOW UP TEN SECONDS BEFORE CURTAIN JUST TO FREAK EVERYBODY OUT!
HE'S PROBABLY LAUGHING HIS BUTT OFF RIGHT NOW!
I CAN'T DO THIS.

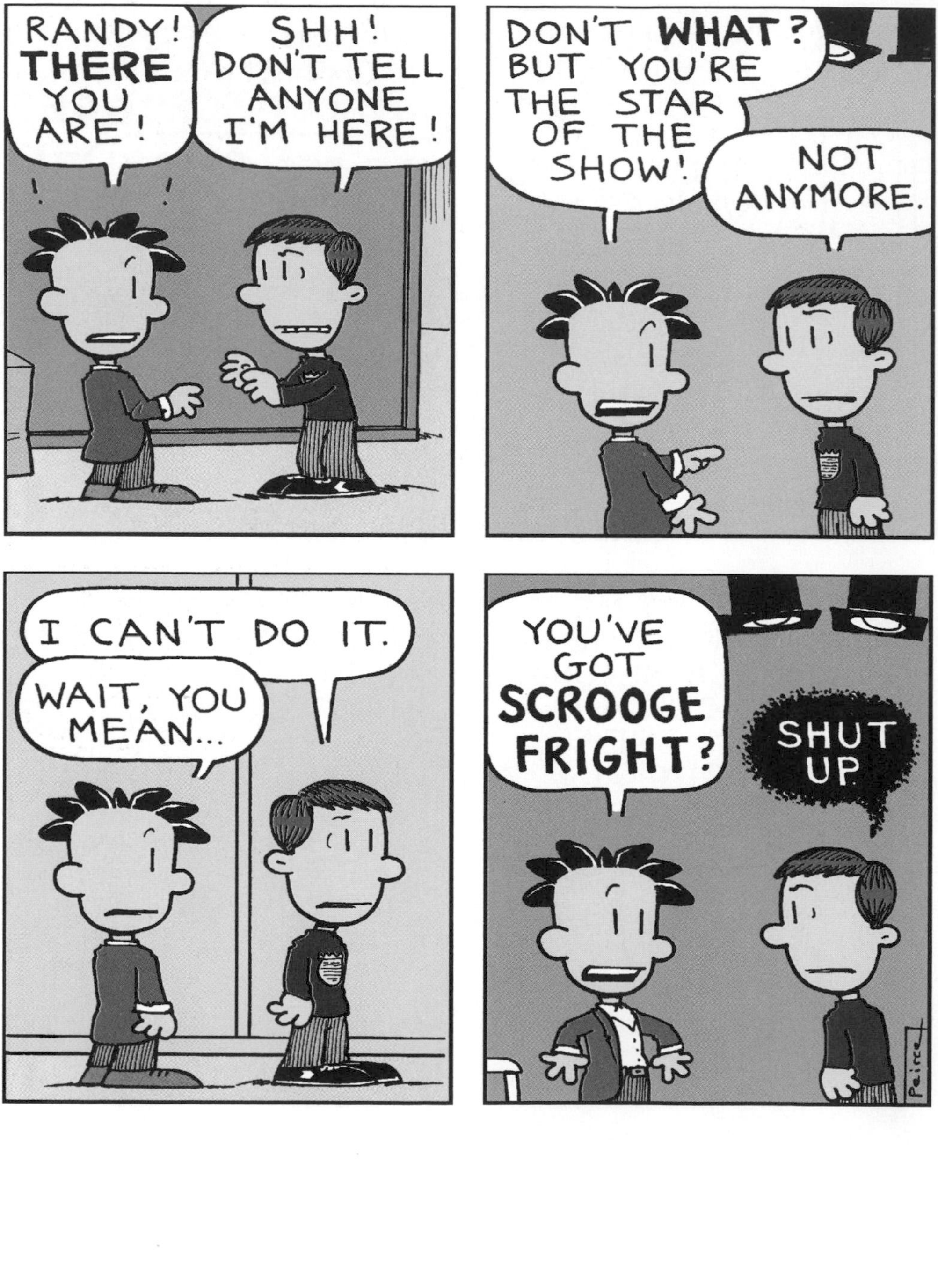
RANDY! **THERE** YOU ARE!
SHH! DON'T TELL ANYONE I'M HERE!
DON'T **WHAT**? BUT YOU'RE THE STAR OF THE SHOW!
NOT ANYMORE.
I CAN'T DO IT.
WAIT, YOU MEAN...
YOU'VE GOT **SCROOGE FRIGHT**?
SHUT UP.
Peirce

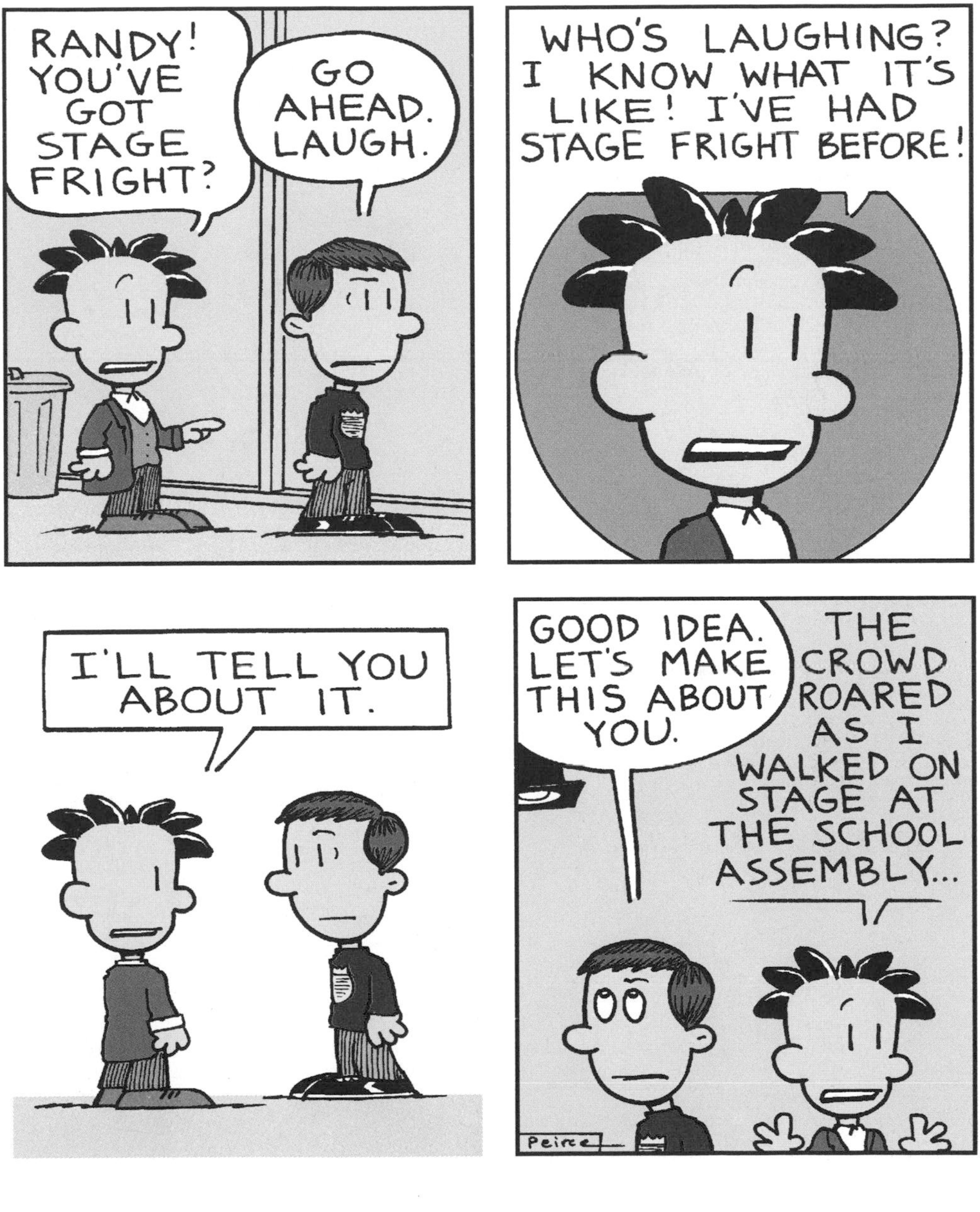
RANDY! YOU'VE GOT STAGE FRIGHT?
GO AHEAD. LAUGH.
WHO'S LAUGHING? I KNOW WHAT IT'S LIKE! I'VE HAD STAGE FRIGHT BEFORE!
I'LL TELL YOU ABOUT IT.
GOOD IDEA. LET'S MAKE THIS ABOUT YOU.
THE CROWD ROARED AS I WALKED ON STAGE AT THE SCHOOL ASSEMBLY...
Peirce

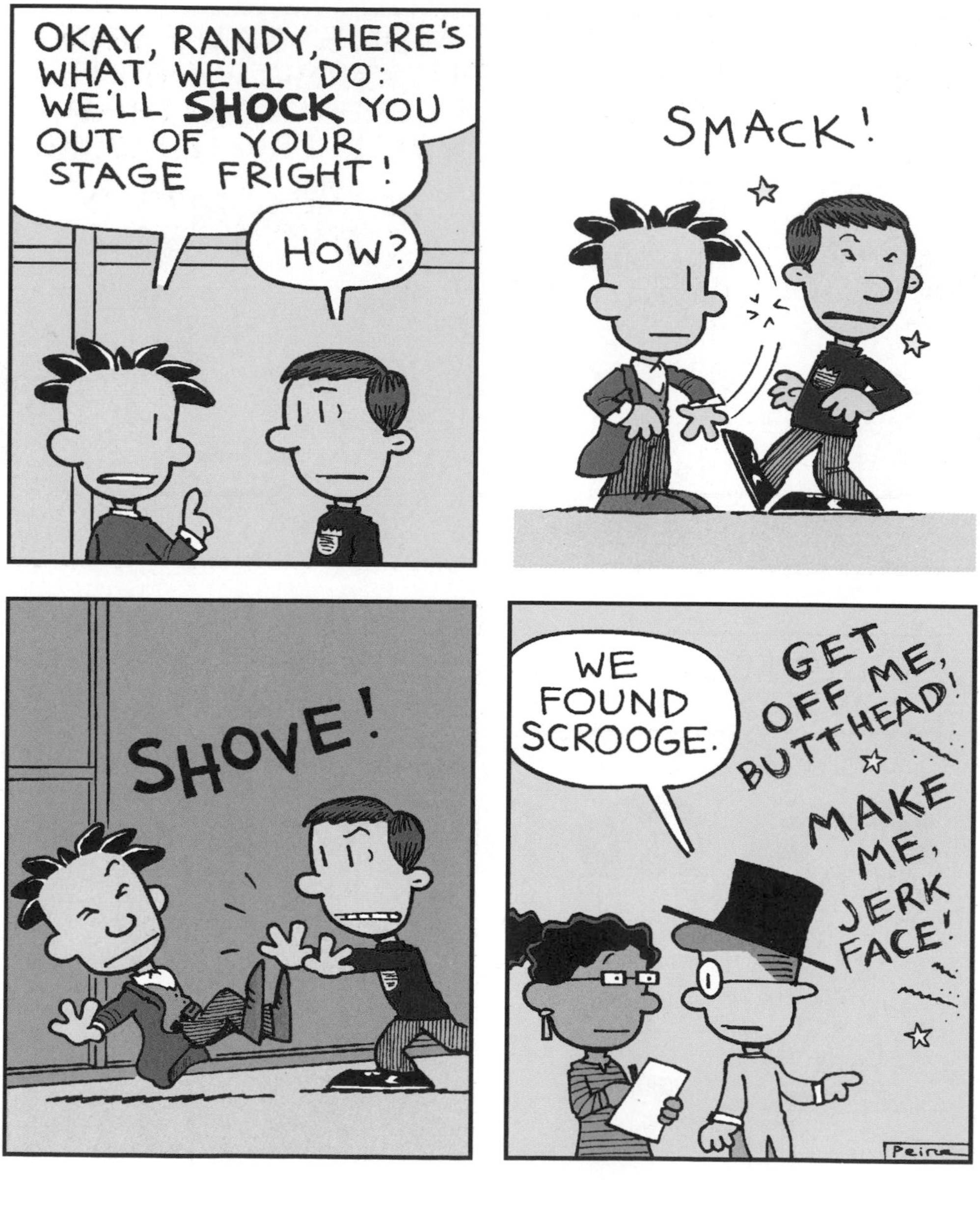
OKAY, RANDY, HERE'S WHAT WE'LL DO: WE'LL **SHOCK** YOU OUT OF YOUR STAGE FRIGHT!
HOW?
SMACK!
SHOVE!
WE FOUND SCROOGE.
GET OFF ME, BUTTHEAD!
MAKE ME, JERK FACE!
Peirce

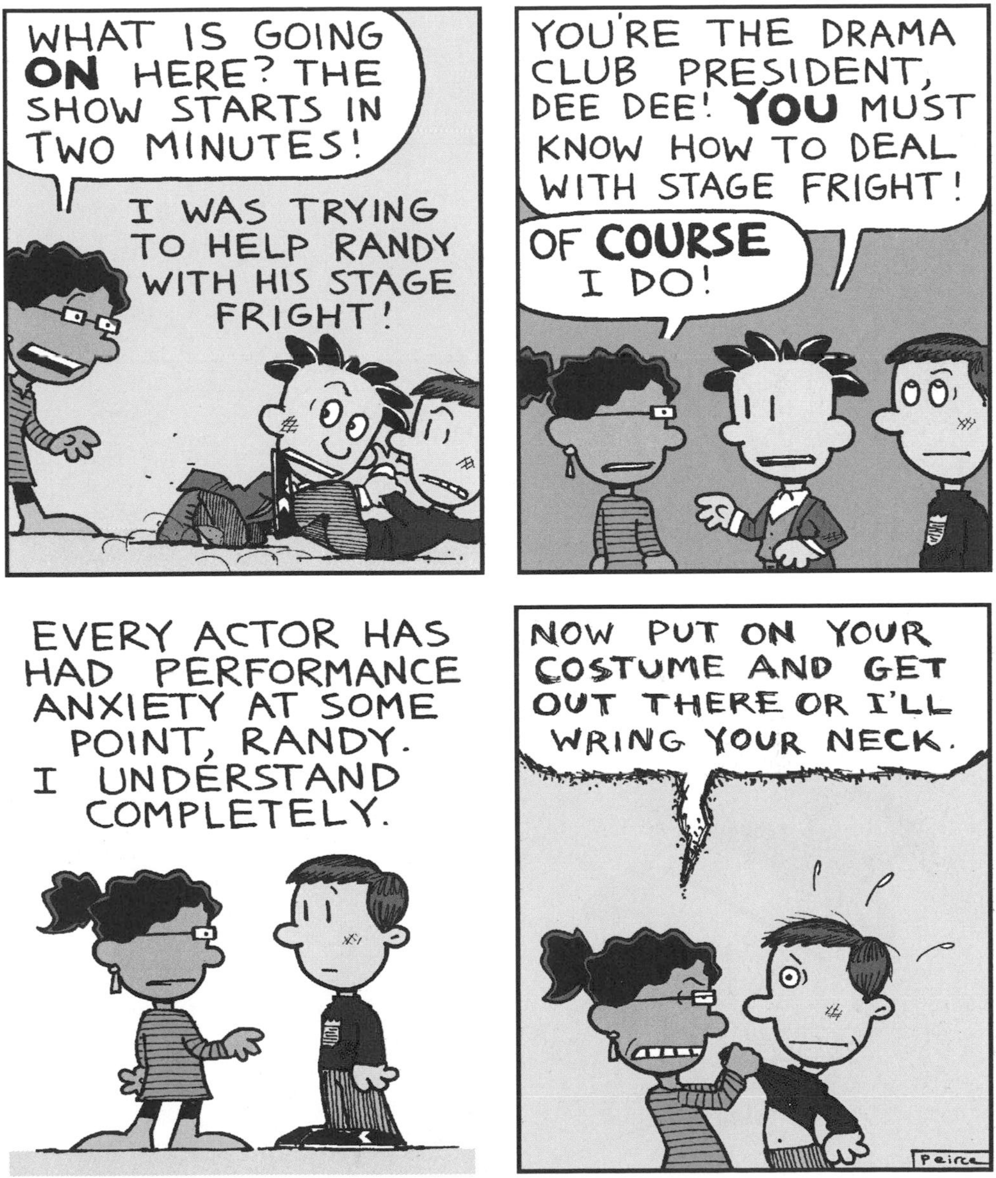
WHAT IS GOING **ON** HERE? THE SHOW STARTS IN TWO MINUTES!
I WAS TRYING TO HELP RANDY WITH HIS STAGE FRIGHT!
YOU'RE THE DRAMA CLUB PRESIDENT, DEE DEE! **YOU** MUST KNOW HOW TO DEAL WITH STAGE FRIGHT!
OF **COURSE** I DO!
EVERY ACTOR HAS HAD PERFORMANCE ANXIETY AT SOME POINT, RANDY. I UNDERSTAND COMPLETELY.
NOW PUT ON YOUR COSTUME AND GET OUT THERE OR I'LL WRING YOUR NECK.
Peirce

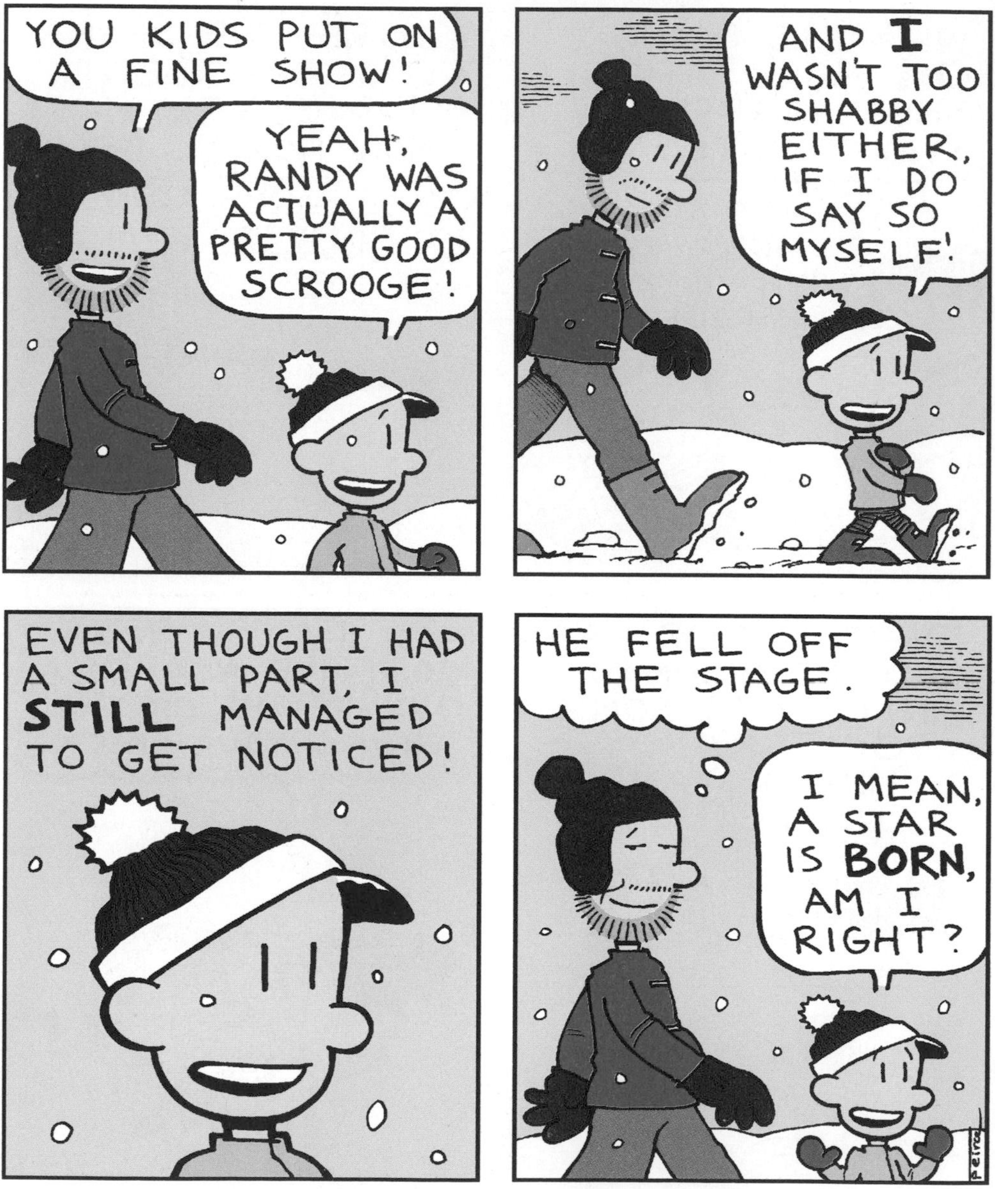
YOU KIDS PUT ON A FINE SHOW!
YEAH, RANDY WAS ACTUALLY A PRETTY GOOD SCROOGE!
AND **I** WASN'T TOO SHABBY EITHER, IF I DO SAY SO MYSELF!
EVEN THOUGH I HAD A SMALL PART, I **STILL** MANAGED TO GET NOTICED!
HE FELL OFF THE STAGE.
I MEAN, A STAR IS **BORN**, AM I RIGHT?
peirce

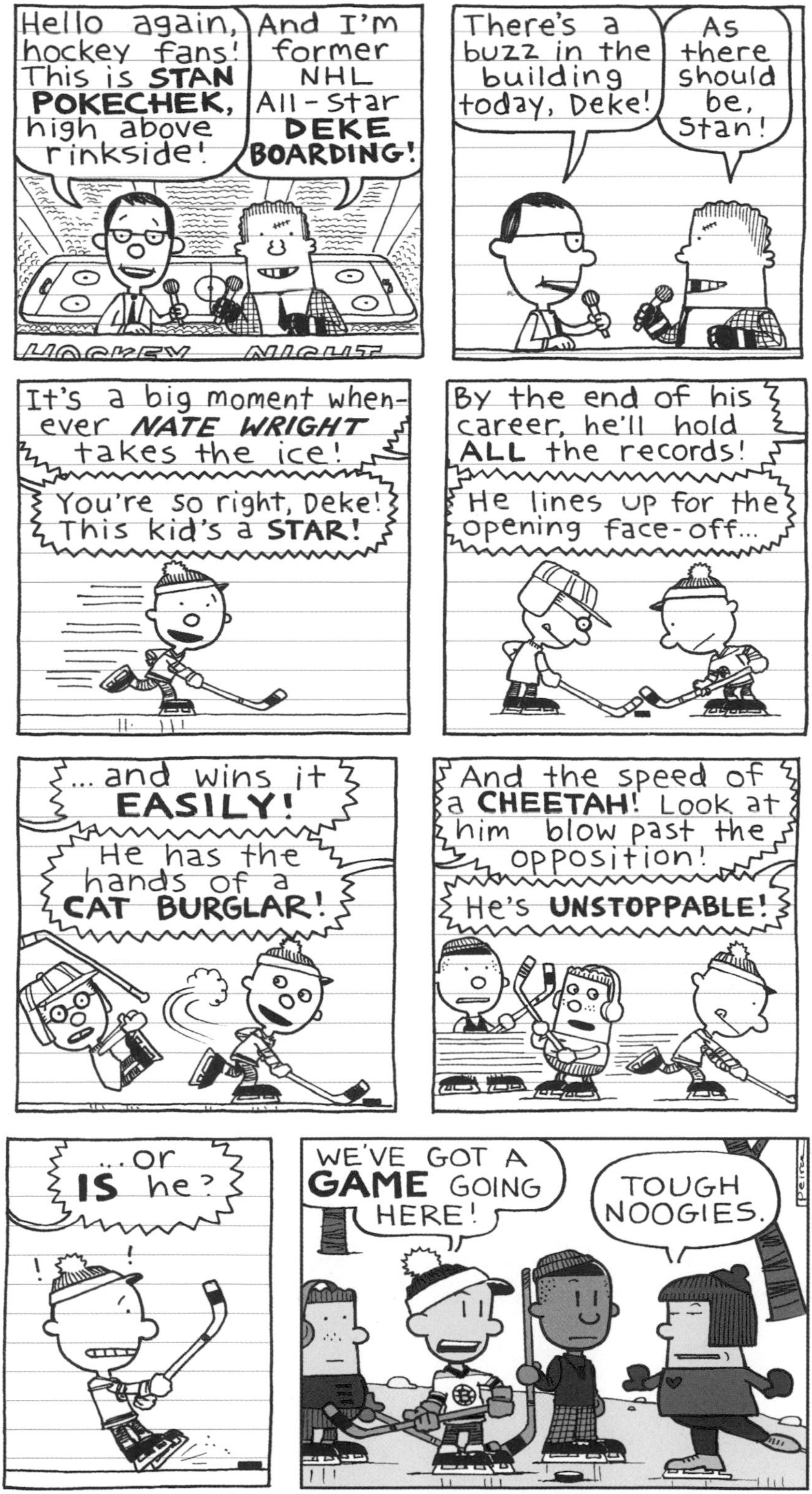
Hello again, hockey fans! This is STAN POKECHEK, high above rinkside!
And I'm former NHL All-Star DEKE BOARDING!
There's a buzz in the building today, Deke!
As there should be, Stan!
It's a big moment whenever NATE WRIGHT takes the ice!
You're so right, Deke! This kid's a STAR!
By the end of his career, he'll hold ALL the records!
He lines up for the opening face-off...
... and wins it EASILY!
He has the hands of a CAT BURGLAR!
And the speed of a CHEETAH! Look at him blow past the opposition!
He's UNSTOPPABLE!
...or IS he?
! !
WE'VE GOT A GAME GOING HERE!
TOUGH NOOGIES.

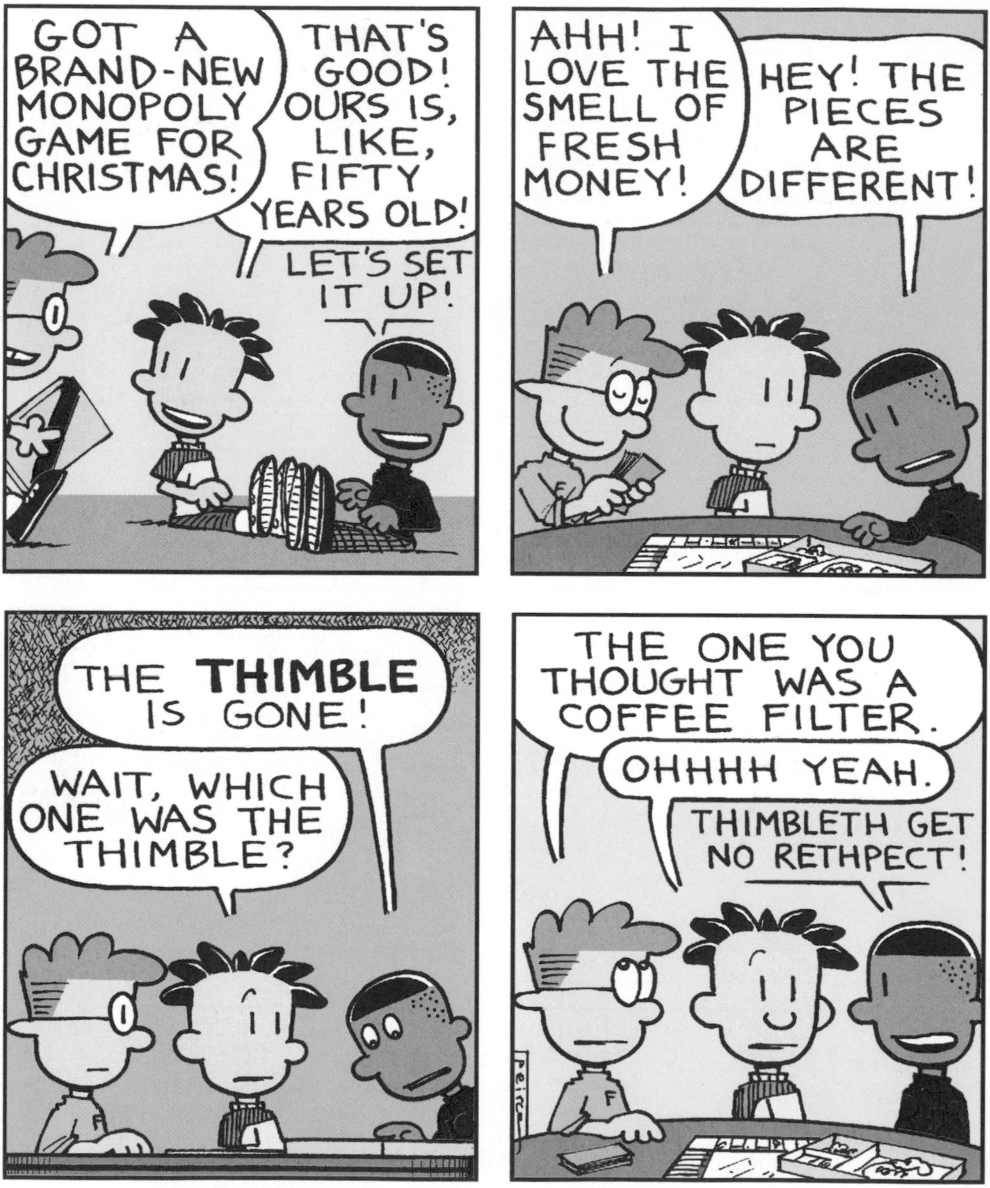
GOT A BRAND-NEW MONOPOLY GAME FOR CHRISTMAS!
THAT'S GOOD! OURS IS, LIKE, FIFTY YEARS OLD!
LET'S SET IT UP!
AHH! I LOVE THE SMELL OF FRESH MONEY!
HEY! THE PIECES ARE DIFFERENT!
THE **THIMBLE** IS GONE!
WAIT, WHICH ONE WAS THE THIMBLE?
THE ONE YOU THOUGHT WAS A COFFEE FILTER.
OHHHH YEAH.
THIMBLETH GET NO RETHPECT!

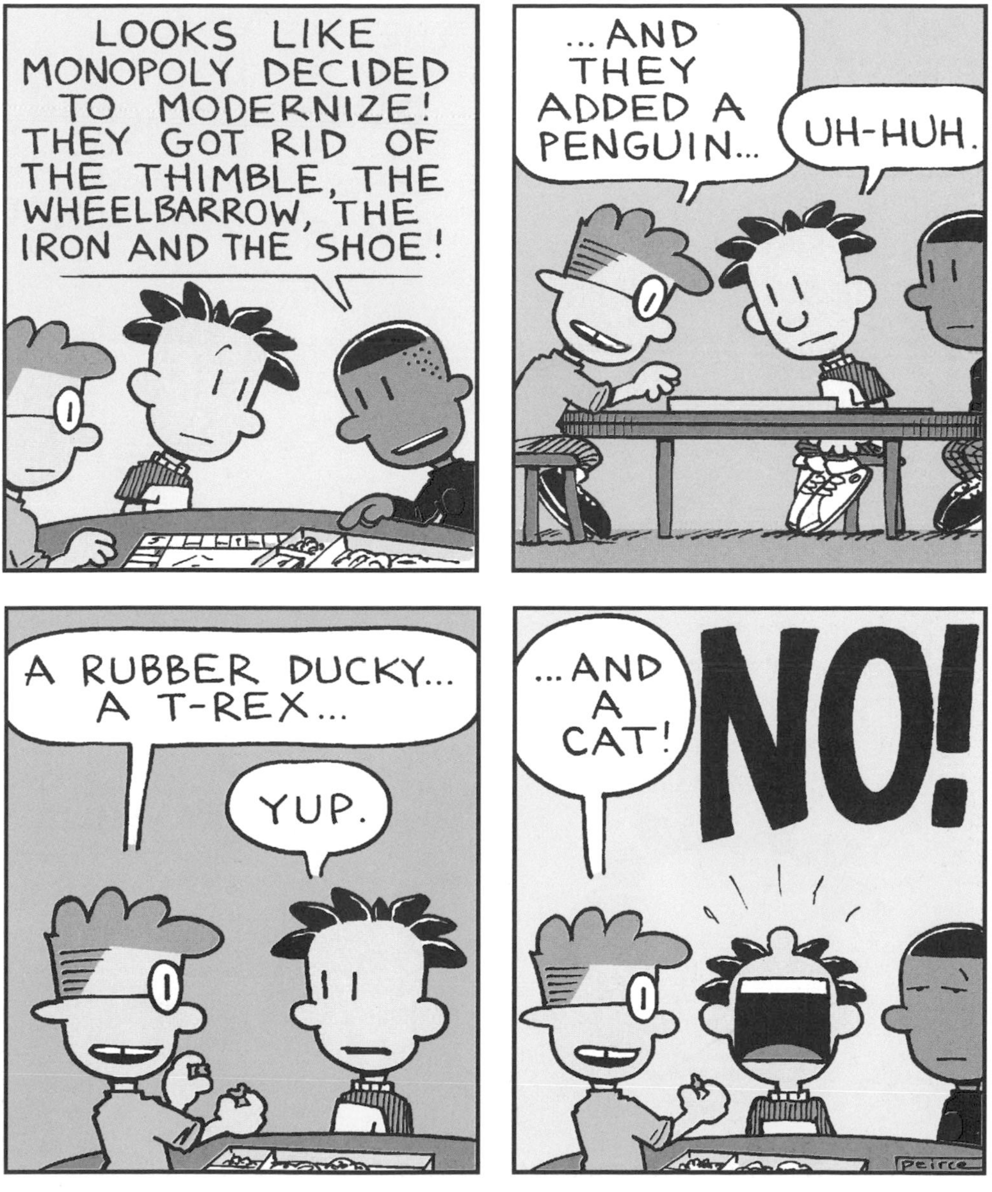
LOOKS LIKE MONOPOLY DECIDED TO MODERNIZE! THEY GOT RID OF THE THIMBLE, THE WHEELBARROW, THE IRON AND THE SHOE!
...AND THEY ADDED A PENGUIN...
UH-HUH.
A RUBBER DUCKY... A T-REX...
YUP.
...AND A CAT!
NO!
peirce

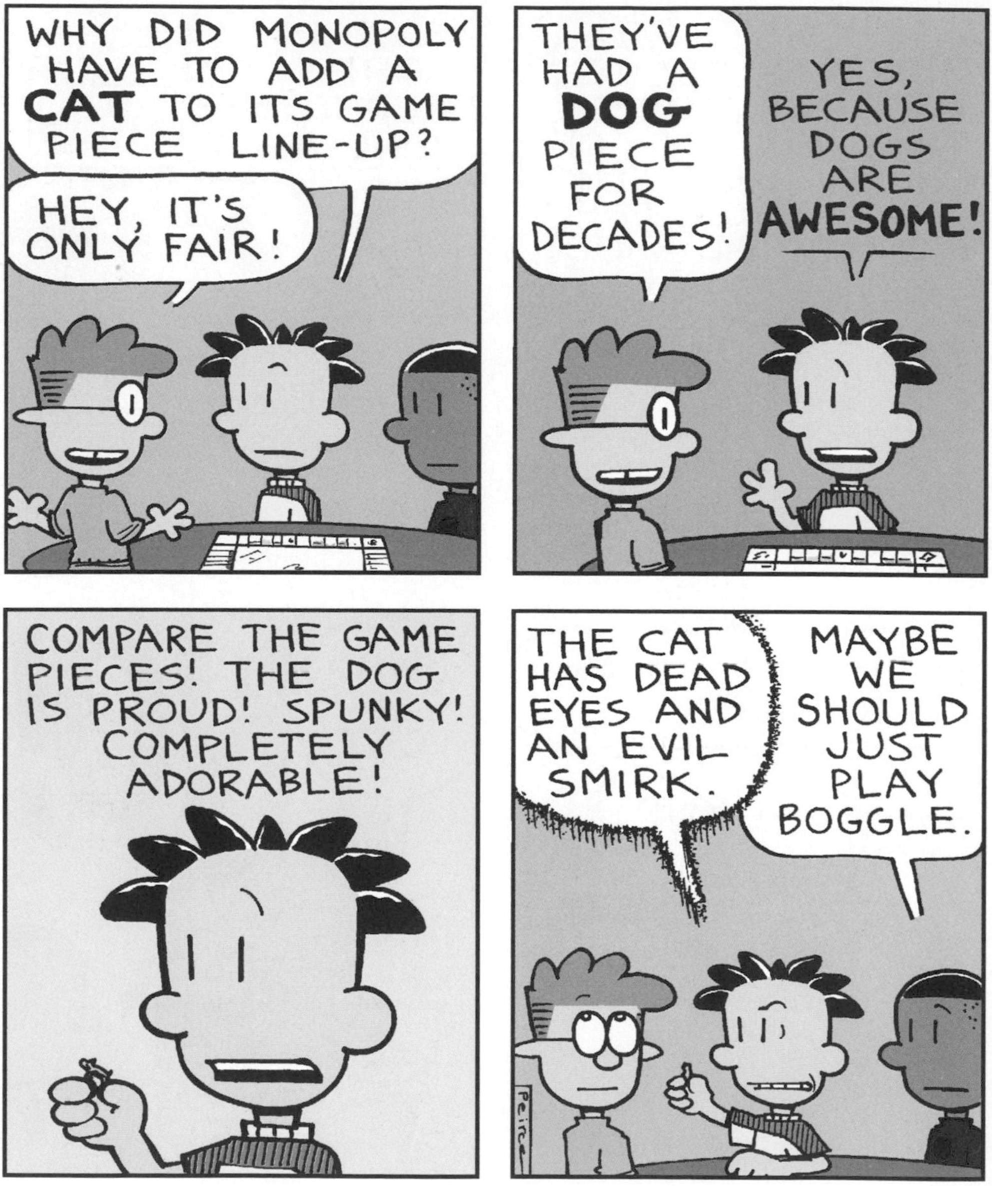
WHY DID MONOPOLY HAVE TO ADD A CAT TO ITS GAME PIECE LINE-UP?
HEY, IT'S ONLY FAIR!
THEY'VE HAD A DOG PIECE FOR DECADES!
YES, BECAUSE DOGS ARE AWESOME!
COMPARE THE GAME PIECES! THE DOG IS PROUD! SPUNKY! COMPLETELY ADORABLE!
THE CAT HAS DEAD EYES AND AN EVIL SMIRK.
MAYBE WE SHOULD JUST PLAY BOGGLE.
PEIRCE

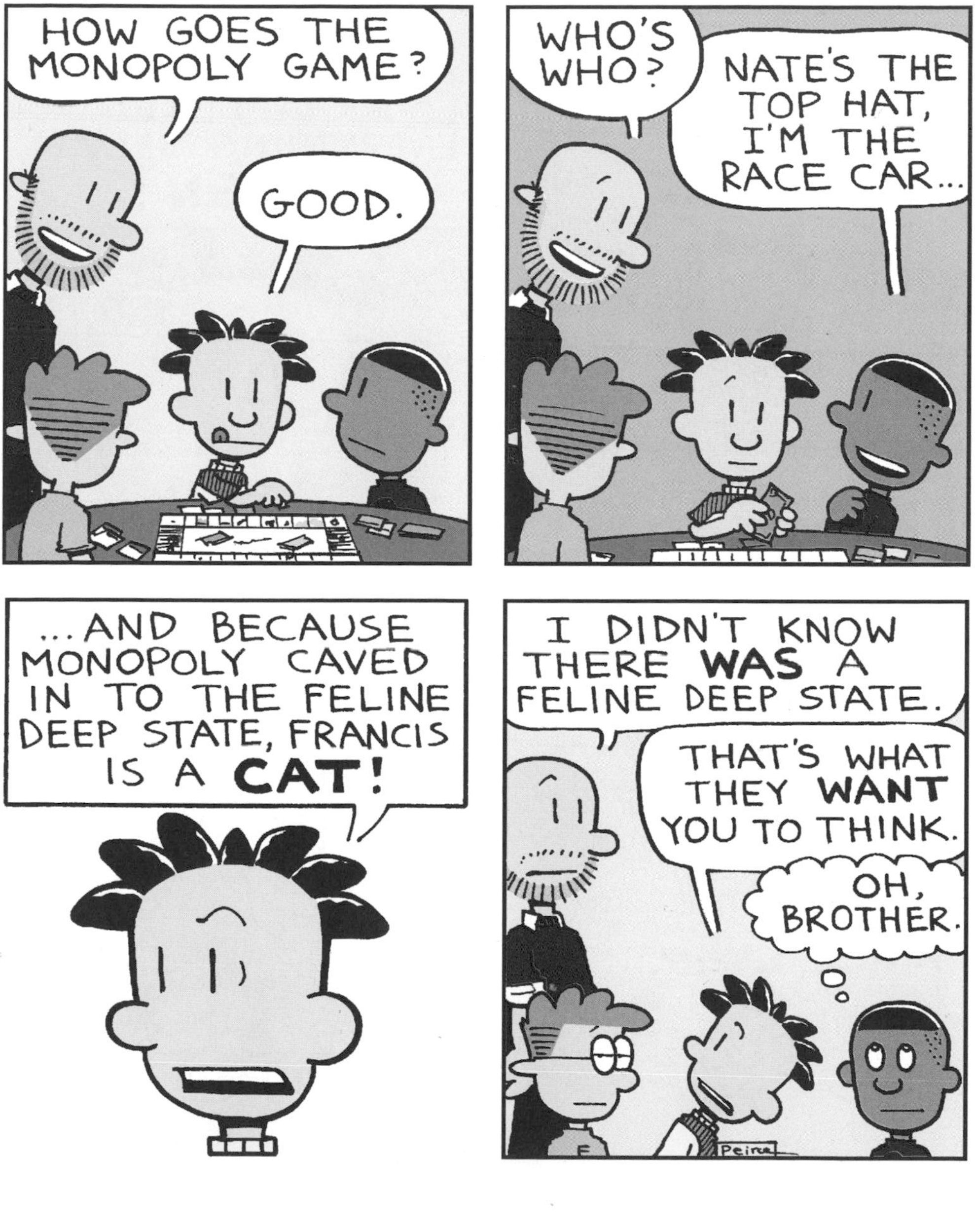
HOW GOES THE MONOPOLY GAME?
GOOD.
WHO'S WHO?
NATE'S THE TOP HAT, I'M THE RACE CAR...
...AND BECAUSE MONOPOLY CAVED IN TO THE FELINE DEEP STATE, FRANCIS IS A **CAT**!
I DIDN'T KNOW THERE **WAS** A FELINE DEEP STATE.
THAT'S WHAT THEY **WANT** YOU TO THINK.
OH, BROTHER.
Peirce

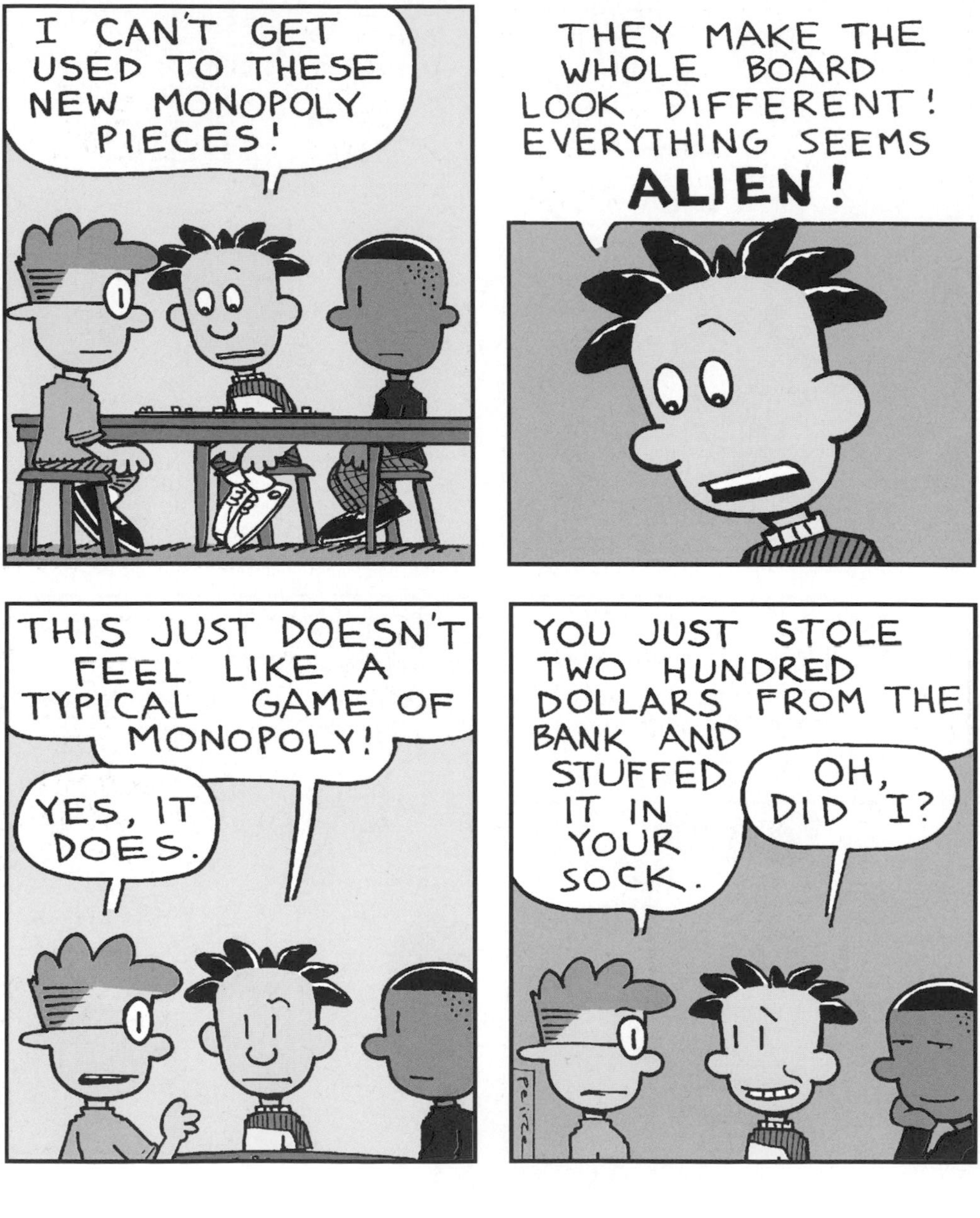
I CAN'T GET USED TO THESE NEW MONOPOLY PIECES!
THEY MAKE THE WHOLE BOARD LOOK DIFFERENT! EVERYTHING SEEMS **ALIEN!**
THIS JUST DOESN'T FEEL LIKE A TYPICAL GAME OF MONOPOLY!
YES, IT DOES.
YOU JUST STOLE TWO HUNDRED DOLLARS FROM THE BANK AND STUFFED IT IN YOUR SOCK.
OH, DID I?
peirce

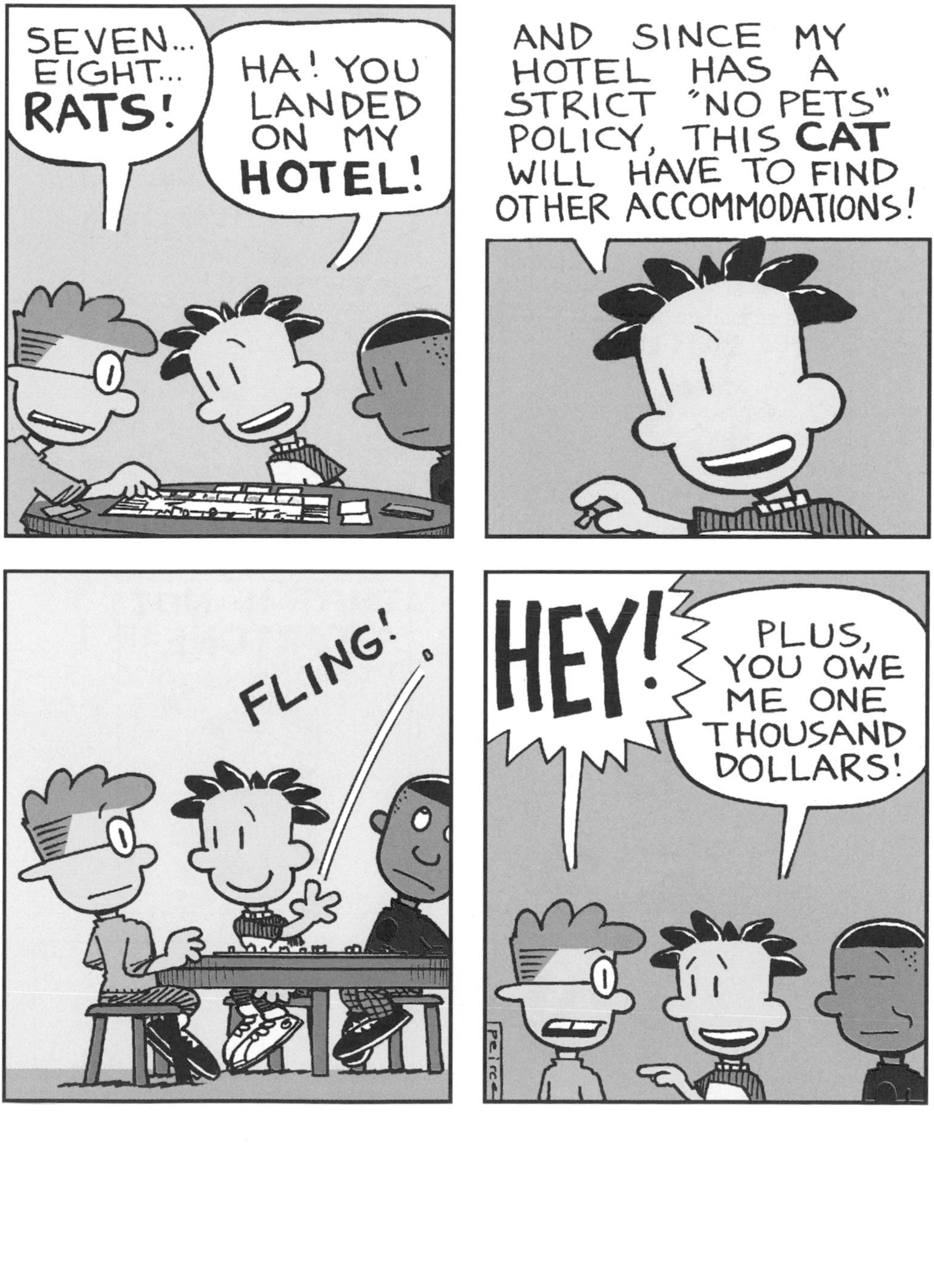
SEVEN... EIGHT... **RATS!**
HA! YOU LANDED ON MY **HOTEL!**
AND SINCE MY HOTEL HAS A STRICT "NO PETS" POLICY, THIS **CAT** WILL HAVE TO FIND OTHER ACCOMMODATIONS!
FLING!
HEY!
PLUS, YOU OWE ME ONE THOUSAND DOLLARS!
peirce

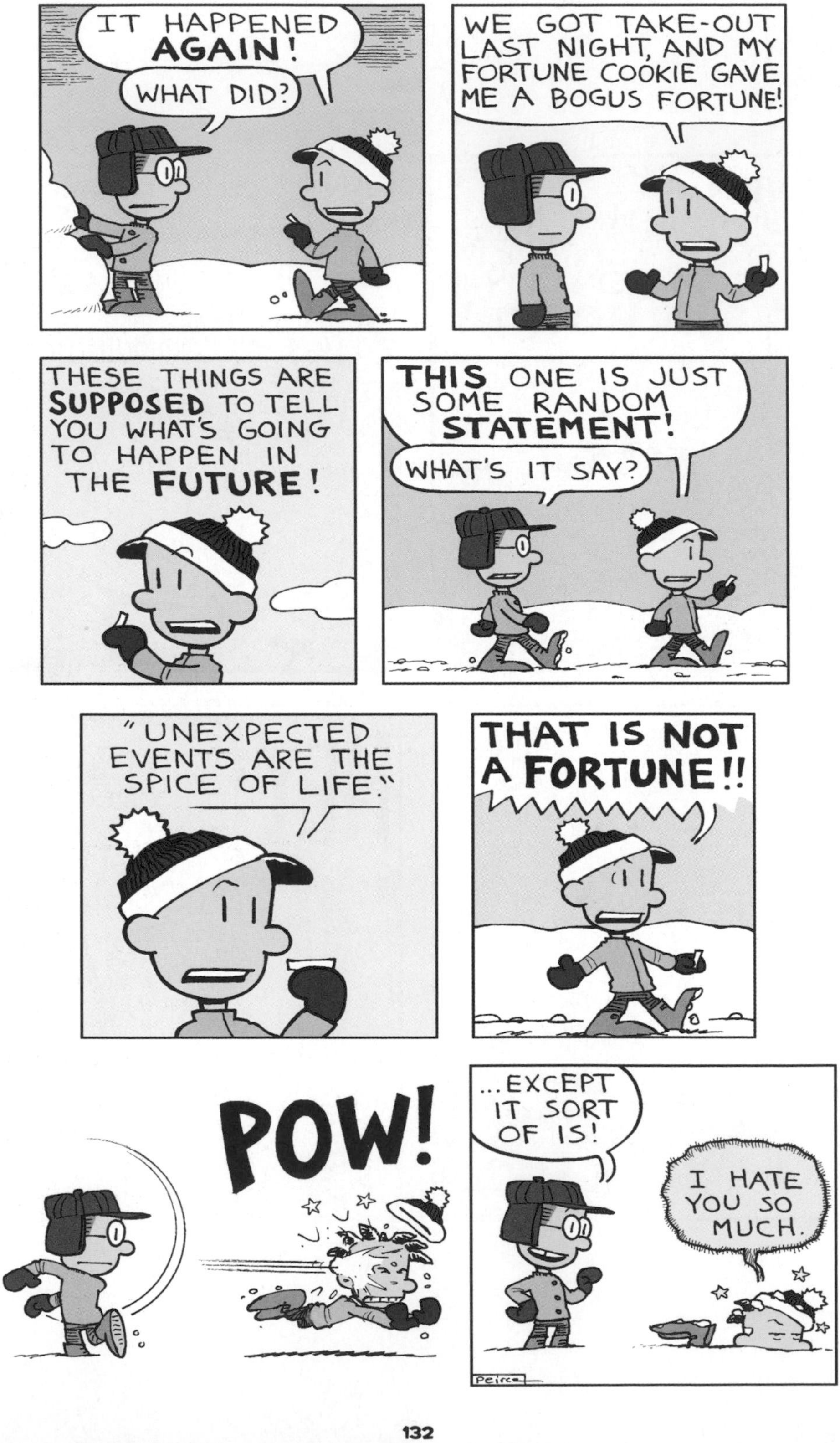
IT HAPPENED AGAIN!
WHAT DID?
WE GOT TAKE-OUT LAST NIGHT, AND MY FORTUNE COOKIE GAVE ME A BOGUS FORTUNE!
THESE THINGS ARE SUPPOSED TO TELL YOU WHAT'S GOING TO HAPPEN IN THE FUTURE!
THIS ONE IS JUST SOME RANDOM STATEMENT!
WHAT'S IT SAY?
"UNEXPECTED EVENTS ARE THE SPICE OF LIFE."
THAT IS NOT A FORTUNE!!
POW!
...EXCEPT IT SORT OF IS!
I HATE YOU SO MUCH.
Peirce

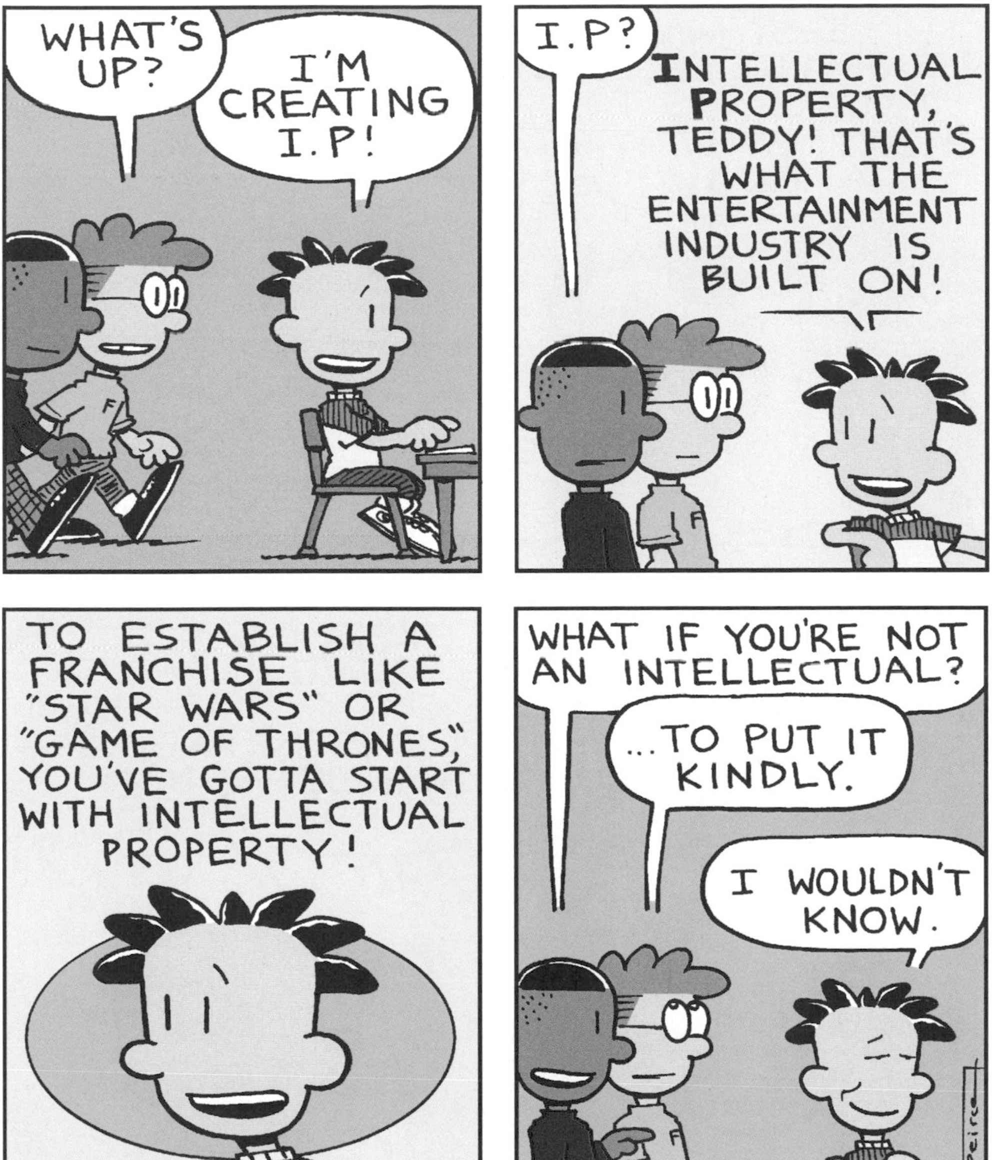
WHAT'S UP?
I'M CREATING I.P!
I.P?
INTELLECTUAL PROPERTY, TEDDY! THAT'S WHAT THE ENTERTAINMENT INDUSTRY IS BUILT ON!
TO ESTABLISH A FRANCHISE LIKE "STAR WARS" OR "GAME OF THRONES", YOU'VE GOTTA START WITH INTELLECTUAL PROPERTY!
WHAT IF YOU'RE NOT AN INTELLECTUAL?
...TO PUT IT KINDLY.
I WOULDN'T KNOW.
Peirce

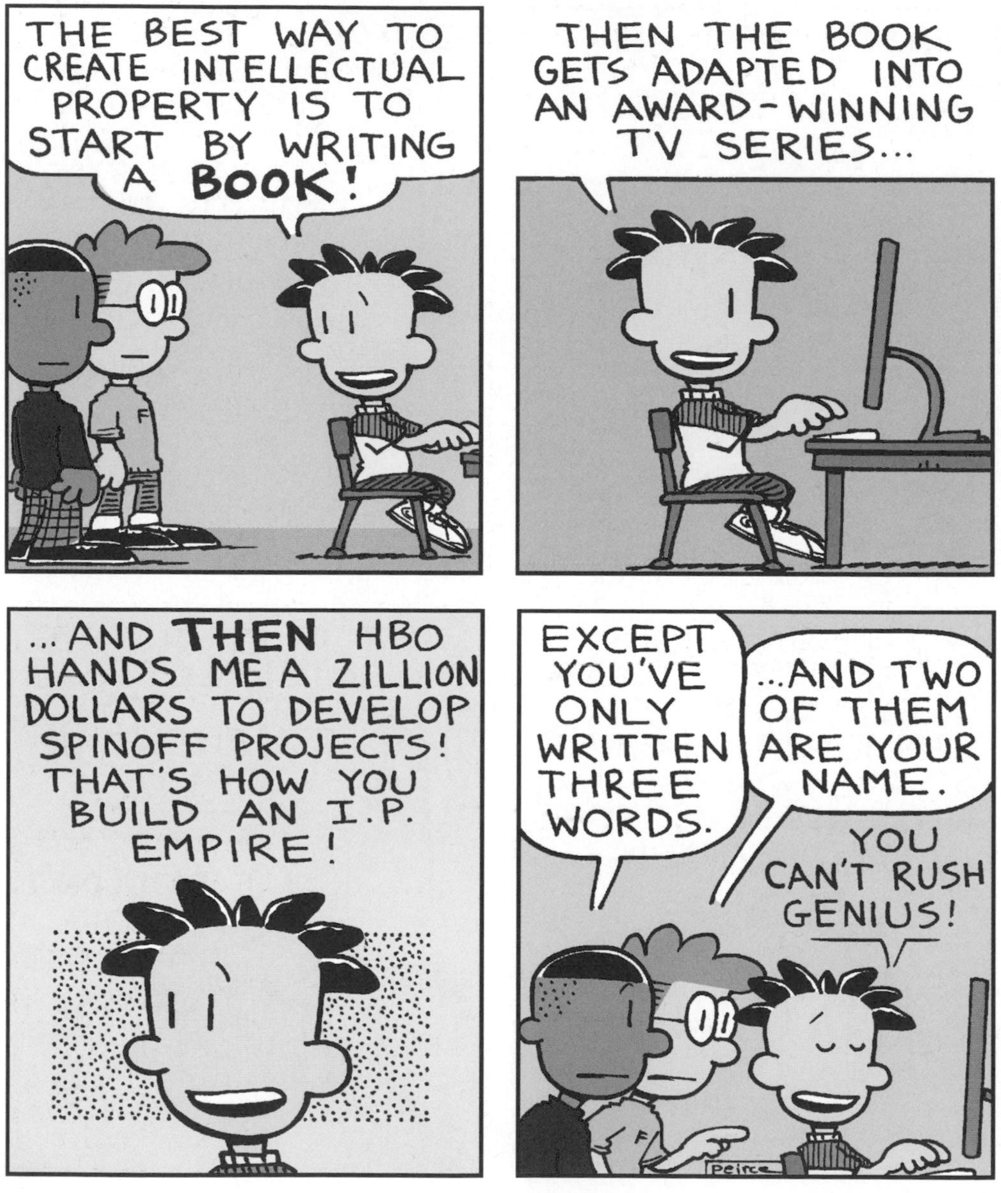
THE BEST WAY TO CREATE INTELLECTUAL PROPERTY IS TO START BY WRITING A BOOK!
THEN THE BOOK GETS ADAPTED INTO AN AWARD-WINNING TV SERIES...
...AND THEN HBO HANDS ME A ZILLION DOLLARS TO DEVELOP SPINOFF PROJECTS! THAT'S HOW YOU BUILD AN I.P. EMPIRE!
EXCEPT YOU'VE ONLY WRITTEN THREE WORDS.
...AND TWO OF THEM ARE YOUR NAME.
YOU CAN'T RUSH GENIUS!
Peirce

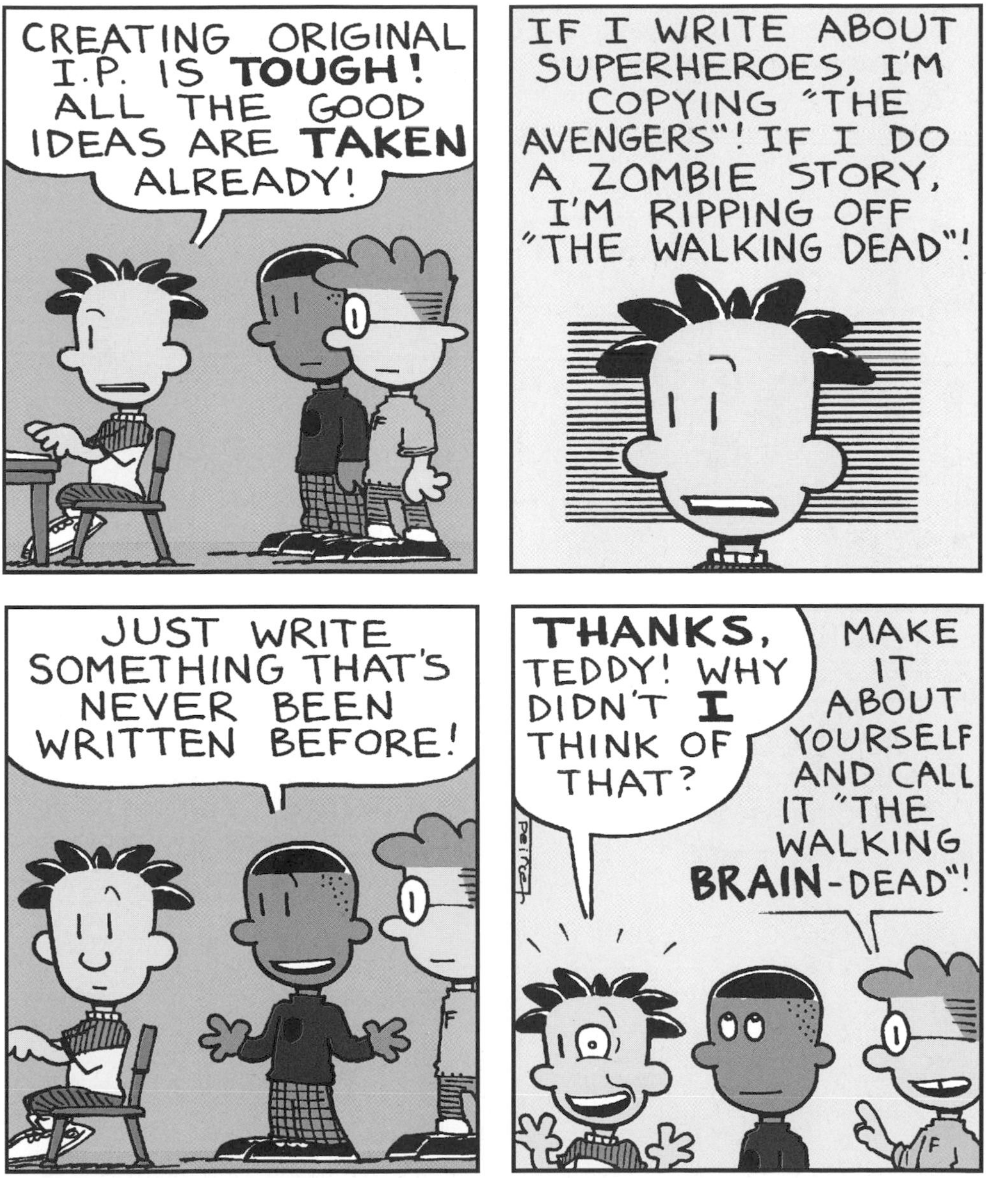
CREATING ORIGINAL I.P. IS **TOUGH**! ALL THE GOOD IDEAS ARE **TAKEN** ALREADY!
IF I WRITE ABOUT SUPERHEROES, I'M COPYING "THE AVENGERS"! IF I DO A ZOMBIE STORY, I'M RIPPING OFF "THE WALKING DEAD"!
JUST WRITE SOMETHING THAT'S NEVER BEEN WRITTEN BEFORE!
MAKE IT ABOUT YOURSELF AND CALL IT "THE WALKING **BRAIN**-DEAD"!
THANKS, TEDDY! WHY DIDN'T **I** THINK OF THAT?
Peirce

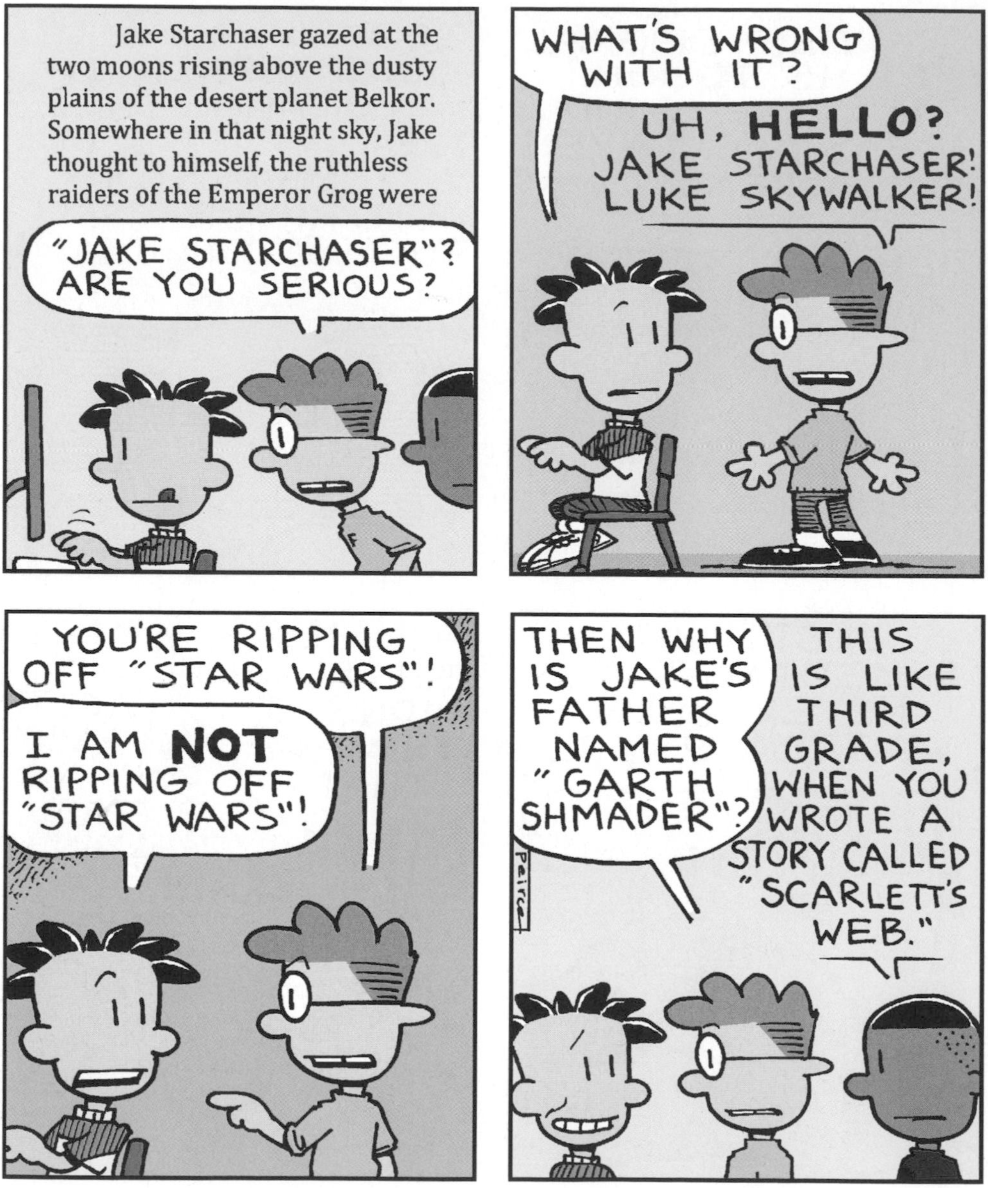
Jake Starchaser gazed at the two moons rising above the dusty plains of the desert planet Belkor. Somewhere in that night sky, Jake thought to himself, the ruthless raiders of the Emperor Grog were
"JAKE STARCHASER"? ARE YOU SERIOUS?
WHAT'S WRONG WITH IT?
UH, HELLO? JAKE STARCHASER! LUKE SKYWALKER!
YOU'RE RIPPING OFF "STAR WARS"!
I AM NOT RIPPING OFF "STAR WARS"!
THEN WHY IS JAKE'S FATHER NAMED "GARTH SHMADER"?
THIS IS LIKE THIRD GRADE, WHEN YOU WROTE A STORY CALLED "SCARLETT'S WEB."
Peirce

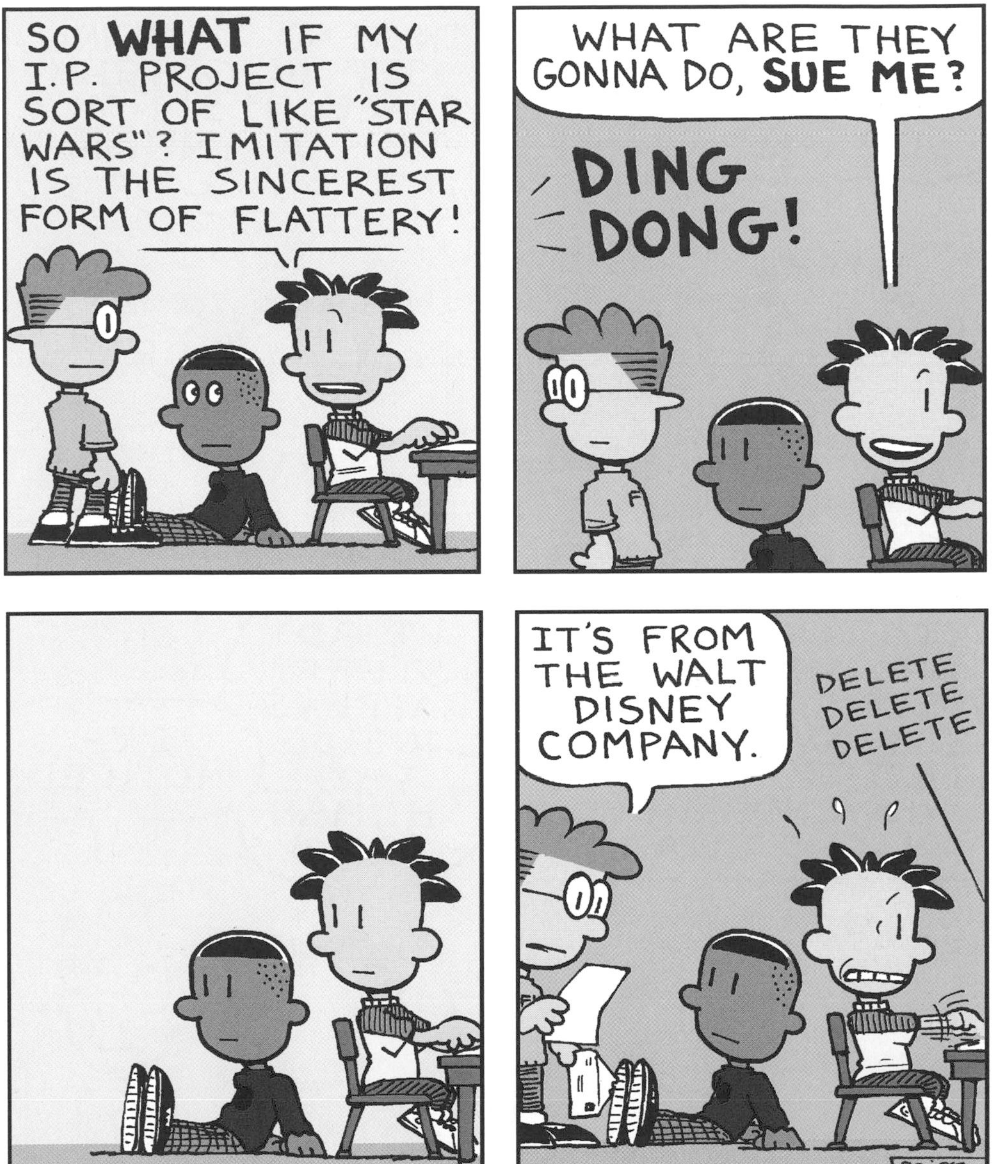
SO **WHAT** IF MY I.P. PROJECT IS SORT OF LIKE "STAR WARS"? IMITATION IS THE SINCEREST FORM OF FLATTERY!
WHAT ARE THEY GONNA DO, **SUE ME**?
DING DONG!
IT'S FROM THE WALT DISNEY COMPANY.
DELETE
DELETE
DELETE
PEIRCE

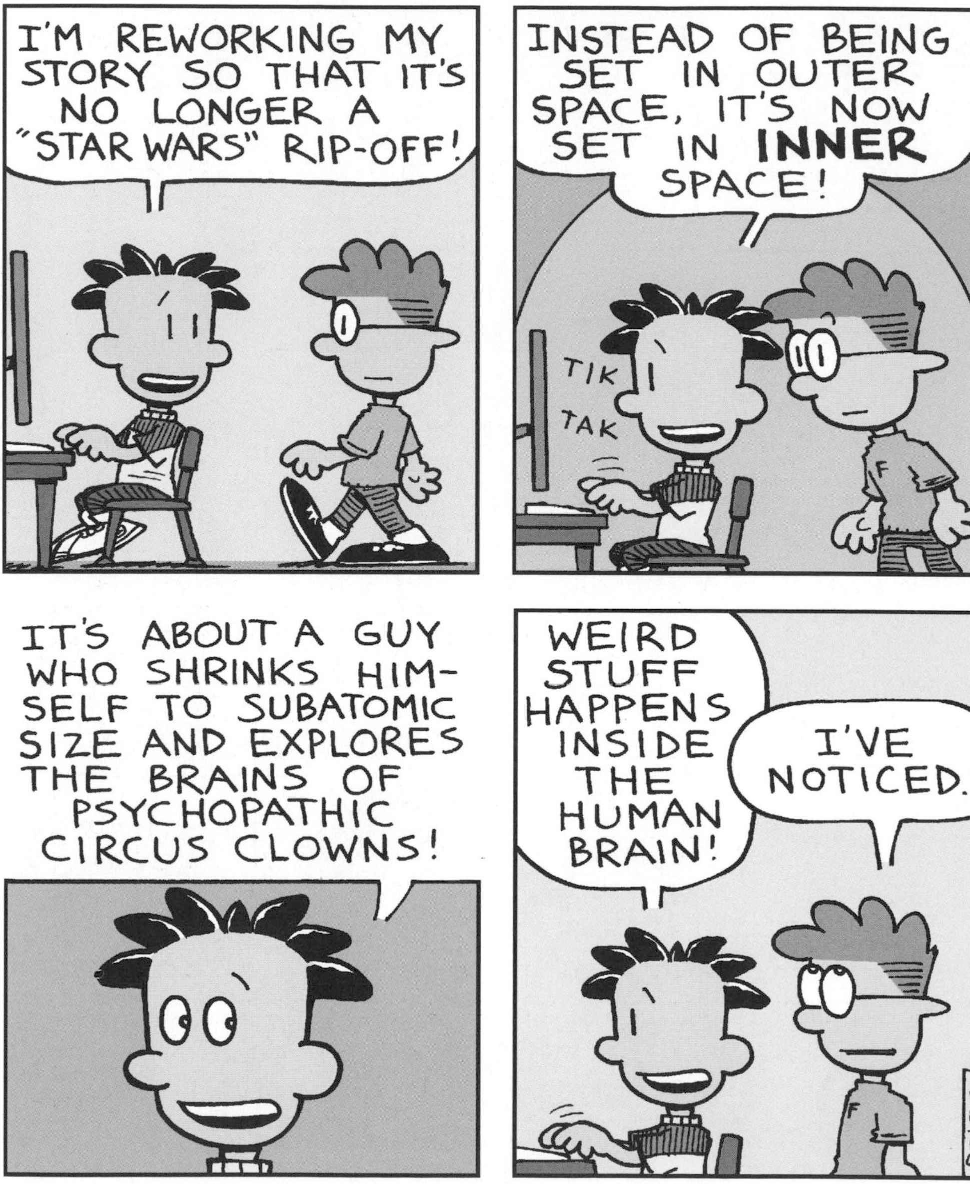
I'M REWORKING MY STORY SO THAT IT'S NO LONGER A "STAR WARS" RIP-OFF!
INSTEAD OF BEING SET IN OUTER SPACE, IT'S NOW SET IN INNER SPACE!
TIK
TAK
IT'S ABOUT A GUY WHO SHRINKS HIM-SELF TO SUBATOMIC SIZE AND EXPLORES THE BRAINS OF PSYCHOPATHIC CIRCUS CLOWNS!
WEIRD STUFF HAPPENS INSIDE THE HUMAN BRAIN!
I'VE NOTICED.
Peirce

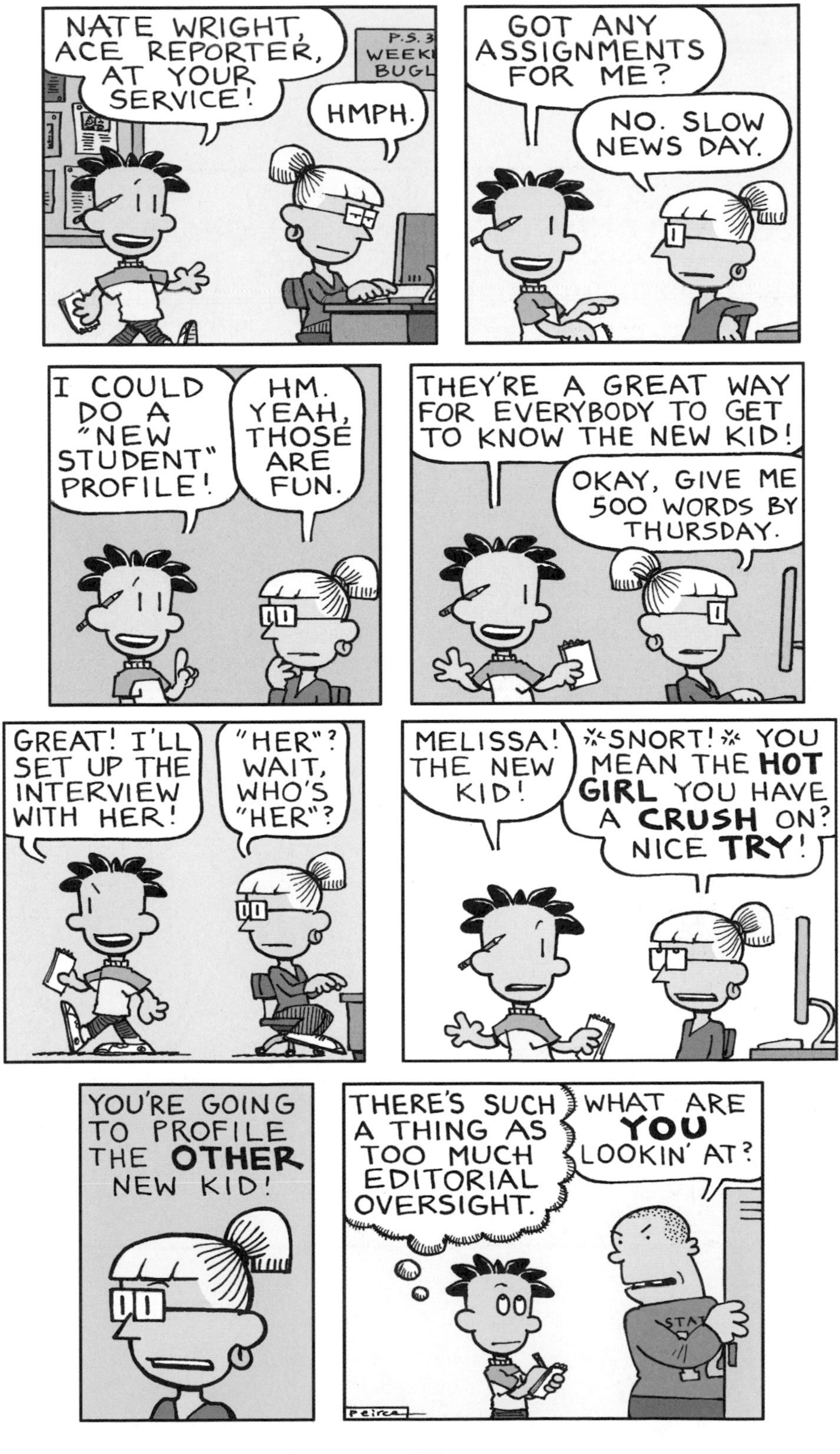
P.S. 3
WEEK
BUG
NATE WRIGHT, ACE REPORTER, AT YOUR SERVICE!
HMPH.
GOT ANY ASSIGNMENTS FOR ME?
NO. SLOW NEWS DAY.
I COULD DO A "NEW STUDENT" PROFILE!
HM. YEAH, THOSE ARE FUN.
THEY'RE A GREAT WAY FOR EVERYBODY TO GET TO KNOW THE NEW KID!
OKAY, GIVE ME 500 WORDS BY THURSDAY.
GREAT! I'LL SET UP THE INTERVIEW WITH HER!
"HER"? WAIT, WHO'S "HER"?
MELISSA! THE NEW KID!
SNORT! YOU MEAN THE **HOT GIRL** YOU HAVE A **CRUSH** ON? NICE **TRY**!
YOU'RE GOING TO PROFILE THE **OTHER** NEW KID!
THERE'S SUCH A THING AS TOO MUCH EDITORIAL OVERSIGHT.
WHAT ARE **YOU** LOOKIN' AT?
STAT
peirce

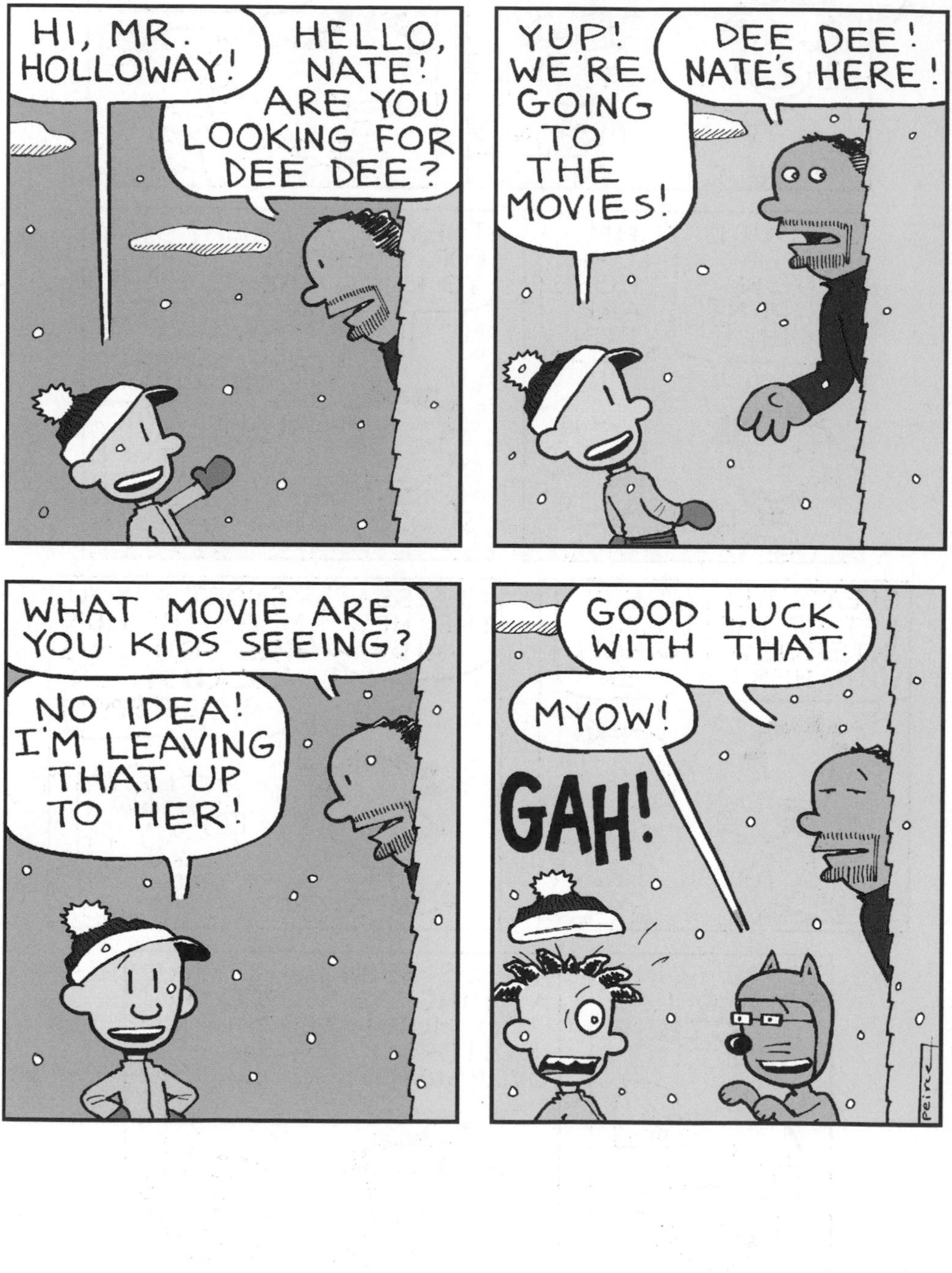
HI, MR. HOLLOWAY!
HELLO, NATE! ARE YOU LOOKING FOR DEE DEE?
YUP! WE'RE GOING TO THE MOVIES!
DEE DEE! NATE'S HERE!
WHAT MOVIE ARE YOU KIDS SEEING?
NO IDEA! I'M LEAVING THAT UP TO HER!
GOOD LUCK WITH THAT.
MYOW!
GAH!
peirce

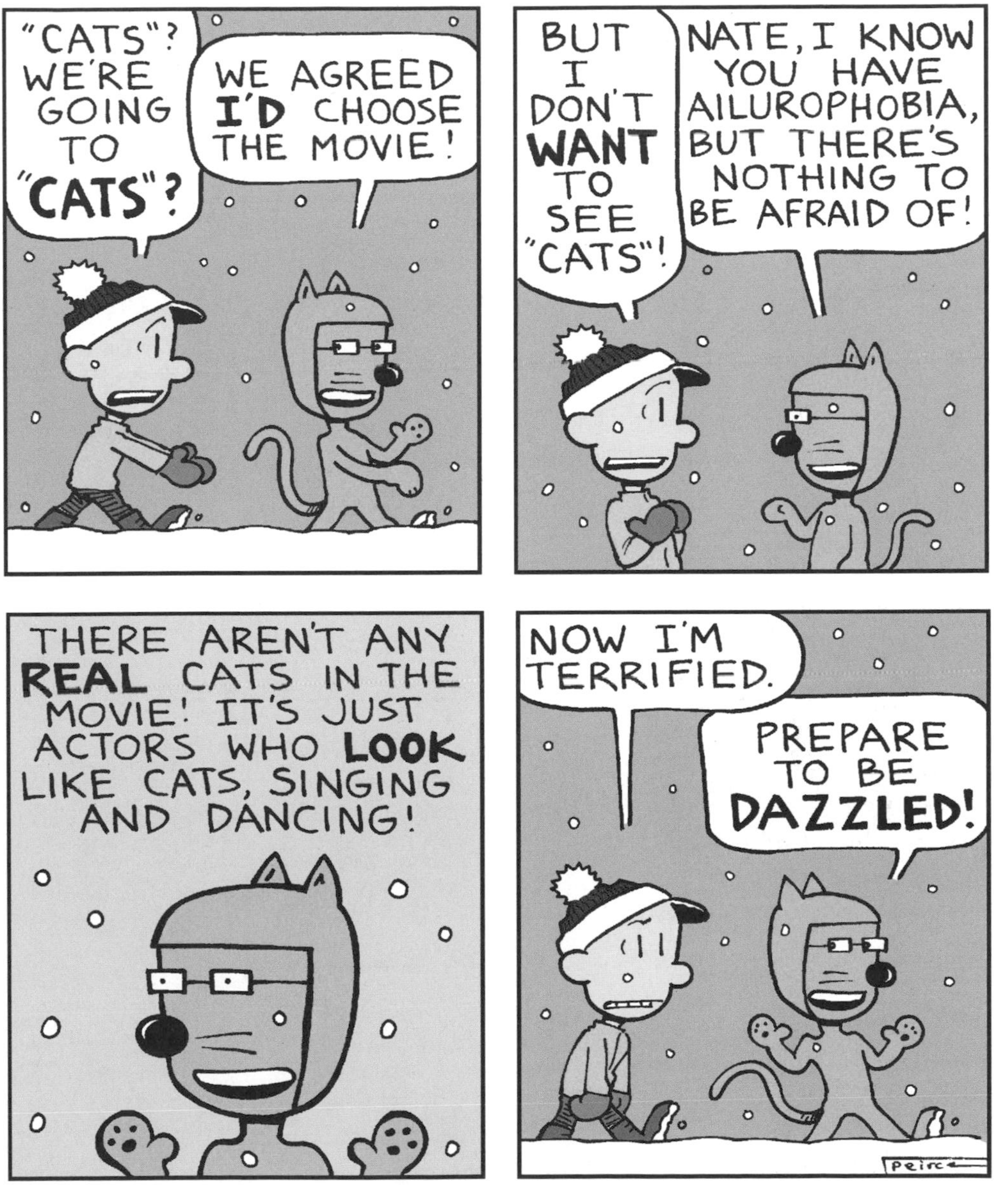
"CATS"? WE'RE GOING TO "CATS"?
WE AGREED I'D CHOOSE THE MOVIE!
BUT I DON'T WANT TO SEE "CATS"!
NATE, I KNOW YOU HAVE AILUROPHOBIA, BUT THERE'S NOTHING TO BE AFRAID OF!
THERE AREN'T ANY REAL CATS IN THE MOVIE! IT'S JUST ACTORS WHO LOOK LIKE CATS, SINGING AND DANCING!
NOW I'M TERRIFIED.
PREPARE TO BE DAZZLED!
Peirce

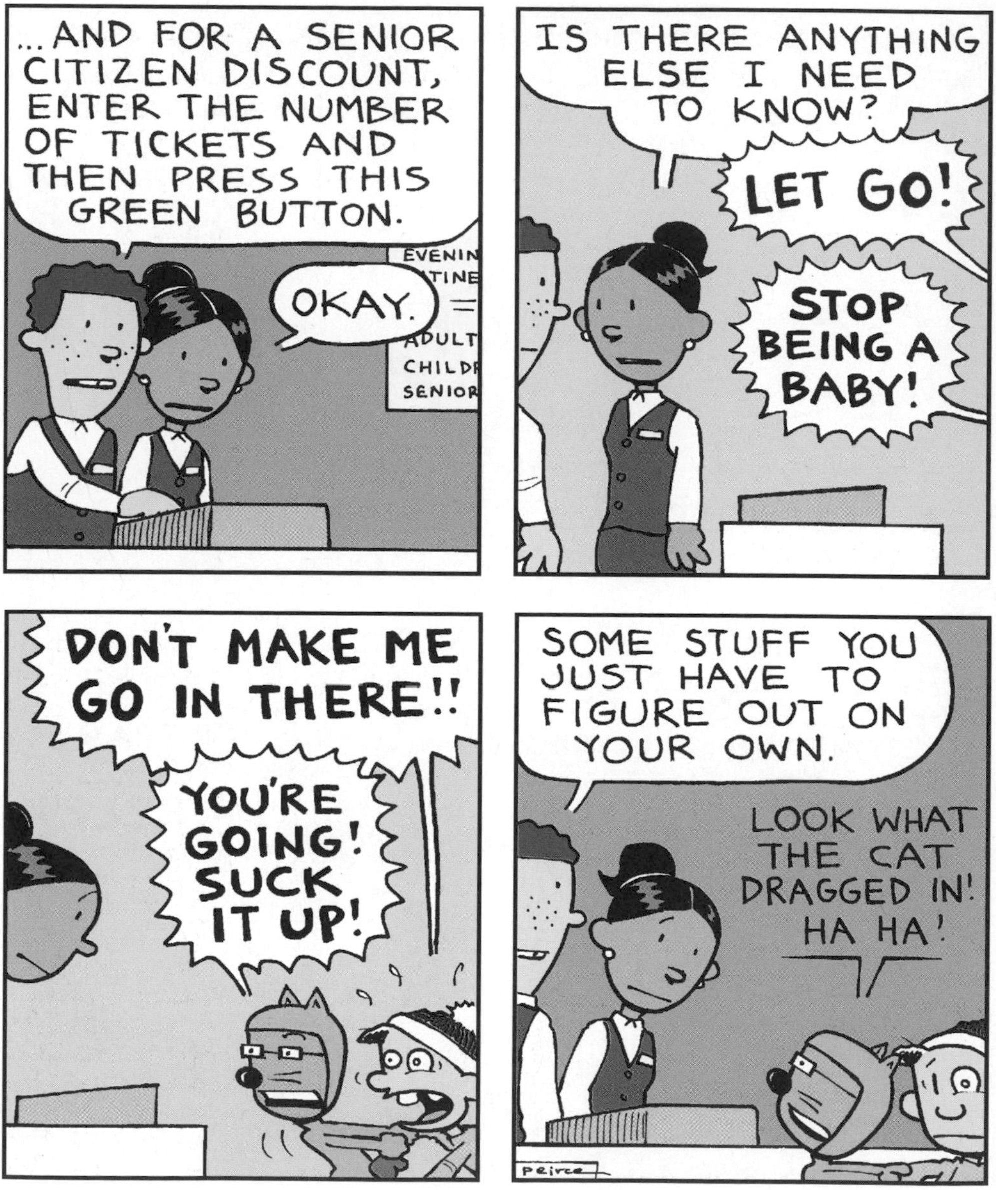
...AND FOR A SENIOR CITIZEN DISCOUNT, ENTER THE NUMBER OF TICKETS AND THEN PRESS THIS GREEN BUTTON.
OKAY.
EVENIN
ADULT
CHILDR
SENIOR
IS THERE ANYTHING ELSE I NEED TO KNOW?
LET GO!
STOP BEING A BABY!
DON'T MAKE ME GO IN THERE!!
YOU'RE GOING! SUCK IT UP!
SOME STUFF YOU JUST HAVE TO FIGURE OUT ON YOUR OWN.
LOOK WHAT THE CAT DRAGGED IN! HA HA!
Peirce

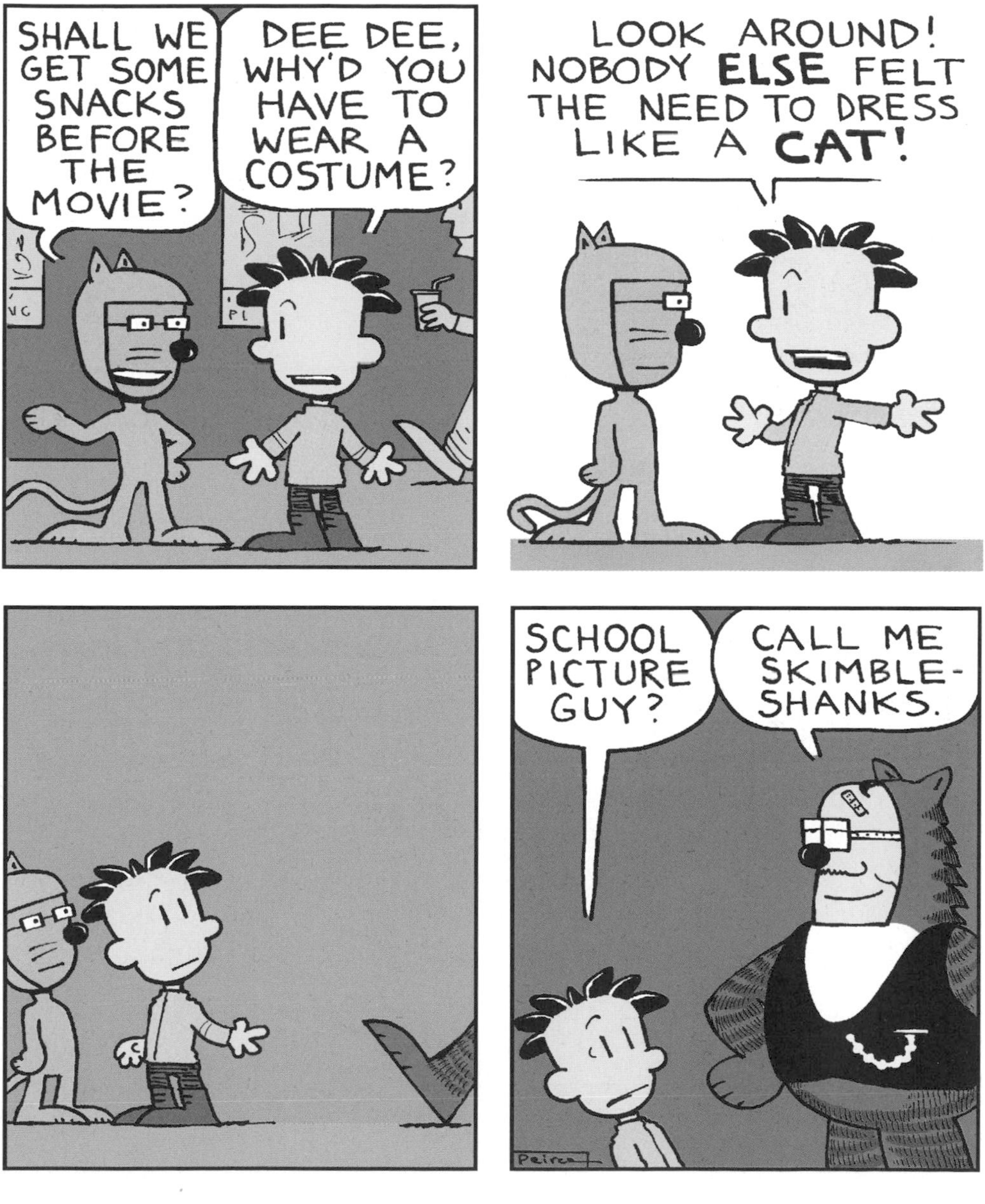
SHALL WE GET SOME SNACKS BEFORE THE MOVIE?
DEE DEE, WHY'D YOU HAVE TO WEAR A COSTUME?
LOOK AROUND! NOBODY **ELSE** FELT THE NEED TO DRESS LIKE A **CAT**!
SCHOOL PICTURE GUY?
CALL ME SKIMBLE-SHANKS.
Peirce

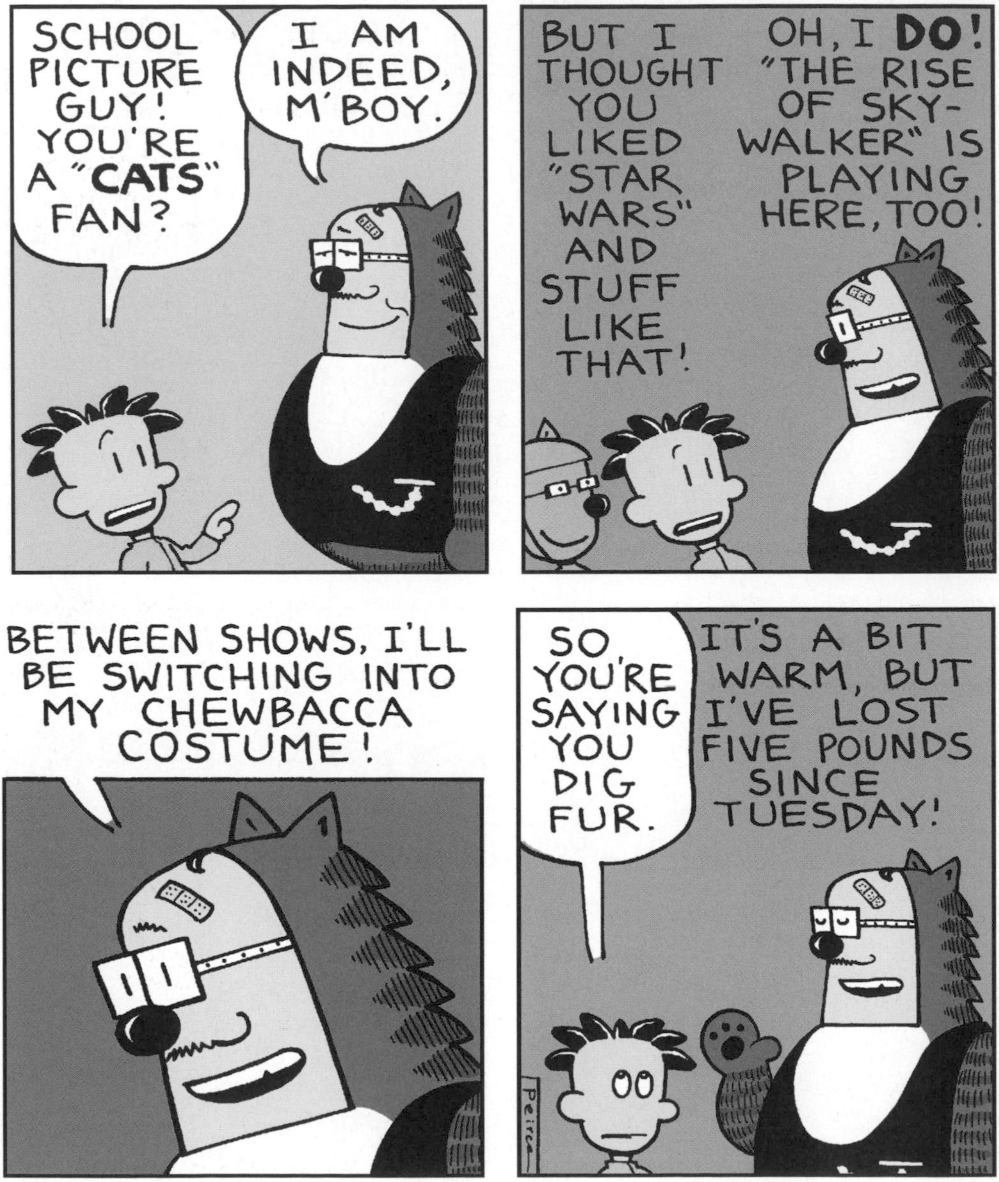
SCHOOL PICTURE GUY! YOU'RE A "CATS" FAN?
I AM INDEED, M'BOY.
BUT I THOUGHT YOU LIKED "STAR WARS" AND STUFF LIKE THAT!
OH, I DO! "THE RISE OF SKY-WALKER" IS PLAYING HERE, TOO!
BETWEEN SHOWS, I'LL BE SWITCHING INTO MY CHEWBACCA COSTUME!
SO YOU'RE SAYING YOU DIG FUR.
IT'S A BIT WARM, BUT I'VE LOST FIVE POUNDS SINCE TUESDAY!
Peirce

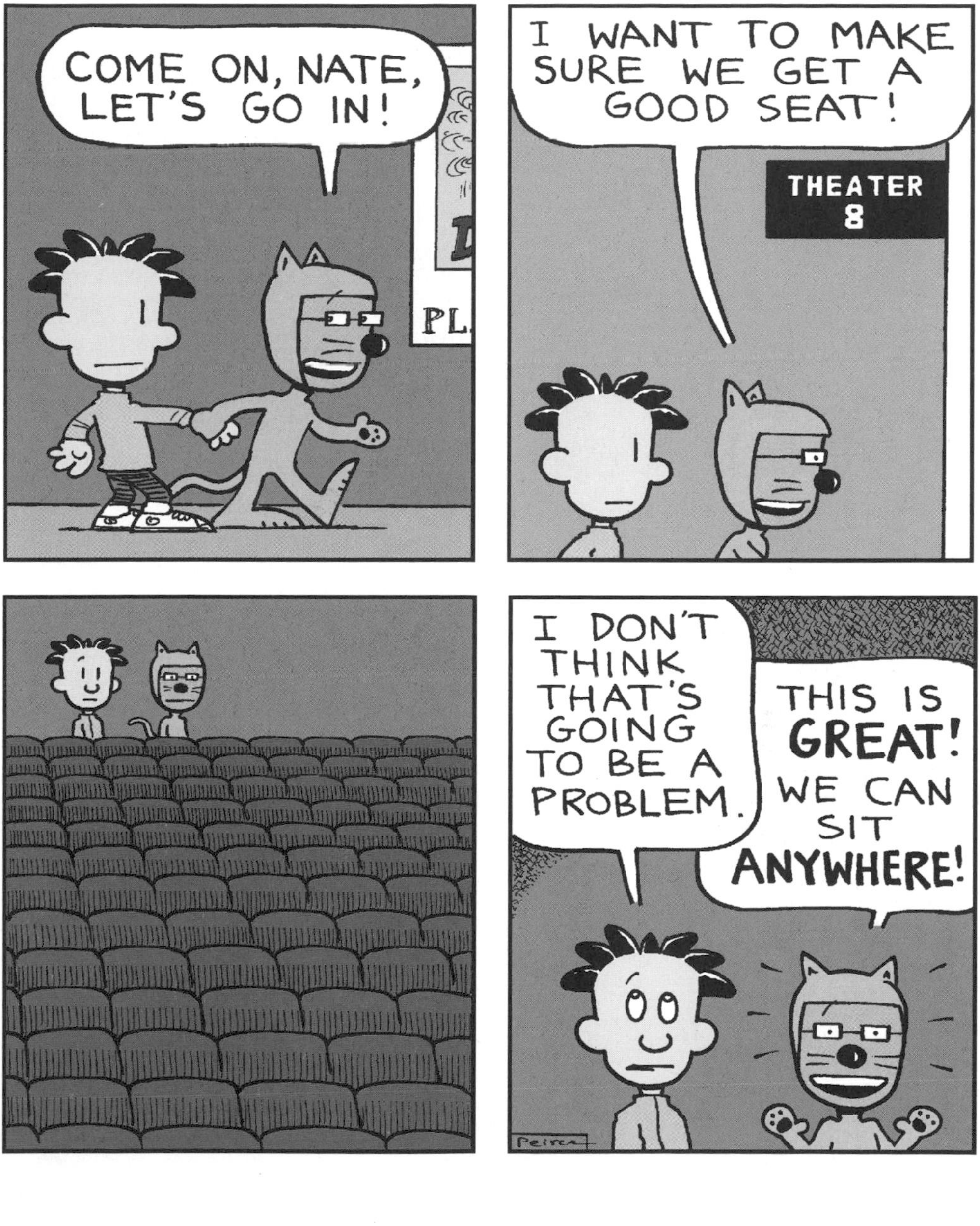
COME ON, NATE, LET'S GO IN!
PL.
I WANT TO MAKE SURE WE GET A GOOD SEAT!
THEATER 8
I DON'T THINK THAT'S GOING TO BE A PROBLEM.
THIS IS **GREAT!** WE CAN SIT **ANYWHERE!**
Peirce

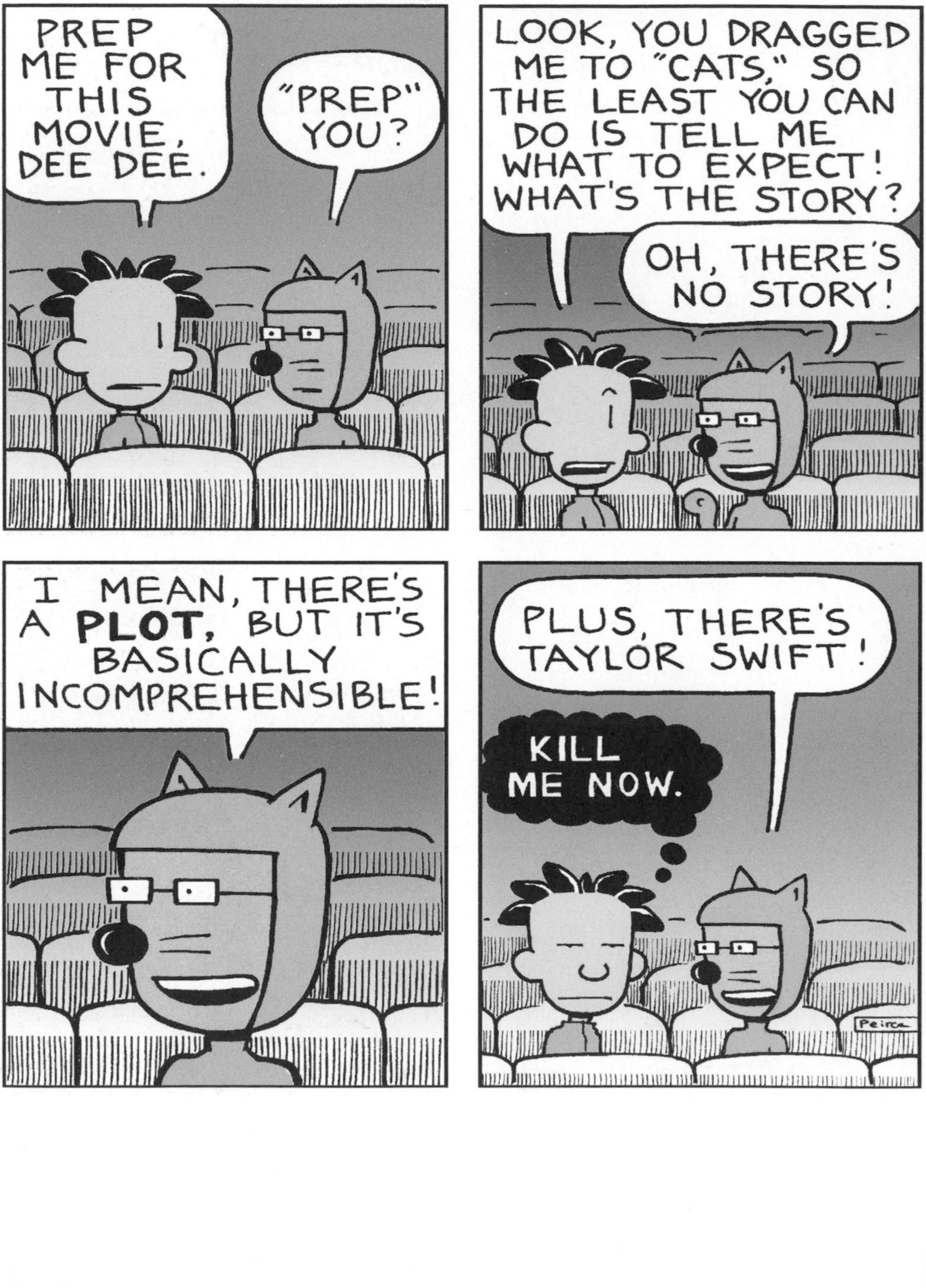
PREP ME FOR THIS MOVIE, DEE DEE.
"PREP" YOU?
LOOK, YOU DRAGGED ME TO "CATS," SO THE LEAST YOU CAN DO IS TELL ME WHAT TO EXPECT! WHAT'S THE STORY?
OH, THERE'S NO STORY!
I MEAN, THERE'S A **PLOT,** BUT IT'S BASICALLY INCOMPREHENSIBLE!
PLUS, THERE'S TAYLOR SWIFT!
KILL ME NOW.
Peirce

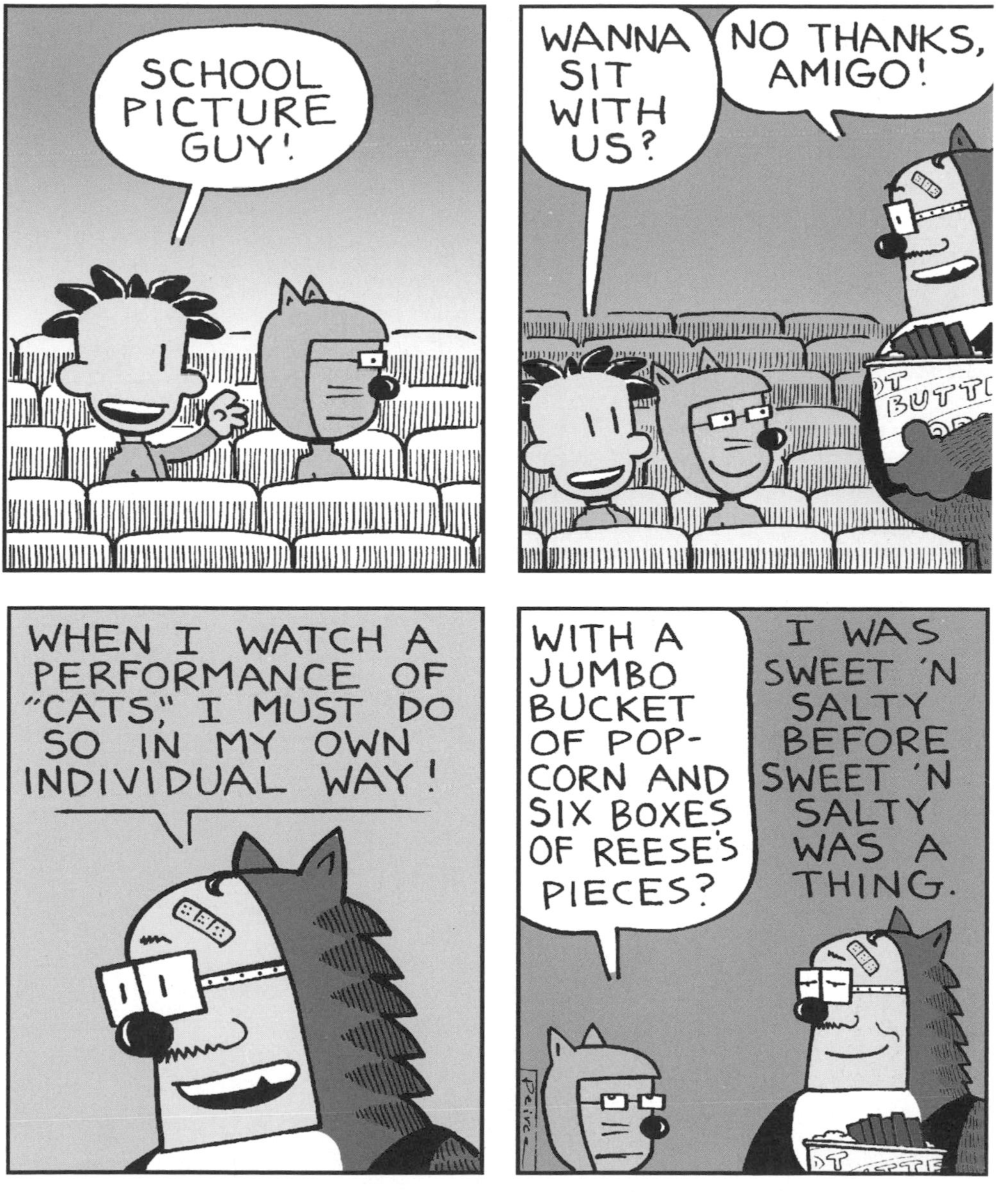
SCHOOL PICTURE GUY!
WANNA SIT WITH US?
NO THANKS, AMIGO!
WHEN I WATCH A PERFORMANCE OF "CATS," I MUST DO SO IN MY OWN INDIVIDUAL WAY!
WITH A JUMBO BUCKET OF POP-CORN AND SIX BOXES OF REESE'S PIECES?
I WAS SWEET 'N SALTY BEFORE SWEET 'N SALTY WAS A THING.

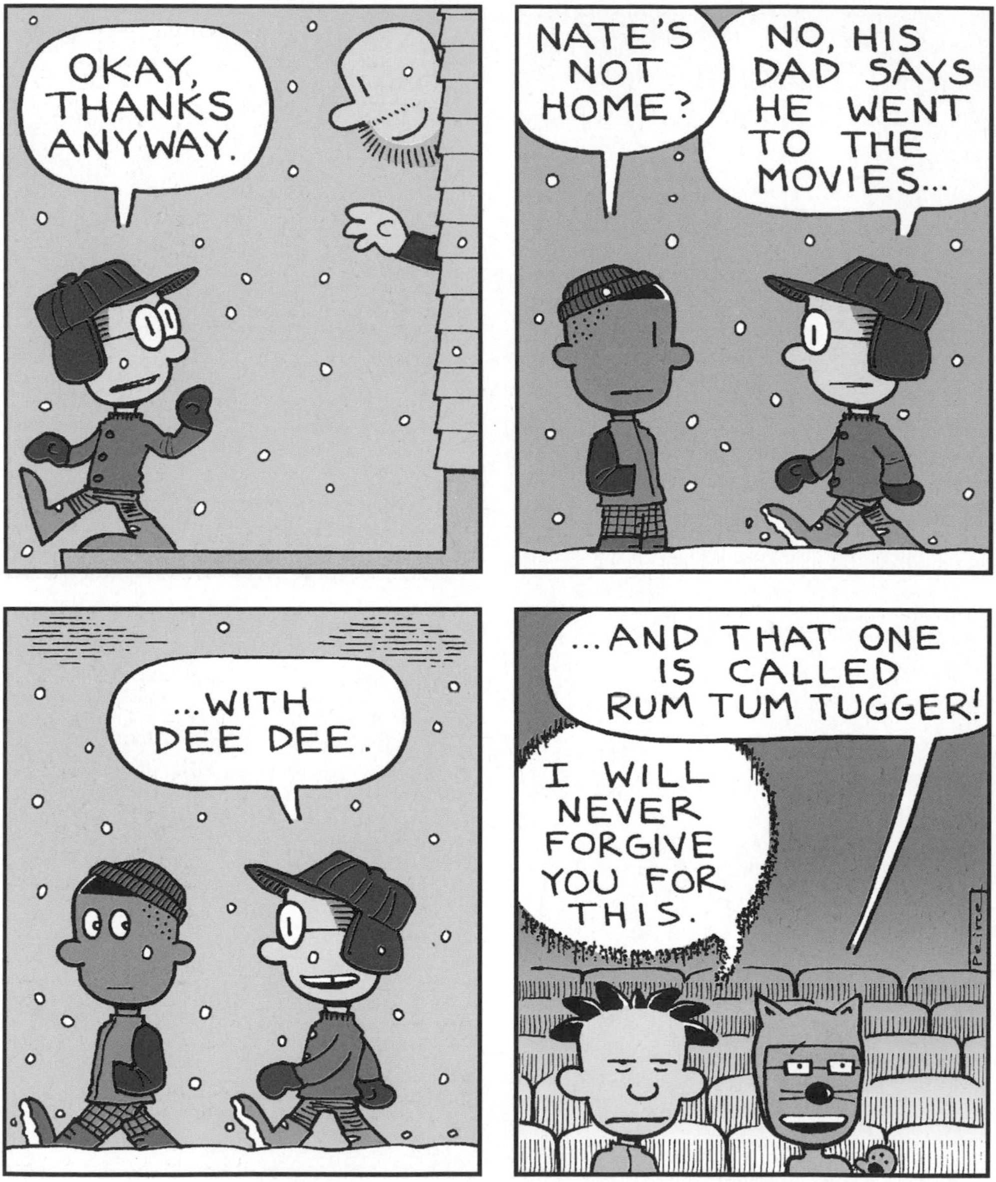
OKAY, THANKS ANYWAY.
NATE'S NOT HOME?
NO, HIS DAD SAYS HE WENT TO THE MOVIES...
...WITH DEE DEE.
...AND THAT ONE IS CALLED RUM TUM TUGGER!
I WILL NEVER FORGIVE YOU FOR THIS.
Peirce

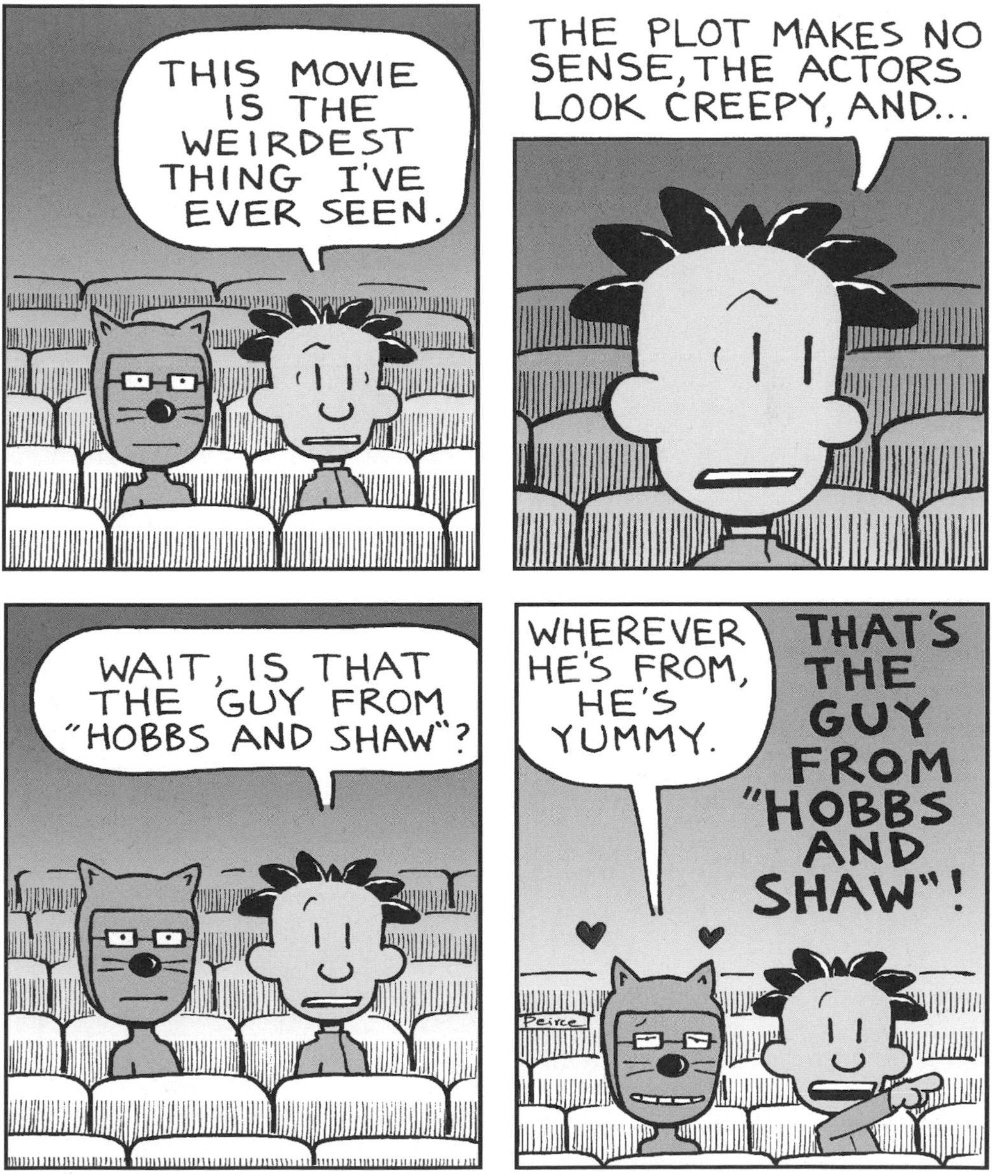
THIS MOVIE IS THE WEIRDEST THING I'VE EVER SEEN.
THE PLOT MAKES NO SENSE, THE ACTORS LOOK CREEPY, AND...
WAIT, IS THAT THE GUY FROM "HOBBS AND SHAW"?
WHEREVER HE'S FROM, HE'S YUMMY.
THAT'S THE GUY FROM "HOBBS AND SHAW"!
Peirce

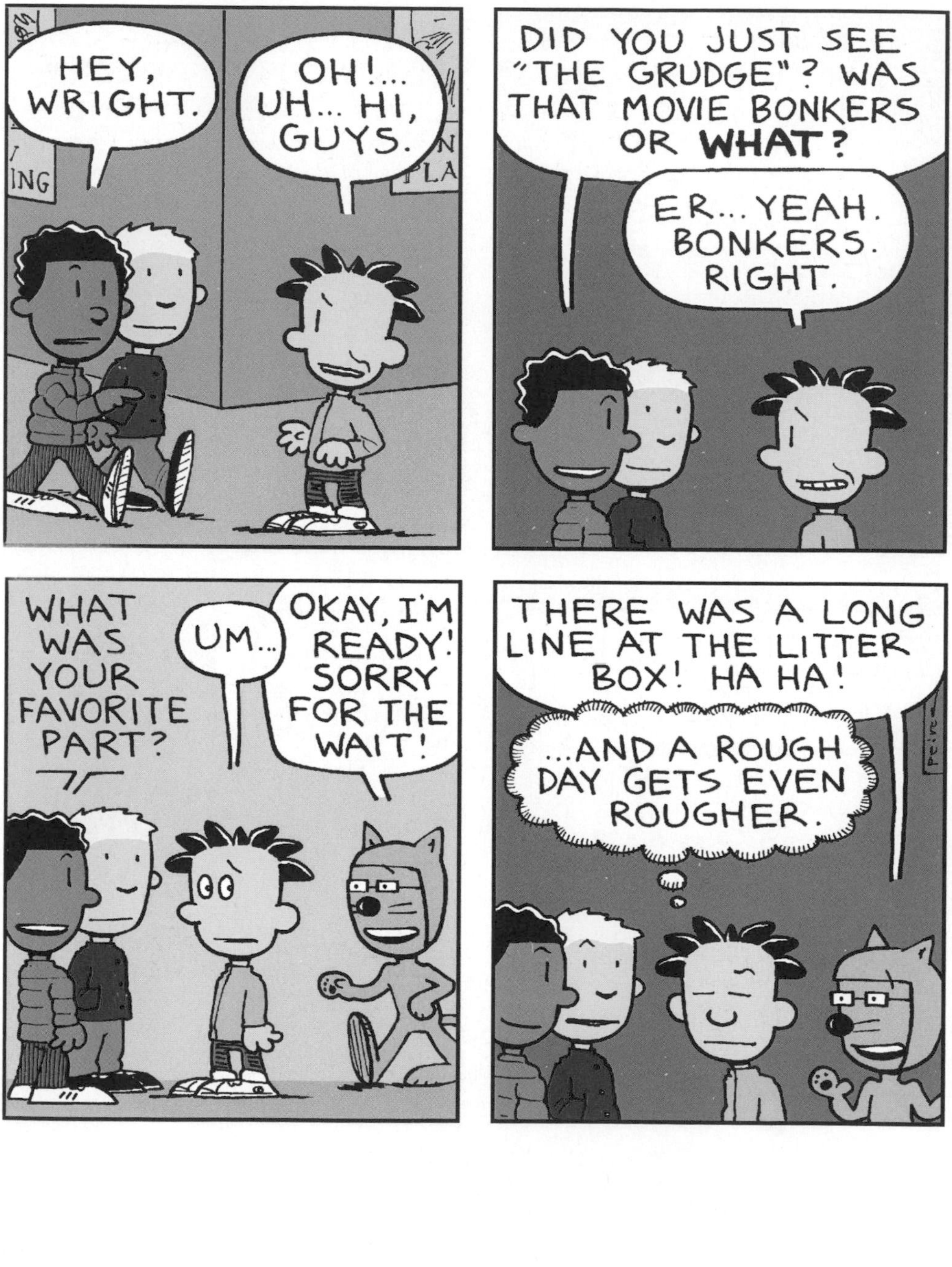
HEY, WRIGHT.
OH!... UH... HI, GUYS.
DID YOU JUST SEE "THE GRUDGE"? WAS THAT MOVIE BONKERS OR WHAT?
ER... YEAH. BONKERS. RIGHT.
WHAT WAS YOUR FAVORITE PART?
UM...
OKAY, I'M READY! SORRY FOR THE WAIT!
THERE WAS A LONG LINE AT THE LITTER BOX! HA HA!
...AND A ROUGH DAY GETS EVEN ROUGHER.

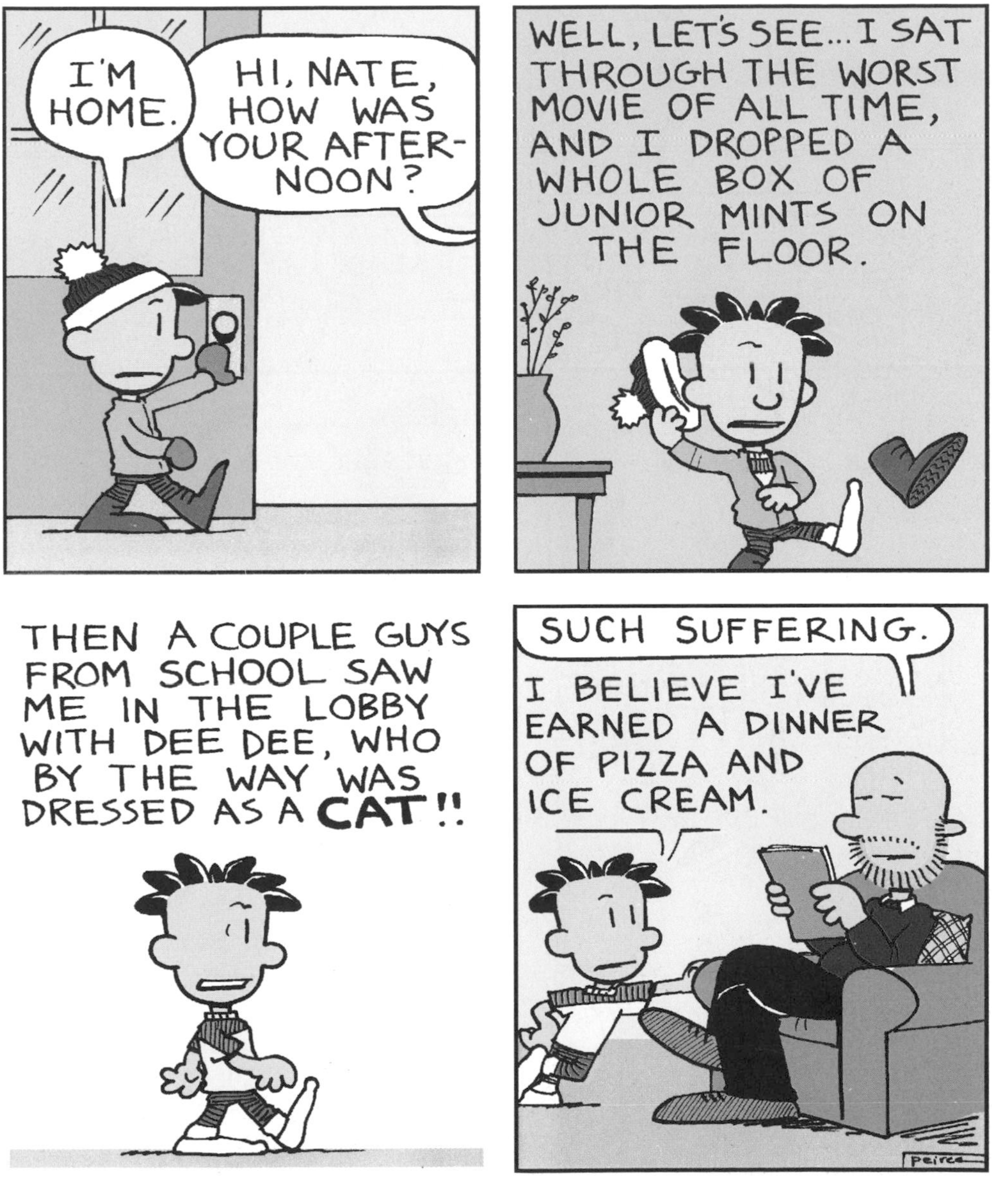
I'M HOME.
HI, NATE, HOW WAS YOUR AFTER-NOON?
WELL, LET'S SEE... I SAT THROUGH THE WORST MOVIE OF ALL TIME, AND I DROPPED A WHOLE BOX OF JUNIOR MINTS ON THE FLOOR.
THEN A COUPLE GUYS FROM SCHOOL SAW ME IN THE LOBBY WITH DEE DEE, WHO BY THE WAY WAS DRESSED AS A CAT!!
SUCH SUFFERING.
I BELIEVE I'VE EARNED A DINNER OF PIZZA AND ICE CREAM.
peirce

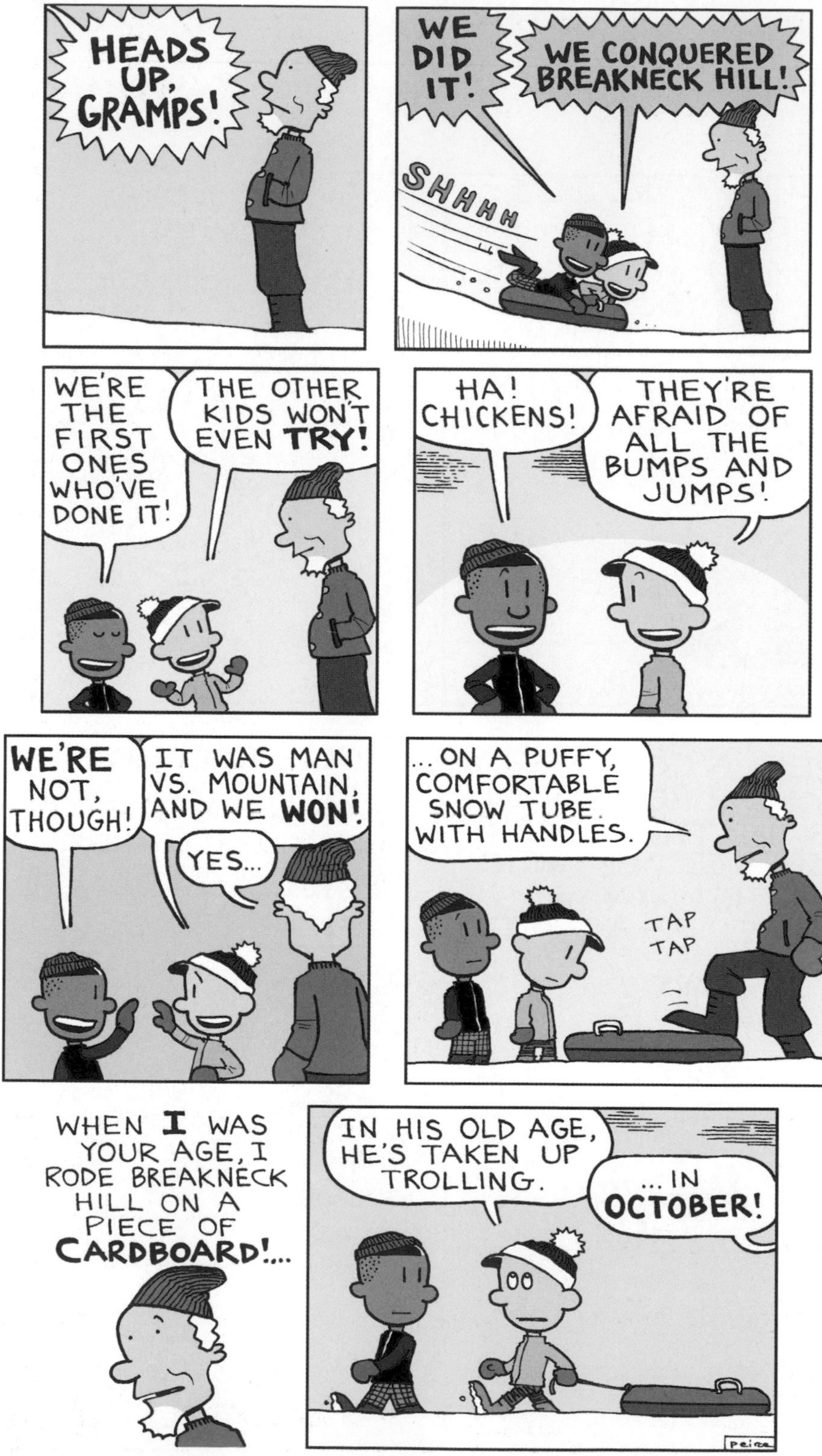

HEADS UP, GRAMPS!
WE DID IT!
WE CONQUERED BREAKNECK HILL!
SHHHH
WE'RE THE FIRST ONES WHO'VE DONE IT!
THE OTHER KIDS WON'T EVEN TRY!
HA! CHICKENS!
THEY'RE AFRAID OF ALL THE BUMPS AND JUMPS!
WE'RE NOT, THOUGH!
IT WAS MAN VS. MOUNTAIN, AND WE WON!
YES...
...ON A PUFFY, COMFORTABLE SNOW TUBE. WITH HANDLES.
TAP TAP
WHEN I WAS YOUR AGE, I RODE BREAKNECK HILL ON A PIECE OF CARDBOARD!...
IN HIS OLD AGE, HE'S TAKEN UP TROLLING.
...IN OCTOBER!
peirce

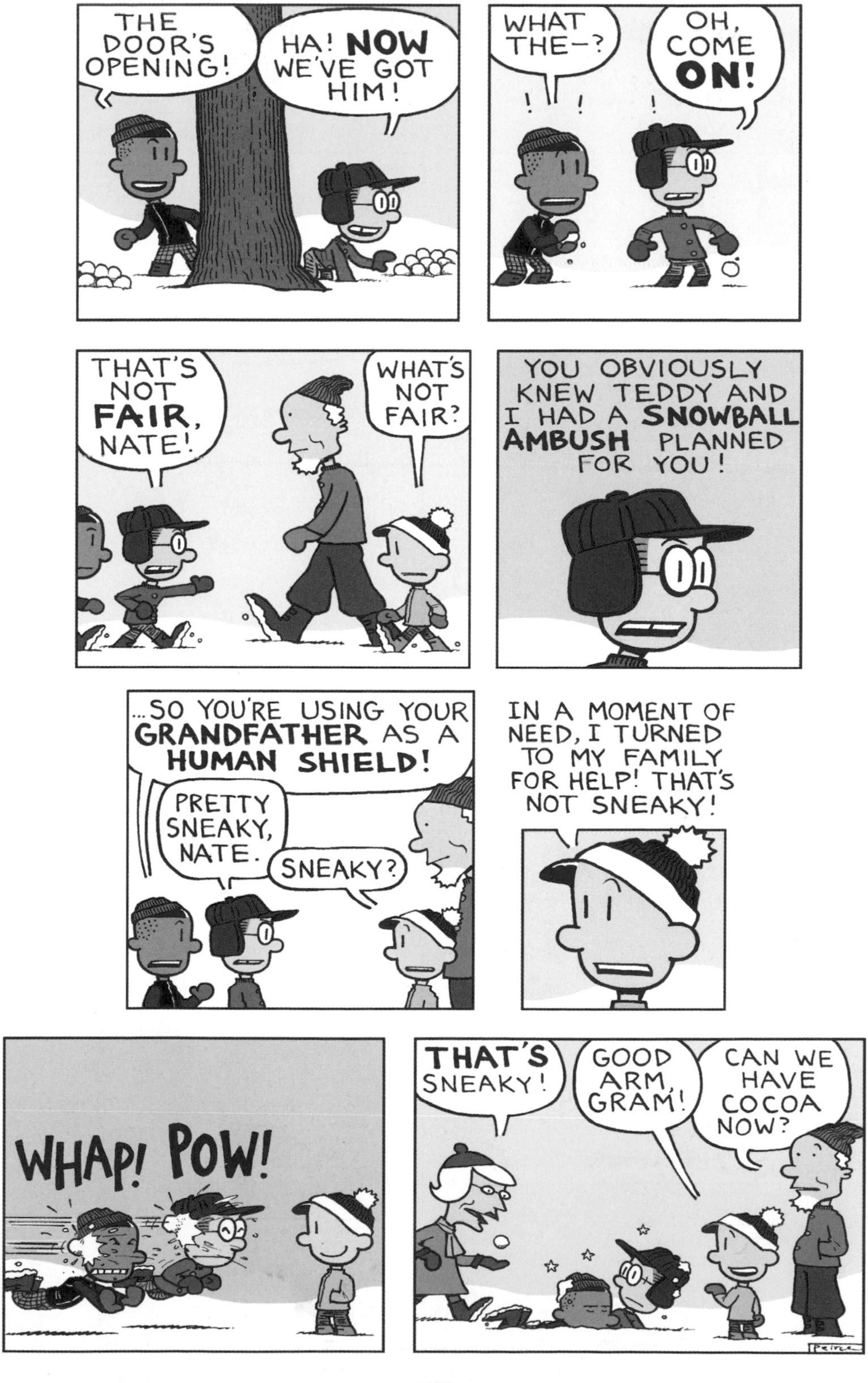
THE DOOR'S OPENING!
HA! NOW WE'VE GOT HIM!
WHAT THE—?
OH, COME ON!
THAT'S NOT FAIR, NATE!
WHAT'S NOT FAIR?
YOU OBVIOUSLY KNEW TEDDY AND I HAD A SNOWBALL AMBUSH PLANNED FOR YOU!
...SO YOU'RE USING YOUR GRANDFATHER AS A HUMAN SHIELD!
PRETTY SNEAKY, NATE.
SNEAKY?
IN A MOMENT OF NEED, I TURNED TO MY FAMILY FOR HELP! THAT'S NOT SNEAKY!
WHAP! POW!
THAT'S SNEAKY!
GOOD ARM, GRAM!
CAN WE HAVE COCOA NOW?
Peirce

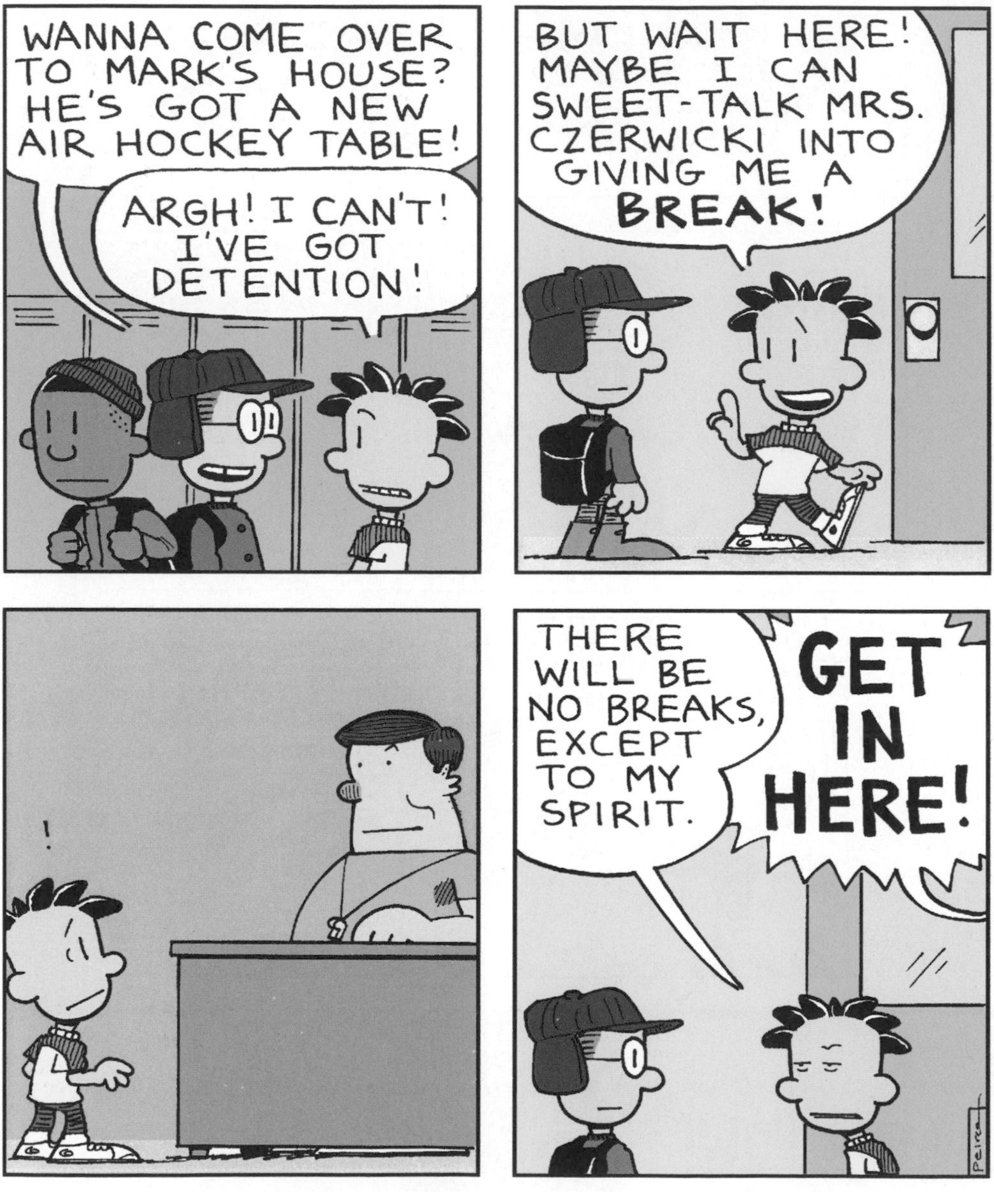
WANNA COME OVER TO MARK'S HOUSE? HE'S GOT A NEW AIR HOCKEY TABLE!
ARGH! I CAN'T! I'VE GOT DETENTION!
BUT WAIT HERE! MAYBE I CAN SWEET-TALK MRS. CZERWICKI INTO GIVING ME A **BREAK**!
!
THERE WILL BE NO BREAKS, EXCEPT TO MY SPIRIT.
GET IN HERE!
Peirce

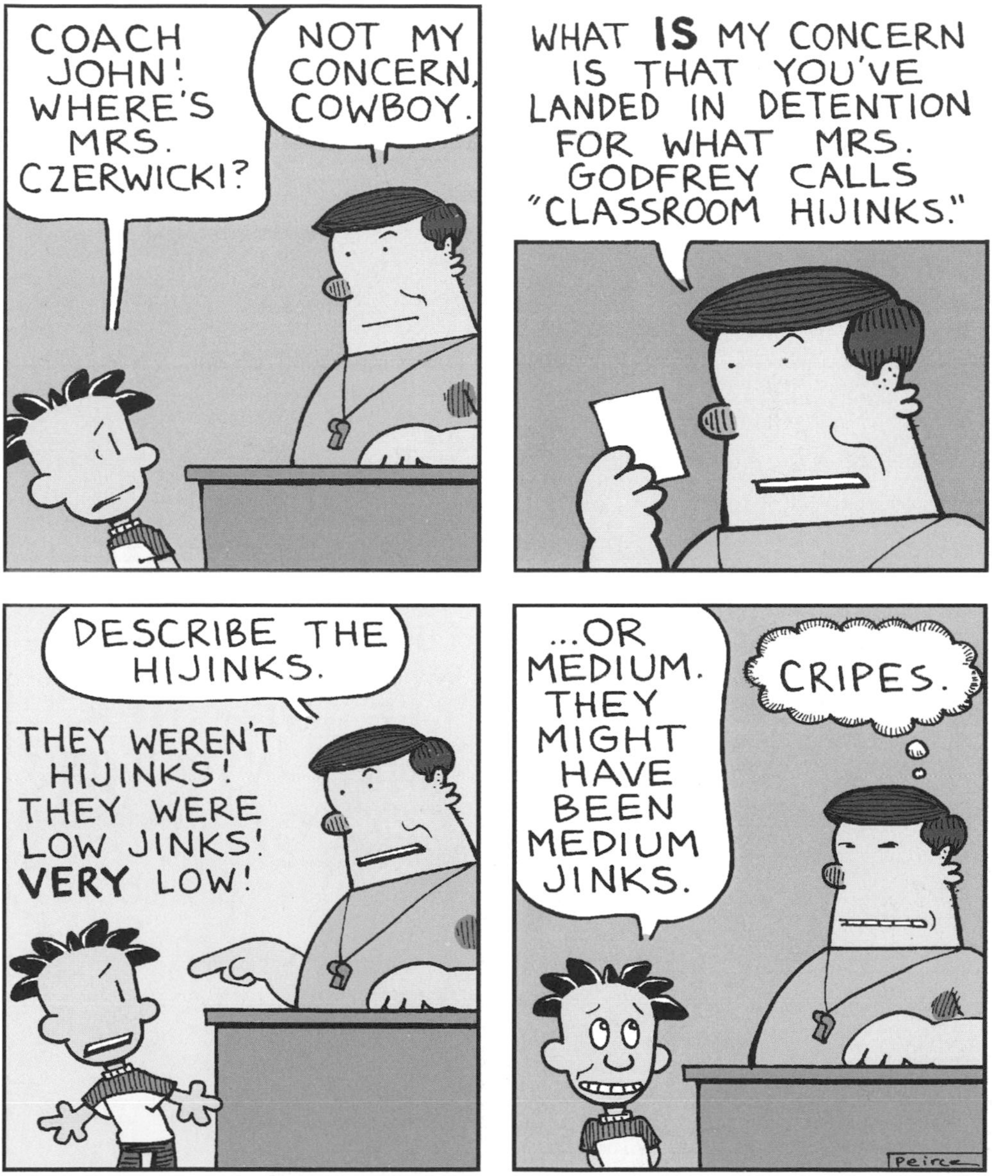
COACH JOHN! WHERE'S MRS. CZERWICKI?
NOT MY CONCERN, COWBOY.
WHAT **IS** MY CONCERN IS THAT YOU'VE LANDED IN DETENTION FOR WHAT MRS. GODFREY CALLS "CLASSROOM HIJINKS."
DESCRIBE THE HIJINKS.
THEY WEREN'T HIJINKS! THEY WERE LOW JINKS! **VERY** LOW!
...OR MEDIUM. THEY MIGHT HAVE BEEN MEDIUM JINKS.
CRIPES.
Peirce

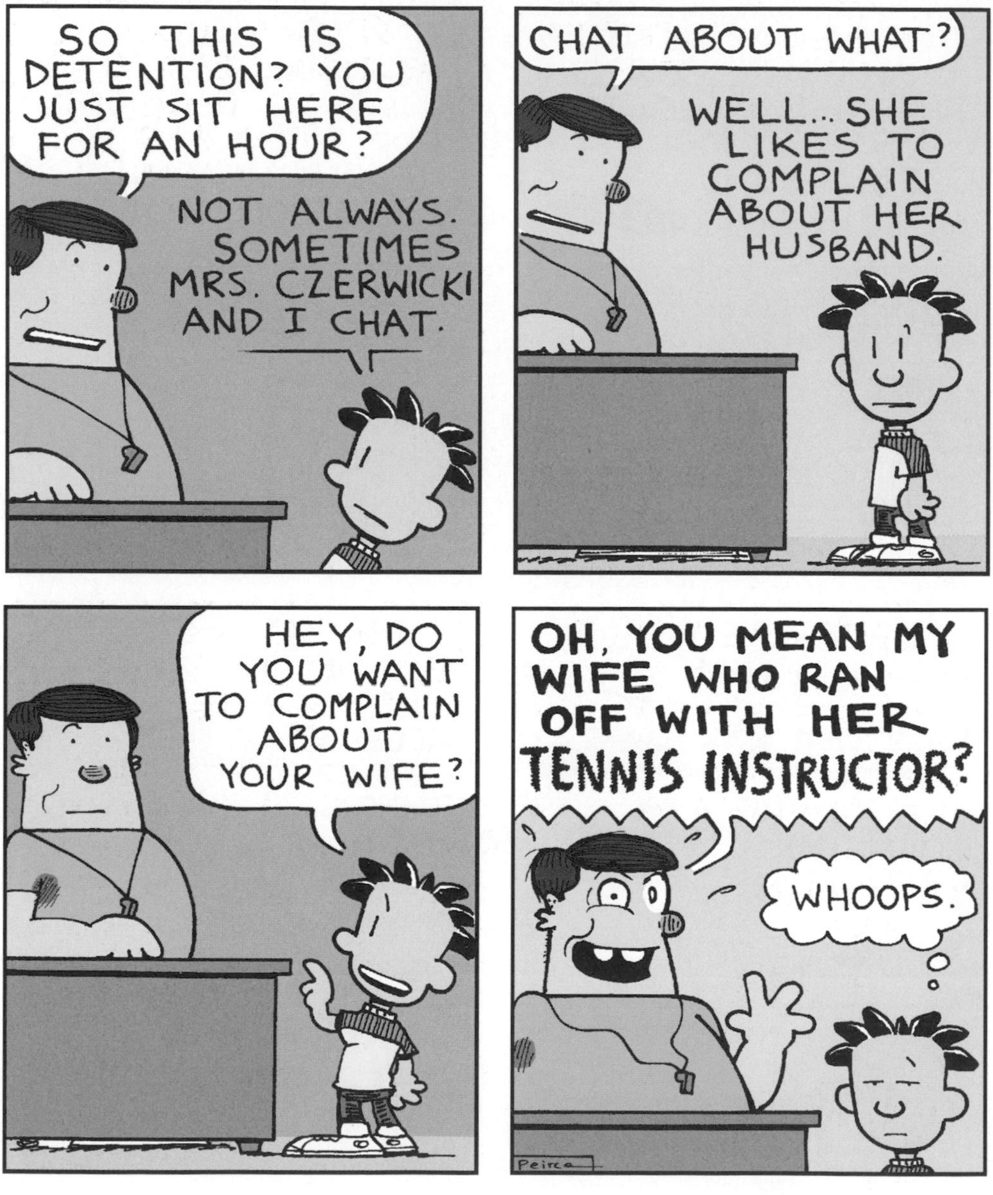
SO THIS IS DETENTION? YOU JUST SIT HERE FOR AN HOUR?
NOT ALWAYS. SOMETIMES MRS. CZERWICKI AND I CHAT.
CHAT ABOUT WHAT?
WELL... SHE LIKES TO COMPLAIN ABOUT HER HUSBAND.
HEY, DO YOU WANT TO COMPLAIN ABOUT YOUR WIFE?
OH, YOU MEAN MY WIFE WHO RAN OFF WITH HER TENNIS INSTRUCTOR?
WHOOPS.
Peirce

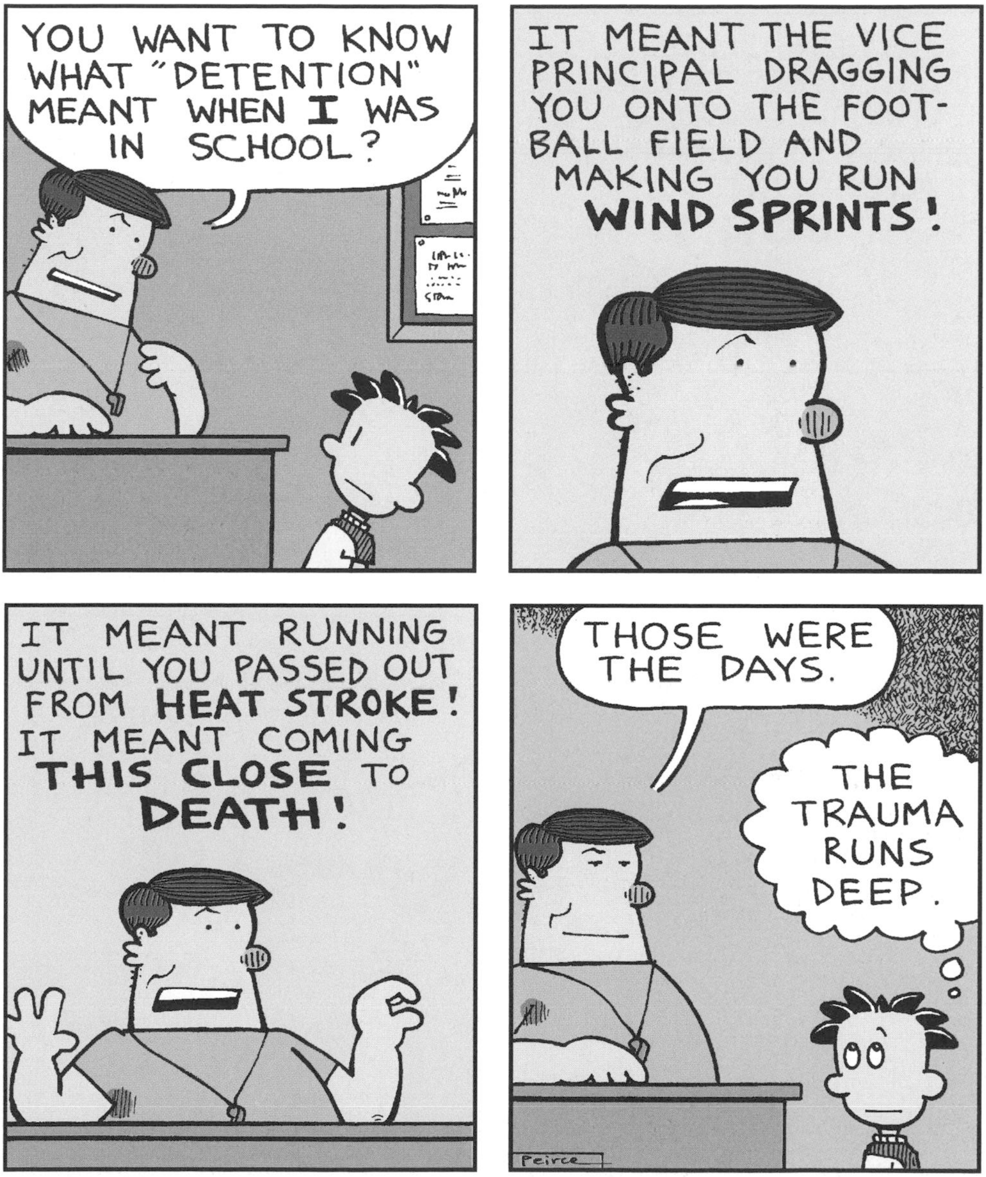
YOU WANT TO KNOW WHAT "DETENTION" MEANT WHEN I WAS IN SCHOOL?
IT MEANT THE VICE PRINCIPAL DRAGGING YOU ONTO THE FOOT-BALL FIELD AND MAKING YOU RUN WIND SPRINTS!
IT MEANT RUNNING UNTIL YOU PASSED OUT FROM HEAT STROKE! IT MEANT COMING THIS CLOSE TO DEATH!
THOSE WERE THE DAYS.
THE TRAUMA RUNS DEEP.
Peirce

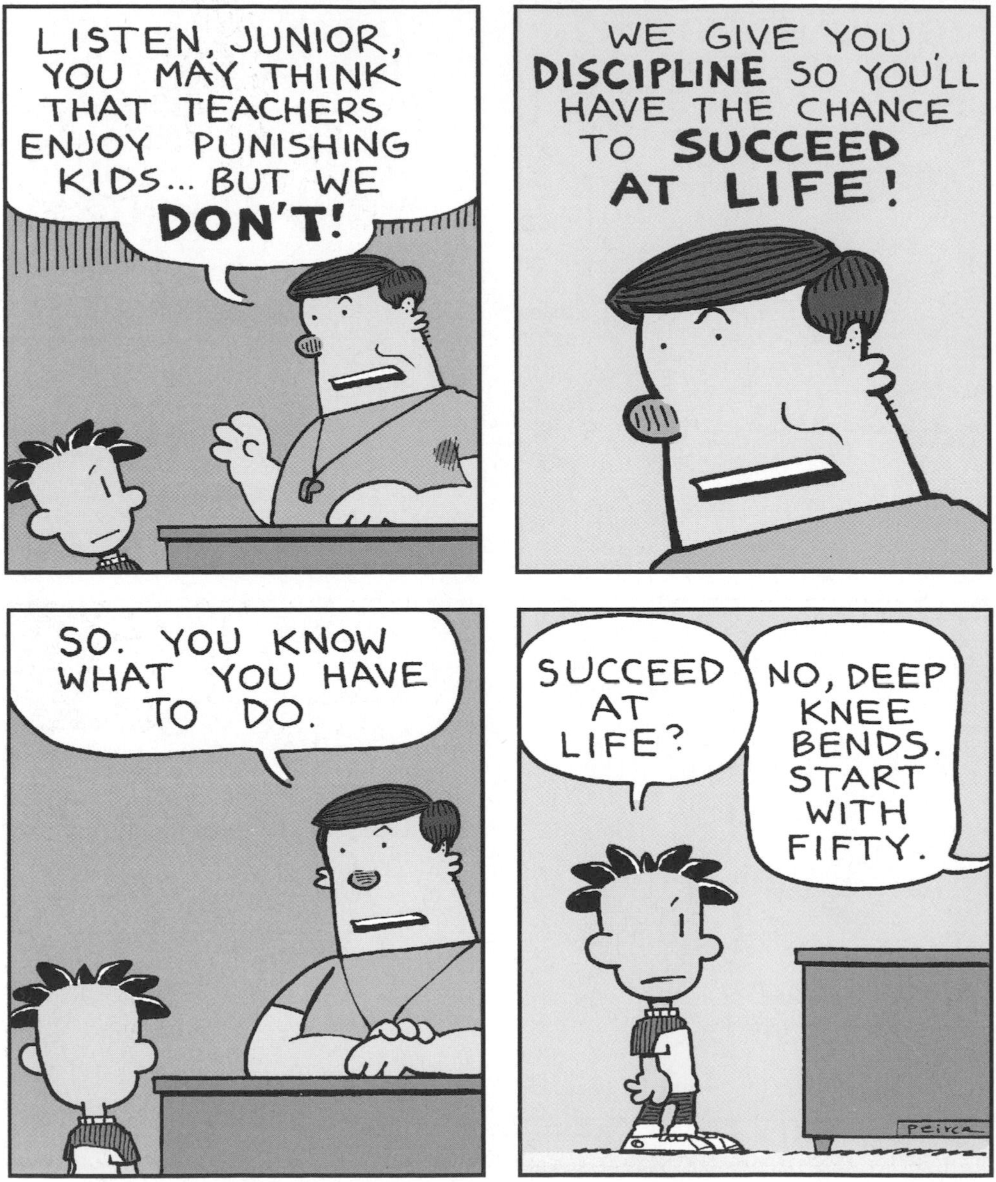
LISTEN, JUNIOR, YOU MAY THINK THAT TEACHERS ENJOY PUNISHING KIDS... BUT WE **DON'T!**
WE GIVE YOU **DISCIPLINE** SO YOU'LL HAVE THE CHANCE TO **SUCCEED AT LIFE!**
SO. YOU KNOW WHAT YOU HAVE TO DO.
SUCCEED AT LIFE?
NO, DEEP KNEE BENDS. START WITH FIFTY.
PEIRCE

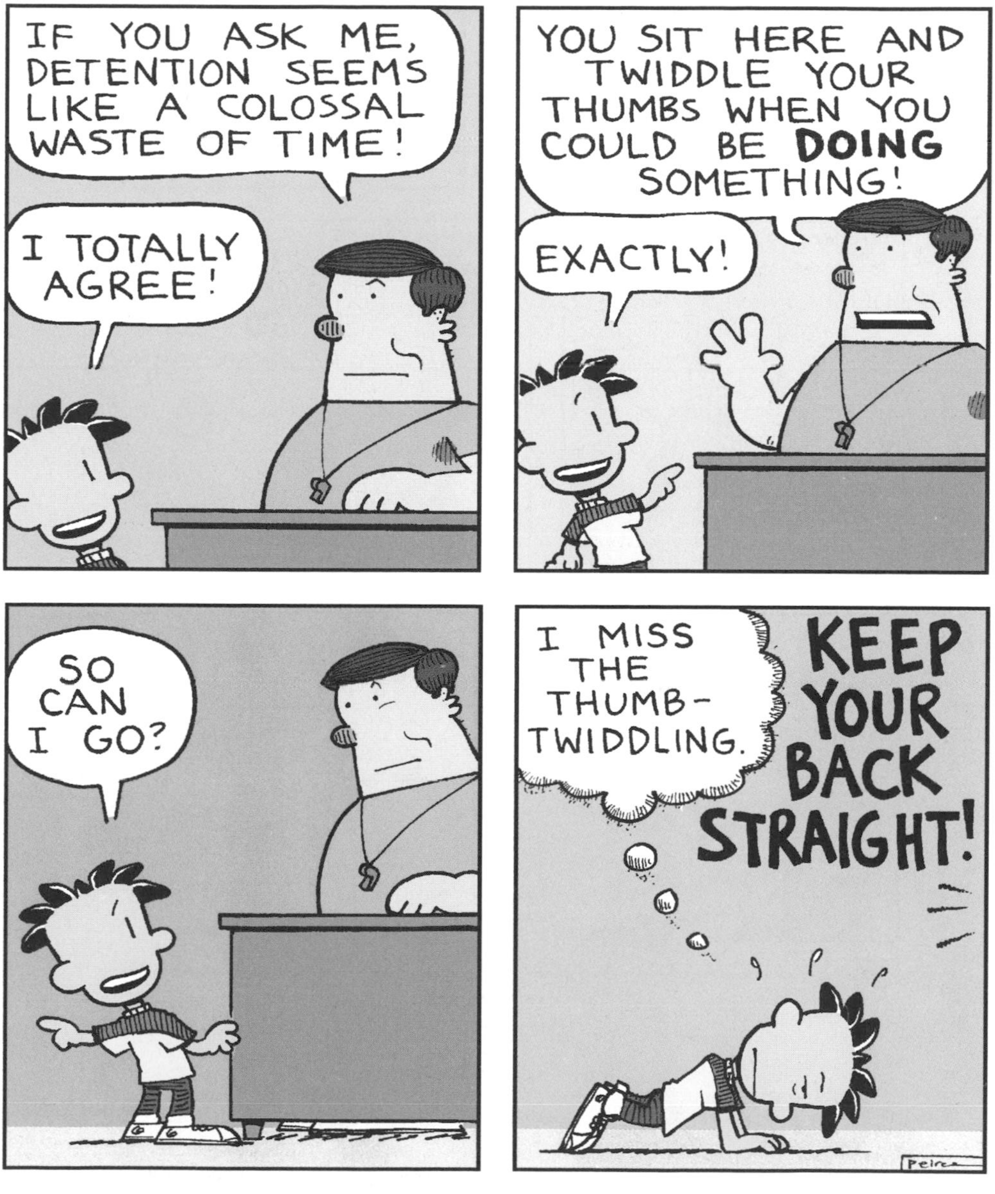
IF YOU ASK ME, DETENTION SEEMS LIKE A COLOSSAL WASTE OF TIME!
I TOTALLY AGREE!
YOU SIT HERE AND TWIDDLE YOUR THUMBS WHEN YOU COULD BE **DOING** SOMETHING!
EXACTLY!
SO CAN I GO?
I MISS THE THUMB-TWIDDLING.
KEEP YOUR BACK STRAIGHT!
Peirce

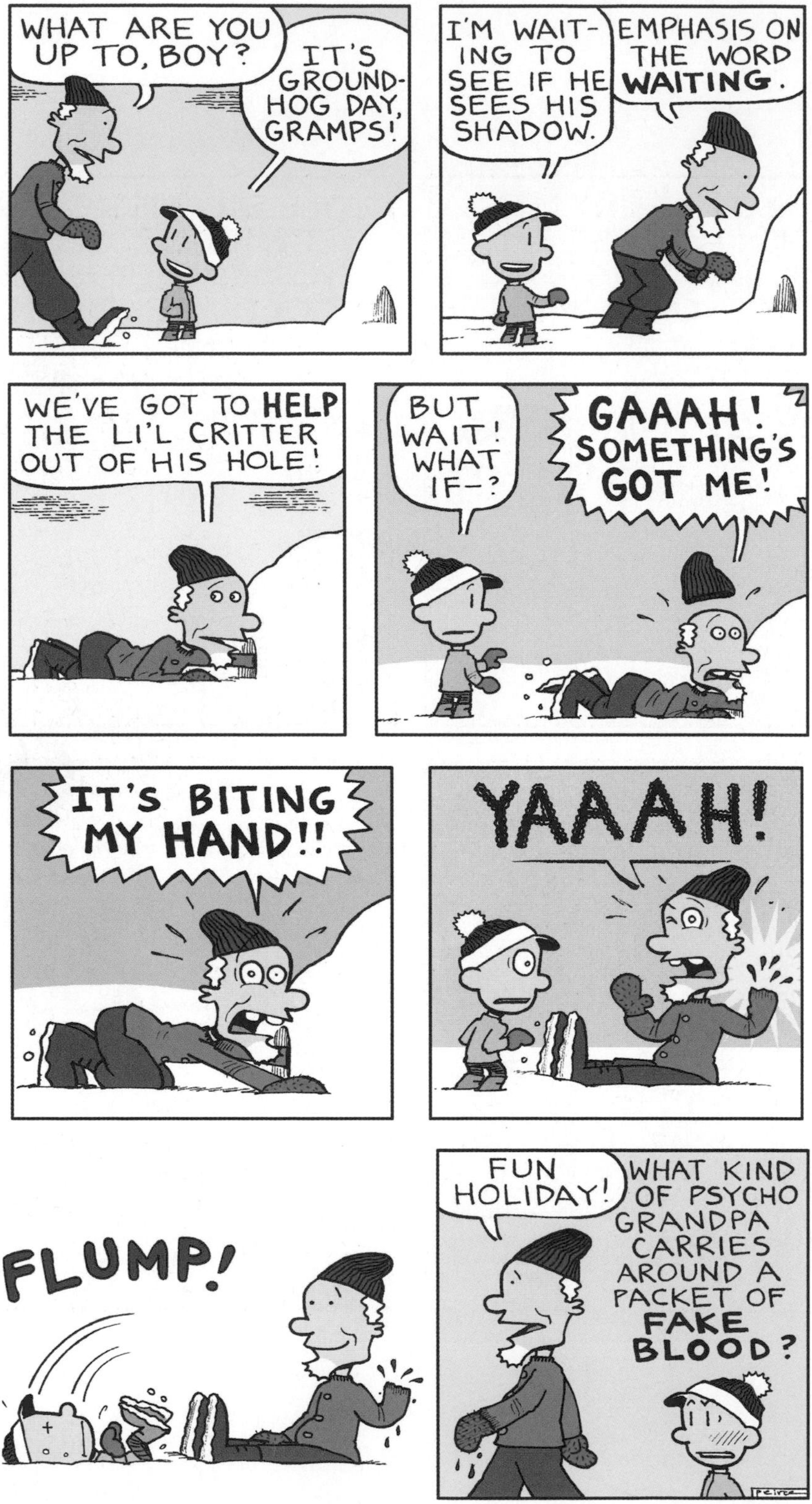
WHAT ARE YOU UP TO, BOY?
IT'S GROUND-HOG DAY, GRAMPS!
I'M WAIT-ING TO SEE IF HE SEES HIS SHADOW.
EMPHASIS ON THE WORD **WAITING**.
WE'VE GOT TO **HELP** THE LI'L CRITTER OUT OF HIS HOLE!
BUT WAIT! WHAT IF-?
GAAAH! SOMETHING'S GOT ME!
IT'S BITING MY **HAND**!!
YAAAH!
FLUMP!
FUN HOLIDAY!
WHAT KIND OF PSYCHO GRANDPA CARRIES AROUND A PACKET OF **FAKE BLOOD**?

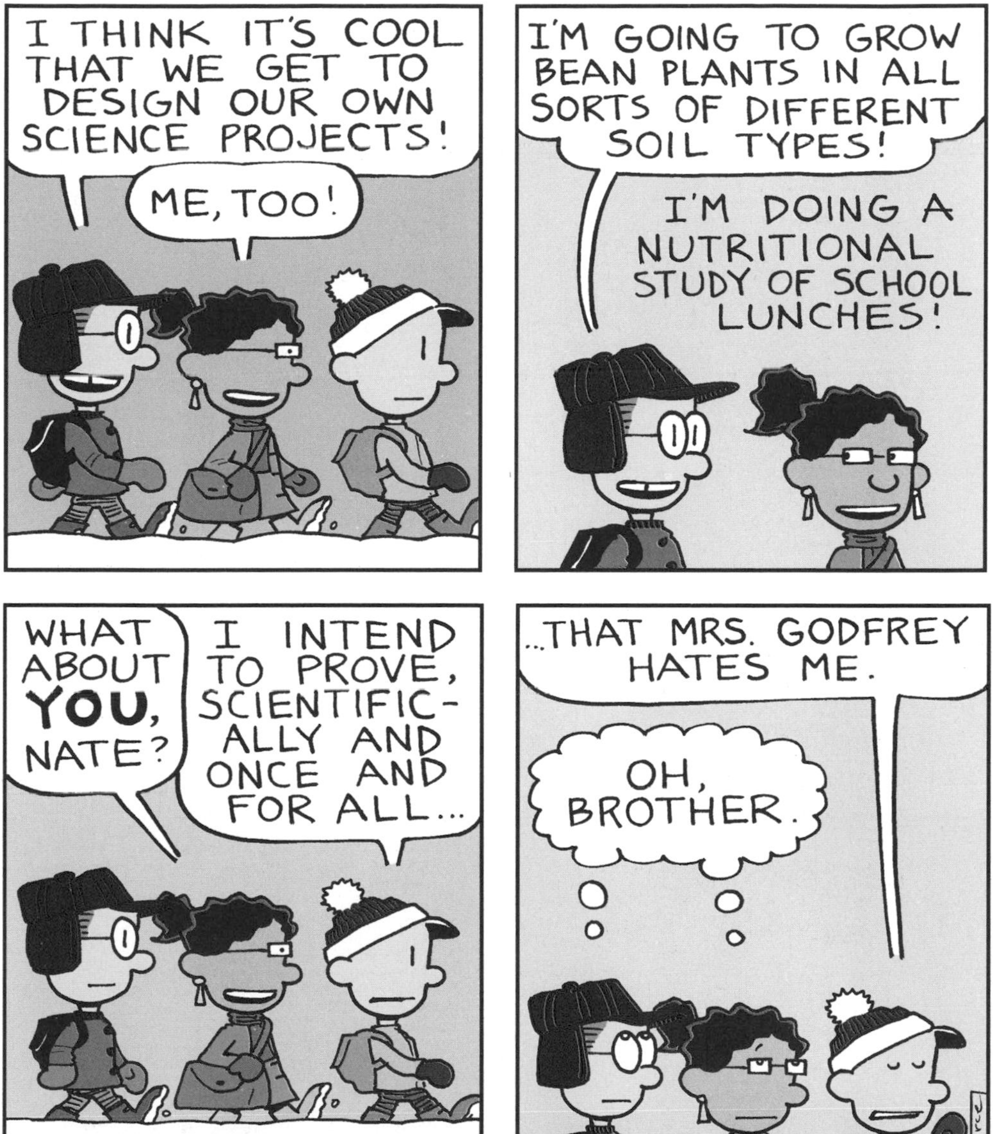
I THINK IT'S COOL THAT WE GET TO DESIGN OUR OWN SCIENCE PROJECTS!
ME, TOO!
I'M GOING TO GROW BEAN PLANTS IN ALL SORTS OF DIFFERENT SOIL TYPES!
I'M DOING A NUTRITIONAL STUDY OF SCHOOL LUNCHES!
WHAT ABOUT **YOU**, NATE?
I INTEND TO PROVE, SCIENTIFIC-ALLY AND ONCE AND FOR ALL...
...THAT MRS. GODFREY HATES ME.
OH, BROTHER.
Peirce

NATE, YOU CAN'T DO A SCIENCE PROJECT CALLED "MRS. GODFREY HATES ME".

WHY NOT? SHE **DOES** HATE ME!

BUT IT HAS NOTHING TO DO WITH **SCIENCE!**

SURE IT DOES! IT'S **PSYCHOLOGY!**

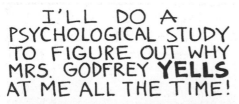

I'LL DO A PSYCHOLOGICAL STUDY TO FIGURE OUT WHY MRS. GODFREY **YELLS** AT ME ALL THE TIME!

PERHAPS SHE YELLS AT YOU BECAUSE YOU KEEP DOING BONE-HEADED THINGS.

IN SCIENCE, WE CALL THAT A "VARIABLE."

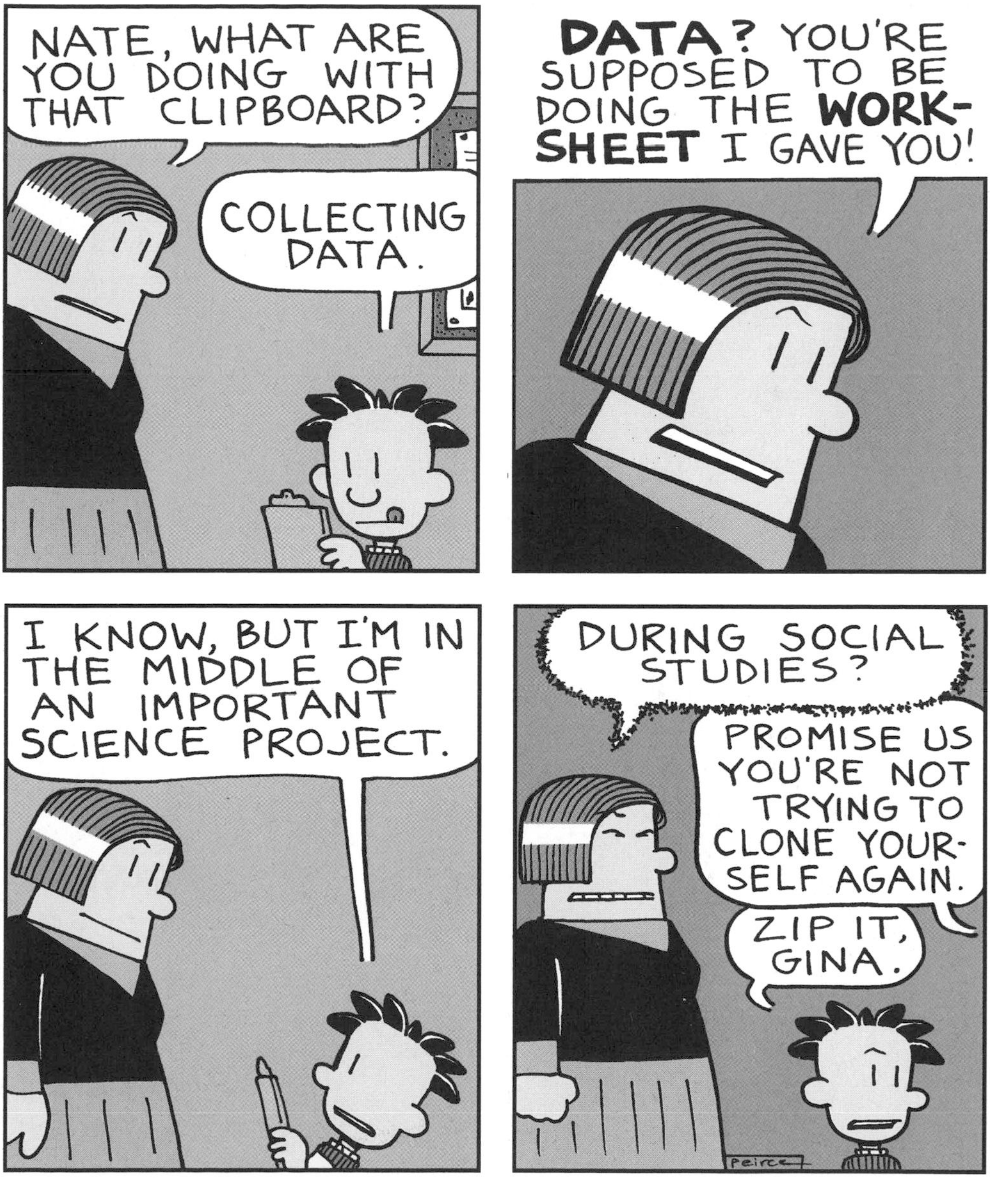
NATE, WHAT ARE YOU DOING WITH THAT CLIPBOARD?
COLLECTING DATA.
DATA? YOU'RE SUPPOSED TO BE DOING THE **WORK-SHEET** I GAVE YOU!
I KNOW, BUT I'M IN THE MIDDLE OF AN IMPORTANT SCIENCE PROJECT.
DURING SOCIAL STUDIES?
PROMISE US YOU'RE NOT TRYING TO CLONE YOUR-SELF AGAIN.
ZIP IT, GINA.
peirce

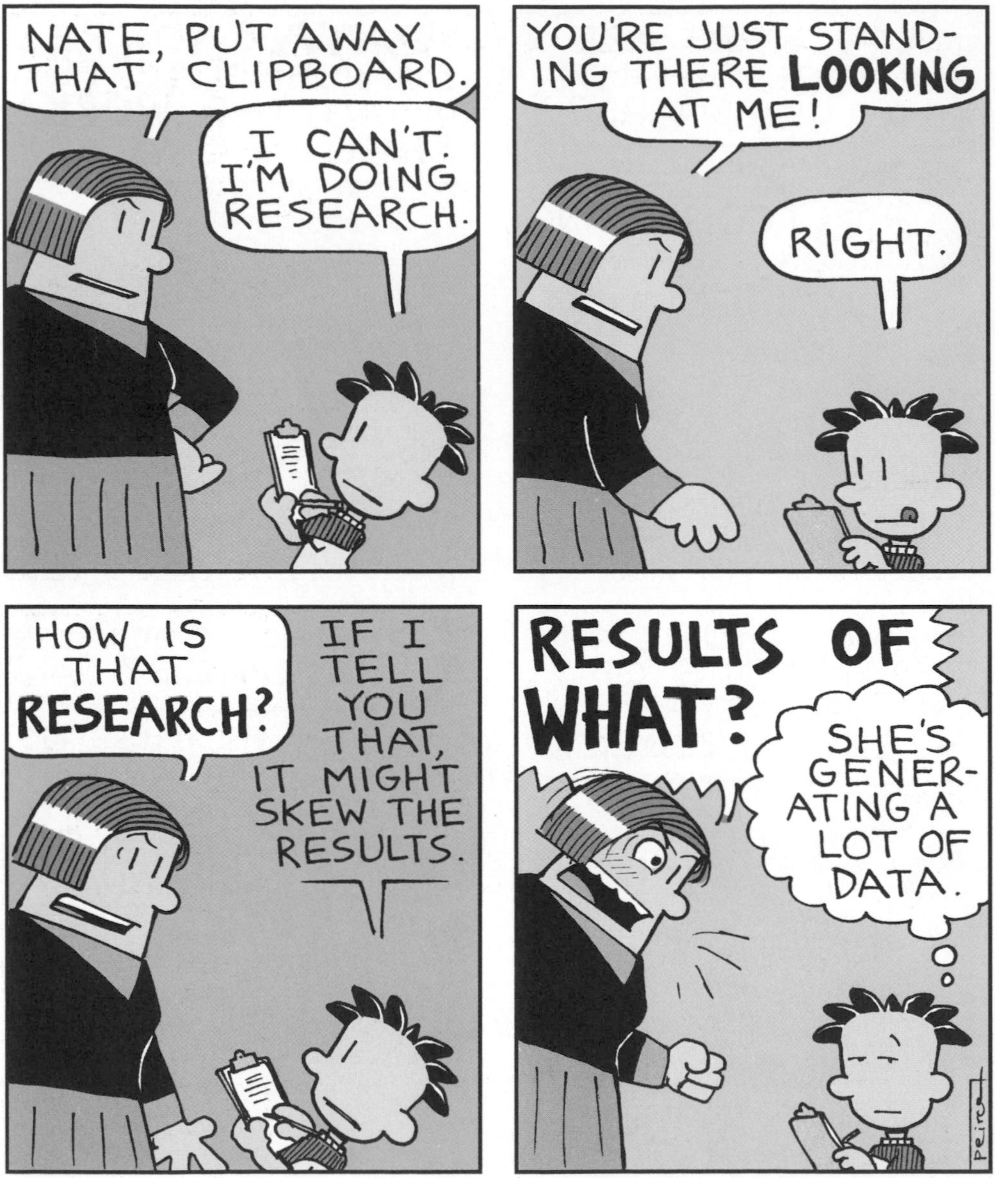
NATE, PUT AWAY THAT CLIPBOARD.
I CAN'T. I'M DOING RESEARCH.
YOU'RE JUST STANDING THERE **LOOKING** AT ME!
RIGHT.
HOW IS THAT **RESEARCH?**
IF I TELL YOU THAT, IT MIGHT SKEW THE RESULTS.
RESULTS OF WHAT?
SHE'S GENERATING A LOT OF DATA.
peirce

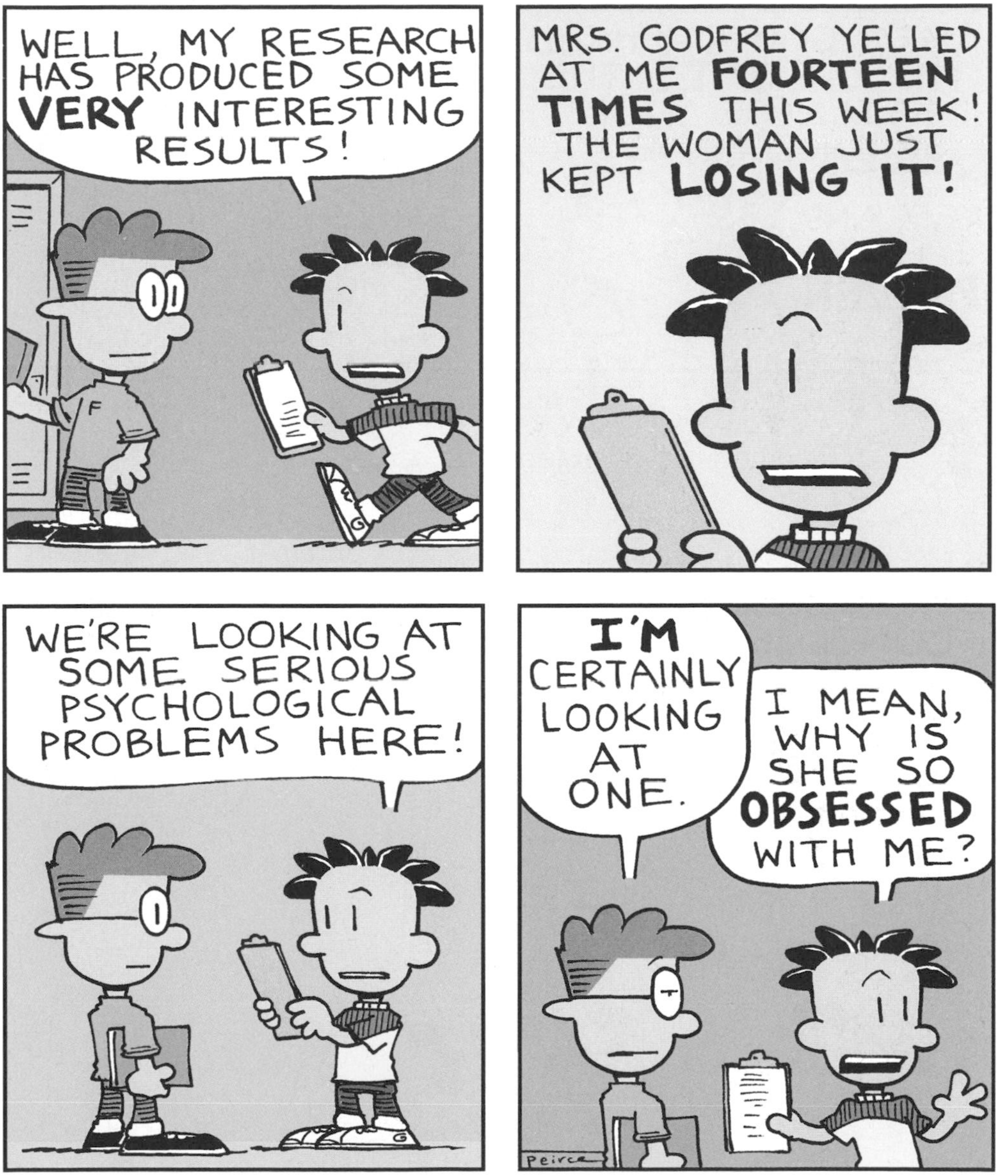
WELL, MY RESEARCH HAS PRODUCED SOME **VERY** INTERESTING RESULTS!
MRS. GODFREY YELLED AT ME **FOURTEEN TIMES** THIS WEEK! THE WOMAN JUST KEPT **LOSING IT!**
WE'RE LOOKING AT SOME SERIOUS PSYCHOLOGICAL PROBLEMS HERE!
I'M CERTAINLY LOOKING AT ONE.
I MEAN, WHY IS SHE SO **OBSESSED** WITH ME?
peirce

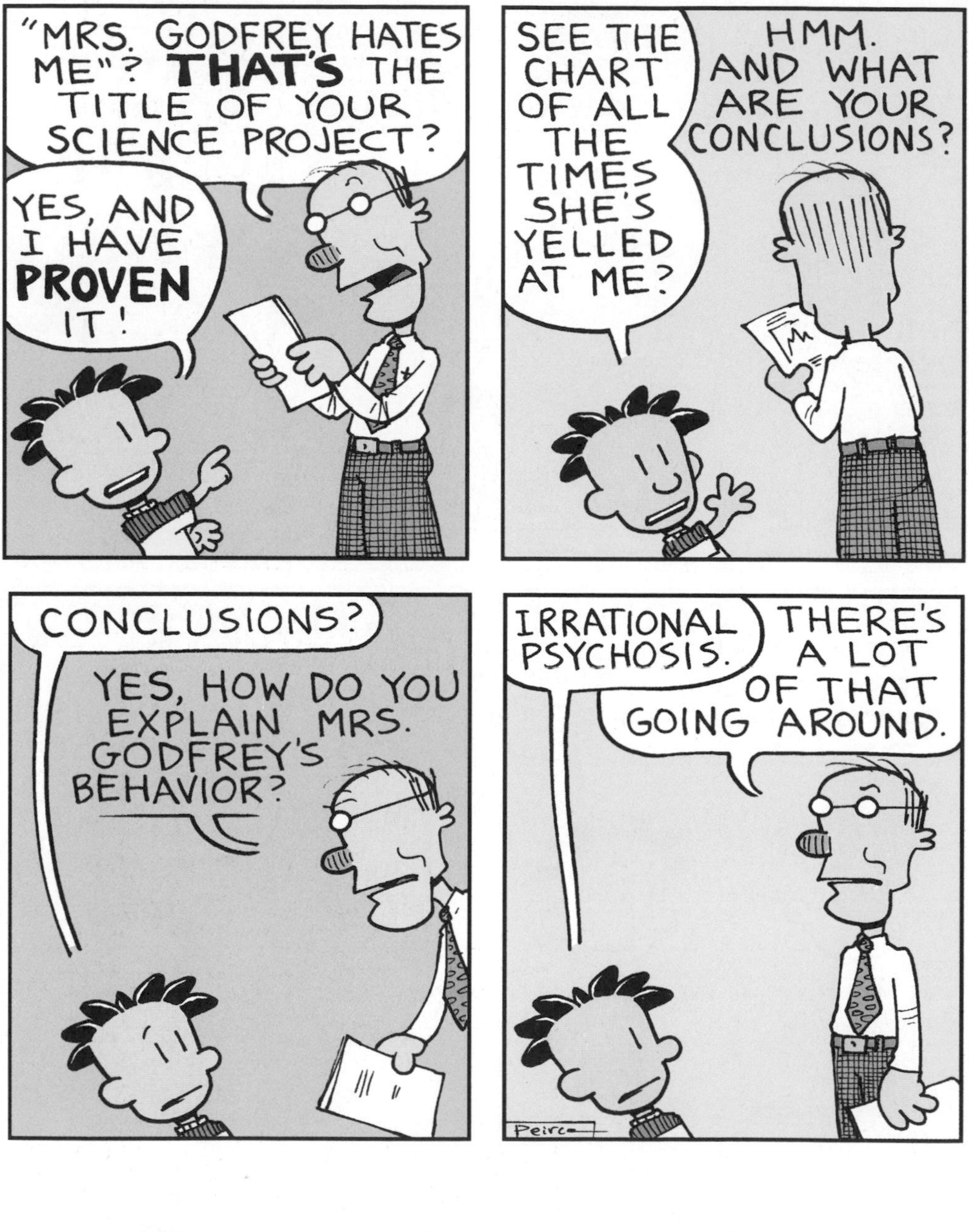
"MRS. GODFREY HATES ME"? **THAT'S** THE TITLE OF YOUR SCIENCE PROJECT?
YES, AND I HAVE **PROVEN** IT!
SEE THE CHART OF ALL THE TIMES SHE'S YELLED AT ME?
HMM. AND WHAT ARE YOUR CONCLUSIONS?
CONCLUSIONS?
YES, HOW DO YOU EXPLAIN MRS. GODFREY'S BEHAVIOR?
IRRATIONAL PSYCHOSIS.
THERE'S A LOT OF THAT GOING AROUND.
Peirce

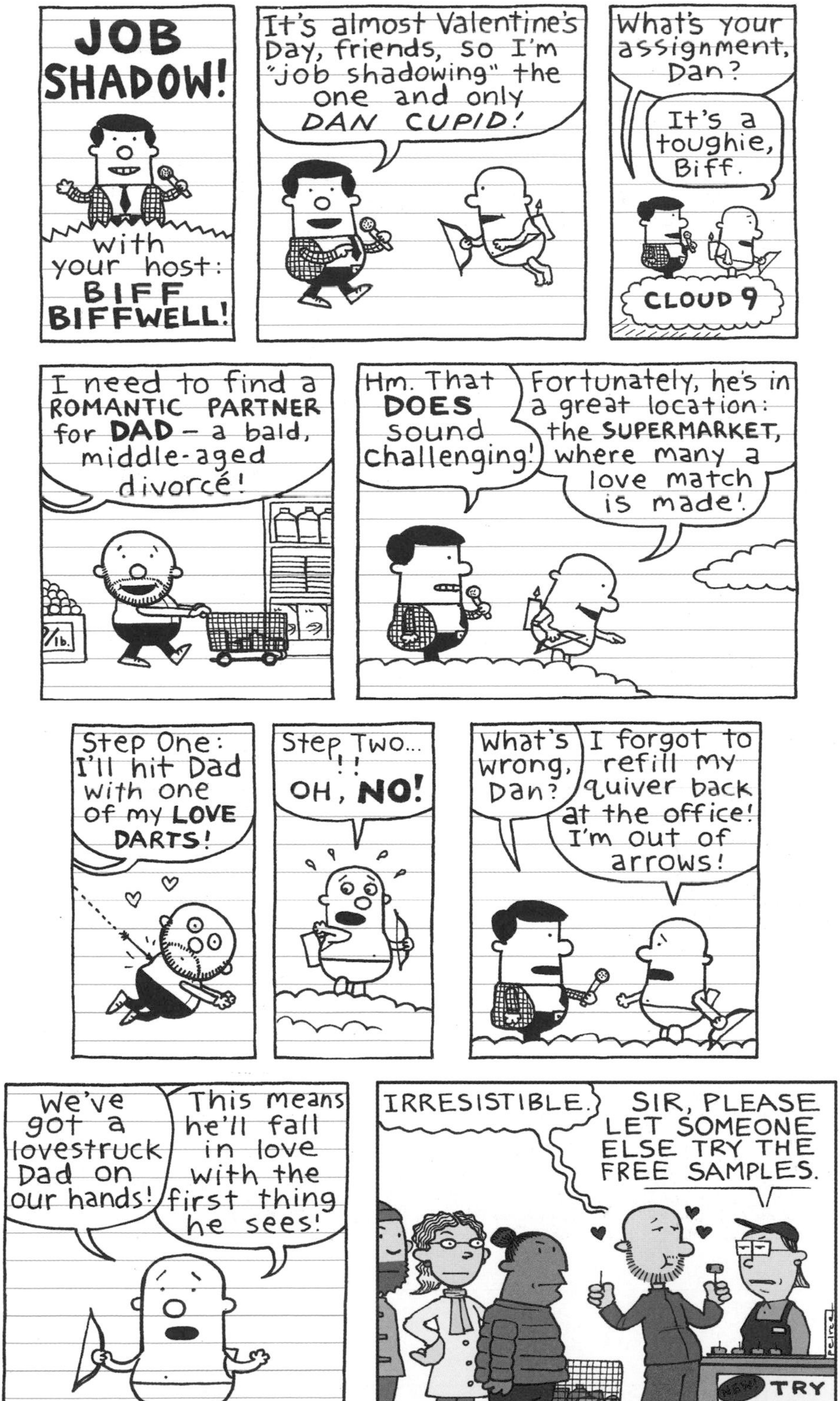

JOB SHADOW!
with your host: BIFF BIFFWELL!
It's almost Valentine's Day, friends, so I'm "job shadowing" the one and only DAN CUPID!
What's your assignment, Dan?
It's a toughie, Biff.
CLOUD 9
I need to find a ROMANTIC PARTNER for DAD – a bald, middle-aged divorcé!
Hm. That DOES sound challenging!
Fortunately, he's in a great location: the SUPERMARKET, where many a love match is made!
Step One: I'll hit Dad with one of my LOVE DARTS!
Step Two... !! OH, NO!
What's wrong, Dan?
I forgot to refill my quiver back at the office! I'm out of arrows!
We've got a lovestruck Dad on our hands!
This means he'll fall in love with the first thing he sees!
IRRESISTIBLE.
SIR, PLEASE LET SOMEONE ELSE TRY THE FREE SAMPLES.
NEW! TRY

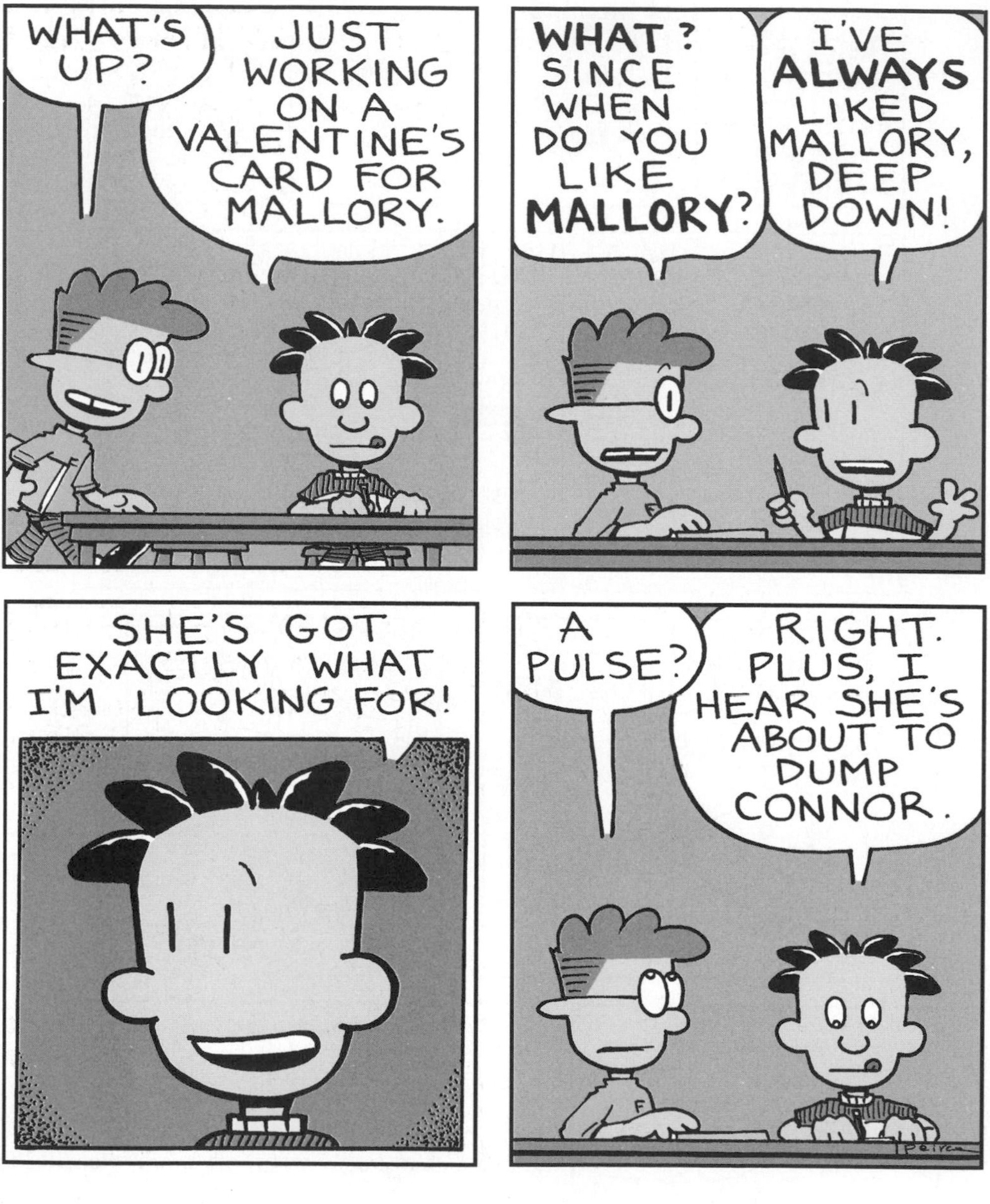
WHAT'S UP?
JUST WORKING ON A VALENTINE'S CARD FOR MALLORY.
WHAT? SINCE WHEN DO YOU LIKE **MALLORY**?
I'VE **ALWAYS** LIKED MALLORY, DEEP DOWN!
SHE'S GOT EXACTLY WHAT I'M LOOKING FOR!
A PULSE?
RIGHT. PLUS, I HEAR SHE'S ABOUT TO DUMP CONNOR.

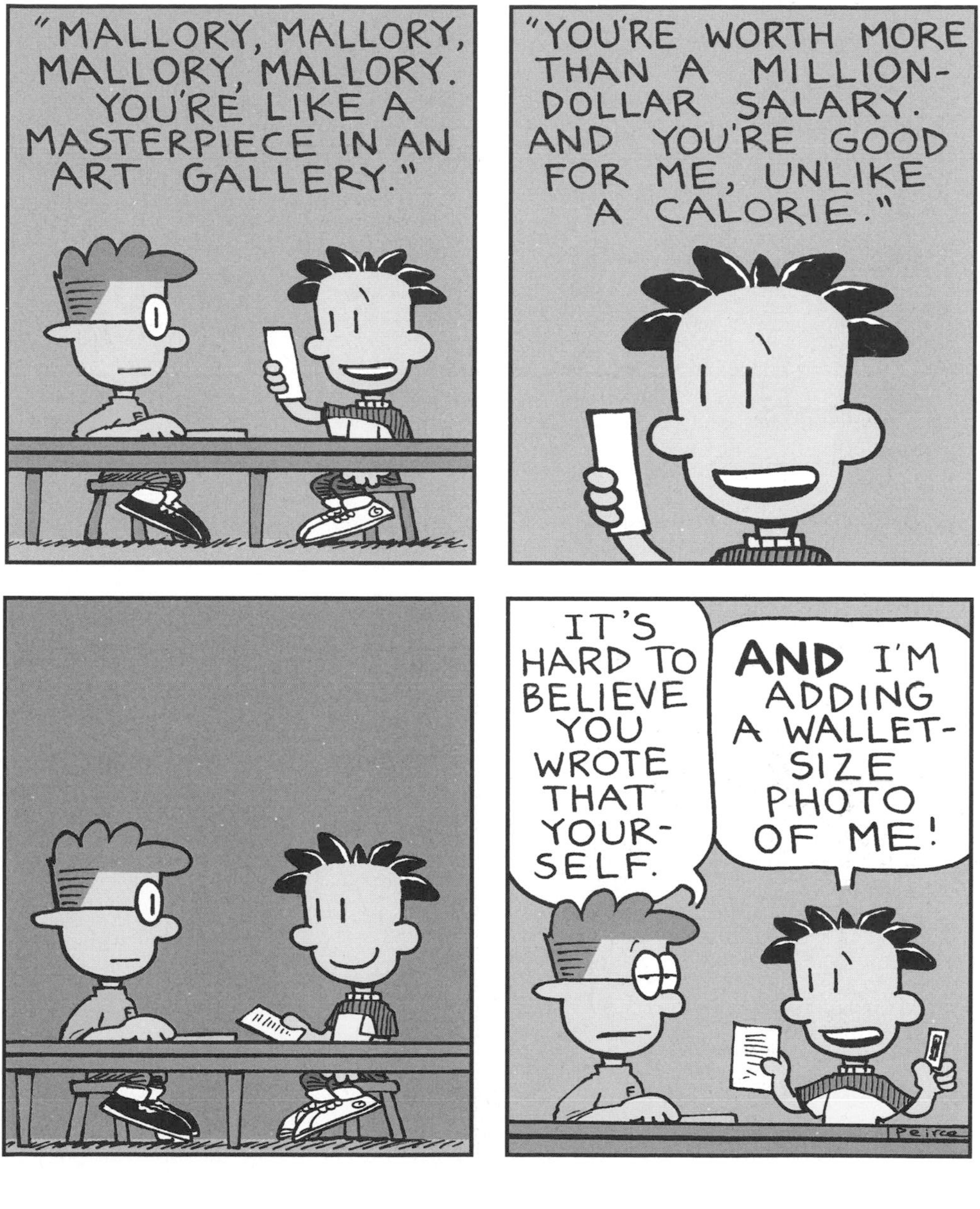
"MALLORY, MALLORY, MALLORY, MALLORY. YOU'RE LIKE A MASTERPIECE IN AN ART GALLERY."
"YOU'RE WORTH MORE THAN A MILLION-DOLLAR SALARY. AND YOU'RE GOOD FOR ME, UNLIKE A CALORIE."
IT'S HARD TO BELIEVE YOU WROTE THAT YOURSELF.
AND I'M ADDING A WALLET-SIZE PHOTO OF ME!
Peirce

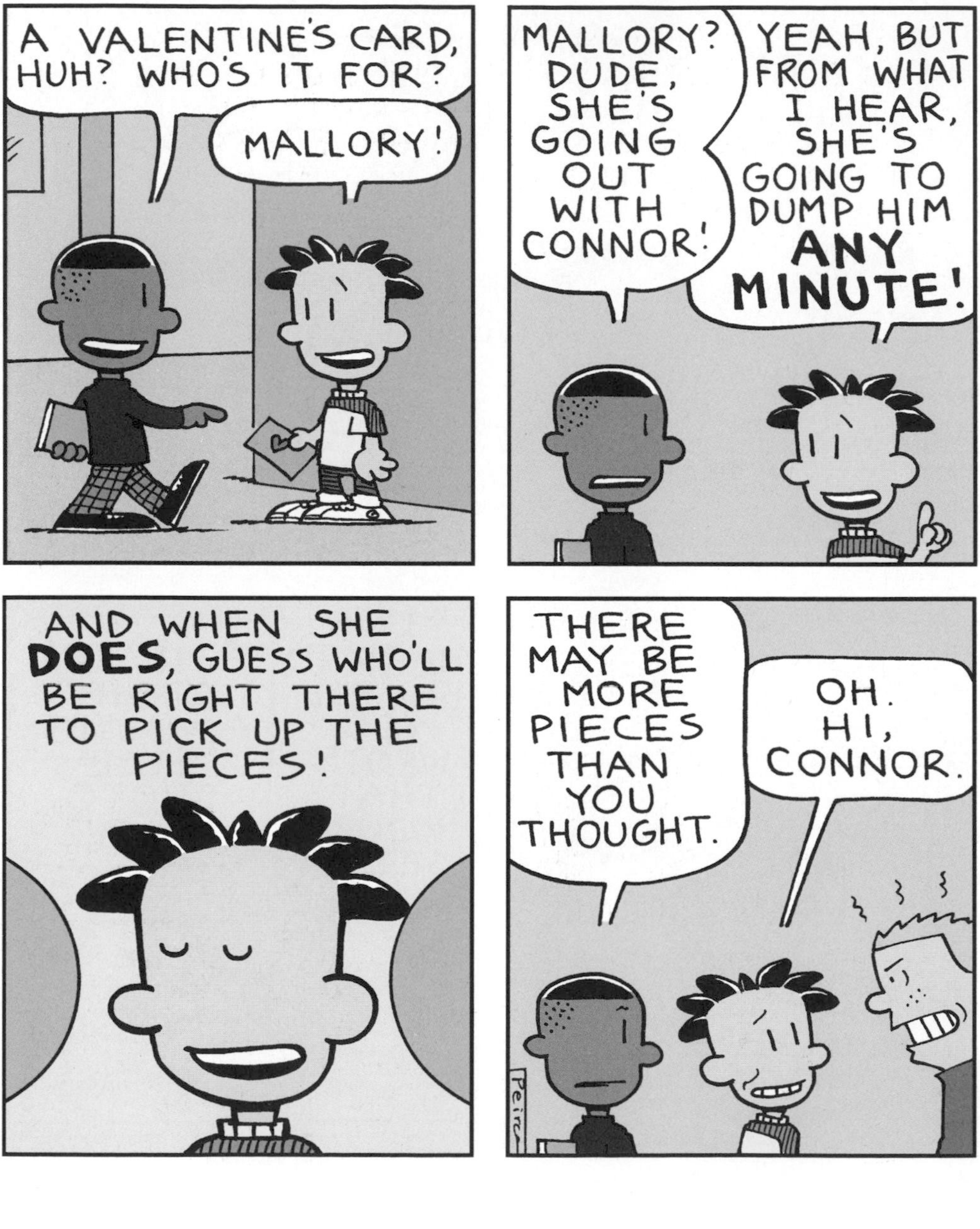
A VALENTINE'S CARD, HUH? WHO'S IT FOR?
MALLORY!
MALLORY? DUDE, SHE'S GOING OUT WITH CONNOR!
YEAH, BUT FROM WHAT I HEAR, SHE'S GOING TO DUMP HIM **ANY MINUTE!**
AND WHEN SHE **DOES**, GUESS WHO'LL BE RIGHT THERE TO PICK UP THE PIECES!
THERE MAY BE MORE PIECES THAN YOU THOUGHT.
OH. HI, CONNOR.
Peirce

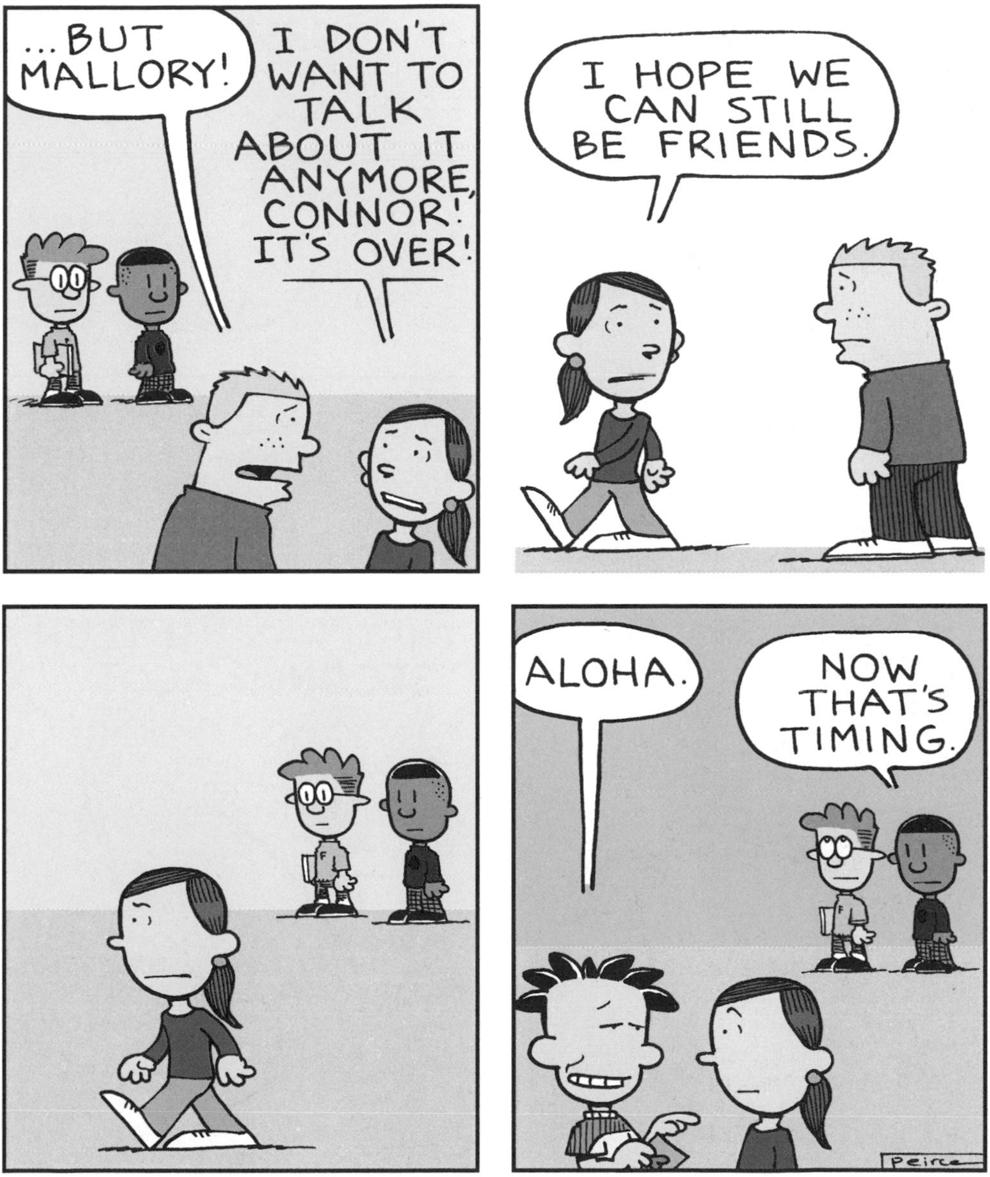
...BUT MALLORY!
I DON'T WANT TO TALK ABOUT IT ANYMORE, CONNOR! IT'S OVER!
I HOPE WE CAN STILL BE FRIENDS.
ALOHA.
NOW THAT'S TIMING.
Peirce

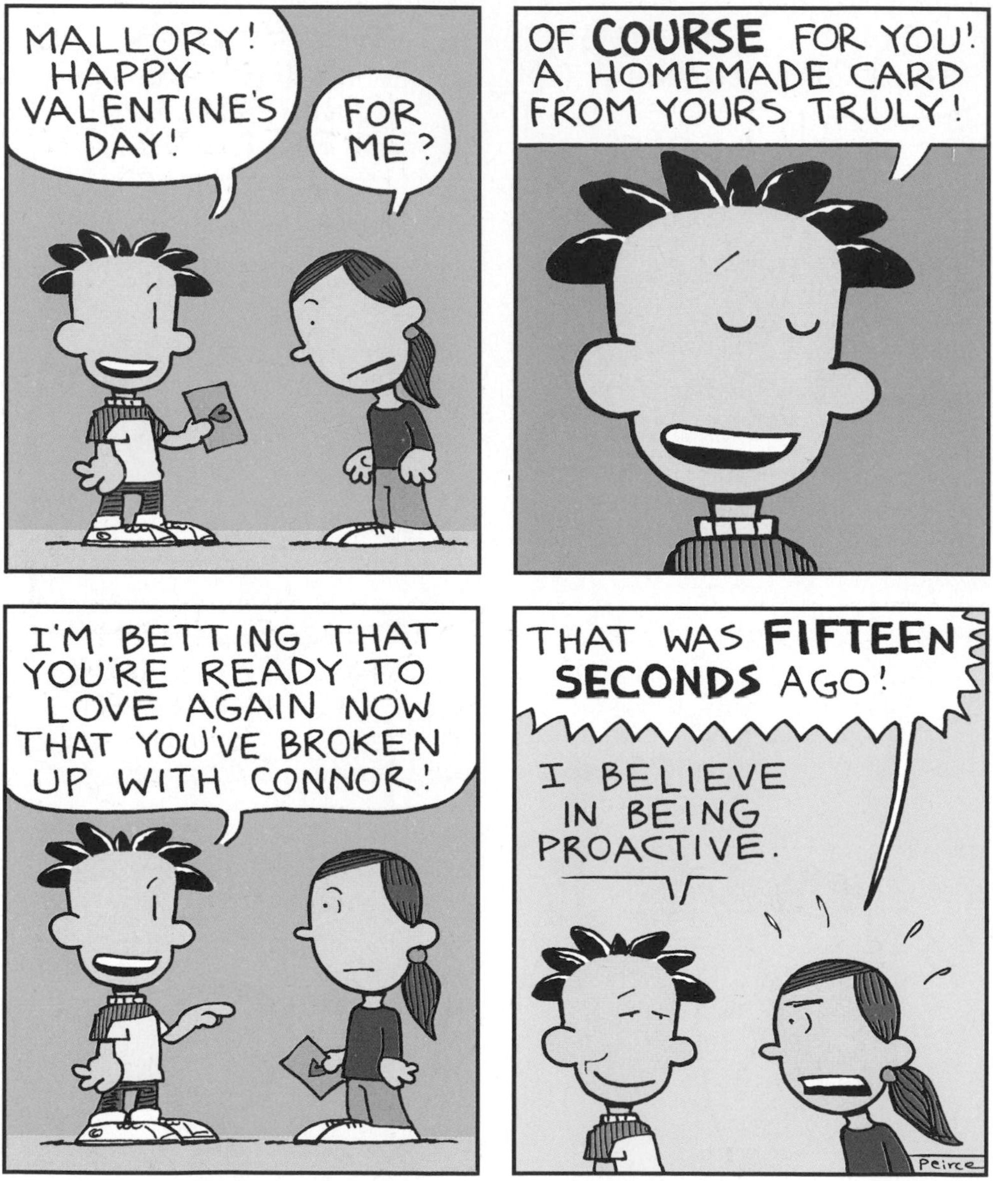
MALLORY! HAPPY VALENTINE'S DAY!
FOR ME?
OF **COURSE** FOR YOU! A HOMEMADE CARD FROM YOURS TRULY!
I'M BETTING THAT YOU'RE READY TO LOVE AGAIN NOW THAT YOU'VE BROKEN UP WITH CONNOR!
THAT WAS **FIFTEEN SECONDS** AGO!
I BELIEVE IN BEING PROACTIVE.
Peirce

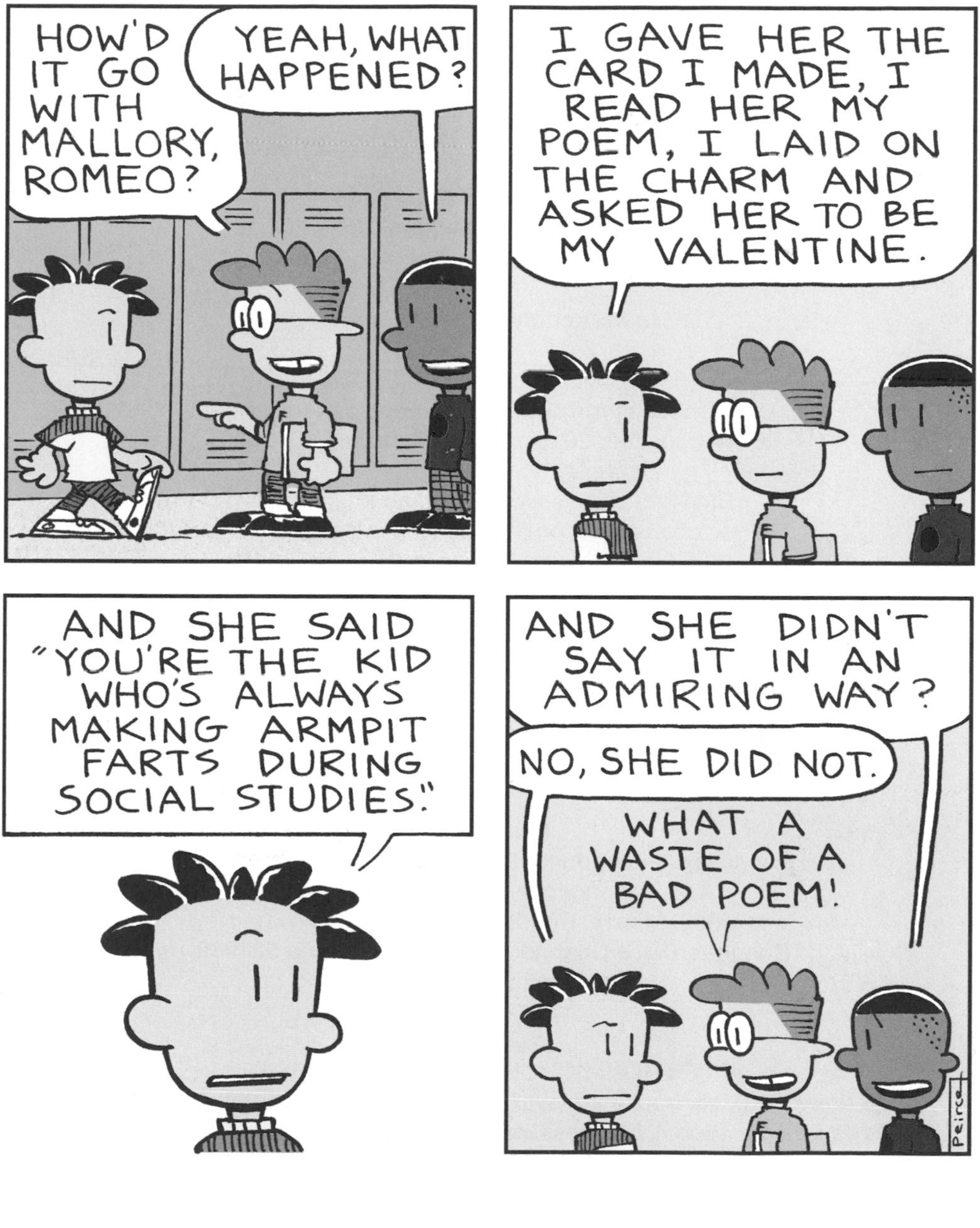
HOW'D IT GO WITH MALLORY, ROMEO?
YEAH, WHAT HAPPENED?
I GAVE HER THE CARD I MADE, I READ HER MY POEM, I LAID ON THE CHARM AND ASKED HER TO BE MY VALENTINE.
AND SHE SAID "YOU'RE THE KID WHO'S ALWAYS MAKING ARMPIT FARTS DURING SOCIAL STUDIES."
AND SHE DIDN'T SAY IT IN AN ADMIRING WAY?
NO, SHE DID NOT.
WHAT A WASTE OF A BAD POEM!
Peirce

Big Nate is distributed internationally by Andrews McMeel Syndication.

Andrews McMeel Publishing
a division of Andrews McMeel Universal
1130 Walnut Street, Kansas City, Missouri 64106

www.andrewsmcmeel.com

These strips appeared in newspapers
from August 12, 2019, through February 15, 2020.

Big Nate can be viewed on the Internet at
www.gocomics.com/big_nate.

23 24 25 26 27 SDB 10 9 8 7 6 5 4 3 2 1

ISBN: 978-1-5248-8129-0

Library of Congress Control Number: 2023930569

Made by:
RR Donnelley (Guangdong) Printing Solutions Company Ltd
Address and location of manufacturer:
No. 2, Minzhu Road, Daning, Humen Town,
Dongguan City, Guangdong Province, China 523930
1st Printing – 4/3/23

Look for these books!

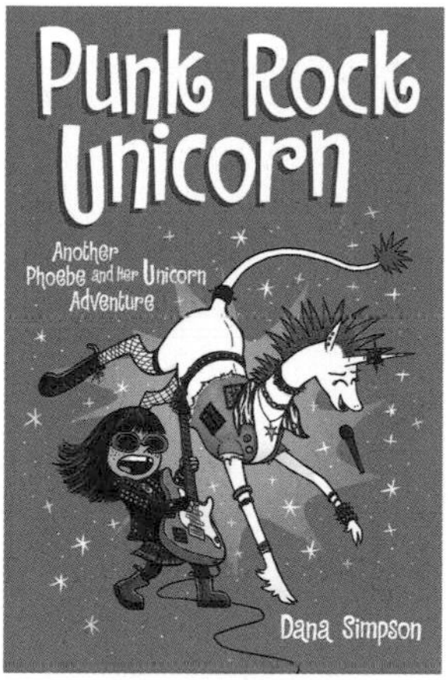
Punk Rock Unicorn
Another Phoebe and Her Unicorn Adventure
Dana Simpson

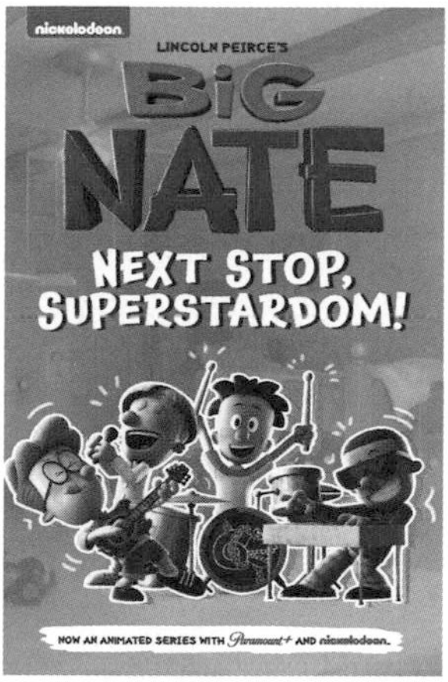
nickelodeon
LINCOLN PEIRCE'S
BIG NATE
NEXT STOP, SUPERSTARDOM!
NOW AN ANIMATED SERIES WITH Paramount+ AND nickelodeon.

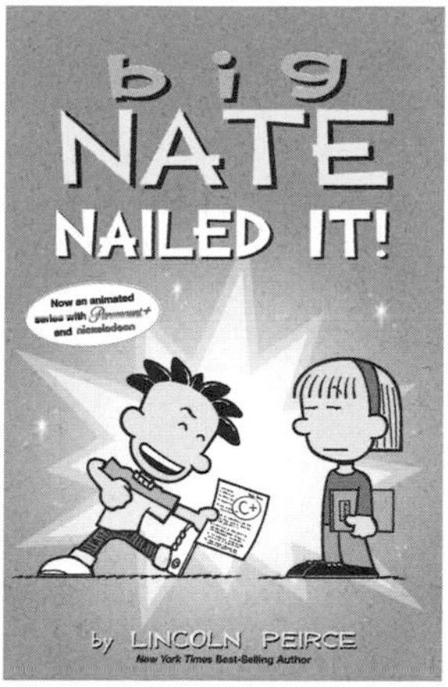
big NATE
NAILED IT!
Now an animated series with Paramount+ and nickelodeon
by LINCOLN PEIRCE
New York Times Best-Selling Author

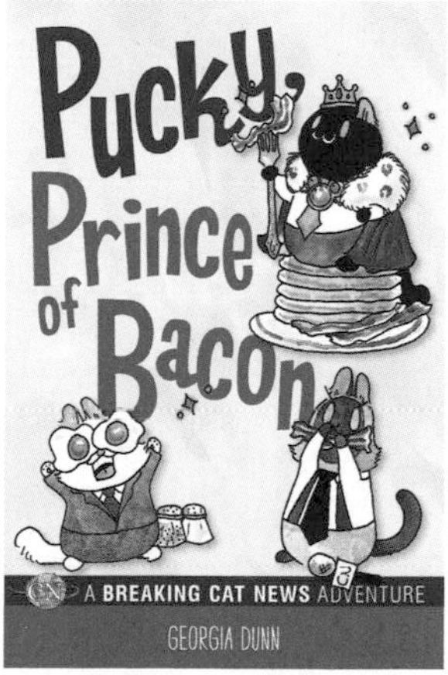
Pucky, Prince of Bacon
A BREAKING CAT NEWS ADVENTURE
GEORGIA DUNN

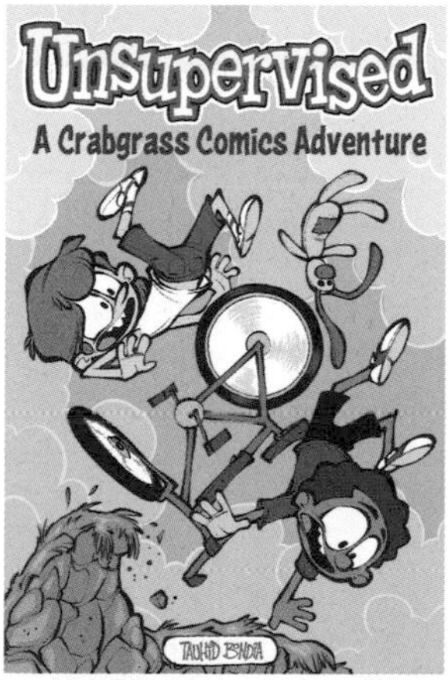
Unsupervised
A Crabgrass Comics Adventure
TAUHID BONDIA

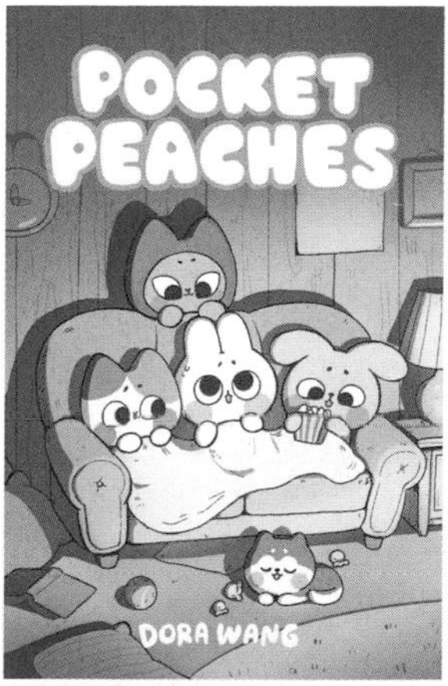
POCKET PEACHES
DORA WANG

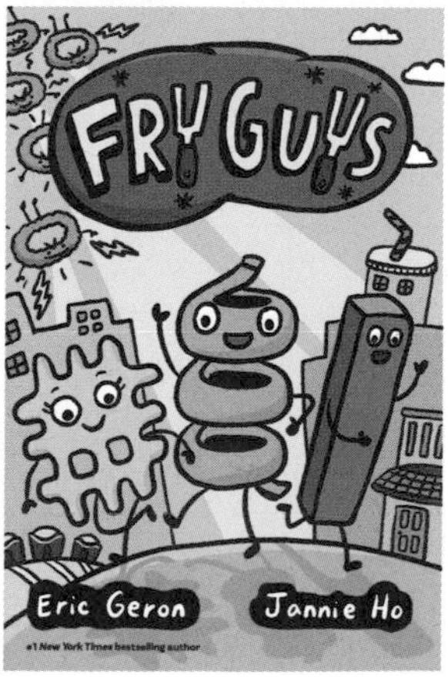
FRY GUYS
Eric Geron
Jannie Ho
#1 New York Times bestselling author

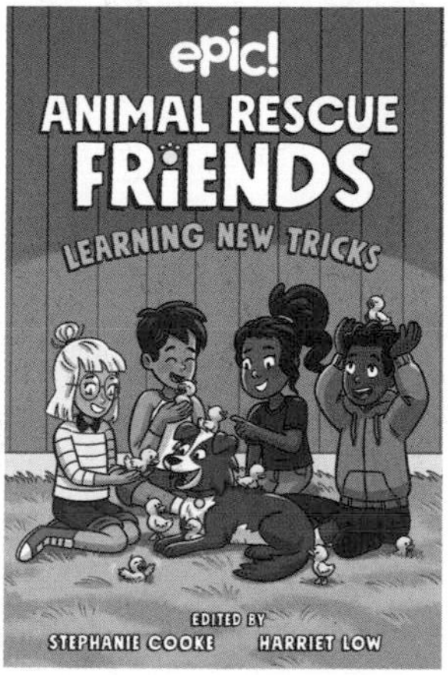
epic!
ANIMAL RESCUE FRIENDS
LEARNING NEW TRICKS
EDITED BY
STEPHANIE COOKE
HARRIET LOW

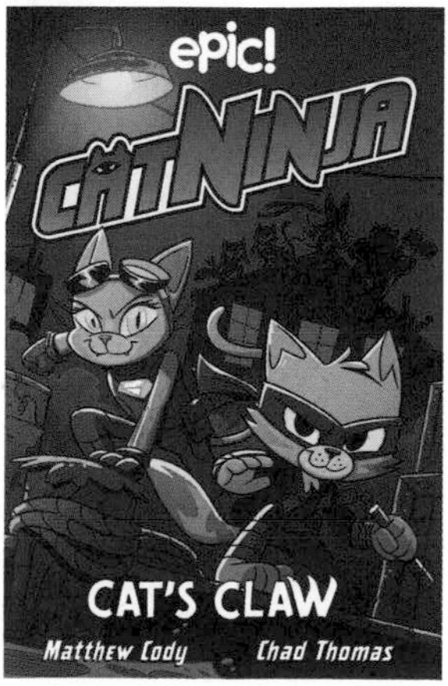
epic!
CAT NINJA
CAT'S CLAW
Matthew Cody
Chad Thomas

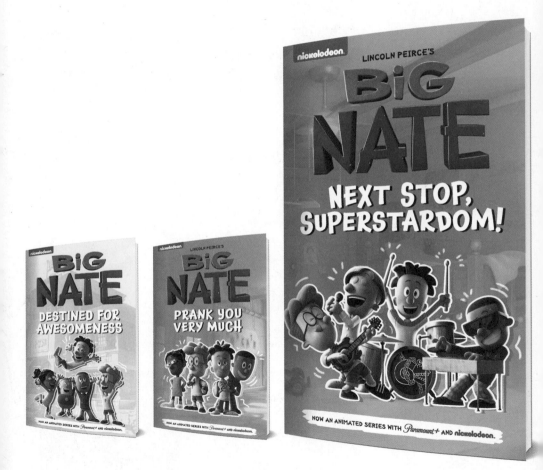